Lorna Cook lives in coastal Essex with her husband, daughters, and a Staffy named Socks. A former journalist and publicist, she owns more cookery books than one woman should, but barely gets time to cook. *The Forgotten Village* is her first novel.

The Forgotten Village

LORNA COOK

avon.

Published by AVON
A division of HarperCollins*Publishers* Ltd
1 London Bridge Street
London SE1 9GF

www.harpercollins.co.uk

A Paperback Original 2019
5

First published in Great Britain by HarperCollins*Publishers* 2019

A catalogue copy of this book is available from the British Library.

ISBN: 978-0-00-832185-7

This novel is entirely a work of fiction.
The names, characters and incidents portrayed in it are the
work of the author's imagination. Any resemblance to actual persons,
living or dead, events or localities is entirely coincidental.

Typeset in Minion by Palimpsest Book Production Limited, Falkirk, Stirlingshire

Printed and bound in UK by CPI Group (UK) Ltd, Croydon CR0 4YY

MIX
Paper from
responsible sources
FSC www.fsc.org **FSC** C007454

This book is produced from independently certified FSC™ paper
to ensure responsible forest management.

For more information visit: www.harpercollins.co.uk/green

For Stephen
Thanks for doing everything and being everything.

PROLOGUE

Tyneham, Dorset, December 1943

Lady Veronica stood shivering in front of the crowd of over two hundred faces in the village square. She desperately hoped none of them had heard the events of last night. Each one of the villagers was a familiar face, and each looked expectantly at her and the handsome man at her side, who was gripping her hand so tightly it hurt. He was expected to say something; a few words of encouragement were all the villagers needed to assure them that they were doing the right thing. It was something they could be proud of – leaving the village, giving it over to the war effort for the troops to use for training. They were doing something that would go down in the history books as an act of incredible sacrifice for the war and for their country.

'Sir Albert?' the vicar prompted, indicating it was time to speak.

The man at her side nodded. He stepped forward a few paces and Veronica moved with him. He gripped her hand tighter. Her fingers felt the thick gold band of the wedding ring he was wearing and she shuddered.

Feeling dizzy, she put her free hand to the back of her head to touch the large lump that had formed. She had managed to wash away most of the blood – of which there had been plenty – but a few traces of thick, oozing red liquid still appeared on her fingers when she pulled them out of her hair. She wiped it off on the black fabric of her dress. Black for mourning. She felt it appropriate given that today marked the death of the village.

He looked down at her, adjusting his grip, his expression blank, as if to check she was still there, as if he still couldn't quite believe what was happening. And then he looked back towards the crowd to speak.

'Today is a historic day,' he started. 'Today the people of Tyneham sacrifice our village for the good of the nation; for the good of the war. We leave, not forever, but until this war is won. We leave together, united in our separation, united in our displacement. This war will only be won by good deeds carried out by good people. You are not alone in sacrificing your home and your livelihood. Each tenant farmer, each shopkeeper, every man, woman and child, including us at Tyneham House – we are all in this together. And when this war is won, we will return together.'

His short speech was met with a sea of subdued faces, but applause started the moment he had finished, despite the sadness of the occasion. Veronica was glad. She knew the speech had to be rousing enough to console the villagers into leaving without a fight, although there was nothing they could do to stop the requisition now. As the residents of Tyneham prepared to gather their few remaining belongings, Veronica closed her eyes, reliving the events of last night over and over until she thought she might scream. But she only had to keep up her façade for a few minutes longer. She would not miss this village and she would not miss Tyneham House.

We will return together, he had said. *No*, thought Veronica. *They would not. She never wanted to see this place again.*

CHAPTER 1

Dorset, July 2018

Melissa didn't know why on earth she was doing this now. It had seemed like a good idea at the time. When she'd read about the 'Forgotten Village' in the local paper, it had sounded romantic: a village lost in time, dramatically stolen from its people in 1943 and given to the troops to prepare for the D-Day landings. And now it was being handed back, in part, all these years later. This vast expanse of derelict land, pub, houses, church, school, shops, and a plethora of other buildings should have been returned as soon as the war had finished, so *The Purbeck Times* had said that morning, but it never was. The villagers had been all but conned. And now Melissa was sitting in a painfully slow mass of traffic on her way to the grand reopening of the village of Tyneham, along with at least two hundred other vehicles – all of which were crawling along. She hadn't been the only one eager to see the latest tourist attraction to open on the Dorset coast.

Melissa adjusted the fan in the car, which she despairingly realised was already at maximum chill factor. It was having no effect on what had to be the hottest day of the year so far. Perhaps it was simply the sitting still, or perhaps it was sitting still in the unbearable July heat. As she felt her sunglasses slide down her nose, she cast them off and threw them onto the empty passenger seat. They bounced off the fabric and clattered onto the side of the door's interior. Melissa reached over to grab them again and shoved them back on her face. The heat was making her grouchy.

'Why is this taking so long?' she asked, thumping the steering wheel with the palm of her hand.

It wasn't really the heat, or even the traffic, that had annoyed her. It was more the fact her boyfriend, Liam, had promised her a romantic fortnight away in Dorset, but he had in fact spent every waking moment so far knee-deep in surf and rip tide, or whatever else he did while paddling in and out of the coast on his board. Where was her romantic holiday? Melissa had tried to understand; agreeing that it was wonderful the weather was so excellent for surfing. Of course he should go and enjoy himself. After all, he'd paid so much money for his weekend pad in Kimmeridge, which he'd bought as an escape from his boring but overpaid job in banking. He deserved to let loose. But she hadn't expected to be alone every day. She'd tried surfing with Liam when they'd first got together eight months ago, but he had no patience with her, especially when it became apparent she was never going to be able to even stand up on the board, let alone master catching a wave. He'd put up no fight when she suggested she leave him to it. But Melissa was a bit surprised that every day since they'd arrived, Liam had gone surfing.

When she'd asked this morning if they should do something together, something touristy, he'd simply said 'maybe another day'. Alone and bored and on the umpteenth walk around the chocolate-box village of Kimmeridge, she'd popped into the newsagent, hoping to pick up a couple of glossy magazines to read while Liam was out. The woman behind the counter had been reading the story on the front page of the local paper.

'Not before time,' she'd said as Melissa approached the counter. 'Utter disgrace, keeping it out of bounds this long. They're still not allowed back there to live.'

'Who aren't?' Melissa had enquired, simply out of politeness.

'The residents of Tyneham, of course. Ex-residents, I should say.' The woman tapped the front cover. 'The village is reopening today.' She shook her head. 'After all this time. That'll be a sight to be seen.'

The bell above the door had sounded as another customer entered and queued politely behind Melissa. And so, without really thinking, Melissa reached over to the newspaper rack and took a copy out for herself, glancing quickly at the headline: *Forgotten Village Returned*. She paid for her magazines and the paper and stepped out into the sunshine to read the lead story. She was no longer interested in the celebrity gossip and overpriced fashion; instead it was the potted history of a long-abandoned village that kept Melissa's eyes on the page. Perhaps it wasn't her usual kind of holiday activity, but it was something to *do*.

Armed with the paper and the crumpled map she kept in the glove compartment, Melissa had ventured into the countryside expecting a quiet day wandering around the so-called forgotten village, perhaps with a handful of pensioners doing the same. But by the time she finally parked, guided into a makeshift parking bay, Melissa fancied she might have made a mistake coming to Tyneham. If the hundreds of cars were anything to go by, it was going to be busy.

The launch day was evidently a big deal to the local area. She wondered if anyone here had been among the people who, the paper had reported, had felt robbed every single day since the winter of 1943 when the army had requisitioned the entire village, every single home and all the surrounding farmland.

Melissa fell in to step with the other tourists along the gravel path and down to a small stage, where she was handed a leaflet and welcomed warmly by a kindly elderly man wearing his luminous yellow jacket with an air of pride. She returned his smile as she took the leaflet and he moved on to the myriad people behind her to offer the same.

Melissa looked past the stage and saw a large red ribbon

stretching from one new-looking gatepost to another. She sighed, realising there was going to be a big song and dance going on before she'd be allowed in to have her five minutes nose around the few decrepit buildings. After that, she'd leave. Maybe Liam would be back from the beach early today and they could go out for dinner or just sit in the cottage garden and drink wine, watching the sun go down. They hadn't done that once since they'd arrived in Dorset.

She was pulled from her thoughts as a man walked on to the stage. The riotous round of applause that accompanied his entrance stopped her thoughts of make-believe wine and sunsets.

Melissa stole a glance at the leaflet she'd been handed. *Tyneham will officially be reopened to the public, for daily summer visits, by TV historian Guy Cameron*, it said. Next to the text was a smiling black and white photo of Guy Cameron: floppy brown hair and laughing eyes. She folded the leaflet up and thrust it into her jeans pocket, none the wiser as to who he actually was – some kind of celebrity, apparently.

History on TV wasn't really up her alley, except maybe in the form of a costume drama. Bonnets and corsets and strapping gents striding in and out of lakes in white shirts were far more her thing.

Clapping along with everyone else to welcome Guy Cameron onto the stage, she slowly edged her way out of the crowd and stood to one side, grateful for a bit of space in the heat.

It seemed this historian was a popular choice as the clapping went on a bit too long in Melissa's opinion. While he talked, Melissa pulled her hair off her sticky neck and up into a high ponytail and pushed her sunglasses back up her nose.

'For so many years I've heard tales about Tyneham and it's always intrigued me,' he started. 'The people who used to live here, what happened to them? Where did they all go? What did they do? How did they react when they were told they had only a month to pack up and leave, not knowing when they'd be allowed back? Not knowing that they *wouldn't* be allowed back. A whole community, displaced . . .' He paused for a few seconds and the drama of his sentence lingered over the entranced crowd.

Melissa looked around briefly as he cast a spell over his audience.

'The village was requisitioned in its entirety,' he looked down at his notes briefly, 'with a promise to be returned during peacetime. Perhaps there should have been a tad more contractual detail about exactly when in peacetime.' He gave a smile and the crowd laughed enthusiastically. Melissa pressed her lips together, stifling a smile.

'Tyneham holds a special place in my heart.' He was sombre now, and the crowd's mood changed with him. 'I was brought up only a few miles from here. My grandmother came from Tyneham, and she was here when the announcement came that she, her friends, family, and employers would all have to leave. I've heard first-hand how she felt, but for everyone involved it was different. I've always thought the coming together of a community as it was being ripped apart was tragically ironic.

'But now we get to see the village once again, not as it was, but as it is now. While you can walk the streets, the buildings are damaged by time. Only the church and school are intact and open to the public and I encourage you inside both, to see photographs of the way the village used to be and other exhibits. But for now, seventy-five years after it was requisitioned, I'm happy to declare Tyneham Village officially open.'

With the sound of clapping once again, he stepped off the stage and a young woman, visibly overjoyed to be part of the proceedings, handed him an enormous pair of ceremonial scissors. He looked taken aback at the sheer size of them and said something to the woman, which made her roar with laughter and flick her hair. He snipped the ribbon and it fluttered to the ground.

At that, the surge started and visitors were shown through by guides in luminous yellow jackets. Melissa watched the crowd head through the gate, but waited for the bottleneck to disperse before she entered the fray. She watched the TV personality as he chatted affably with a handful of visitors. He posed easily with people for photos and signed copies of books, which Melissa assumed he must have written. He smiled throughout and she thought it must be exhausting being a celebrity: the permanent smile and the demands on you by the public. As soon as one doting fan left Guy Cameron's side, another appeared. Melissa cast him a final glance before she slipped past him and through the gates, into the forgotten village.

An hour and a half later, a golf buggy whizzed by Melissa and took a turn ahead past the derelict village square. She was rifling inside her bag looking for a non-existent bottle of mineral water to quell the beginnings of a headache. Her head snapped up to see the historian, whose name she had already forgotten, on the buggy, looking incredibly embarrassed as he overtook the tourists. He gave a few of them a little wave of recognition and Melissa laughed, half wondering why he didn't just go the whole hog and give them a royal wave.

Melissa trudged on up the hill and stopped to look at her map. She was now ragingly thirsty as she wiped stray strands of her ponytail off her neck. All that was left up here was Tyneham House, more affectionately known as the Great House, the leaflet told her. The note against it simply stated that it had been home to the Standish family, who had owned it for over three hundred years until they, like the villagers, had found their home commandeered from underneath them. They had been given a month to leave.

What's good for the goose, Melissa thought as she folded up her map and tucked it into her back pocket. She'd been walking for ages and had become ridiculously hot while looking inside the farm buildings and dilapidated cottages. Many of the ramshackle buildings were hidden within the woodlands that surrounded the village and the whole atmosphere was proving deliciously eerie. Wiping her forehead with the back of her hand she chastised herself that in the impromptu act of getting in the car for a day out, she had forgotten water. Her mouth was dry, but there wasn't a café or gift shop on site from which to buy a drink. She couldn't believe what an oversight it was given the amount of tourists present. They were never going to make any money this way. She resigned herself to giving the church and school a miss and calling it a day – just after she'd had a little peek at the manor house.

Two tourists on their way back passed Melissa as she arrived at the end of the tree-lined avenue that led to the house and she smiled at them politely, envying them their bottled waters. There was no one else up here and she was grateful for the peace and quiet. She was ready to soak in the atmosphere, undisturbed.

As with most of the other houses in the village, a permanent display board had been placed at Tyneham House, positioned by the entrance to the front drive. There was a potted history of the house and where the bricks used to build it had come from, which Melissa skipped over.

There was very little detail about any of the prior residents, which seemed odd. But there was a picture of the last owners, Sir Albert and Veronica Standish. At least that's what the picture caption said. There was no information printed about them other than the fact they had been the last residents of the house, and with the image printed crudely onto the strange plastic board they could have been anyone.

Melissa stepped forward to look closer. The couple in the small black and white photograph looked unremarkable. But, despite the heat, she shivered. Her mum would have said that someone had walked over her grave. Melissa wasn't sure she believed in that sort of thing.

She pushed the thought away and walked through the wide

red-brick entrance into the front drive. She could see holes in the brick walls on both sides where wrought-iron gates would once have been fixed but had long since been removed. She put her hand against the warm brick wall to steady herself for a minute or two as the sun beat down on her head. The heat was making her nauseous and she fanned herself with her leaflet for a few seconds before ploughing on. She wasn't usually this feeble. Just a few quick minutes glancing in the windows of the house if they weren't boarded up, and then she'd head off.

But as she let go of the wall and walked towards the large pale-bricked Elizabethan building in front of her, her vision blurred and her stomach churned. Melissa reached out to grab the wall again, but it was too far behind her and her fingers grabbed pointlessly at the air. She started to stumble forward, her legs gave way and the ground rushed up to meet her. As her eyes flickered shut, she was only vaguely aware that a strong pair of arms had grabbed her, breaking her fall.

CHAPTER 2

Melissa opened her eyes slowly and looked up into a man's face.

'Are you all right?'

It was the historian. He was crouched over her; his face full of concern, laced with a hint of panic. He was very attractive up close, but then Melissa wondered why he was so close. And why was she on the ground?

'Are you all right?' he repeated. 'I could see you falling from all the way back there.' He pointed over her head towards the avenue. 'I don't remember the last time I had to run that fast.'

Melissa nodded. 'I'm fine,' she said out of good old-fashioned British politeness, although it was clear she wasn't fine at all. Her head still hurt and her raging thirst hadn't diminished. And she was still on the ground.

He narrowed his eyes. 'Hmm. Stay still for a few minutes at least,' he said. 'You just passed out. There must be a first-aider here who can take a quick look at you.'

She sat up slowly, ignoring his protestations. 'How long was I out?'

'Not long. About thirty seconds or so.'

'Oh.' Melissa coughed dryly.

'Here, have this.' He offered her his chilled bottle of water and Melissa sipped, then offered it back. He shook his head. 'It's yours.'

She put it on the ground, where it rolled to one side and came to rest against a piece of fabric. 'What's that?' she asked.

'My sweater. I put it under your head when I laid you down.'

'Did you catch me?' She looked into his eyes. They were a startling shade of blue that the photograph on the leaflet hadn't done justice.

He nodded. 'When I caught sight of you wobbling, I ran so fast I almost careered into you.'

Melissa spied her sunglasses a few feet away. She felt lucky they hadn't smashed. They must have fallen off her face as she passed out.

He looked in the direction of her gaze; stood and scooped them up, then handed them back before looking at his mobile phone.

'There's no signal out here. No phone mast for miles; the village never needed one. So I can't summon any help. You're stuck with me, I'm afraid, until you feel well enough to walk.'

'I feel fine now,' she said, only half-fibbing. 'I think I was just a bit dehydrated.'

Melissa looked around, hoping the golf buggy might return for its celebrity passenger so she could hitch a lift, but she didn't mention it.

He sat down next to her and eyed her carefully. 'OK. Well, we'll give it a while before we move. Just rest for a bit.'

Melissa nodded and reached for the water again before taking another sip. 'That's much better,' she said, screwing the cap back on. She looked at the house properly and felt a strange kind of sadness.

'Are you interested in this sort of history?' Guy nodded towards the house.

'Not usually,' Melissa admitted and then felt a bit guilty admitting this in front of a historian. 'I was curious about this though and I had the day to kill. I seem to have accidentally come on a surfing holiday, but I hate surfing, so I've been finding other things to do with my days. I've never even been to Dorset before. I had no idea about Tyneham.'

'I'd imagine you wish you hadn't come now,' the historian said.

She turned to look at him. 'Why do you say that?'

'Well, you passed out for one. And you look pretty down. Although that's possibly on account of the fainting.'

'I don't know how anyone could be anything other than sad here. It's just so . . . abandoned,' she said. 'Although this house has fared better than the rest. It's still got a roof for a start.'

'It's a beautiful building.' He pointed at the top floor. 'My gran used to work as a maid here, up until the requisition.'

Melissa made an appropriate noise and looked at the gabled servants' quarters on the second floor. It was the only level that didn't have any window boards. Every window on both the first and ground floor had metal sheets with *Danger, Keep Out* emblazoned across them. The studded dark wooden front door inside the arch was still in place and looked original. And uninviting. It all gave off a depressing and cold air, even in the heat of the summer sun. But Melissa was sure that in its prime this house would have been something else entirely.

'I'm not sure Gran really enjoyed her time here,' the historian said. 'I must remember to ask her if she lived at the house' – he lifted his gaze towards the second-floor windows – 'or if she walked up from the village every day.' He snapped back from his meanderings. 'How are you feeling now?' he asked.

'Better, thanks.' Melissa wondered if Liam would be back from surfing and worried as to where she was. No, of course he wouldn't. But with no phone signal she couldn't tell him she'd be late. In fact, she hadn't even told him where she'd gone.

She stood up slowly and then reached down for his sweater. She handed it to him and he thanked her, putting it over his shoulders and tying the arms loosely round his neck.

'I'll walk you back,' he offered.

Still feeling woozy, Melissa didn't argue. 'I'm so sorry, I've completely forgotten your name.'

He smiled and introduced himself, holding out his hand.

'Thanks for taking care of me, Guy.' Melissa shook his hand and then introduced herself before continuing to walk beside him.

'Nice to meet you, Melissa.' Guy laughed. 'It's been one of the more interesting ways I've made a new acquaintance.'

The church came into view. 'I'm sure I'll be fine from here.' Melissa pointed towards the car park.

'Oh.' He sounded disappointed. 'Are you not coming into the church? There are meant to be loads of great photos of the way it all was. And a talk, not given by me this time, you might be pleased to hear.'

Melissa laughed and looked towards the old stone church. 'Maybe another day. I'd better be getting back.'

One of the guides appeared at the stone wall dividing the churchyard from the lane. 'Excuse me, Mr Cameron. We're starting the talk now if you would like to join us. We waited for you.'

'I'm not speaking am I?' he sounded concerned.

'No, no. But we didn't want you to miss it.'

'That's very kind of you. I'll be right there.'

The guide walked back towards the church and Guy turned to look at Melissa.

'Bye.' She gave him a small wave as she moved towards the car park. 'Enjoy the talk.'

He nodded. 'Bye. Take care of yourself, Melissa.'

As she drove to Liam's cottage, Melissa glanced at her watch. She'd been wandering around Tyneham for the best part of the day and she had only meant for it to be a flying visit. She was tired and hungry.

Melissa opened the front door expecting to hear something along the lines of 'Where the hell have you been?' But Liam was leaning on the arm of the sofa. A sports channel was on in the background broadcasting a surfing competition somewhere warm and sunny. He was playing with his phone and didn't look up when she entered.

'Hi,' she said from the door.

'Y'aright?' he mumbled, his fingers tapping away on his mobile.

'Yeah. Good day?' Melissa asked, but Liam didn't answer. The tapping on his phone continued.

She went towards the kitchen and downed two glasses of tap water. Finally feeling better, she glanced up at her boyfriend, who hadn't even looked at her yet, and she wondered why she had bothered rushing back. She grabbed a yogurt and a spoon from the kitchen.

Were they in a rut? How had this happened so soon? Admittedly they'd not been going out that long, but at eight months, this was Melissa's longest relationship yet. It was a fact she wasn't exactly proud of given she was twenty-eight and felt she should probably have worked out how to hold down a relationship long before now. But at this relatively early stage, wasn't it still supposed to be a bit more exciting? She had no idea what she was doing. She wondered if she was messing it up, playing it too cool, but she knew from watching the breakdown of her parents' marriage that men didn't like women who nagged. Her mum had found that out the hard way, leading to perpetual arguments. But maybe Melissa had gone too far in the other direction. When she and Liam had first got together, they'd been great – or so she'd thought. They'd met in one of those awful bars in Canary Wharf where bankers drink champagne costing £160 a bottle. She hadn't been used to that kind of flamboyance on her admin assistant salary. She'd only been there to celebrate a friend's birthday after work. Maybe she'd been out of her depth from the start.

She toyed with telling him she'd passed out today. But what would be the point; to make him look up, to force him into paying some attention to her? Melissa cringed thinking about it.

There were other ways, surely, to try to save a relationship and the sympathy vote wasn't it.

'Shall we go out for dinner?' she asked when she'd finished the yogurt. She was holding the fridge door open and enjoying its cool temperature.

'What?' He sounded harassed. 'Oh, I've already eaten.'

Melissa was taken aback. 'Really?' She closed the fridge. 'I thought we would eat together.'

'We didn't say we would, did we?' The tapping had resumed.

Melissa's eyes widened and she looked at the back of his head. 'No,' she said slowly. 'I suppose not.' She folded her arms, trying not to rise to the argument. 'What did you have?'

'Crab cakes, those sexy skinny chips, sticky toffee pudding. And a fabulous bottle of Sauvignon.'

'Wow. Where'd you get all that?'

'The Pheasant and Gun.'

'Oh.' Liam had eaten at the swanky gastro inn a few miles down the road that Melissa had been wanting to visit since they'd driven past it at the start of the holiday. 'I thought we were going to go there together?' she asked pointedly.

He finally put the phone down and turned to her. 'I was hungry.' He shrugged. 'We can still go there another day. We've got plenty of time before real life beckons and we head back to London.' He picked up his phone again, indicating the end of his participation in the conversation.

Melissa shook her head. Unbelievable. She was too livid to speak. When it was clear Liam wasn't going to look back up and engage, Melissa stalked over to the table where she'd thrown her car keys, grabbed them and slammed the front door behind her. She needed some thinking time.

Her stomach rumbled. In a fit of annoyance, she decided that, for the first time in her life, she was going to have dinner in a swanky restaurant by herself.

On the drive over to the Pheasant and Gun, she tried to work

Liam out. Who goes to a top gastro pub on their own, on a Saturday, when they are on holiday with their girlfriend? What on earth? It was like she wasn't really there. Like she wasn't actually on holiday with him. He didn't seem to care what she did with her days or whether they actually spent any time together at all. This was turning out to be the worst holiday she'd ever been on, but, as she thought this, she remembered two weeks in Magaluf with her parents when she was eighteen. Perhaps this week in Dorset was coming in a very close second.

By the time she pulled into the car park of the Pheasant and Gun, Melissa was starting to question her impulsive move. She was nervous. Other than a quick sandwich in a café, Melissa had never eaten out by herself before. Catching sight of herself in the rear-view mirror, she pulled out her make-up and made her face presentable.

On the walk across the gravel car park, she hastily pulled the band out of her long brown hair and let it fall down around her shoulders, fluffing it up a little for good measure. She'd never walked in anywhere and asked for a table for one. Maybe she could eat inconspicuously at the bar. She wished she'd brought one of her glossy magazines so she had something to read.

As she pulled open the door of the inn and walked through, she regretted her decision to dine solo. The bar was heaving with drinkers and all the dining tables were full. What was she doing? She should have just gone to the fish and chip shop.

'Can I help you?' the lady behind the bookings desk asked.

'Table for one?' Melissa asked uncertainly.

'Have you booked?' The woman eyed Melissa's outfit of jeans and T-shirt with a look of disdain.

Melissa's face fell. 'No, sorry.' Oh, what was she doing here?

While the hostess spent a long time looking through the diary in front of her trying to find a vacant timeslot, Melissa looked around self-consciously, mentally preparing herself to leave. As she did so, she caught the eye of a man sitting at one of the window tables. She glanced back and did a double take when she realised it was the TV historian.

Guy waved hello and gave her a look that said 'what are you doing here?'

'We don't have anything available until 9.30,' the fierce woman behind the desk said.

Melissa looked at her watch. That was hours away. 'Okay, don't worry.' She turned to leave, shrugged, mouthed a goodbye to Guy and gave him a small wave in return.

He shook his head and mouthed, 'No, come here.'

She stopped, confused, and gave him an awkward look.

He stood up and said loudly, 'Yes, come here.' Melissa saw him visibly cringe when he realised he was drawing attention.

She approached his table, feeling equally awkward.

'Hello,' he said, still standing.

'Hi,' Melissa replied, tucking a lock of hair behind her ear.

Guy looked behind her. 'Are you on your own?'

'Yes, but they've got no tables for ages, so I think I'm going to have to head to a takeaway.'

'Well, I've got a spare seat here and I've not ordered yet,' he said, glancing at the dark wooden chair opposite his.

'Oh no, I couldn't,' she returned. *That would be too weird.* She tucked her hair behind her ear again, wondering why she'd taken it out in the first place. She hated her hair being down. It just got in the way and she longed to shove it back in a ponytail again.

'Have dinner with me? What's the absolute worst that can happen?' he asked. 'You get a decent meal while being bored rigid by history chit-chat?'

Melissa laughed but couldn't think of a valid excuse. Plus she was really rather hungry now. 'Okay. Thanks,' she said on impulse.

They both sat down and a waitress appeared instantly. She

fawned over Guy as she discussed their drinks options and thrusted Melissa a menu. The waitress looked at Guy almost the whole time, even when asking what Melissa wanted. Melissa ordered water and Guy ordered a glass of Sauvignon.

'Are you having one?' Guy asked.

'Why not?' she said, then added, 'I'm driving, so just the one.' Something struck her then. Liam had said he'd had a bottle of Sauvignon at dinner earlier. Who orders a whole bottle of wine to themselves? Why had it not occurred to her to ask Liam if he'd had dinner alone or if he'd been with someone? And had he driven the little car he always kept in Dorset or had someone else driven him home?

No. She was being silly. He hadn't mentioned dining with anyone. And it was perfectly feasible to drink a whole bottle by yourself. She'd done it, more times than she cared to admit. But then drive home? No way.

'I take it you're feeling better now?' Guy interrupted her thoughts.

She nodded. 'Thank you for walking me back down the hill. How was the presentation?'

They were interrupted by the waitress again, who came back to give them their drinks and take their food order. With no time to look at the options, Melissa panic-ordered what Liam said he'd eaten. 'Crab cakes and skinny chips please.'

'That was quick,' Guy mumbled. 'You haven't even looked at your menu.' He quickly looked at his and ordered a steak.

When the waitress had gone, Guy continued, 'The presentation was good actually. Fascinating. Even for someone like me, who thinks they've heard it all before.'

Melissa studied him while he spoke. His brown hair fell over his eyes and he pushed it back every few seconds. Melissa thought he was good-looking – in a posh boy kind of way.

'I didn't get to look at the schoolhouse though,' he said. 'I didn't leave enough time. I think I might nip back tomorrow, just to satisfy idle curiosity. What did you think of the school? There's meant to be some of the children's work still on the walls, exercise books and coat pegs with their names on. It sounds rather moving.'

'I didn't see it either actually. I was rushing around quite quickly to get back for . . .' Melissa trailed off. Why exactly had she been rushing around to get back for Liam? He hadn't been bothered. It occurred to her now that he hadn't even asked where she'd been all day.

Guy waited for her to finish her sentence and when she didn't, he asked, 'Come with me tomorrow if you like? The photos in the church are wonderful too. A real eye-opener. You should see them before you finish your holiday.'

What would she be doing tomorrow, waiting about for Liam to grace her with his presence after surfing? And she did want to take a better look around.

'All right then, yes,' Melissa said, 'if you don't mind me tagging along?'

He beamed. 'It would be a pleasure.'

She looked at him and wondered how she'd got into this position. She was sat having dinner with a minor celebrity, albeit one she'd never heard of, who she'd only met a matter of hours ago and she was arranging to meet him again tomorrow.

Melissa felt a stab of guilt about Liam and then tried to quash it immediately. Liam was making her feel, well, a bit crap actually and Guy Cameron was making her feel very at ease. They were only going to look at some photos. It was hardly a date.

They ate their dinner and talked. Guy revealed he lived on the fringes of London where town just about met country and she confessed that she lived in a very unsexy part of town where London met Essex.

'And what do you do, when you aren't holidaying in Dorset?' he asked while they waited for pudding.

'I'm currently in between jobs,' she said, trying not to sound too embarrassed. She didn't really fancy telling him she'd jacked in her job in a fit of idealistic madness and was now temping.

'Oh right?' He was clearly waiting for more.

'Just office work. Admin really. Nothing very exciting. How did you get into TV presenting?' Melissa asked, attempting to move the conversation on quickly. She just couldn't admit to this incredibly successful and rather good-looking man how much of a failure she was.

The waitress brought their pudding over. They'd decided to share one of the restaurant's famous soufflés. Guy didn't have a sweet tooth, but he was happy to make the meal last a bit longer. He was enjoying Melissa's company. It was the first time he'd been out with a woman in a long time.

'I don't know, really. I suppose I sort of fell into it. Someone suggested I'd be good on a radio segment and it all spiralled from there.'

'I've got to confess that I've never actually watched any of your programmes,' Melissa said, pushing her spoon into the soft, pillowy pudding and obviously avoiding his eye contact.

He smiled. 'Well, thank you for being honest.' He was so used to people approaching him because he was in the public eye, believing they already knew him. It was refreshing talking to Melissa. She didn't gush compliments at him.

'And also, until I read your name on the leaflet this morning,' Melissa continued, 'I hadn't actually heard of you either.' He watched her spoon soufflé delicately into her mouth.

He laughed now. 'Believe it or not, that's music to my ears.'

'Really?' she asked. 'I did wonder if it was exhausting being a celebrity?' Guy grimaced at the word celebrity and Melissa continued. 'Whether you had to watch your back all the time in case someone papped you; whether you could go on a real bender in the pub without someone telling the *Daily Mail*?'

'Ah, no one cares about a Z-lister like me,' he said. 'I get photographed a lot by lovely middle-aged women who just want a nice picture to show their friends. And I'm far too clean-cut to have anything I do end up in the gossip rags,' he said with a wink.

'Shame.' She gave him a sideways smile. They looked at each other for a few seconds before she turned to signal the waitress for the bill. 'I should be getting back.'

'I'll get this,' Guy said. 'I insist.'

'Are you sure?'

He nodded, pulling out his wallet.

Melissa put her purse away with a reluctant look. 'All right,' she said slowly. 'But you have to let me buy you lunch tomorrow then. Even if it's only a plastic sandwich from a service station after we've been to Tyneham.'

'It's a deal.'

Melissa stood to leave and he held out his hand to shake hers to seal the deal.

She shook it with a smile. 'Erm, 11 a.m. okay for you? At the main entrance?'

'See you then,' he said.

She turned and gave him a little glance from the door. He waved goodbye and then sat down and cringed at himself when she was out of sight, pushing the rest of the pudding away. Who shakes hands after a nice dinner like that?

He glanced around him. A few people had recognised him and were smiling as he caught their eye. He nodded to politely acknowledge them. One lady was taking a sneaky picture of him on her phone. Oh well, not giving Melissa a friendly kiss on the cheek had perhaps done him a favour.

Melissa stood by the bookings desk for a few seconds, rifling in her bag for her car keys. The keeper of the bookings diary was off wielding her power over someone else and so Melissa did something she knew she was going to regret. She grabbed the diary and scanned through the list of names. She found what she was looking for in seconds and then put the book back before leaving the restaurant.

As she walked to her car, she felt cold and it wasn't due to the temperature. Liam's name was in the book, listed against an earlier booking. Table for two.

CHAPTER 3

Melissa knew what she had to do. She and Liam needed to have 'The Talk'.

But the idea of speaking to him about it created a hollow feeling in her stomach. This kind of thing had never gone down well at home. As a child, she'd spent far too much time in her room listening to her parents fight, listening to her mother plead with her father over one thing or another. The muffled tones rarely gave away what the argument was about, but her mother's crying at the end of almost every row had certainly been audible. But Melissa was stronger than her mother. She was sure of it. And at least there were no children hiding in an upstairs bedroom if a fight did break out between her and Liam.

She stood in the shower the following morning, thinking for far too long, letting the hot water run over her. Melissa considered her track record with men. It wasn't great. She knew that. Before Liam, six months had been her absolute personal best when it came to relationships. She knew it must be something she was doing. Or not doing. Perhaps that was a throwback to watching her parents kill their own relationship one fight at a time.

Liam had been asleep by the time she'd got in last night and Melissa was secretly grateful that he'd already left to go surfing by the time she'd woken up this morning. Although whether they spoke about their issues, including Liam's mystery restaurant booking, tonight or tomorrow, this delay was only putting off the inevitable. Things weren't working and Melissa wanted to know why.

She had hoped this holiday was going to fix whatever it was that had already gone so horribly wrong, but it was only high-lighting that they really weren't very compatible at all. Somehow, none of it seemed quite so horrific during the daily grind of working life when they only saw each other a few evenings a week.

Maybe that was the problem. Maybe he'd lost respect for her having jacked her job in. But she hadn't been out of work for *that* long and she was on the hunt for something more suitable. It certainly didn't help that Liam was silent a lot of the time these days and that Melissa did most of the talking, often to fill the silence. He'd never been a big chatter and his silent brooding was one of the things that Melissa had originally found attractive about him. But now his inability to actually talk about anything meaningful was doing neither of them any favours. She sighed and turned the shower off, knowing that when they did eventually speak, she couldn't expect much from Liam. It would be her doing most of the talking anyway.

The clock on the car radio showed 11 a.m. by the time Melissa was finally on her way through the country lanes, passing quaint traditional white fingerpost signs every few miles. In the distance, over the green hills littered with sheep, she could see the coastline and out to sea as she drove. The sun glinted off the water brightly. She was going full pelt in her hatchback, eager to keep the appoint-ment she had agreed to. It felt like an old-fashioned sort of meeting; the kind people made before mobile phones and email meant you could casually cancel moments before and hope it would be okay. Why hadn't she taken Guy's mobile number? With her outrageous timekeeping, she wasn't going to be there for at least another fifteen to twenty minutes. And that was assuming she didn't get stuck behind a tractor.

As her car eventually skidded to a halt in the car park, kicking up a bit of turf, Melissa could see Guy leaning against the gatepost. She smiled. He had waited.

'I'm so sorry I'm late,' she said as Guy pointed to his watch and raised his eyebrows with a grin. 'I couldn't find my car keys and I thought my boyfriend might have moved them and then I almost forgot I promised to buy us some lunch. But it's not from a service station. Oh no, it's from a lovely little deli, so I think you'll like it. But I don't have a picnic mat, so we'll have to just sit on the grass, which I don't mind, if you don't. And look,' she said, presenting a huge bottle, 'ta-da. I remembered to bring water today!'

During her little speech, his face took on a confused expression, but Melissa couldn't work out why. She lowered the water.

'I really am sorry I'm late,' she said again.

He smiled thinly, but she still couldn't read his expression; his eyes were hidden behind mirrored Ray-Bans, which meant Melissa could only see her own flustered reflection.

'What's wrong?' Melissa asked.

'Nothing.' His expression lifted. 'I'm glad you're here. Let me carry that.' He reached out and took the water bottle and the bag of shopping from her hands.

'Thanks.' Melissa locked the car and they walked together into Tyneham. 'I thought we could eat the picnic up by the Great House. I realise you didn't get to see it yesterday. You were too busy escorting a dehydrated woman back down the hill.'

He laughed. 'True.'

They walked on a few paces.

'No golf buggy today?' Melissa ventured.

He looked sheepish. 'Not today. God, I felt like a complete idiot yesterday, whizzing past everyone in that bloody buggy. I absolutely loathe things like that.'

She looked at him through her sunglasses and they fell into a companionable silence.

'So,' he said after a while, 'how long have you been with your boyfriend?'

'How do you know I have a boyfriend?'

'You just told me. He was one of the reasons you were late.'

'Oh. Did I? About eight months.' Melissa looked at Guy. Was it her imagination that Guy looked a bit annoyed?

'Shall we look in the schoolhouse first?' Guy asked, seemingly changing the subject.

Melissa nodded, wondering why Liam's existence might be bothering Guy. He didn't think this was a date, did he? Of course he didn't. She was being silly. He was a famous historian and she'd seen the way he had women practically falling at his feet.

Guy opened the large wooden door to the schoolhouse and held it for her. If there hadn't been a few tourists in front of her, Melissa could have sworn she'd been transported back in time. Everything inside the bright, airy room was cleanly scrubbed, but the original open-lid desks and chairs were still on the dark wood floor. Pieces were displayed around the walls: drawings of famous landmarks, old charts showing capital cities and times tables. It was all very atmospheric. The few tourists inside the room were whispering, out of a sort of respect.

Melissa walked around, grateful that it wasn't as busy in the village today as it was yesterday. She might have struggled to have actually seen any of the items inside the room otherwise. She thumbed through some of the textbooks on the shelves before stopping at the curved metal coat pegs on the far wall, still showing the names of the last of the children to attend the school before it had closed for requisition.

'My gran came to this school.' Guy stood beside her and looked at the coat pegs.

'Really?' Melissa raised her eyebrows. 'Wow.'

'It's mad to think she sat at one of these desks and copied out tasks from that chalk board.' He nodded to the front of the classroom.

'How old was she when she left the village?' Melissa turned to face him.

'Seventeen. She was working up at the Great House by that point, so she'd long since left the school.'

Guy moved off and Melissa flicked through a few of the children's exercise books, trying to decipher the old-fashioned handwriting. She wondered why she'd never really bothered to explore museums and the kind of houses the National Trust owned before. Perhaps she'd never really known anyone who was interested enough to go with her, but now she was here, she was fascinated and enjoying herself.

Out of the corner of her eye, she saw Guy leaning back against the wall, fully engrossed in reading an old leather-bound encyclopedia. A few teenage girls arrived, clearly bored on a day out with their parents, and were making themselves busy, trying to catch his eye. Melissa smiled. Even if they had no idea who the man hidden behind the mirrored shades was, he was incredibly attractive. He looked up and gave them a quick smile before looking down at the book again. The girls giggled and nudged each other. Guy was completely oblivious.

'Melissa, are you ready to go and look at Tyneham House?' He put the book back on the shelf. 'There's not as much to see as in here, but it's a sunny day and we can eat our picnic.'

Melissa agreed, put the exercise book down and accompanied Guy out the door. She gave the girls a polite smile as she edged her way past them and tried not to laugh when they shot her daggers.

'Those girls were eyeing you up,' Melissa teased.

Guy looked around blankly. 'Which girls?'

'Never mind.' She laughed.

'They probably thought I was someone else. People often

assume I'm some A-lister when they think they recognise me, and then try hard to hide their disappointment when they realise "Oh, it's just you off the telly."'

'Oh, I feel so bad for you.' Melissa nudged his arm and Guy found himself laughing.

They walked through the rest of the village in companionable silence. Now Guy wasn't being driven around in a golf buggy with the organisers chatting to him non-stop, he could see the village properly, for what it was. A bloody mess. He had been waiting to see the village without quite realising it, for most of his adult life; ever since his grandmother had talked quietly about Tyneham years ago and her idyllic childhood there. As a historian, his specialist subject was World War Two and so he knew of the few villages up and down the country that had been taken over by the army during the war. Whole communities had been forcibly ejected. His grandmother had been part of one such community and now he was seeing where she'd grown up. He'd been amazed that she hadn't wanted to come with him, see the village and walk, very literally, down memory lane. 'It would be too painful,' she had said. 'Best not go back.'

He and Melissa strolled past shells of pubs, farm labourers' cottages, and what used to be shops. Guy sighed at what he saw and was grateful his grandmother hadn't come along. She'd have hated this. Inside, he was reeling. He shook his head. This had been his grandmother's village and now it was a ruin. Crumbling brickwork, boarded-up windows, great chunks of roofs missing, and the occasional *Danger – No Entry* sign. His grandmother had been stoic when discussing it. 'It helped win us the war,' she'd said. It was best she'd remember it how it was then and not how it looked now.

By the time they reached Tyneham House, Guy was miserable. Melissa had been right when she'd said it was all just so depressing. It really was. He'd not felt like this yesterday. The schoolhouse was charming and it was clear the guides had made an effort in sprucing it up for visitors. But he was more interested in the house, which gave off an air of absolute abandonment, despite the fact it was one of the very few buildings in the village still intact.

The village had been weeded and the grass cut, but the grounds of the Great House were in need of some love. They stood on a large patch of trampled grass in front of the manor. So this was it then. Tyneham House. He stood back to look at the once-great building. He noted the boarded-up doors and windows with their words of warning emblazoned across. For a reason he couldn't quite pinpoint, he felt as if a heavy weight was on him.

While his grandmother didn't have especially fond memories, he'd found it enchanting to know she'd turned up for work here during the early war years before she'd had to leave Tyneham behind. In the village, he'd tried picking out her family home she'd described to him, but those that were still standing all looked the same. He couldn't locate any individual property out of the identical ones from the long row into the village, towards the market square and back out towards the coast. He'd taken pictures in the hope she'd be able to spot her former home, but he was rather against showing them to her now. Her once lovely village home was in tatters.

'I'd love to see inside.' Melissa looked up at the house. 'I can just imagine that front door leads on to a large and ornate entrance hall complete with fireplace and sweeping staircase,' she said. 'I used to dream of living in a grand old country house in the unlikely event I ever became a millionaire.' Melissa blushed.

'It's a pity it's not for sale,' Guy mused. 'It's run-down of course, but with a hell of a lot of money and TLC, it could be a home once again. It's a shame it can't be.'

'Why can't it be?'

'The house and village are still owned by the Ministry of Defence,' he said. 'The army uses the land around it for artillery and tank training. The village and this house were in the way then and still are now. Not during summer though. They stop their training exercises over summer.'

Melissa's face fell. 'Oh, right. So it's just going to stay like this then? Until it falls away to rubble?'

'I suppose all we can do is appreciate it as a piece of social history now and endeavour to understand the huge sacrifice the residents made,' he said. 'That's just the way it is with all those villages requisitioned during the war. Some of them were given back, but they were often unliveable by the time the army had finished with them. They're mostly tourist attractions now.'

Melissa sighed and then busied herself getting the picnic food out of the paper bag. She'd bought some breadsticks and various dips, a crusty loaf, two kinds of cheese, some delicious-looking sliced ham, and paper plates and empty takeaway coffee cups for the water. She looked quite pleased with the little array until, 'Oh damn. I forgot to ask for plastic cutlery to slice the cheese and ham with. We'll just have to use fingers, I'm afraid.'

Guy sat down next to her on the grass and drew his eyes away from the building and down to the feast in front of him. 'Impressive.'

'Tuck in,' Melissa encouraged.

Guy ripped off a bit of Brie. He held it between his fingers and narrowed his eyes at the building.

Melissa glanced at where he was looking and then back to him. 'What?' she asked.

He shook his head. 'Nothing,' he said and put the cheese into his mouth and chewed. When he finished, he asked, 'Did you know the owner of the house, Sir Albert Standish, was an MP?'

Melissa shook her head and rolled up a piece of ham. 'Gosh, that was unfortunate. Being an MP and still having your home whipped out from underneath you, same as your constituents. No special treatment for *him*. Bet he wasn't too chuffed. Was that who your grandmother worked for?'

'He and his wife, Lady Veronica. My gran doesn't speak very

highly of him though. Bit of a bastard from what I can gather. Gran was one of their maids. I think she was the last one to leave.' Guy frowned, trying to remember what his gran had said. 'She loved Lady Veronica though. The family owned the entire village and all the surrounding farmland. Everyone rented their properties from the Standishes.'

'Where did they all go? The villagers, I mean. How do you rehouse a whole village in the middle of a war?'

'Temporary accommodation in the nearby towns. Some went to stay with family,' Guy said. 'My great-grandparents went to stay with relatives, I think, and then my gran joined the war effort and was posted away for a while.'

Melissa looked at the house again and then dipped a breadstick into some hummus. 'Where did the Standishes go?'

'Good question. They probably had a London home.' He rolled up a piece of ham and looked back at the house.

They shared small talk and when they had finished their picnic, tidied up and walked slowly down towards the church.

'I'm looking forward to seeing these pictures now,' Melissa said. 'You've really built this up, so it had better be good.'

'You won't be disappointed.'

He opened the heavy wooden door and showed her into the church, removing his sunglasses and hooking them into his shirt pocket. The church was beautiful on the inside and out. Built of the same pale brick as the Great House, it had huge stained-glass windows that dripped an array of sunlit colour onto the flagstone floor. Tourists milled about and an elderly guide whose name badge read 'Reg' acknowledged Guy immediately and started fussing. Guy shook the man's hand and then raised his finger to his lips, indicating the tourists. The guide smiled knowingly, pleased to be in on the secrecy, and left Guy and Melissa to it.

Melissa pushed her sunglasses up onto her head and looked up at one of the stained-glass windows. The light was streaming through and casting glorious colour onto her, her face raised up intently, studying the glass. She was beautiful, Guy thought as he leaned against one of the pews. Almost ethereal in this light.

She turned to look at him and walked slowly towards him. He felt like his heart had lurched into his mouth.

'Come on then, Mr Historian,' she said quietly. 'Show me these photos.'

He led her over to a series of boards that had been staggered around the nave of the church. Each one showed a group of properties, their owners, and had a bit of information about their family histories and what had happened to them after they had left Tyneham.

'That's Gran.' He looked proud as he leaned over her shoulder to point to a photo of a teenage girl in a pinafore, her hair up in a loose bun with a few front sections falling down by her face.

'She was very pretty,' Melissa said and turned to smile up at Guy. He was only a few inches from her, and he smiled, a lovely smile that made the corners of his eyes crinkle.

Melissa read each of the boards with interest and scanned the pictures of the various houses, the vicarage and the post office. At the final board, Melissa saw the same bit of blurb about the Great House that she'd read in the leaflet and looked at pictures of the house in its heyday taken from various angles. A few black and white images of the staff and owners throughout the years were on display. And then there was the portrait shot of Sir Albert Standish and his wife Veronica taken outside their house. It was larger, much more clear than the miniature version on the board at the Great House. She could actually see their faces. The caption said it had been taken by the local Historical Society. Melissa was taken aback by Veronica and Albert. They were much younger than she imagined they would be; they looked no older than their early thirties. She wasn't sure why, but Melissa had imagined they'd be at least middle aged.

She raised an eyebrow. 'Lady Veronica was beautiful,' she said to Guy, who turned to look. Veronica had dark hair, possibly red, but it was hard to tell in the black and white of the photo, swept over on one side so a thick waterfall of fashionable rolled curls fells down to her shoulders. She had thick eyelashes, fairly high cheekbones and was wearing a dark lipstick that Melissa guessed might be red. Melissa turned her gaze to the man standing by Lady Veronica's side, Sir Albert. 'Her husband was a looker too.'

'Yes, I suppose. If you like that sort of thing,' Guy said jokingly.

Sir Albert had a chiselled jaw and dark hair that looked like it should have fallen to his eyes but was instead firmly Brylcreemed, giving it a bit of height.

'Imagine what their children must have looked like. Supermodels,' Melissa marvelled.

'I don't think they ever had children actually. My gran never mentioned children when she worked there.'

'That's a shame. So there was no one to inherit the house?'

'No. But like the rest of the village, the house was subject to a compulsory purchase order after the war. It didn't matter that he was an MP.' Guy nodded towards the picture of Sir Albert. 'He never got it back.'

Melissa looked at Albert and Veronica Standish. The photograph was dated December 1943 – the same month the village had been rendered a ghost town. Had they already known when the picture was taken that they were being kicked out?

There was something about Albert Standish that Melissa couldn't put her finger on. He looked stern, but not only that, he looked . . . Melissa couldn't work it out. The body language was normal enough for a formal photo, but the hand that was holding Veronica's was clenched; as if he were holding on to her far too tightly. Melissa tried to see past his ridiculous good looks and wondered if he didn't have a bit of a domineering edge to him.

Melissa peered at Lady Veronica again and tried to work out Veronica's expression. Her mouth was set in a straight line and her eyes were slightly wider than was normal, but there was something else . . .

'Look at Lady Veronica,' she said. 'Look at her face. Does she seem a bit odd to you?'

Guy looked. 'Maybe. Perhaps she's not happy having her picture taken?'

Melissa wasn't sure. She read the words that accompanied the picture to see what had happened to the couple after they had left Tyneham. It didn't say. All the other boards had little stories about each family, but the Standishes had no information at all.

'What happened to them after the requisition?' she asked Guy. 'It doesn't say.'

'Yes, I wondered that,' he replied. 'I'll ask my gran, she might know.'

Melissa turned back to the photograph of the couple. After a few seconds she'd worked out what the expression was on the woman's face: fear.

Lady Veronica Standish looked scared to death.

CHAPTER 4

Tyneham, December 1943

'Hurry. Put that in there.' Veronica threw her leather jewellery box through the air to her maid, Anna. Anna pushed it into one of the trunks that was open in the middle of the bedroom and looked up at her employer, ready to catch the next item. Veronica rifled in drawers and grabbed whatever she could that she thought she could either use or sell.

With nothing else flying through the air, Anna dashed past Veronica and yanked open the wardrobe doors, helping to pull clothes from rails and piling them into the middle of the room. Both women knew there was no time to sort, simply to stuff suitcases and trunks and get Veronica out.

'I'm sorry I can't take you with me.' Veronica was breathless, quickly throwing fur stoles that she knew she'd get good money for into the trunks.

'I understand. Don't worry about me. I'll go back to my parents after you've left. And then, in a few days, we're all leaving the village anyway . . .' Anna trailed off as she picked up a beige booklet from the floor. Her eyes were wide. 'Why have you collected your ration book from Cook?'

'I'll need it,' Veronica said.

Anna frowned and put it inside the trunk.

'What's wrong?' Veronica asked.

'I don't think that was a good idea. What if she tells Sir Albert you've got it?'

'I told her I had to take a quick shopping trip to London. She can't possibly know what I'm doing.'

Anna looked worried. 'Let's hope not. Will you be going to London in the end? I mean, really?'

'I don't know where I'm going yet,' Veronica said. 'Anywhere will be better than here. I'll get a hotel first near a station and then I'll make plans to move on.'

'Don't write to me,' Anna said. 'He'll know.'

Veronica nodded and wondered how a seventeen-year-old was so wise beyond her years. Living with Veronica and Sir Albert had obviously opened Anna's eyes to the harsh realities of human behaviour.

'All right, that's everything I think I'll need.' Veronica stuffed the last of her clothing into the trunk, snapping the clasp shut. 'Your brother's still coming with the trap, isn't he?'

'He'll be here any minute.' Anna took down the eighteenth-century marble and gold clock from above the mantelpiece and held it out. 'You might get a few pounds for this.'

Veronica shook her head. 'It belongs to Bertie. It's a family heirloom. Best to put it back.' She didn't want to give her husband any more reason to hate her. She knew he'd be enraged and would begin hunting her down the moment he realised she was gone. Any further excuse would add to whatever sentence Bertie had in store when he found her.

If he found her.

The sound of a horse and cart crunched rhythmically over the sweep of the gravel drive.

'Is it your brother? Is it William?' Veronica asked.

Anna dashed to the window and her hands flew to her face.

Veronica's head shot up and she pushed her long auburn hair out of her eyes. 'What? What is it?'

37

'It's not William.'

Veronica dashed to the window. The house had been so quiet for ever so long. Visitors were few and far between since the war had started. 'Who on earth is it? No one is expected. Not today. Why is someone visiting today?'

Veronica peered down as the cart approached the front door. A well-dressed man in a suit was sitting next to the driver, but from the bedroom window, the angle made it impossible to see his face.

'I'll go down and tell them no one's at home. William will be here any minute and . . .' Anna trailed off. William's horse and cart had come into view at the end of the driveway and was on its way towards the house.

'Oh, dear God, it's too late. Anna . . .' Veronica closed her eyes and tried not to let panic get the better of her.

'No, it'll be all right. We can still get you away. Just wait here for a minute.' Anna turned and left the room.

Veronica clutched the thick curtain so hard that the whites of her knuckles showed. She stared at the first cart, hoping for it to turn and leave with its passenger still on board.

Veronica saw Anna rush round from the side of the house and spin her fingers in the air, indicating to William to turn around and go. Halfway down the drive, William threw his hands in the air to his sister, indicating the task was an impossible one. He continued towards the house in order to sweep past and exit through the other entrance and, as he did so, acknowledged the passenger of the first cart with a tip of his hat. Veronica strained her eyes downward to try to identify the suited man but was unable to get a glimpse of his face.

William's cart continued away from the house and out of the space where the large iron gates had once stood. Veronica had loved those gates. But having been taken in the metal drives in 1940 to help build weapons and Spitfires, they had not yet been replaced. It didn't matter now. She would not be here to see them remade.

From the latticed window of her bedroom Veronica watched as Anna stopped momentarily in front of the visitor. Anna started to speak and then narrowed her eyes as if in confusion.

Anna opened the front door, indicated for the man to come inside and then disappeared inside herself.

What on earth was Anna doing? Why was William leaving? And why was she showing that man inside?

Veronica left her bedroom and descended the main staircase, almost tripping as she moved. Her mind was a whir. She was supposed to be in William's cart, making her way towards the train station with her belongings. She was supposed to be leaving Bertie. There might still be time. If she could get rid of the visitor quickly, they might have time to summon William back before Bertie returned from his appointment in Dorchester. Veronica tried to take control of her nerves.

Anna stopped and looked up at Veronica, a frightened expression on her face. Veronica looked past Anna and into the eyes of a man she recognised but had not seen for years. She stopped on the final stair, let out a large breath and gripped the bannisters for fear of collapsing.

'No,' she whispered and then collected herself. 'Anna,' Veronica said, forcing the words out with as much calm as possible. 'I think . . . perhaps today . . . I think that some of the trunks may need . . .'

Anna searched her employer's eyes. Veronica knew she looked lost. She didn't have the answer.

Not now. How would she ever leave now?

Anna shot Veronica a desperate look as the maid walked past. But there was nothing either of them could do.

The man smiled up at Veronica, a wide smile that reached his eyes as she eventually descended the stairs towards him.

'Veronica Hanbury, as I live and breathe,' he said.

'Freddie?' she whispered. She was looking into the eyes of Bertie's brother.

CHAPTER 5

'In the flesh,' he said with a grin. 'Although I should have called you Veronica Standish, but I'm afraid old habits die hard.'

Veronica stepped off the final stair slowly and stood in front of Freddie, looking at his features before throwing her arms around him. Freddie staggered back a pace and slowly lifted his arms to embrace her.

'It's so good to see you,' she whispered into his neck. He was warm, despite the cold of the day and memories flooded back to her of the last time he'd held her like this; so long ago when things were simple. Before everything had changed and she'd married his brother. Before it had all gone so horribly wrong.

He pushed her back gently, holding her at arm's length, and studied her. 'You're still as beautiful as the last time I saw you. Feels like years ago.'

'It was,' she nodded. 'Nearly five.'

'Well, there we are then,' he replied and let go of her.

She searched his face. He looked the same, but now his eyes creased at the sides when he smiled and the beginnings of frown lines had appeared on his forehead.

'I can't believe you're here,' Veronica said.

'Really? I wrote and told Bertie I was coming. Or rather, I replied to his strongly worded demand.'

'I had no idea. He didn't tell me.'

'Strange. Maybe he didn't think I'd come.'

'But you are here,' Veronica said, smiling.

He nodded. 'Is there anyone about to lend a hand with suitcases and trunks and whatnot?'

'No. I'm sorry. We've packed up all the things that are going to the London house and sent them on already. We've only got Cook, and the maids Rebecca and Anna, who you just saw, until we go. We've got a removal company coming to help load the last remaining things when we all leave in a few days. Can I help you with your cases?'

Freddie laughed. 'Of course not. I'll manage. Bertie ordered me to clear my things out on the off chance the army sneak off with my possessions while they've got free run of the place. I've only brought a few suitcases to fill. I can't imagine there's much left of me here really.'

Veronica knew all too well how true that last statement was. Bertie had removed almost every trace of his brother from the house years ago. It was as if Freddie had never existed at all. The strange mix of dislike and misplaced jealousy Bertie had always felt towards his younger brother ran as fresh now as it had always done. So it was odd that Bertie had ordered Freddie all the way down to Dorset for the purpose of clearing out his possessions. She was sure Bertie knew there wasn't much left.

'Am I in my old bedroom?'

'I . . . I'm not sure what's made up. I didn't know you were coming. Most of the furniture has gone to London or into storage.'

He put his hand softly on her arm and she looked down at it. Her breathing slowed. He'd always had a calming effect on her. He removed his hand and made a fuss of looking at his watch. 'Any chance of some lunch and a stiff drink? I've been travelling

41

for bloody ages. The trains were a nightmare. Full of troops and the Navy. I stood almost all the way from London.'

While Freddie collected his cases from the cart and paid the driver, Veronica went off to see if Cook could rustle up a meal. Most of the vegetables from the kitchen garden had been dug up in preparation for departure. Bertie was adamant if they were leaving the house to the army, they'd already taken enough from him. The army could grow its own food, Bertie reasoned. He was determined to leave nothing behind for the soldiers. Veronica was appalled at Bertie's unpatriotic stance, especially as the stews Cook had been providing over the past week were far too plentiful for the household and most of it was being wasted. But she knew that to say anything would lead to what her mother would call 'unpleasant behaviour that should not be mentioned again'.

Veronica thought of her mother. The idea of running to her had crossed her mind but had quickly been eschewed in favour of going it alone. Mrs Hanbury idolised Bertie. She'd never quite got the hang of calling him by his nickname, instead preferring the way 'Sir Albert' felt on her tongue and how it sounded to her bridge club friends when she spoke of her son-in-law, the MP. When Veronica had tried to discreetly mention that Bertie took to drink and was a little free and easy with his fists, Mrs Hanbury had told her never to mention it again. In that moment Veronica knew that in marrying Bertie she had made her own bed and had to lie in it.

Bertie hadn't always been this way. It had been subtle at first, so subtle Veronica had managed to brush her fears under the carpet. Slowly, over the first months of their marriage, the honeymoon period had crossed seamlessly into silence and surliness on Bertie's part. And what Veronica now saw as desperation on her part to get Bertie to engage with her. Perhaps that had been what pushed him over the edge. There had been many a time Veronica had worried Bertie disliked her. But whenever she had found her mind wandering in that direction she had accused herself of going mad.

There were many 'firsts' in Veronica's life she could remember with utmost clarity. Her first day at boarding school and the fear of leaving her family behind; the first time she saw Freddie and how remarkably wonderful he had been – unlike any other man she had ever met. And the first day Bertie hit her. The memory of that day had burnt itself into her mind with the same ferocity as that which his fist had landed on her cheekbone. She would never forget it. It heralded the beginning of the end of their marriage, such as it had ever been.

The argument had been short and the violence had come from nowhere. Although if Veronica had analysed Bertie's behaviour over the preceding months, she would have seen the layers of it thickly building within him.

They had been going to a party. Her dress had been too low-cut and in it, Bertie said, she had looked obscene. She had laughed, not at him, but because she thought he'd been making a joke. She hadn't taken him seriously and had touched his arm to soothe as she had looked past him towards the wardrobe to choose her shoes. And then suddenly she was on the floor, wide-eyed and holding her cheek. Looking up at him, she saw a flash of satisfaction in his eyes before he issued his monotone apology. She didn't go to the party. It had taken a fortnight for the bruise to fade enough for her to be able to cover it with powder and eventually be able to leave the house.

The next time he did it he didn't apologise.

Bertie was not the man she thought he was. After the shock of realising this had worn off, she had felt so lost and alone. His violence was unpredictable and linked to his ever-increasing thirst for alcohol. But she knew now that if she was going to summon the courage and the strength to do anything about her situation, she would be doing it entirely alone. She thought of Anna. Thank God for Anna. Veronica was not quite so alone.

As Veronica made her way to the kitchen, her heart sank. She had almost left. She had almost tasted freedom. It was too late now. In the confusion of Freddie's arrival, William had gone and with him her lifeline. She felt in her pocket for the little purse of pin money she'd scavenged together from coins Bertie had left scattered in his study over the last few months. It wasn't much. She'd been summoning up the courage to leave him for the last six months – ever since she fully realised his drinking was now entirely out of control. He'd been drinking for as long as she had known him, but it was as Bertie had grown disheartened with the war and his place in the wider world that he had really upped his daily allowance to unprecedented levels. And with the drink came the madness and the violence he couldn't keep at bay.

After she'd had a few words with their reluctant cook, Veronica moved into the sitting room that faced the front drive. The large room now only housed oversized settees, the wireless, a drinks trolley and a few old copies of *The Tatler* piled up on a coffee table. All the ornaments, portraits and Chinese rugs from the ground floor had been packed up and sent on. As such, the room echoed.

Veronica went to the fire and prodded it, sending sparks onto the hearth. She hugged herself against the cold of the December day and stared blankly into the flames. Her mind moved back to a simpler time. She and Freddie dancing together on the threadbare carpet of the little flat he'd just bought but hadn't had time to furnish. How they'd both tried hard in his kitchen to master cooking something from a battered copy of *Mrs Beeton's Book of Household Management*. It had been the only cookery book they'd ever heard of and they had bought it together from a second-hand bookshop on a whim. They'd laughingly discarded the Victorian tome, wondering what on earth had possessed them, before Freddie had bicycled off for fish and chips.

A log shifted in front of her and sparks flew high in the grate, snapping her back from her memory. She could have cried thinking about how happy she had been then, how happy she thought he had been. But she'd been wrong about Freddie.

Why the hell was he here? And what in God's name was she going to do now?

Freddie lugged his two small cases and his gas mask in its cardboard box up the stairs and deposited them at the top. He had intended to stay until the end, to see all his childhood friends from the village and leave when they all left together on the final day; if any of his friends were left. He knew many would have been called up. Or, like him, would have joined up at the first available opportunity. But he felt like a fraud. He'd not been back to the village in years and to stand with those that were here at the end in an act of solidarity didn't feel quite right somehow. Unlike them, he wasn't losing anything. He hadn't lived in his family home for a long time. He wouldn't miss it either. He told himself he was only here for his things. Perhaps he shouldn't have responded to Bertie's letter. Perhaps he shouldn't have come at all.

A noise of something heavy being dropped onto the floor down the hall grabbed his attention and he glanced quickly to the right to see what it was. The maid Anna was in one of the bedrooms, picking up items that had fallen out of a black leather jewellery box. Around her were trunks that looked as if they had sprung open and had spilled their contents around the solid wood floor. She looked as if she was in the midst of chaos.

On seeing him, Anna moved towards the bedroom door and, with her gaze cast to the floor, closed the door gently but pointedly.

Strange girl, he thought.

Freddie turned his attention back to his suitcases and wondered what he'd actually left here all those years ago that Bertie, in his short and clipped mandate, demand he now remove.

On the train down from London, he'd been rather nervous about seeing Veronica. It had been so long. He'd pictured her face the whole way down. Imagined what he'd say to her. He compared

45

her now to how he remembered her, before his brother had swooped in and set his sights on her. Back then she'd been fun, exciting, a breath of fresh air. He remembered the party where they'd met. He smiled as he recollected the moment he'd spotted her instantly across the room. She had been drinking champagne from a cut-glass saucer, laughing raucously and spilling it everywhere. A gaggle of men surrounded her, offering to mop up her spillage. Of course they had. She was the most beautiful woman he'd ever seen. But she'd locked eyes with Freddie as he walked in to the party and it was as if his world had changed forever.

The woman in front of him now as he entered the sitting room was not the Veronica from back then. Her hand shook slightly as she chewed her nails and stared wide-eyed but unseeing into the fire. He watched her silently, wondering what had happened to her since he'd last seen her that had changed her quite so much.

She spotted him out of the corner of her eye and forced a smile. 'Gin and tonic?' Her voice almost broke as she spoke and she knew she had to work harder to keep a tight lid on her emotions. She wasn't used to men other than Bertie being in the house. She told herself it was just Freddie, but that only made it worse.

'How'd you get hold of decent gin?' he enquired. 'Black market?'

Veronica shrugged. 'I assume so. Bertie always finds a way of getting what he wants.'

He nodded and made his way over to the drinks trolley, glancing around the room as he did so. 'I will, thanks. This room's empty.' It was an obvious comment.

Veronica didn't answer.

'I assume all my old things are in the attic?'

'I think so.'

'It's probably just an old cricket bat and a trunk of books, but I'll go up later and take a look,' he said. 'I think I'll get out of your hair tomorrow.'

She turned quickly from the fire to face him. 'But you've only just arrived.'

He made an apologetic face and then shrugged. 'The factory doesn't run itself, you know.'

She looked into the fire again, forcing herself to breathe calmly. 'Are you . . . very busy?' She was on the edge of asking him if he was happy.

He threw himself into one of the few remaining overstuffed settees and stretched his legs out. 'I shouldn't complain. But we're struggling to keep up with the demand for munitions.' He rubbed his eyes, which looked tired. 'Bertie shows no interest in the business. So I'll just keep at it in the office on my own.' He put his head back against the settee. 'How are you?' He stared up at the ornate plasterwork. 'It's been a while.'

She followed him to the settees and sat opposite him. 'It has.'

Veronica felt suddenly nervous. The joy of seeing Freddie again after all this time had hit her unexpectedly, guiltily, even if his arrival had ruined her chance to leave. She still didn't understand what had happened between her and Freddie all those years ago. There had been a fleeting moment when she thought it was they that would marry, not she and Bertie. How stupid she'd been to think that.

Freddie had put up no fight when she'd left him. He'd not loved her after all. He'd made it too easy for her to walk away. And now here he was, as dangerously handsome and as charming as ever. Why didn't he look as nervous as she? How could he sit there looking so . . . confident?

She avoided his question. How was she? She was a shipwreck of a person. And she was sure he could see that.

'I'm just going to check on Anna. I left her with rather a lot to do. Lunch won't be long.' Veronica left the room with Freddie looking at her retreating figure.

*

'What's happening?' Anna asked as Veronica entered the room. She shoved the last of the clothes away and pushed the empty trunks into the corner.

'He's going tomorrow, he says.'

'Good. We can try again after he leaves.'

Veronica sat on the bed and put her head in her hands. 'It's no good, Anna. That was it. That was my only chance. Bertie's not planning on going anywhere else. He's only out today because he's at his solicitors attempting to fight the requisition order on the house. I'll have to wait until we get to London. Perhaps I can slip out one day when Bertie's busy. It'll be easier in London. There I can disappear into a crowd instantly.'

Anna was silent for a moment and then said, 'He's not here now, is he? Just go. Now. We can walk down to the village. We'll see if William's still able to drive us to the station. You've got your money? And you can just take the jewellery box in your handbag. You can sell the jewels. What will they fetch?'

'I've no idea.' Veronica felt hope rise within her. 'Enough to find somewhere to rent, I think, while I look for some kind of job. Although heaven knows what I'll do. I must do something. But I'm sure I can work all that through later.' Veronica stood. 'Yes,' she smiled, clutching Anna's hand. 'Let's go. Let's find William.'

Anna grabbed the jewellery box while Veronica cast her eyes over her bedroom one final time. But as Veronica turned, she stopped dead and gasped. Freddie was standing by the open door.

CHAPTER 6

Veronica tried to force her face into a normal expression, but Freddie's look was one of uncertainty. Veronica panicked: how much had he heard?

'I just came to put my cases in my room,' he said, looking from Veronica to Anna and then back again.

'Right, yes.' Veronica snapped to attention. 'Of course. I'm sorry I haven't checked to see . . .'

Anna spoke up. 'The Blue Room is still made up, sir. The others have been emptied.'

Veronica threw her maid a helpless look as Freddie bent to pick up his suitcases.

Inside the Blue Room, Freddie dumped his cases just inside the door while Veronica threw open the thick blue curtains and removed the blackout frame from the windows. She couldn't remember the last time anyone had slept in this room. It had been so long since they'd had guests. So long since Bertie had allowed Veronica to have any of her remaining friends to stay. And now all their friends were in far-flung locations, playing their individual parts in beating Hitler; something she longed to do but which Bertie would never allow if it meant her being out of the house for long periods of time. She wasn't sure her old friends from London would have come if she had invited them. Not just because they would be doing vital war work somewhere or other, but because they'd never really liked Bertie, had never really accepted her marrying him. As such, she hadn't kept in touch with them. Bertie had discouraged it, feeling the same disdain towards her friends as they felt towards him. Inviting them to a party at Tyneham House wasn't worth the argument with Bertie. And he no longer invited any of his friends, preferring privacy and quiet. They had been shut up alone in Dorset for so long, Veronica thought she was going to go mad.

Winter sunshine penetrated the room. Veronica stood by the window, reluctant to turn and look at Freddie. When she eventually did, she attempted a smile and hoped it masked the fact that she felt like the stuffing had been knocked out of her.

Freddie looked at her and a worried expression appeared on his face.

'Veronica, I hope you don't mind my saying. You look very thin. You look like you've had no sleep. Are you unwell? Are you ill? I mean, really ill?'

'I'm fine,' she lied. 'It's the stress of the requisition. It wouldn't be so bad, but Bertie's still trying to fight it. It's hopeless, of course. Even he's conceded we should pack up, but he's fighting it nonetheless.'

Freddie sat on the edge of the four-poster bed, crumpling its dark blue eiderdown. Dust motes fluttered into the air. 'I don't believe you. Or rather, I don't believe the requisition order is what's done this to you. Tell me what's really wrong,' he said. 'There was a time when you could tell me anything,' he finished quietly.

'I know.' Veronica raised her eyes to meet his and then quickly blinked back tears.

Freddie stood and rushed towards her, stopping himself only a few feet away. But as a tear rolled out of her eye and down her cheek she found herself being pulled into his arms.

He just held her, resting his head on top of hers, while she cried into his chest, dampening his shirt with her tears. Her head still fitted neatly underneath his chin and for a few precious moments it was as if nothing had ever changed – as if the years hadn't simply rushed past them both, grabbing hold of them and pulling them in different directions. Although embarrassed, she tried to stop her tears from falling, but it was no use. Her body shook. Freddie held her, making no further demand for her to divulge what it was that was making her cry, and for that she was grateful. She couldn't tell him. Not now. If she was able to get away from Bertie, she couldn't envisage having to ever tell anyone.

She lifted her head gently from the warmth of his chest and wiped her face. Freddie looked down at her and as their eyes met Veronica felt her heart pound. He was just the same as he'd ever been. It all felt too familiar, despite the fact it had been so long. The silence between them was tinged with emotion and the expression on Freddie's face moved from concern to one of fresh pain. Veronica felt it too.

Downstairs, Cook rang the lunch gong and Veronica heard Anna pad past the Blue Room on her way downstairs to serve. Veronica sprang back from Freddie. She looked at his shirt, damp around his collarbone from her tears. 'I'm so sorry,' she said. 'I don't know quite what came over me.'

He looked at her intently, but she wouldn't meet his eyes.

'Lunch,' she said in far too bright a voice and left the room.

While Anna hastily laid the table and then served, Veronica turned to Freddie and attempted to make polite conversation to counteract what had happened in his room. 'We're at sixes and sevens since we had the order to leave. It's all been rather a rush, packing up and sending things on to the London house. We're lucky, of course, at least we have another house to go to.' Veronica knew she was prattling.

'Where is the rest of the village going?' Freddie asked.

'Those that aren't going to family are being rehoused around Purbeck,' Veronica explained. 'Until hostilities end. Until they can return.'

'They'll hate that. Most of those families have lived here for generations.'

'Your family has lived here for generations,' Veronica countered.

'Yes, I suppose so.' He looked around but appeared unbothered by the prospect of his family home being requisitioned. 'This house doesn't feel like part of me anymore though.' He shrugged. 'Hasn't in years.' He looked at Veronica pointedly, but as she opened her mouth to speak, he asked, 'Any wine?'

Anna disappeared, reappearing minutes later with a bottle of red. She fumbled with the corkscrew and Freddie leaned forward and delicately took it from her hands with a smile. 'It's all right, I'll do it,' he said. Anna shot him a grateful look and left the room.

'She's not used to serving,' Veronica explained. 'She's my lady's maid. All the male staff have gone to fight.' Veronica didn't like to say that the moment war had been declared, every single male member of staff had joined up immediately, as if they couldn't wait to be gone from the house.

Freddie nodded. 'How's Bertie?' he asked.

Veronica's knife and fork stalled halfway up to her mouth.

Freddie plunged the needle of the corkscrew into the wine bottle and then started winding.

'Fine,' she said dismissively and then she asked quietly, 'When did you last see him?'

Was it her imagination or did Freddie clench his jaw? He poured wine into both their glasses and then his next words cut through the room. 'At your wedding.'

Veronica's eyes widened. The wedding. The wedding she never wanted to think about ever again. 'You've not seen him since then? Almost five years? That can't be true.'

Freddie nodded. 'We've spoken of course. But not often. He

likes to know I'm not messing it all up at the factory. But communication has been . . . sporadic. One year has just drifted into the next. And here we are, five years on and the village is being requisitioned and your house is being taken.'

Veronica looked away at the dark wood panelled walls, now devoid of any portraits.

'It's not my house,' she said quietly.

Freddie didn't know then. He had no idea what Bertie was like now; the change that had slowly ravaged him. Although, Veronica supposed she had no real idea if Bertie had always been so violent, so full of hate. Perhaps he had but he had overtaken her senses when she'd met him. It was in the darkest moments of Bertie's behaviour that she forced herself to remember how he used to be. She'd been swept along in the wake of Bertie's forceful presence and hadn't had time to fall in love with him. His intensity had taken her breath away and she now wondered frequently whether the signs of madness had always been there, under the surface. Had he simply hidden them away? Perhaps she was just blind and hadn't wanted to see the start of the behaviour that would eventually destroy their marriage and almost kill her. She'd never know now.

A car crunched on the gravel and Veronica's head rose. She stiffened. Bertie. There were no other cars in the village. Petrol rationing had put paid to that. Bertie, as an MP, believed it was necessary to the war effort that he swan around in his Morris Eight.

Veronica sat rigidly and pushed her lips one against the other, creating a thin line. She heard Anna run down the hallway to open the front door.

Anna shouldn't still be here. Veronica was supposed to be on a train to London and her new life, such as it would be. She had made Anna promise she'd leave Bertie's employment the very moment Veronica left, come what may. Anna had promised that she wouldn't stay in the house alone with Bertie. Veronica knew

53

Bertie's sexual predilections and while, so far, they did not stretch to the staff, if Veronica had gone and Anna stayed, it would only be a matter of time. Veronica couldn't bear to think about the poor young girl failing to fight Bertie off.

But Veronica was still here and so was Anna. And now so was Freddie. The nightmare was only getting worse.

The front door banged and she could hear muffled voices. Moments later, the dining room door was thrown open and Bertie walked in.

Freddie tossed his napkin on the table and stood, moving towards his brother and greeting him warmly. Bertie smiled thinly by way of reply and reciprocated the handshake. He stood beside Veronica.

'Not going to kiss your husband?' he asked.

Veronica stood and he pulled her towards him, placing his lips firmly on hers and clasping her around the waist. Veronica was stunned. This wasn't for her benefit. Bertie pushed his lips harder onto hers until it started to hurt. She made a small noise and Bertie kissed her harder to mute her. Freddie shifted uncomfortably next to them.

'Well,' Bertie said to Freddie when he'd finished embracing Veronica, 'my reprobate brother has returned.'

Freddie moved back towards his seat. 'As commanded.'

'Good. All your things are in the attic. Take what you want and anything you want destroyed by the bloody army you can leave here.'

'Understood.' Freddie sat down again.

'Welcome back, little brother,' Bertie said. He looked down at Freddie's wine glass and picked it up, drained it and placed it back on the table.

Freddie made no comment but waited until Bertie had turned before he rolled his eyes.

'Aren't you going to ask me how it went?' Bertie turned to Veronica.

As Veronica opened her mouth to speak, Bertie cut in, 'It was a bloody disaster,' he said. 'There's not a damned thing we can do about this requisition order. We leave as planned.'

'I see.' Veronica stared at her food.

'Joining us for lunch?' Freddie suggested when the awkward silence grew.

'No. I ate. I'll be in my study.'

A few moments later Bertie's study door slammed shut.

'The requisition has put him on edge?' Freddie asked and then stopped talking as another young woman came into the room to remove their empty plates. She stopped short and stared at him.

'Rebecca, Sir Albert's brother will be staying with us for the night,' Veronica said.

'Very good, m'lady,' Rebecca said. 'Cook has custard and stewed fruit she can offer if you'd like pudding?' she asked, not meeting their gaze. She removed their plates.

'Not for me,' Freddie grinned. 'I'm full. I've not eaten this well in a long time.'

The maid glanced back at him and took in his features with a shocked expression on her face. Freddie smiled back uncertainly at her scrutiny.

'No thank you, Rebecca,' Veronica replied. 'Please tell Cook that was delicious, as usual.'

Rebecca turned and left.

'Well,' Freddie said. 'I'm going to take a look in the attic while the light's still good. See what I've left behind from my misspent youth.'

'Freddie?'

'Mmm?'

'About the crying.' Veronica felt unable to meet his gaze. 'I'm sorry.'

He crouched beside her and glanced down the hall towards Bertie's study. 'Are you going to tell me what's wrong?' he whispered.

She could feel his presence next to her as he crouched. Affability and warmth emanated from him. She'd always wondered what it would be like when she saw him again. After five long years being married to Bertie, she'd tried not to think about Freddie. It was too painful. She had tried not to regret the way it had all ended between them. It had been for the best. She'd been devastated when she'd learnt he didn't love her, when she'd discovered he was casually playing her off against other women. But it felt as if her heart hurt even more now he was here than it had ever done in the long absence since she'd wed Bertie.

She tried to swallow down the uprising combination of guilt and love that she always felt when she thought of Freddie. She couldn't help it. His head was almost level with hers and she risked a glance at him. The kindness in his eyes only served to wound, not to heal. She'd missed him, more than she cared to admit, but she'd have given anything for him not to be here now.

Veronica brought herself back to the present, back to the dire situation she'd unleashed upon herself, and tried seeing things through Freddie's eyes. To the untrained eye, Bertie's behaviour looked relatively normal. It was the most horrifically believable act. He'd been playing it for years. Freddie would never believe her if she told him the truth.

Veronica shook her head and looked down at the floor.

'I can't force you,' Freddie said gently, taking her hand. 'But you know where I am if you want to unburden yourself. You know I'll always listen to anything you have to say, Veronica. I'm sorry for you. And I'm sorry for Bertie. This departure, it must have hit you both very hard.'

Veronica felt a lump forming in her throat. But it wasn't tears; it was regret. She'd cast Freddie aside for Bertie. She only had herself to blame. Veronica knew that everything she'd suffered at Bertie's hands was her comeuppance for leaving Freddie without an explanation. She shook her head. 'There's nothing wrong.'

CHAPTER 7

As Freddie ventured upstairs towards the attic, Anna entered the dining room and pushed the door closed behind her.

'You're not leaving?' Anna asked.

'How can I get away?' Veronica threw her hands up in the air. 'How can I go now? Every time I try . . .' she trailed off.

Anna sighed and glanced towards the dining room door. 'I don't know.'

Veronica pushed out the chair next to her with her foot and gestured to Anna to sit. Anna sat gingerly on the edge, ready to leap up if Bertie entered the room. It wouldn't do for staff to be seen looking comfortable.

The women sat in silence. Veronica looked at Anna and felt her heart surge with gratitude that she was there. Bertie had hired her on a whim in place of a regular lady's maid, reasoning that she was untrained and therefore cheap. Over the years, the young Anna had seen and heard too much to ignore and Veronica had been in dire need of a confidante. It had been a shock to both women that they had forged a friendship.

'The brother's nice,' Anna said absent-mindedly. 'I almost had a heart attack when I caught a quick glance at him in the drive. I thought it was *him* at first.' Anna pointed towards Bertie's office.

'Freddie's not been back here in a very long time,' Veronica said.

'What will you do now?' Anna returned to the subject that was plaguing them both.

'I think I'm going to try to leave on the last day, when the whole village leaves. But I'm going to have to go before anyone notices. I can slip away in all the confusion of the exodus.'

Anna stood up. 'Cutting it fine. It won't be easy. But I can run down to the village and tell William he's needed again. We just have to get through these last few days.'

Freddie rifled amongst the detritus in the attic and found a few things he wanted to take as mementoes but nothing that warranted the uncomfortable train journey he'd just made. Although he did whoop for joy when he found his old cricket bat. He knew he'd left it here. He was sad to see moths had ravaged his comfortable cricket jumpers. He was sure he'd left them in his old bedroom when he'd last been at Tyneham House, but Bertie had obviously seen fit to banish Freddie's possessions to the attic. He threw them back into the dusty trunks. He'd leave them; along with everything else, except the bat. His old school exercise books and sporting manuals were of no interest to him now. The army was welcome to them. He wondered where everything else was. He suspected Bertie had had a clear-out long before he arrived. There was barely anything left. This was classic Bertie behaviour.

Whistling as he descended the stairs two at a time, he realised the house was eerily quiet. He stopped and listened, twizzling the cricket bat around in his hands as he reached the front hall. There was the faint sound of scribbling in Bertie's office and Freddie knocked and entered.

Bertie looked up from behind his desk and glanced at the cricket bat. 'Found something?'

Freddie looked down at his prized bat. 'I brought two suitcases with me, thinking I'd fill them up. But there's just this.'

He walked over to the large brown leather chesterfield settee that was situated in front of Bertie's desk and sat down. He stretched his legs out in front of him lazily and looked around the study. Bertie watched him.

'Sad to see the old place go?' Freddie attempted conversation.

'Absolutely bloody livid,' Bertie exploded. 'I had no idea they were going to take the house.' Small bits of spittle flew from his mouth as he spoke.

'It's war, they can do what they like,' Freddie reasoned. 'You and I are lucky though. We're both of us here, still alive, not dying in some foreign field.' Freddie looked around at the shelves wondering why the account ledgers hadn't yet been packed away. Bertie obviously really believed he could put the requisition off and hadn't yet packed the smaller items. 'We've got to make sacrifices somewhere.'

'What sacrifice have you made exactly?' Bertie put his fountain pen down on the table and stared at his brother square in the eye.

Freddie narrowed his eyes. *I left this house, I stayed away and I didn't fight hard enough when you stole Veronica from me.* There was no point hashing all that up now. She'd made her choice and it hadn't been him. Instead, Freddie said, 'I got shot, remember?'

'Oh yes, the famous bullet that put you out of the war on day one,' Bertie said, looking down at his papers again.

Freddie shook his head disbelievingly and rubbed self-consciously at his chest. The bullet he'd taken fighting in France in 1940 had nearly killed him.

Bertie looked as if he was spoiling for a fight and as he opened his mouth to speak, Freddie quickly interjected. 'How's Veronica? She seems . . . different.'

'She is. She's not the same woman I married,' Bertie said sourly.

'Is it the requisition?' Freddie volunteered.

'No. It's been happening ever since we got married. Slowly,

here and there, I'll notice small things about her that make me more than a little curious about her sanity.'

Freddie's mouth fell open. The Veronica he fell in love with all those years ago had been a vivacious, energetic woman, full of life and love. He'd fallen head over heels instantly, but he was too slow off the mark at proposing. That had been his undoing.

'I sometimes wonder if I should have just let you have her back?' Bertie mumbled.

The grandfather clock chimed in the hallway, breaking the silence that had fallen in the room. Freddie knew better than to reply. This was not the first time Bertie had alluded to his less than brotherly behaviour. After six months of stepping out with Veronica, Bertie had used his position as the older brother to full advantage with her father, convincing him to turn Veronica's head. The lure of Bertie inheriting the estate and the London house was too much for Veronica's father. No matter which way it was dressed up or justified, Bertie had stolen Veronica – and Veronica had obviously been willing to go.

Freddie often wondered how different his life would have been if he'd been the older brother; if he'd have held more sway. He blamed himself for Veronica's switch of affections. He should have proposed the moment he knew he was in love. But he had been too late. Freddie remembered the words Bertie had used when he'd broken their engagement news to him, slapping him on the back. 'It's the greatest compliment, old chap. She wanted you. Only better.'

Choosing not to engage, Freddie stood and picked up the cricket bat. 'I'm going to pack this and then I'll walk around the grounds for a bit. Visit my old haunts. Is the beach hut still there?'

Bertie was writing again and looked up impatiently. 'What? I wouldn't know. I've not been down there in years.'

After an hour of walking around the formal gardens and the wood, Freddie decided he needed sea air. He walked towards the long cliff path that led to the estate's private cove. He stopped at the top of the cliff and peered over the edge. The steps were still there, naturally formed unevenly into the cliff face. He stared out to sea, listening to the waves crashing down below. Glancing around the coastline, he could see across towards the next bay, where a square stone observation post had been built in readiness for preventing a German invasion. His heart sank as he looked below and saw the stone 'dragon's teeth', ruining the beach but forming a necessary part of the coastal defences.

He stretched lazily and looked about. As a boy, he'd played here with Bertie in summer, had rowed the dinghy to the rocks and they had thrown their fishing nets out, catching nothing. Freddie smiled, remembering how they used to steal bottles of Father's port from the cellar when no one was watching and throw the empty bottles into the sea, returning back to the house drunk and happy. God, they were tearaways. They'd been so similar back then. Or had they really? It had always been Bertie encouraging Freddie to steal the wine. But somehow it had always been Freddie who got the blame.

If the little beach hut was still there, it would probably be a miracle. His mother had installed it where the steep cliff met the sand so they could store their belongings, deckchairs, parasols and fishing paraphernalia. It had been Freddie's safe haven when life in the shadow of his brother got too much and he needed some peace and quiet.

Freddie descended the steep cliff steps, which wound down to the pale sandy beach, and went to look at the dragon's teeth. Waist-height, they resembled stone pyramids that had been squared off at the top. How things had changed since he'd last been here. Still, he'd rather look at his beloved cove braced for war than covered in Germans. He'd seen enough of them in France while he was narrowly escaping with his life. The dragon's teeth were a small price. *These will certainly stop a few tanks*, he thought as he raised his hand to shield his eyes from the low December sunshine.

He stopped, bending over to catch his breath and to try to alleviate the pain that exercise brought to his ravaged chest. Scrambling up and down the cliff path wasn't easy at the best of times. He damned the German who had shot him three years ago as he ran towards the beaches at Dunkirk. That was the last time he'd been on a beach. Until today. Feeling the soft sand underfoot brought back memories of men screaming in pain, along with the madness of the songs being sung by the troops as they waited for the long-promised boats to arrive. He thanked whichever God it was that had seen fit to save him. He'd been one of the lucky ones, even with a bullet lodged inside. He'd survived. He rubbed his chest. It always hurt more in the cold.

Across the sand, the beach hut was still there. And Freddie was pleasantly surprised to find it was prettier than ever. The wood had been scrubbed and painted fresh, not too long ago by the looks of it. It used to be a yellowing beige colour, the wood on the verge of rotting when he'd last seen it. But now it was cream and varnished to a shine. The little porch had a brass hurricane lamp hanging from it with a candle inside. The wood of the decking was a brilliant white. He smiled. Someone had been taking care of his little hut.

He walked closer to it and wondered if it was unlocked. As the beach was private to the estate, there had been no need to lock it in his day. But times changed and who knew what orders his brother had put in place in the last few years since his parents had passed away and Bertie had inherited the lot.

The wooden decking creaked gently under his feet and he reached out for the door handle. But as he looked through the window of the door, he caught a sudden movement from within. Veronica was sitting inside, staring at the floor.

He wasn't sure what to do. She was probably here because she wanted to be alone. Would his intrusion be welcome or not? After a few seconds he decided he couldn't stand out here all day in the cold, so he knocked gently. She looked up sharply. A flash of worry hit her face and then it faded as fast as it had appeared, replaced with a smile that reached her eyes.

Freddie opened the door. 'Mind if I join you?'

'No. Not at all.' She gestured for him to come in. The hut was small, the majority of the room having been given over to a small daybed on which Veronica sat.

Freddie leant against the doorway, his muscular frame filling the space. She was entirely aware of him.

'Did you find anything in the attic?' she enquired.

'Not much. You've made this look nice,' he said, looking around at the books on the little shelf and the daybed with a cream eiderdown printed with little blue flowers. 'I assume it was you? I doubt very much it was Bertie.'

Veronica laughed. It sounded alien to her. It was the first time she'd laughed in weeks. She was almost surprised she still could. 'No, I don't see Bertie as the floral eiderdown type, do you?'

Shuffling along the daybed, she made room for Freddie. He sat down slowly, awkwardly, as far away from her as possible. She wondered suddenly if this was entirely appropriate. He was well built and she could feel his proximity to her even though he was at the other end of the seat.

She slid a bit further along until she reached the metal bars of the headboard and then cursed herself for her obvious retreat. She watched him turn slightly so he could see her better. She felt stiff all of a sudden and he looked the same. What had he been doing all these years? Had he been happy? Had he fallen in love? The thought made her feel sick. They should have been indifferent to one another given the easy way their relationship had ended. But even now, after all this time, it didn't feel that simple.

He was watching her thoughtfully and when he didn't speak, Veronica felt the need to break the unbearable silence.

'Where have you been?' Veronica shivered in the cold of the December afternoon and pulled her cardigan around her.

'In the attic. I've—'

Veronica cut him off. 'That's not what I meant. Where have you been, Freddie – these past few years? Why haven't I seen you? Not even once since . . .' She was quieter now, 'Since the wedding? Bertie told me you've been busy at the factory. But you never came back here. Not once.'

'I'm sorry,' Freddie said. Veronica noticed him bristle. 'When I got back I just threw myself into work and there never seemed time to make the journey down here. And then it became even more complicated as the war dragged on, especially when petrol went on the ration.'

'Oh,' Veronica said. And then after a few seconds, 'When you got back? From where?'

Freddie pulled a cigarette out of a little silver case and put it between his lips. He offered her one and she shook her head. 'From France.' He snapped the case shut. She watched him flick a silver lighter out and light his cigarette. He ran his finger absent-mindedly over his engraved name. Veronica recognised the lighter and case. Bertie had an identical set bearing his name. Both had been gifts from their parents when they had each turned twenty-one. Freddie snapped the lighter shut and put it back in his trouser pocket.

'When were you in France?' she questioned.

He pulled a small piece of stray tobacco from his tongue and flicked it away before looking at her strangely.

'When?' he replied. 'I joined up just after you and Bertie got . . .' He trailed off and avoided her glance. 'At the end of '39.'

She looked at him, her eyes narrowed and then she sat up straighter. 'You joined up? The army?'

He laughed and then stopped abruptly, returning her gaze equally as questioningly.

'You didn't know?' he asked.

She shook her head slowly, her mouth open. 'Bertie didn't tell me.'

'Bloody hell.' He narrowed his eyes and looked out the window of the beach hut, towards the rough sea.

'Why didn't he tell me? Why would he keep that from me? I knew he wasn't called up because he's in government, but I assumed you were in a reserved occupation too, with the factory. I thought you were working. This whole time.' She couldn't believe it. Freddie had been fighting. In France. He could have been killed. Would Bertie have told her *that*? 'How long were you fighting?'

'Not long. I came home in June 1940.'

'Oh my God,' she exclaimed quietly. 'Oh my God,' she repeated louder as she suddenly realised the significance of the date. 'Dunkirk. The beaches. Were you . . .?'

He nodded slowly and then closed his eyes tightly shut. He muttered something under his breath that Veronica didn't catch. She looked at him but didn't know what to say. The thought of Freddie on the beaches made her stomach lurch. She'd read the ministerial reports Bertie had left lying around his study about the horrors of the evacuation and then the rather different version in the news shortly thereafter.

'But you're not in the army now?'

He shook his head. 'I assume if Bertie didn't tell you I went to the front, then he also didn't tell you I got shot?'

She stood up, staring down at him, horrified. 'Shot? You got shot? At Dunkirk?' She could hear the hysteria in her own voice. Freddie was nodding and laughing. 'Why are you laughing?' she squeaked.

'I just can't believe he didn't tell you . . . any of it.'

'I can.' Veronica sat back down with a thud. 'It's the kind of thing he would do.'

Freddie's eyebrow shot up. 'Really? No, don't answer that.'

'I'm so angry with him.' Veronica was almost shouting. She hated Bertie. She'd hated him for so long, she could barely remember a day when she didn't. Freddie could have died. Freddie

65

had gone to fight and been shot and Bertie had kept it all from her.

'How long?' she enquired.

'How long what?'

'How long were you on the beaches for?'

The smile fell from his face. 'Long enough.'

'My God, Freddie. I'm so . . .' She wasn't sure what she was – sorry, angry, frightened? She was almost shaking with the overwhelming emotions that engulfed her.

'Should we ask Bertie why he didn't tell you? I want to know now.' Freddie gave her a sideways smile as he exhaled cigarette smoke.

'No!' Veronica was emphatic. There would be hell to pay and Veronica would be on the receiving end. 'Don't ask him. Don't! Promise me. Please.'

Freddie looked into her eyes, nodding slowly. 'I was just pulling your leg. I won't ask him. Of course I won't. I promise.'

They sat back against the wall of the hut. Veronica stole a glance at him every few seconds. He was as handsome now as he'd ever been. Perhaps more so. Briefly she was transported back to an easier time, before the war, before things between them had gone so awry so suddenly. Before Bertie. When Freddie and she had talked, when they'd kissed, when she had been so in love with him it hurt. But he hadn't loved her. How stupid she had been. How easily she'd been talked out of waiting for Freddie to act. And how easily she'd allowed Bertie to lead her away; so forcefully, so assuredly. She wasn't sure who she hated more, Bertie or herself? There was no point now wishing everything had been different. It was too late for all that.

'Where did you get shot?' Veronica ended the silence that had fallen between them in the beach hut.

He pointed to the right side of his chest.

She closed her eyes, letting the horror of the whole situation sink in. She'd tried not to think about him over the years. But perhaps if she had allowed herself to think about him, really think about him, she could have somehow kept him from getting shot. She knew it was a stupid thing to think.

And now he was unavoidably here and still alive.

'Are you all right?' she asked in what she hoped was her calmest voice.

'Now? Yes, just about. I get by on one and a half lungs,' he joked. 'It rather put me out of action. I'm like some sort of horse that's been put out to pasture. Not able to do anything useful. Just the factory.' He looked downcast.

'I'm so sorry, Freddie.'

He smiled at her, taking her hand in his. 'Don't be. I'm still alive.'

Her heart lurched at his touch, once so familiar and now so alien, and she fought her instinct, which was to pull her hand away. Instead, she let it rest inside his gentle grip, closed her eyes, and for a brief moment pretended the last five years hadn't separated them.

'I think I should like that cigarette now please,' she said.

Veronica and Freddie climbed the cliff path back to the house in silence. Freddie walked behind her on the narrow climb and she wondered what he was thinking but didn't dare turn round to glance at him. Could he tell just by looking at her how she really felt, how she'd always felt about him? She knew he didn't feel the same way. He never had done.

'We have a couple of hours before dinner.' She turned towards him as they both made their way inside the gothic porch. He was so close he almost bumped into her as she turned round. Her first instinct was always now to defend herself and, flinching, she put her hands up. But she was in no danger of an attack from Freddie. She knew that. Her hands were still on the thick wool of Freddie's coat and he glanced down at her touch against his chest. She cursed herself for waiting a fraction too long before letting her hands fall. They stood under the arch, shielded from any possible onlookers. As he moved his hand a fraction, Veronica half-thought he might be reaching for hers, but he let it fall by his side and neither of them spoke. The expression on his face had softened. She wanted to pour her heart out. Even if he was long past caring now – even if he had never cared – she wanted to apologise for the way things had ended. There was nothing she could say that would undo the damage she'd caused.

She tried desperately to recover herself and recall what it was she'd originally turned to say to him. Eventually she remembered.

'You'll need to change for dinner, I'm afraid. Have you brought suitable things?'

'Oh, good lord, Bertie still doesn't go in for all that bother, does he? Is he not even marginally aware the world is drastically changing around him?'

'He thinks if we uphold the old traditions then nothing will change.'

Freddie laughed and threw his hands up. 'The house is being requisitioned. Everything is changing.'

Veronica hushed him. 'Freddie, please,' she begged. 'You don't know what he's like. Don't let him hear you.'

'Fine, fine.' Freddie looked down at his crumpled trousers and conceded defeat. 'I'll change.'

'We have drinks at six and dinner at seven, precisely. Please don't be late. Bertie doesn't like it,' Veronica said.

As she turned towards the front steps, she thought she saw Freddie roll his eyes.

CHAPTER 8

Dorset, July 2018

Guy was at the front door of his grandmother's bungalow, knocking for the fifth time in ten minutes. She wasn't deaf or slow on her feet and he'd given her more than enough time to get to the front door from wherever she was inside the house. But now he was starting to get worried. He dialled his grandmother's landline and heard the phone ring inside. It went to answerphone and he hung up. It was a blisteringly hot day and he wondered if she might be in the garden, so he tried the side gate and when it didn't budge, he reached over and fumbled in vain for the bolt but couldn't quite reach it. Moving back, he gave himself a few feet for a running jump and leaped up the gate, hooking the front of his shoes into the thick wooden cross-bar so he could vault over. He was half over when his grandmother's neighbour appeared.

'Oh, it's you,' the elderly man said. 'Thought I could hear a lot of noise round here.'

'Mr Hunter. How are you?' Guy said from his awkward position, straddling the gate.

'Looking for your gran?' Mr Hunter asked. 'No one told you?'

'Told me . . .?'

'She went in to hospital this morning. Fell over and broke her hip. Your mum was with her. Went in an ambulance she did.'

Guy wobbled on top of the gate. 'No!'

'She was talking and telling everyone to stop fussing, so I doubt she's a corpse just yet. Had one of those little mask things on. Very annoyed at being stretchered into the ambulance though.' Mr Hunter gave a chuckle.

'Oh God,' Guy said, throwing his leg back over and landing with a thud on the crazy paving. 'Thanks.' He rushed towards his car.

'Get your mum to let me know how she is, will you?' Mr Hunter called as Guy slammed the car door and sped towards the hospital.

Melissa had wandered around Tyneham again to soak in the atmosphere after Guy had left to have tea with his gran. And then she'd run out of things to look at and had forced herself into the car and back to the cottage. Hours later, she looked at her watch. Where was Liam? She exhaled loudly as she thought about what to say to him about the restaurant booking. And everything else. She had no idea how she was going to begin and yet she knew she couldn't put it off any longer. She suddenly felt nervous and tried to think about something else.

And then Guy popped in to her head. He had promised to ask his gran where Veronica and Albert Standish had ended up after the army requisitioned the village. Melissa couldn't now unsee Veronica's eerie expression in the photograph. There was something about it that was bothering her and would do until she knew what had happened to the woman.

Veronica and Albert had probably gone to London and lived happily ever after, but Melissa just wanted to *know* now.

She pulled her laptop out of its case. With any luck, she could connect to the internet and wait the interminably long time for a page to load. One quick search would provide the answer to her short-lived quest to find out where Veronica and Albert Standish had gone.

While she waited for the laptop to connect with the online world, she went to the kitchen to flick the kettle on. It had been hours since she'd been at Tyneham and so she pulled her phone out of her jeans pocket to check for any messages, but there was still no news from Guy, so she shoved it back again and wandered over to the computer screen.

Melissa tapped 'Veronica Standish' into the search engine. Over 100,000 results appeared and Melissa clapped her hands together in anticipation until she reached page three of the search results and realised absolutely none of them were the Veronica Standish she was looking for. She added '1943' to the search term and a few results appeared, but none of them looked particularly relevant. Then she deleted '1943' and input the word 'Tyneham'. A mention of Veronica and Albert in reference to the 'ghost village' of Tyneham simply listed them as among the two hundred and twenty-five residents who were displaced during the requisition of the Dorset village. There was nothing there that she hadn't already found out from Guy or from the boards in the church.

She pulled her phone out to look again. Still nothing from Guy. Melissa clunked it face down on the table and then reached forwards and turned it over so she could see the screen. Just in case.

With no further information about Albert or Veronica Standish on the website, Melissa was left half wondering if she'd hit a dead end. She searched just for the husband's name instead. A plethora of information came up.

'Oh, here we go,' Melissa said, and edged forward on the sofa to look at the results. There were a lot of parliamentary speeches he'd made and she read a few of the summaries. They were dull and mainly about issues related to farming or fishing in Dorset in the war. There were other references to the house and to him and then she found something interesting that she didn't quite understand in a link to an old newspaper article. In January 1944, Sir Albert Standish had quit as an MP. A by-election had been called and he'd been easily replaced by the looks of things. The newspaper article was short and fairly tedious and Melissa got up to make a cup of tea, feeling strangely disappointed. One month after they had left Tyneham, Albert Standish had stood down as an MP. Perhaps it was a protest at having his home requisitioned. Perhaps it was just a perfectly normal thing to do, quit when you no longer lived in your own constituency. Perhaps Albert and Veronica had gone to live in London after all, happily ever after.

She sipped her tea and sat back down on Liam's terribly stylish, uncomfortable sofa. The article was unsatisfying. There was no mention of Veronica, but then why would there have been? If it wasn't for the fact that Veronica had looked a bit odd in the photograph, Melissa wouldn't care that there had been no information about the couple on the boards in the church. Perhaps that was just Veronica's un-photogenic smile and Melissa was barking up the wrong tree. But no, she knew she wasn't. She wished she'd taken a picture of the photo on her mobile phone. Remembering Veronica's face, even a few hours later, was difficult, but it had been fear on her face. Veronica looked utterly frightened, that much Melissa *could* remember.

Melissa closed the laptop lid and then looked at her phone again. She tapped her fingers on the table and looked around guiltily. Even though she knew she was alone, she was embarrassed by what she was about to do. Melissa reopened the laptop and when the screen lit up, she typed 'Guy Cameron' into the internet search engine and waited for the results to load.

Then, suddenly, the front door opened and Liam walked in, stopping when he saw her.

'Oh, hi, you're home,' he said.

Melissa jumped. 'I thought you'd still be surfing,' she blurted.

'Not today no. Too much wine yesterday. Thought a day out of the sun was wise.'

The wine. The table for two. And where had he been today if not surfing? Melissa took a breath.

'Listen, Liam, I need to talk to you.'

'Why are you looking him up?' Liam interrupted, moving closer to Melissa's computer. 'That bloke off the telly,' he clarified.

Melissa was flustered. She'd not seen Liam long enough to even mention Guy to him. She'd spent two days with another man and hadn't so much as told her boyfriend where she'd been or who with. She realised now it was also because she'd been worried, not wanting to get into an argument. But it wasn't like Liam had asked either. She felt even guiltier when she realised the two days with Guy were the nicest days she'd had in ages and certainly the best she'd had on this particular holiday.

Liam nodded towards the computer screen as a row of attractive, smiling press shots of Guy littered the page. 'He does those boring history programmes on TV.'

Melissa looked at the screen. 'Oh, right, yeah. I wouldn't know. I haven't watched any.' She shut the laptop quickly and turned to face him again.

He shifted from one foot to the other and she dared a question. 'Where have you been today, Liam?'

It took her boyfriend of eight months a few seconds to respond.

'You're right.' He ignored her question, sinking down on the sofa opposite. 'We do need to talk. This, us, I'm not sure it's working anymore,' he said, looking sheepish.

'You're seeing someone else.' It was out of her mouth before she could stop herself. But the moment she said it, she knew it was the truth.

'Shit.' Liam reddened. His head shot up to meet her gaze. 'How do you . . .?'

'For how long?' Melissa demanded.

Liam ran his hand through his hair. 'Don't take it personally,' he started.

Melissa's eyes widened. 'What? What do you mean by that?'

'It's not you,' Liam started.

'Are you serious?' Melissa raised her voice. '*It's not you it's me,*' she mimicked. 'Exactly how long has this been going on?' she asked again.

'That's why you shouldn't take it personally.' Liam looked at the floor. 'A while.'

'Specifically?' Melissa ground her teeth.

Liam's brow had more furrow lines today than she'd ever seen on his forehead. 'I was seeing her before you. We've known each other a while. And then it ended.' Liam shrugged.

'And then it started up again, clearly.' Melissa couldn't believe how stupid she'd been. They hadn't been stuck in a rut at all. He'd been seeing someone else. 'Is she here, in Dorset?'

Liam nodded.

'I don't believe this is happening.' Melissa shook her head. 'Not like this. I knew we weren't getting on. But I had no idea you'd been . . .' She thought of Liam sneaking off this week, presumably to sleep with this other woman and then to come back and sleep with her. 'Oh God,' she said and swallowed down bile.

'I'm so sorry,' Liam said. 'I didn't think it was going to be a real thing this time with her and so that's why—'

'That's why you agreed to a holiday in Dorset with me? So you could see her at the same time? I thought this holiday would . . . fix . . . whatever was obviously broken with us. I couldn't see how we'd gone so wrong so quickly. But your heart was never even in it. You've just led me on.' She put her hand to her mouth. 'I'm such an idiot,' she said, marvelling at how thick she could be sometimes.

A stale silence descended on the room. Melissa had no idea what to do now. She felt thoroughly alone all of a sudden. She'd been cheated on. She was miles from home. She had nowhere to go, but she knew she couldn't stay here. She couldn't be in Liam's proximity. Not for one minute longer. Her hands started to shake and she wiped a tear from her eye.

74

'Don't cry,' Liam pleaded.

'I'm not crying,' Melissa snapped, angry with herself that she was indeed crying. She needed to get out of here and go somewhere. But where could she go at this time of night?

He glanced at his watch. 'I suppose it's too late to drive back to London.'

'Oh wow,' she said, shocked now. She started shaking. 'I'm being kicked out?'

'No, no! Not at all. Not right now! I'm not a monster. I'll sleep on the sofa and you have the bedroom and, you know . . . tomorrow . . .' he trailed off.

Melissa stood up and walked stiffly towards the bedroom. 'No, it's fine,' she said. Her voice caught in her throat. 'I'll go now.'

'Don't be silly, Melissa. It's late.'

But Melissa was already in the bedroom, gathering her things. The holdall zipper stuck, so she yanked it open, pulling the zip off its runner but stuffing her clothes and cosmetics inside all the same. It didn't take long to locate her belongings. He'd given her a single drawer to put her clothes in and that had probably said everything. If only she'd really been paying attention. She finished packing and thought about the single drawer he'd also allowed her to have in his flat. It had taken a lot to negotiate that. And the toothbrush, which she left in his little glass holder in the bathroom but which she always found had been put back in her drawer whenever she returned to stay the night. Melissa shook her head. What an idiot she'd been. There was no way she could have fixed their relationship, such as it was. He'd never wanted it to work in the first place.

Her laptop cable was trailing on the floor and as she entered the sitting room Liam unplugged it and handed it to her, along with the laptop.

'I really am sorry,' Liam said. 'I mean it. Don't go now.'

Melissa looked up at him through the tears in her eyes. She

wished she could stop shaking. How was this happening? Liam suddenly felt like a total stranger. She couldn't be near him a moment longer.

She reached the front door, turning to look at him one last time. He was already pulling his phone out of his pocket by the time she'd closed the door.

The car was stifling from the hot day and Melissa wound the window down and started the engine, desperate to be out of the drive and gone; despite the fact she didn't know where she was actually going. He was right. It *was* too late to drive home. He'd put his phone down long enough to appear at the sitting room window with a concerned expression on his face. She wasn't sure how much of that was for show. It was probably the most caring he'd ever been towards her. It only served to make her feel numb. She fumbled for her sunglasses, despite the sun dipping low in the sky, hoping to hide her crying eyes from Liam as he watched her leave.

Eight months with Liam and it was over in under ten minutes. She waited a respectable distance until she was out of sight of the house and pulled over. She put her hand to her mouth and looked blankly around the car, but she couldn't focus on anything through the tears that were falling freely down her cheeks. She wiped them away and breathed deeply, trying to collect herself. Where was she going to go?

When she'd finally gathered her thoughts, Melissa started a search for hotels on her phone. The signal was dire and the page loaded painfully slowly. It was with a start that Melissa felt the phone vibrate and watched the screen flash to signal an incoming call. She jumped and stared at the screen before swiping to answer the call from Imogen, her best friend since childhood.

'Oh good, you're not dead,' Imogen deadpanned as Melissa said a teary hello.

Melissa swallowed down the tears and laughed, ever so slightly. 'What do you mean?'

'I've sent you a few emails, but you haven't replied. Wondered if you might be dead, that's all.'

Melissa sat back in the car seat and exhaled loudly. 'No. Not yet. I've not had much reception on my phone for the past couple of days.' She wasn't in the mood to describe where she'd been and who with, or why. And then there was the unavoidable subject of Liam.

'Are you all right?' Imogen asked. 'You sound . . . flat.'

'I'm all right,' Melissa fibbed. And then the truth. 'Liam and I have broken up.'

The comment was met with silence as Imogen digested the news and then, 'Hmmm.'

'What does that mean?' Melissa asked warily.

'What happened?' asked Imogen. 'I know you said you were worried he seemed disinterested.'

'He was seeing someone else.'

'I knew it,' Imogen sounded triumphant. 'Sorry, I didn't mean it like that. I never liked him.'

Melissa struggled not to laugh. 'That's not what you said at your birthday party.'

'I was drunk. He'd just bought me a really expensive bottle of gin as a present. It was hard not to like him right then.'

'He's a banker,' Melissa countered. 'Everything he buys is really expensive. Oh, Imogen, what the hell's wrong with me?'

'Nothing. It's not you. It's them.'

The near-repetition of Liam's break-up speech had not been what Melissa wanted to hear at all.

'Plus, you won't say boo to a goose when it comes to men. They walk all over you.'

'Cheers.' Melissa sniffed. But she knew it was the truth.

'I would say that you need to really learn to stand up for yourself a bit more, but when someone's cheating on you there's very little point. Best to just walk away.'

'Yeah, that's what I thought,' Melissa sniffed and wiped the last remaining tear from her face. She glanced at the clock on the car radio. 'I need to dash. I've got to find a hotel for the night.'

'Has he kicked you out? For God's sake! If I ever see him again, I swear—' Imogen started.

'No. Nothing like that. I had to get out of there. I'm all right, honestly.' And it was true. She felt all right now, slowly.

Imogen sounded uncertain. 'Okay, well, if you're sure. Text me later to let me know you're okay, won't you?'

Melissa smiled. 'I will. Thanks, Immy.'

'Oh, by the way, you know our mums are meeting for lunch tomorrow, don't you?' Imogen said.

'Christ, don't tell your mum about Liam and I. She'll tell my mum and I don't think she can hear about yet another of my failed relationships. She only blames herself for various reasons every time I mess another one up.'

Imogen promised to keep quiet and the women said goodbye. Melissa looked at the screen. While the signal had held long enough to sustain a phone call, loading a hotel listing on the web page was still too much for her ageing phone. She shook it madly and hit refresh five times in quick succession. The page refused to appear. 'I just need one hotel listing.' She resisted the urge to slam it into the steering wheel in a mix of frustration and upset.

Melissa tried to think and then remembered the Pheasant and Gun had rooms. It was swanky, too swanky for an out of work admin assistant, but Melissa felt too empty to drive around looking hopefully for a budget chain hotel. 'It's only for one night,' Melissa reasoned and pointed her car in the direction of the inn.

CHAPTER 9

As the sun dipped behind a thick band of cloud, Melissa took off her sunglasses and looked at her pale reflection in the rear-view mirror. She looked a state – exactly like a caricature of someone who'd just been cheated on and then dumped. The drive had given her time to calm down, but she still felt like crap. She held on tightly to the steering wheel, forcing herself to breathe in and out a few times.

The pub looked comforting with its latticed windows displaying a surge of low light from inside and Melissa tried to guess what the room would cost. She sat there debating what to do. Hopefully it wouldn't be more than £150 a night. Yes, there was a nice little savings pot she'd got from her voluntary redundancy – being stuck in the same dead-end job for the best part of a decade had turned in to a nice little earner when she'd quit – but Melissa was acutely aware she'd been strangling that fund. It was supposed to see her through her 'thinking time' until she found a job she loved. God only knew when that day would come. All the jobs she was qualified for were essentially the same job she'd just left. Dipping into the redundancy wasn't supposed to be a habit and so she was grateful it *would* only be for the night.

She entered the building through the hotel entrance and

dropped her holdall onto the flagstone floor with a thud. No one was present to check her in at the wooden reception desk. Melissa tapped her foot impatiently. There was a small silver bell, but politeness prohibited her from actually touching it. She stood and coughed a bit, hoping that might hail someone instead.

'Are you looking for me?' A man's voice came from her right.

Melissa swung round, a bewildered expression on her face until she realised who it was. A smile broke out when she saw Guy sitting on the large leather sofa; a broadsheet spread out on his lap.

'No. I'm looking for a room. You're here again?' she asked.

Guy pointed to the ceiling. 'I'm staying here.'

'Oh,' Melissa said simply.

Guy looked pointedly at her holdall and angled his head to one side. 'You all right?'

Melissa nodded. 'Yes. No . . . Yes.'

'What's happened?' He folded his newspaper and threw it on the coffee table in front of him.

Melissa looked behind the reception area again and into the back, but no one was coming. She walked over to Guy and sat down on the sofa opposite him.

'My boyfriend and I. We've . . . I just need somewhere to stay for the night.'

'You've had a row?' Guy asked gently.

'Yes. And then we broke up.'

'I'm sorry to hear that.' He did in fact look genuinely concerned and Melissa relaxed a fraction into the sofa.

'Don't be. We weren't right for each other.'

The receptionist returned to the desk and fumbled with papers before starting to move away. Melissa jumped up to grab her before she left. It was the woman from behind the lectern the night before. Great.

'Hi, do you have a room for the night? It's a bit last minute, I know.' Melissa aimed for an apologetic tone.

Lectern-woman surveyed her. 'I'll check,' she said and then scrolled up and down on the computer screen for a few agonising minutes. 'Sorry. No,' she said eventually.

'Oh, no. Nothing at all?' Hope died and Melissa chewed her nails.

'Sorry,' lectern-woman repeated, not looking sorry at all.

'OK. Not to worry.'

Guy gave Melissa a questioning look as she turned round. She shook her head and sat on the edge of the sofa, trying to work out how far it was to the nearest budget hotel.

Melissa pulled out her phone and, with a few more bars of signal, started to search for hotels again. She glanced up at a silent Guy and noticed his brow was furrowed.

'Stay with me,' he suddenly said.

Melissa's head shot up all the way this time. 'What?'

'I'm in their only suite. It's rather lovely, with a little sitting room and a separate bedroom. I was upgraded for free. Don't ask,' he said with an embarrassed look on his face. 'You take the bedroom and I'll sleep in the sitting room.'

Melissa shook her head slowly. 'No. I couldn't ask you to do that.'

'You're not asking.' He sat forward to take a sip of his pint. 'I'm only too happy to offer.' He met her gaze and she looked back, thinking.

'Um. Okay,' Melissa agreed and then instantly regretted it. What the hell was she doing?

'Great,' Guy said. 'That's my good deed done for the day,' he smiled. 'Fancy a drink?'

Guy sipped his pint and Melissa tried not to chug her gin and tonic down in one desperate go while she explained what had happened between her and Liam.

'He was always coming down to Dorset. He told me it was lads' surfing weekends, but he's been seeing someone else almost the entire time.'

'Well, the man's clearly a moron,' Guy said. 'I mean, you're lovely. And, well, look at you.'

Melissa's eyes widened as Guy looked back down and studied his pint.

'Thank you,' she said quietly.

There was silence and Melissa felt a slow tension. 'Anyway. Enough about my crap love life. How was your afternoon?'

He raised his eyes and looked at her. 'Pretty diabolical actually. My gran was taken to hospital. She's broken her hip.'

'Oh no, Guy, I'm so sorry. I'm rattling on about being dumped and . . . Will she be okay?'

'I hope so. She can't move. She's waiting for surgery. But she's elderly, she's already got heart disease and I'm not sure the doctors like the idea of operating on her. I've just extended my hotel booking for a week so I can be nearby. I'm going back to the hospital again tomorrow,' he said. 'If my gran's up for talking, I'll see if I can find out where the Standishes went, if you like?'

'Oh no, don't do that! Let her rest. Oh your poor gran. I'm so sorry,' Melissa repeated.

'Thanks,' Guy said.

Melissa sipped her gin. 'I did have a little look on the internet and I found a fairly boring newspaper cutting that showed Sir Albert in London standing down as an MP a month after they left Tyneham.'

'Really?' Guy mused. 'I wonder why he did that.'

'It didn't say, but then I didn't look any harder after that. I was too busy being dumped.'

Guy gave her a sympathetic look. 'Any mention of the frightened-looking Veronica?'

'No. I tried on the net, but I didn't get anywhere with her and, to be honest, I've got enough on my plate right now. I've got to get back to London and sort out a job. My holiday is over.'

'When are you leaving?'

'Tomorrow. I've got to. I've seen the tariff sheet here and at

£200 per night exclusive of breakfast I need to get the hell out of here and back to my life.'

Not that she really knew what her life looked like right now.

Melissa refused the offer of the main bedroom and Guy helped her pull the sofa bed out in the sitting room of his suite, protesting almost the entire time that he didn't mind if she took the bedroom. With the lateness of the hour, both were grateful the sofa bed was already made up and just needed pulling into place. Guy found two extra pillows in one of the wardrobes and he handed them to Melissa as the two said an awkward goodnight.

He pulled together the little doors that separated the bedroom from the sitting room and she gave him a grateful smile. God, this was weird. As he closed the doors all the way with a soft click, she felt incredibly embarrassed. What was she doing here? Walking into his suite with him had been the height of humiliation. No one had been about to witness, but going into a hotel room with a man was usually indicative of something untoward. It said everything about Guy that there weren't any crossed wires and that he was being an absolute gentleman. She'd only known him two days, but he was incredibly easy to be with. It certainly didn't hurt that he was hot. She put that thought to one side as she climbed in to the sofa bed, reminding herself that she'd only been single for a matter of hours.

Melissa rubbed her eyes and blinked in the morning sunshine. It took her a few minutes to remember where she was. The doors dividing the sitting room from Guy's bedroom were open. His bed was empty and tidy and he appeared to have gone. She glanced over to the coffee table in front of her sofa bed. In the middle of the table was a large silver tray bearing a basket of fruit, croissants and Danish pastries with an assortment of little pots of jams and preserves and a pot of coffee. Melissa put her hands around the coffee pot and rejoiced at finding it still warm.

She looked around the room as she poured herself a coffee.
Her eyes fell on a little note on the hotel's headed notepaper.
She picked it up.

Melissa,

I hope you slept well. I've gone to the hospital to see
Gran. I didn't want to wake you. I won't be long. Please
don't leave until I've had the chance to say goodbye. Also,
I had a look at some archives online and found something
interesting out about both Sir Albert and Lady Veronica.
There are no death records for either of them!

Be back soon, Guy. X

CHAPTER 10

Tyneham, December 1943

After they returned from the beach hut, Freddie went off to fix himself a drink and Veronica went upstairs to have a bath and choose a dress for dinner. Veronica's feelings about Freddie's arrival were so mixed that she didn't quite know what to think. With Freddie now among them, it would be the only night in recent memory that she and Bertie wouldn't be alone at dinner, taking part in a silent charade of a marriage, one where she sat in fear waiting for him to verbally destroy her, or hit her in a temper caused by a storm of alcohol to his system. Veronica prayed that with Freddie here, Bertie might control himself. For show. But, likewise, with Freddie here, she felt even more of a wreck than she had been over the last few weeks, especially as she wasn't even supposed to be here. She should have been long gone, halfway to her new life. Whatever that would be. Wherever that would be.

She pulled out her bedroom key from her pocket to unlock the door. Bertie was a stickler for tradition and the ingrained idea of separate bedrooms in a house this size was one Veronica hadn't fought against. Keeping hold of her key had become a necessity against Bertie's drunken arrivals in the dead of the night. But the door was already unlocked. Perhaps Anna had forgotten to lock it with her key after her toing and froing this afternoon. Or perhaps Veronica had. Which of them had been the last to leave? She couldn't remember now.

Veronica entered her room and stopped. Something wasn't right, but she couldn't put her finger on exactly what. She looked around the room slowly, finding nothing obvious. She locked the door behind her, took her shoes off and went to her bathroom, throwing in some bath salts and stirring them into the hot water with her foot as she sat on the side of the tub. She waited for it to fill up to its regulation five inches, slipped her clothes off and slid into the scalding water.

After a few minutes of lying in the claw-footed bath, she heard her bedroom door handle start to turn. She held her breath. The handle rattled a little and Veronica sat up straight in the bath and listened. Her heart thumped. The door was locked. But that fact had not always stopped Bertie before. It had been weeks since Bertie had tried to gain access to Veronica's bed. But before that his attempts had been becoming angrier, more violent. And often in the past, just when she dared rejoice, thinking he had given up permanently, the inconsistent, frenzied attempts would start all over again. She felt as if she was living on the edge of a breakdown, teetering on the precipice of going utterly mad with fear.

The door handle rattled again louder and more forcefully. She was silent, her fingers gripped the edge of the bath. He knew she was inside. Suddenly the noise stopped and she heard movement outside the door. From the end of the hall, she could hear Freddie hailing Bertie, who moved away from her door.

Veronica lay back against the cold of the enamel bath and breathed out slowly, wondering what would happen now. Her heart was racing. Bertie would try again, later, after dinner. She knew that. The thought dripped fear into her heart.

After her bath, Veronica dried herself and, trying not to shake through cold and panic, mentally evaluated her wardrobe, intending to pick out her cream silk dress. Bertie always expected her to make an effort. She'd never been one for being dressed by a maid, but as she lined up her hairpins on her dressing table and let her auburn hair fall down about her damp shoulders, she knew she'd have to ring for Anna to help her style her hair. She could climb into the dress all by herself.

Veronica held her towel in one hand and rubbed at her eyes in the mirror with the other. She looked haggard, and it was no wonder. She closed her eyes. How was it possible, after all the weeks of meticulous planning, that she was still here? She'd pinned her hopes on leaving today, ever since Bertie announced his intention to visit his solicitor and fight the requisition order for the house. Neither Bertie's fight nor her departure had been successful. Both had come to nothing. Ironic, that it was only now, at the very end, that they shared common ground.

Tugging on the bell pull with one hand, Veronica opened the top drawer of her large chest of drawers with the other and gasped. It was empty. *No.* She yanked it out and threw it out onto the floor in her haste to check the very back of it and saw that the one underneath was also empty. Had Anna done this? She couldn't have. She'd only just unpacked from earlier in order to stave off any suspicion. But the entire unit had been emptied. Every drawer in her bedside tables, bar one, was bare. Her furs, her jewellery box and the expensive trinkets she'd kept ready and waiting – gone. The room had been cleared.

She pulled the cord again, harder than before, and listened for the sound of Anna's light steps. Anna declared herself at the door and Veronica unlocked it and threw it open.

Anna looked at the empty drawers scattered on the floor. 'What's happened?'

'All my things . . . . all my things are gone,' Veronica said, sitting on the bed. 'They've all gone.'

Anna opened the mahogany wardrobe doors. Inside were enough day and evening dresses to see Veronica out until the planned departure. The remainder of the wardrobe was barren;

only a handful of discarded wooden hangers remained. Anna fumbled on the floor of the wardrobe to check what else had been left, while Veronica ransacked the rest of the room. Veronica's anger and fear were growing in equal measure. Anna stood rigid, realisation clearly dawned on her face, and Veronica came to the same conclusion. When Veronica finished fumbling under the four-poster bed for any trace of her suitcases, she stood and stared at Anna. Bertie had taken everything.

'He knows,' Veronica said. 'He knows I'm leaving him.'

Freddie was buried in a good book and a gin and tonic by the time Veronica appeared for pre-dinner drinks. He put the book down and stood to greet her, pulling at the collar of his dinner suit. 'No Bertie?' he questioned.

'Not yet,' she said. 'He'll only be a few minutes, I'm sure. It's not quite six yet.' She glanced at her watch and braced herself for the arrival of her husband. She felt hollow, unsure as to what he knew about her plans. It was the uncertainty that worried her the most.

She glanced at Freddie out of the corner of her eye. He had resumed reading his book, only she noticed his eyes weren't moving. He was staring very hard at a place at the top of the page. His gaze lifted very gently towards her and both of them quickly averted their eyes. She couldn't help herself. A few moments later, she looked back at Freddie, who glanced up and smiled this time. And then the smile fell from his face completely as he looked past Veronica. She turned to see what he was staring at. Bertie had arrived silently and was leaning against the door frame, arms folded, watching them.

'You'll have noticed some of your things have gone, darling,' Bertie addressed Veronica, his face impassive.

'Yes.' She winced at his false term of endearment, clamped her teeth shut firmly together and waited for the inevitable bilious lies. 'Where are they?'

'They've gone up to London,' he said innocently, a hint of a smile on his face. 'No point waiting until the bitter end. Most of mine have gone too. I had Rebecca do it. I've kept back what we need for the next few days.'

'My jewellery, my furs? My suitcases have gone too.'

'You don't need them, do you?' his tone was innocent. 'The jewellery has gone to the bank, where it should have been all along. I don't trust it at the London house. It's too susceptible to bombs and looting – people taking things they shouldn't.' He looked pointedly at Veronica, who thought quickly of the clock on her bedroom mantle that she'd chosen to leave behind. She steeled herself against anything further, but there was only an accusing silence.

Dinner was a mute affair. Veronica pushed her food around her plate as Bertie drank glass after glass of wine, ringing the bell for a fresh bottle. Veronica had lost count of the amount of glasses she'd watched Bertie sink.

When dinner was over, Bertie sat back and watched Anna clear the plates. Veronica's expression turned to a worried frown as she noticed his glazed eyes resting on Anna as she moved around the table.

'Port? Cigars?' Bertie asked Freddie, his eyes still trained firmly on Anna.

'You sly dog. How are you still getting hold of those?' Freddie asked. But Bertie offered no reply. 'No, thank you,' Freddie continued. 'I thought I'd wander down to the pub actually. See if William and some of the old lot are down there. I assume they're all away fighting. It's been too long.'

At the mention of Anna's brother, Veronica's head shot up.

'Most of the farmers are here. Reserved occupation,' Bertie said, his words coming slowly. 'But I'm afraid I couldn't tell you exactly who's still here. Why do you want to mix with them?' Bertie made a disgusted face. Veronica threw Anna an apologetic look.

Freddie laughed. 'They were my friends once upon a time.'

'Heaven knows why,' Bertie said and refilled his glass.

The front door closed with a loud, satisfying thud and from the dining room Veronica heard Freddie's feet crunch on the gravel towards the village in the chilled December night.

'I don't like you smoking, you know that.' Bertie's voice was thick with warning. 'Did you think I wouldn't notice?'

'I wasn't smoking,' Veronica lied. 'Freddie had a cigarette earlier and I—'

'Don't lie, Veronica. I could smell the smoke. It lingers.'

Veronica didn't reply. She would have liked to have closed her eyes and counted to five to calm herself and formulate a better lie, but she didn't trust him not to hurl himself at her. Like last time. She looked up and met his gaze. He was staring blackly at her. He looked halfway to a snarl, his top lip curling back ever so slightly from his teeth.

'I tried your bedroom door today. I couldn't get in.'

It was not phrased as a question. Veronica tried to get away with ignoring it.

'You appeared not to hear me.'

'I was in the bath,' she said.

'So you did hear?'

'I—'

He cut her off. 'Cook asked me an interesting question yesterday.' Veronica stopped breathing.

Bertie continued. 'She wanted to know if I would be needing my ration book too. She wanted to know if I was accompanying you on . . . what did she call it . . . your short trip.' Bertie angled his head to one side. 'Where were you going, Veronica?'

'Nowhere,' she said quietly, clenching her fists in her lap, poised for his attack. She could feel the blood draining from her face. She could no longer hold his gaze.

'I'm sure you are right. I'm sure Cook was simply mistaken.

90

I'll be coming to your room again tonight, Veronica. This time I expect you to open the door. I expect you to oblige.'

Veronica watched him drain his glass and then refill it. He started slowly drinking it again. With any luck he'd be far too gone to perform, which had been her salvation for the past few months as Bertie descended further and further into his alcoholic stupors. She would not ask him if he'd had enough. She knew better. Let him drink. Let him be unable. She could deal with the hate and the venom he hurled towards her. She could even deal with his fists, which, when drunk, sometimes missed their mark. It was his sexual taste for inflicting pain and distress that Veronica feared the most. What he wanted to do to her, what he wanted from her . . . She would rather be dead. A husband wasn't supposed to want to hurt his wife with such severity. She was past wondering what she had done to deserve this.

Suddenly Bertie stood and Veronica pushed her chair back slightly, bracing herself, expecting a reprisal for the ration book fiasco. But, instead, Bertie staggered past her and towards his study without a word.

She only had to make it through the next few days, then she would be gone from him forever.

If there were no further setbacks.

Veronica went to her bedroom, pulled the key from her pocket and firmly locked the door behind her, listening over the sound of her heart beating faster than ever for the noise of Bertie's footsteps outside her door.

She wouldn't let him touch her anymore. Not tonight. Never again. The thought repulsed her. But more importantly it frightened her to death. If it was the last thing she ever did, she would stop him.

Hours later, Freddie left the pub with William and staggered a few paces. Anna's brother lurched to try to support his old friend, but it was no use. The two men were as inebriated as each other.

Freddie leant against the wall of the old stone pub, pulled his cigarette case and lighter out and lit two cigarettes as he hummed Vera Lynn's 'We'll Meet Again'. As he offered one through the darkness to William, the younger man baulked, cutting Freddie's tune short.

'You can't light that out here. The blackout. What if we get seen? By them?' William pointed up to the sky.

Freddie waved his cigarette in a circle above his head. 'Oh, they can't bloody see us from all the way up there. We're like a needle in a . . . something. Can't remember the phrase.'

'It's good to see you again,' William said.

'No, that's not it,' Freddie joked.

William laughed. 'The wanderer returns.'

Freddie inhaled on his cigarette and his mouth changed shape as he blew a series of smoke rings.

'You've been away too long,' William said. 'You've been missed.'

'I doubt it, but I appreciate the lie.'

'Why have you been keeping away?' William probed. 'Is it her? Them?'

Freddie shot him a warning look.

'Your brother . . .' William started. 'I'm not entirely sure . . .' He stopped speaking and shook his head, clearly struggling to find the right words. Eventually he sighed and gave Freddie an apologetic look.

Freddie pushed himself away from the wall, patted William's shoulder amicably and started to stagger in the direction of the Great House. 'Goodbye, old friend,' Freddie called over his shoulder, waving his cigarette around.

William turned and walked back towards his home.

It had been news to Freddie to find out tonight that the Anna living and working in his brother's house was little Anna, William's sister. Little shy Anna who never used to speak. She'd only been a child back then. He'd been a bit obtuse about that. He didn't realise how much he'd missed at Tyneham. And how much he missed William, his friend of old, his partner in petty childhood troublemaking, when Bertie wasn't leading him astray that was. William and Freddie had crossed the class divide. Not that, as children, either of them had realised such a thing really existed until it was brutally pointed out by a disgusted Bertie. Even Freddie's parents hadn't cared. Much.

Freddie was debating what William had said. Had he been away too long? Or had he been away not nearly long enough? As he approached the house he stopped where the gates once stood. He looked back down the avenue of trees, empty of their leaves in midwinter and saw the village in blackout but bathed in pale moonlight. Nearby all was silent, but if he strained his ears, he could hear the sea in the distance; the waves crashing against the rocks by the cove. He'd moved on. It was time to leave. As he mentally said goodbye to the village of his childhood home, he jumped, startled, as a blood-curdling scream came from inside the house.

CHAPTER 11

Dorset, July 2018

Melissa re-read Guy's note. There were no death records for either of them? What did that mean? Could Veronica and Albert still be alive? In the shower, Melissa used her fingers to try to count up how old they would be now. They looked in their early thirties in the picture, so they'd be in their early hundreds now. Unlikely, but not impossible.

By half past one, Melissa was growing hungry again. She'd been in Guy's suite for most of the morning, searching in vain for death records on websites that required a subscription and a credit card. Housekeeping had already come in to clean. She regretted letting them take the breakfast things away. She could murder a leftover croissant right now. The drive home would take about four hours if traffic was at its usual unpredictable level. Guy had asked her to stay to say goodbye. It was the least she could do, seeing as he'd kindly let her crash in his room, so she shut the lid of the laptop, tapped her fingers on it and waited.

A while later, a key jangled in the door and Guy walked in, looking handsome and well-dressed in chinos and a fitted shirt, but harassed. 'I'm so sorry. That took a bit longer than I thought it would.'

'It's perfectly okay. How's your gran?'

'Stable, I think. Sleeping a lot, which is good, I guess.'

'Oh I'm glad.'

'Um, did you see my note?' he asked.

She nodded and looked at him expectantly.

'Interesting, isn't it?' He grinned.

'I don't really understand what it means, if I'm honest.'

He joined her on the sofa.

'Well, simply, it means that either they are both still alive, which is probably not the case, or they both died, maybe in an air raid, but they might not have been accounted for. So there are no records. It's not as exciting now I say it out loud,' Guy said, moving on quickly. 'However, what I did find out that *is* pretty exciting is that after they left Tyneham, there are no official records for either of them anywhere. Other than that newspaper article you found where he quit as an MP and a by-election was called. And that is it. At first glance, on a few of the subscription services I use . . . there's just nothing. No record of them at all.'

Melissa was quiet while she thought. 'What does that mean?'

'Can't be sure. Maybe they died. Maybe they lived. Either way, the plot thickens.' He sat back and looked at her expectantly.

She didn't look convinced, so he tried again.

'It's not normal to have no official records at all.' He looked excited by his discovery. 'Especially for someone like Sir Albert: wealthy, a former MP. I mean, there's birth and marriage, but we know about all that, it's the bit after that's missing. Electoral roll, boat passenger lists, death records . . . There's usually something to hang on to and work back from. But for both of them there's nothing. Absolutely nothing whatsoever. It's as if, officially, they completely vanished.'

Melissa sat back and crossed her legs. 'So, your guess is that they both died soon after. In an air raid or something like that?' she asked.

'Who knows. I've got to go and pick up some bits from Gran's house. Come with me? We'll ask if she remembers hearing anything when we drop them off. Hopefully she'll be a bit more alert this afternoon.'

'Won't your gran mind?' Melissa asked. 'If she's recovering, she's not going to want me there.'

Guy gave her a knowing smile. 'If I turn up with a girl, my gran will be over the moon. Trust me.'

Melissa smiled and looked at her watch

'We can grab a bit of lunch on the way,' he prompted.

She nodded slowly. 'Go on then. But then I really will have to get going after that.'

Guy grinned.

They ate sandwiches from a petrol station as Guy drove his shiny black Range Rover down the country lanes towards his gran's bungalow at Sandford – about twenty minutes' drive from Tyneham. Guy explained that Anna and her husband had moved here after she'd been demobbed when the war had finished. Melissa glanced at him as he spoke. In a gleaming car and with expensive Ray-Bans on, he looked like a different person, like an ultra-sleek proper celebrity. She could see how easy it might be to bask in the celebrity glow.

Guy parked outside the bungalow. He walked around to the passenger side to open Melissa's door, but she was already out of the car by the time he got to her.

'I just need to pick up a few bits. We won't be long.'

He opened the bungalow's front door and held it open for her. Melissa couldn't remember if Liam had ever held a door open for her.

The bungalow was neat and tidy inside, a few bits of paramedic debris and oversized empty plaster wrappers were the only sign that anything untoward had happened. Melissa picked them up as Guy closed the front door. She went towards the small, yellow-tiled kitchen to find a bin in which to put the rubbish. Looking around, there were heaps of books piled up on the shelves that ran around the edge of the kitchen underneath the raised cupboards. Cookery books jostled for space between scrapbooks, which in turn fought for plots between gardening books.

Behind her she could feel Guy watching her. She glanced at him over her shoulder.

'Gran tried to teach me to cook in this kitchen.' He sounded wistful. 'She failed. Or I did. I'm still awful.'

Melissa laughed and Guy fumbled in his jacket pocket, producing a small scrap of paper with a list. He frowned.

'Could you grab a few of these things for me? Er, knickers et cetera. I feel a bit strange going through Gran's underwear drawers.'

Melissa smiled and walked past him, taking the paper from his fingers as she went.

'Her bedroom's first on the left,' he called after her.

Guy went to the sitting room to find a few paperbacks to take to hospital and Melissa slowly started searching in the bedroom. There were photographs of a young Guy next to the bed and a black and white one of a man in a British Army uniform who looked uncannily like Guy but who, Melissa thought, had probably been Guy's grandfather.

She pulled open the drawers and found the first few items from the list. Glancing around at the wardrobes in search of a dressing gown, Melissa opened the doors and pulled out a soft pink fluffy robe, folded it up and put it on the bed to take to the hospital. Next on the list was writing paper. On the shelf was a cream box. With no sign of writing paper in any of the drawers, Melissa lifted the box down and took a look inside to see if any was lurking in there. There were a few locks of baby hair tied neatly with ribbon and a few picture postcards from various British towns that shared the box with birth and marriage certificates and old passports with the corners clipped off. It was a memory box. At random, Melissa flipped over a black and white postcard of Inverness Castle. The postcard was blank where the message should have been. Anna's name and address were present and the postmark showed 1949. Melissa picked up a few other postcards: there was one for 1950 and 1951 and then one a year until 1970. Each was blank. There were more postcards inside, but Melissa heard Guy cough and she hastily shoved everything back in the box and almost threw it up onto the shelf for fear of being caught snooping.

Guy was by the front door holding a bag when Melissa emerged from the bedroom. She put in the bits she'd gathered and they left for the hospital.

'Gran, this is Melissa.'

'Hello, dear, how are you?' Anna asked, her eyes crinkling as she smiled. 'As you can see, I'm in a bit of a pickle.' She winked and her heavily wrinkled eyelid closed and opened slowly. Her grey hair was long and piled up into a loose bun on her head. Melissa could see a faint trace of the seventeen-year-old girl in the photograph from the exhibition.

Melissa liked her instantly. 'I hope you don't mind my coming along. I met Guy at the opening of Tyneham a few days ago.'

'I know, dear,' the older lady said. 'He's talked about nothing else since.'

'Gran!' Guy sounded like a horrified schoolboy.

Melissa misunderstood. 'Well, Tyneham is a very special place. It's pretty much all I've thought about since I visited too.'

Anna gave Melissa a curious smile and put her head to one side.

'We brought the things you asked for,' Guy hurried on.

'Are you in any pain?' Melissa asked. 'Is there anything else we can get for you?'

'No, No. I'm drugged up to the eyeballs. It's marvellous actually.'

Melissa laughed.

'So, what did you think of Tyneham?' Anna smiled.

'Amazing. I've never been anywhere that atmospheric before, even with all the tourists. We went to the Great House, where Guy said you worked.'

'Oh yes?' Anna stiffened and looked down at the white sheet covering her bed. 'I'm afraid I don't have very fond memories of that house. I miss the village and my home, the church on Sunday, the friends that scattered far and wide. But the Great House . . . It's a beautiful building. Not a nice place though . . . not in the end.'

Guy exchanged a look with Melissa.

'Why?' he asked, reaching to the bedside table on wheels to pour his grandmother a glass of water.

'The owner wasn't very nice. Thank you, dear,' she said, taking the glass and sipping.

'To you?' asked Melissa.

'To anyone,' Anna returned. 'Anyway . . .'

Melissa looked wide-eyed at Guy to nudge him on.

'Erm, Gran, we were wondering, and this may seem a bit strange, but Melissa's got a bee in her bonnet about Lady Veronica.'

'What about her?' Anna asked with a kind smile, before taking another sip.

Melissa spoke up. 'This sounds so bonkers when I say it out loud. But the photo in the church display shows her looking a bit odd, a bit frightened maybe.'

Anna stayed very still, her lips just touched the rim of her glass, but she had stopped sipping.

Melissa continued, 'All the display boards tell you what happened to each family and their general whereabouts after the requisition, but there's nothing about Lady Veronica, or her husband for that matter actually. I just wanted to know that she was all right, I suppose. I think only because she looked a bit strange in the photo. Oh I don't know. I feel mad now. Just ignore me.'

Anna's voice sounded strange. 'She was fine, dear.'

'Do you know what happened to her? Where she went?' Guy asked.

'They went to London for a short while and then they moved away. I heard from her occasionally. She wrote. Only a bit, mind. But she was fine.'

'Oh phew,' Melissa said. 'Great.'

'This is a bit strange, Gran, but how did they die?'

Anna's smile faded. 'Die?'

'They aren't still alive are they, her and her husband?' Guy asked. 'I mean, they'd be in their hundreds now if they were.'

'I'm not sure. They were much older than me. Lady Veronica was in her early thirties when she left Tyneham. I was only seventeen. I imagine they must both be dead by now,' she said. 'Comes to us all.' She looked pointedly around the hospital ward.

Guy had a frown on his face. 'But you didn't hear that they'd died, in an accident or something like that?'

Anna shook her head. 'No. I lost touch with them a long time ago.'

Guy nodded thoughtfully.

'They probably died of old age,' Anna reasoned.

Guy stopped nodding. 'Well, no. They can't have. That would mean they'd have died in the nineteen eighties or nineties in all likelihood. Records were kept better. Their deaths would have been logged.'

Melissa's eyes flicked back and forth slowly from Guy to Anna throughout the exchange. Melissa thought Anna looked lost. Actually, Melissa was starting to feel lost.

'What do you mean?' the elderly lady asked.

'They have no death records, which is odd by today's standards. But not back then, in the forties, in the confusion of war. Lots of records went missing or deaths weren't logged as people were buried alive in bomb craters or not identified after the damage was cleared. I mean, the entire 1931 census records were destroyed during the war. Completely obliterated. But that kind of thing doesn't happen now. It's all logged electronically these days. I assumed perhaps Veronica and Albert had been in an accident together for both their deaths to have been—'

Anna cut him off. 'No, dear. They were both fine. They didn't die in the war. We lost contact in the 1970s, so I think perhaps they might have died then, or perhaps she did as I never received a . . . The communication stopped then. They were both fine. I last saw them the day they left Tyneham and that was a long time ago. I don't know what happened to them after that, but they were fine.'

There was silence while Guy and Melissa digested the information.

Melissa's brain kicked into gear. Why, if they had outlived the war and the administrative confusion that could have easily missed two people dying in some kind of bombing accident, had their deaths not been recorded if they were still alive and writing letters to his gran in the 1970s? Melissa looked at Anna, who in turn was looking into her half-empty water glass. Melissa refilled it. Anna looked at her gratefully.

'You said Sir Albert wasn't very nice to everyone. Did that include his wife?' Melissa started.

'Do you know, my dears, I'm quite tired now. Would you mind if I had a little rest?'

'Oh gosh, of course not. Sorry, Gran, we've tired you out,' Guy said, and he and Melissa stood up.

'Thank you, my darling. Your mum should be here for the evening visiting hours, so don't feel obliged to pop back, will you?'

Guy had been dismissed. 'Erm, all right. Get some sleep. I'll pop in tomorrow.'

They headed back to the hotel and for the first ten minutes Guy drove in silence. Melissa stared out of the passenger window, her lips pursed together, itching to say what she was sure Guy was thinking. Every now and again she glanced at him. His brow was furrowed and he had a puzzled expression on his face.

Melissa was impatient, unable to remain silent for much longer.

'So, what do you think?' she asked him tentatively as he pulled into the Pheasant and Gun's car park.

Guy blew out a puff of air from his cheeks. 'I think,' he said slowly, shaking his head, 'that she's hiding something.'

CHAPTER 12

Tyneham, December 1943

From inside the house, Anna's scream pierced the night. Behind her bedroom door, a chair had been wedged under the handle, but it was starting to show the strain, its back legs creaking with every crash that Bertie's body made against the other side. Madness had gripped him and he was thrashing his way through the wood, attempting to either break the door down by snapping it from its lock or forcing a hole through the wood panels. It was clear he didn't care which. If only she had something to fight him off with.

He'd tried before but never like this. Never. She was frightened. Why now? Why at the end? What had she done?

There had been plenty of times when he had caught her alone, when he had put the fear of God in her, but had never followed through. But now he was drunk. Horrendously drunk. Worse than she'd ever seen him before. And he was coming for her.

In the corridor, the thrashing stopped momentarily as raised voices started up from the end of the hallway in the servants' sleeping quarters.

'What the hell are you doing?' Veronica screamed at Bertie. 'Anna, are you all right?' Veronica shouted down the landing towards Anna's bedroom.

Anna was against the far wall in her room, too scared to scream back that she was fine. Sir Albert was a man possessed and in this state he clearly didn't care who he had in front of him, as long as he had someone. And now Veronica was out there with him.

'Run, Lady Veronica!' Anna eventually managed to shout, although the words that left her mouth sounded rasping and not her own. 'Run!'

In the dark of the hallway, Veronica backed away from Bertie. His staggering body lurched towards her like some kind of demonic entity. His eyes were narrow and black, his face unreadable and still, although Veronica could see from the splintered door what his intentions had been.

'You've had too much to drink again, darling.' The tone of endearment sounded wrong, misplaced, about a year too late. Veronica tried to use her calmest voice, but it wavered amid the fear. Bertie smiled dangerously and Veronica moved along the dark of the hallway, with only the chink of light from underneath Anna's door to guide her back to the servants' staircase.

As she turned and ran, she crashed into something tall, muscular and smelling faintly of cigarette smoke.

'What on earth . . .?' Freddie said as Veronica thudded against him. 'What's going on? I heard screaming.'

'Oh, thank God. Thank God,' Veronica replied, burying her face into Freddie's chest. She'd never been so happy to see him in all her life. 'It's Bertie. He's . . . he's . . . mad,' she finished in a whisper.

Freddie grabbed Veronica and moved her behind him.

'What's he doing? What are you doing, old chap?' Freddie called down the hall in a placating voice.

Bertie staggered towards Freddie slowly, his fists raised. But his foot caught on the rug and he stumbled, falling face forward onto the floor. He was still.

Veronica stood clutching Freddie's wool coat, as if it was a safety blanket, looking out at the scene in front of her. Her eyes had adjusted to the darkness and she moved round Freddie and stepped forward.

'Good God, he's out like a light,' Freddie murmured. 'I hope he's all right. What the hell's he doing all the way up here?'

Anna unbolted her door and appeared, shaking, in her nightdress.

Veronica ran to her. 'Anna, I'm so sorry. I'm so sorry.'

'It's all right, Lady Veronica.'

'No, it's not. He's never done this before. Has he?'

Anna shook her head. 'Not *this*, no.'

'Then I don't know why he ... I don't know what he ...' Veronica trailed off.

Freddie unbuttoned his coat and put it around a shaking Anna. 'Put this on, you're cold.'

Anna accepted it, nodding; her face grim.

Freddie reached out and took Veronica's hand within his. It felt like the most natural thing in the world, the two of them, hand in hand. Bertie's absurd actions in front of Freddie forced Veronica to admit defeat. There was no hiding Bertie's behaviour now. She felt ashamed, so ashamed, that this was her marriage. This was her husband, on the floor in front of them.

Freddie was mute. He slowly removed his hand from Veronica's, bent down and with an effort of will picked Bertie up and threw him over his shoulder. 'Help me get him to bed, will you?' His voice was strained with the weight of his brother on his shoulder.

Veronica walked behind him, but made little effort to stop Bertie's head from bashing into the bannisters as Freddie stumbled and staggered his way to Bertie's bedroom. Anna followed at a slow pace.

After depositing Bertie on his own four-poster, Freddie turned to face the women who had both silently refused to enter Bertie's room and were standing in the doorway. Veronica was still in her cream silk dress from dinner; her face like thunder. Anna, drowning in Freddie's coat, looked small and younger than her seventeen years. The two women were holding hands. He looked from one to the other and then sat on the edge of Bertie's bed with a thump. The move roused Bertie, who stirred and rolled over in his sleep. Both women stepped back, fearful of the consequences of him waking.

'Veronica, what the hell is going on in this house?' he asked.

Veronica spoke to Anna, ignoring Freddie's question. 'Stay in my room tonight. The door is stronger.'

Anna nodded and walked towards Veronica's room.

Freddie's eyes widened. '"The door is stronger?" Veronica?'

Veronica closed her eyes. She needed time to think before she told Freddie the truth. But he had resumed scrutinising his brother.

'That was quite a fall. Do you think he'll be all right?' He looked back at Veronica for an answer.

She tried to hold the tears in, but the relentless emotions brought about by Bertie's violence, the requisition, and her failed departure were too much. Her nerves were fraught and the tears she'd been attempting to hold back poured forth. She put her hand over her mouth to stifle the sobs, but it was no use.

Freddie walked towards Veronica and pulled her into his arms. He turned so he was facing Bertie, watching, waiting for any sign of resurgence. Freddie stroked her hair while she cried. The movement felt wonderful, soothing and she allowed herself to rest against him. What must he think of her? How she had fallen from grace. How ridiculous must she look to him now – frightened to death of her own husband, isolated, her maid her only friend. She wanted desperately to know he thought well of her. But she didn't think well of herself. Not anymore.

Gently he moved back from her, causing a bereft feeling to hit her. He looked into her eyes; his gaze held so much sympathy that Veronica couldn't bear it. But then Freddie's expression slowly softened and he reached out and touched her face. She closed her eyes, guiltily relishing his touch. The intimate gesture forced her to involuntarily draw in a sharp breath. She wanted to tell him to stop. It was cruel.

He whispered her name. As she opened her eyes, he moved slowly towards her, dipping his head. His face only a slight distance from her own, he slowly closed the gap and softly kissed her.

Her mind raced and her body surged with electricity. Freddie held her gently as he continued to kiss her, faster, more urgent. She felt the full weight of his passion and she returned it. She had no time to understand why it was happening, only that it was, after all these years. There was no time for happiness; no time for anything at all.

Behind her, Bertie stirred. Veronica sprang back from Freddie and swung round, her eyes wide in fear. But Bertie slept on. What they had just done was so incredibly dangerous. She couldn't believe it had happened. It must have been sympathy driving Freddie to comfort her. She daren't hope it was anything else. She daren't hope it was a flicker of love.

As Bertie snored and rolled over, safely in his slumber, Veronica turned back to Freddie. He was running his hand across his forehead, his expression one of anguish.

'I'm sorry,' he said. 'I'm so sorry. I shouldn't have . . . I'm sorry.'

Veronica touched her lips; they were warm where his lips had pressed against hers, deliciously, familiarly. The love for Freddie that she thought she'd buried came to the fore. She looked at him and mustered the only words she felt able to utter without a lump forming in her throat. 'Please don't worry.' Her voice sounded stiff and not at all like her own.

He looked like hell and stared at the floor, nodding by way of reply as Veronica left the room and went back to her own.

In the morning, Freddie awoke to a blissful, false state. The memory of last night's awful events hadn't yet wormed into his mind. But the sedate waking moment was swiftly replaced with a sick feeling. Whatever was happening in this house was wrong. To say he was uneasy would be an understatement. And then there was the kiss. He couldn't have her. She would never be his again. He shouldn't have done it. He shouldn't have kissed her. It was spur-of-the-moment and stupid. More than that — as good as it had felt, it was wrong.

After bathing and dressing, he walked down the hall and knocked quietly at Veronica's door. There was no answer and all sounded quiet within.

He encountered Anna in the dining room.

'Good morning, sir. Breakfast is warm in the dishes if you'd like something.' Anna pointed towards the sideboard. He was ravenous, but was more interested in finding Veronica. He wondered if he should go and look for her. But given how he had acted last night she was probably avoiding him.

'Anna? Are you quite all right?'

'I'm fine, sir, thank you for asking. I've hung your coat up again.'

Freddie shook his head in disbelief. So that was to be the only reference to Bertie's antics last night.

Freddie helped himself to kedgeree and what passed for coffee these days and sat quietly. He ate nothing and fiddled with the handle of his coffee cup.

Bertie appeared moments later and helped himself to the dishes. 'I suppose I'm not getting my newspaper in my room,' he sulked.

Freddie's eyes were wide and he extended his head forward with shock. 'After last night?'

'Bloody servants,' Bertie uttered.

'What were you doing last night, Bertie? I arrived to find you scampering about upstairs on the servants' landing. I know I was drunk, but you were something else entirely.'

Bertie put his cutlery down and looked his brother directly in the eye. Bertie's eyes were bloodshot and his skin was pale. Freddie retreated a little in his seat.

Anna appeared with a fresh pot of coffee. 'May I get you anything else?' she asked, studiously avoiding looking at her employer.

Both men shook their heads and Freddie looked up at Anna to find her staring at him. He looked at her enquiringly and then glanced at his brother to check he wasn't watching. Anna left the room clutching the empty coffee jug.

Freddie was beyond frustrated and threw his napkin on to the table as he stood. 'I'm finished.'

'You're leaving today, aren't you?' Bertie said in a tone that made it clear he wanted his brother gone.

'I'm not entirely sure yet,' Freddie said, thinking of the events of last night. Before he left he needed to speak to Veronica. After what he'd done, she would probably want him long gone.

Bertie nodded and looked around frantically. 'Where's the bloody newspaper?'

Instead of replying, Freddie simply left the dining room.

Anna was waiting for him in the hallway. Wordlessly, she passed him a small scrap of folded paper and then left.

Freddie glanced behind him to check Bertie hadn't moved like a wraith to creep up on him. He opened the paper. In Veronica's handwriting, there were two words: *Beach hut.*

CHAPTER 13

Veronica could hear crunching on the mix of pebbles and sand and she stood up from the daybed in readiness. She'd been waiting in the beach hut for what felt like hours, but in all probability hadn't been more than half an hour at most. She steadied herself against the bedpost. She felt sick from the lack of breakfast and sleep, petrified about seeing Freddie in the cold light of day and overwhelmed at how the situation with Bertie had risen to this horrific new state. She wondered what she could have done earlier in their marriage to stop Bertie becoming this bad. What would he have allowed her to do? With every attempt to quell him, his violence had risen.

Veronica had tried every approach under the sun to get Anna to leave, but she'd always refused. 'We can handle him together. It's only until we all leave anyway,' Anna had said.

But this was new. Surely she'd go now.

Veronica knew she had to explain things to Freddie. He had saved them both last night, she was sure of it. In the corridor, Bertie's attentions had swiftly turned from Anna to Veronica. Perhaps that's what he had planned all along, luring her from behind her locked door knowing she would go to Anna's aid? Perhaps he had been tricking them. Veronica narrowed her eyes, wondering how he could have executed a plan like that while staggeringly drunk.

Freddie appeared at the door and Veronica smoothed her skirt down nervously. She wished her heart wasn't beating so fast. He shook his head and rubbed his hand over his forehead.

'Oh, Veronica,' he said.

She couldn't mention the kiss that shouldn't have happened. She was too embarrassed by how guilty yet mistakenly hopeful she'd felt. And she didn't want to embarrass him by mentioning something he'd seemed ashamed and regretful of almost the very moment he'd done it. Instead, she launched into the speech she'd been rehearsing in her head for the best part of the morning.

'Don't leave.' She spoke quickly. 'I'm begging you not to leave today. Please stay until the end. Please stay. If not for me . . . you owe me nothing of course . . . but for Anna. She refuses to leave me and I'm not sure I can protect us both. I can protect myself, I think. I've learned how. But Anna, she's too young.'

Freddie's face went slack. 'My worst fears . . .' he murmured, but then he looked at her, his eyes questioning, unsure. 'Bertie tried to get into Anna's room? But it was a mistake? He didn't know what he was doing? He can't have. He's sitting at the breakfast table as if nothing's happened.'

Veronica gave a bitter laugh. 'Of course he is. Freddie, he's your brother and you don't want to hear this, but please, please believe me. He's not normal. Not anymore. He was fine when I married him, I think. Or at least as close to fine as I thought he could be, given that he wasn't . . .'

'Wasn't . . .?' Freddie raised an eyebrow.

'Wasn't you,' Veronica said, ploughing on before she could acknowledge what she'd admitted. 'But he's not right. I swear he's not. He's been like this for some time.'

'It's the requisition order,' Freddie murmured. 'It has to be.'

'It's not.' She was forceful. 'It's the drink. He's getting worse. He drinks bottle after bottle of whatever he can, every night. He drinks so much, he can hardly stand and then, on the nights he *can* stand, he comes for me. Although he can't . . . you know . . . unless I'm scared, and he makes me pay for that.'

Veronica went quiet and Freddie screwed his face up and looked at the bookshelf, clearly trying to work out what she meant.

'He can't, what?' he asked, looking back at her.

Veronica breathed in and out loudly and then whispered, 'Don't make me say it.'

His face was still puzzled. And then realisation dawned. 'Jesus Christ,' he said when he finally understood. He slumped against the door frame and rubbed his hand across his jaw.

Veronica looked at the floor. 'At first I thought it was me; that I wasn't enough. Then I thought it was the alcohol. Now I think it's both. He hates me. He hates me so much, he won't divorce me. He'd rather keep me, trapped, like a caged animal.' She fought back tears.

Freddie appeared unable to speak.

'He's never been the loving sort, or particularly gentle,' Veronica continued quietly. 'He left me alone more often than not until he really started drinking a few months after we got married. It all changed then. He started taking out whatever frustrations were bothering him on me. I took it to begin with. Each time, I thought, he won't do this again, I'm sure of it. He said he was sorry, at first. And I forgave him. I was sure he would stop. But every time was the same. Until it got worse and he started hurting me. He struggled to . . . you know . . . and I realised he needed more and more violent ways. I tried to oblige, until I finally knew that I wasn't an active participant. When I tried to fight him off, he enjoyed it. My fear. Then I tried to stay silent, thinking that if I didn't show fear, he'd struggle, but he hit me so hard, I passed out and since then I don't trust him not to kill me. Now I refuse to unlock the door.' The tears she'd been holding back fell.

Freddie was silent, his face lost all colour. He looked like the bottom had fallen out of his world. He couldn't move, couldn't seem to go to her and comfort her. He was rooted to the threshold.

He groped for the door frame to steady himself. 'My own brother.'

'I'm sorry. I'm so sorry,' Veronica wiped tears from her face. 'I shouldn't have told you. He's your brother. I'm sorry. I just need you to promise to stay. For Anna. She won't leave me. I've tried to get rid of her. But she won't go. If Bertie gets to her, she won't know how to stop him. She'll be frightened. She'll show fear. She won't know it, but she'll be giving him all the things he needs to . . . Oh God.'

It appeared to take all of Freddie's strength to move his body away from the door frame and walk to Veronica, pulling her towards him. He held her tightly against him and her body weakened, her arms hanging limply by her side.

'I don't know what to do.' His eyes were wide.

'Please don't leave,' she begged.

'I'm not going anywhere,' he promised.

Veronica cried tears of relief into Freddie's chest. 'Thank you. Thank you.'

'What happened last night? Why doesn't he remember anything?'

Veronica wiped her eyes. 'He remembers. I'm sure of it. It suits him to act relatively normal during the day and to turn into a monster after a few drinks at night. I've tried to stop him from drinking,' she sobbed. 'I've paid for it with his fists.'

'Jesus Christ,' he said. 'I know he always used to like a drink. We both do. But I had no idea he was so out of control.'

Veronica looked up at him, but he was looking over the top of her head to the wooden beach hut wall.

'Everything will be all right. You know that, don't you, Veronica?' Freddie led her to the daybed and they sat down.

Veronica nodded in agreement, although she had no idea how

it would ever be all right again. She was so tense, her stomach was aching.

'Why Anna? Why last night? I'm sorry, I'm struggling to understand all this.'

'I don't know. To punish her for being loyal to me? Because she's young and innocent? Because he knew I'd come running for her? Because he failed to get to me earlier in the day? Because she's an easy target?'

They were quiet then with nothing but the winter wind whipping around the old beach hut. Freddie clearly couldn't believe this. He looked as if he was in a nightmare from which he hoped he'd soon awake. They sat back against the painted white wood, rough where it had not been sanded before the paint had been applied.

'How often . . .' His voice sounded strange, strangled. 'How often does this happen? How often does he . . .' He trailed off, swallowing loudly.

Veronica's voice was quiet. 'He used to try once or twice a month. Then the rest of the time he wouldn't even look at me. But it's more frequent now. Freddie, I thought I was going to die the last time. He was killing me. I was so scared and that was what spurred him on. It's what's driven him for months. Getting that reaction from me. It's his addiction. I can't take it anymore.' The more she thought about it, the more despair whirled inside her.

His face was ashen.

'Why haven't you just left him, Veronica?' he asked. 'Why are you still here?'

She couldn't tell Freddie; couldn't admit that the reason she was still here was because he had suddenly arrived, changing her escape plans and forcing her to stay longer in the presence of her violent husband. She looked at Freddie's face, full of concern and, she wasn't sure, something else that she couldn't quite read and knew he'd never forgive himself if she told him.

'I am leaving. I'm going the morning the requisition takes effect. There's bound to be so much commotion that no one will miss me for a while. The vicar has asked Bertie to say a few words to the villagers. I'm going to try to get away during that.'

Freddie reached over and held her hand. 'I'll help you.'

Her eyes widened. 'You will? How?'

'I'll help you get away. I have money. I'll find you a flat, somewhere you can be safe. He won't take his wife leaving him lightly. He'll try to find you, you do know that, don't you?'

'I know.'

'We'll leave together. I'll protect you. If he comes for you, if he finds you, I'll kill him,' Freddie said, leaning towards her, his voice meaningful.

'Freddie, you don't mean that. Don't say such things.'

'Veronica, you have no idea, do you?' he said under his breath.

'About what?'

He turned towards her, his face full of pain. 'About how I feel about you. How I still feel about you. Nothing's changed, you know.'

'Don't. Don't, Freddie. I wasn't anything special to you. Don't pretend otherwise. It's not fair.'

His face fell. 'What? You were the only important thing in my world. I was in love with you. Why do you think I kept away all this time?'

She shook her head, reliving the pain of what she'd found out so long ago. 'You weren't in love with me. I was just one in a long line of women. I was just one among many, all at the same time. I fell in love with you, Freddie. I fell in love with you the night we met at that party. But you didn't want me. Not really. Not in the end.'

Freddie's mouth fell open and he stood up in front of her. 'You were the only one in a very very *short* line. There was *only you*. There has only *ever* been you.' He looked down at her unblinkingly.

'But . . . Bertie told me . . .' Veronica looked at the wooden floor and fought down the urge to be sick. She felt the colour drain from her face.

'Bertie told you what?' Freddie demanded through gritted teeth.

'He told me that you were making a fool of me, that you'd never marry me, that you had a different woman on your arm every night of the week and that I was best to get away now, dignity intact, and not to make a further fool of myself by clinging on to something that was quickly dying.'

Remembering Bertie's words brought her fresh pain. The way Bertie had told her, so forcefully, so convincingly. At first, she hadn't believed him as she thought of the way Freddie would look at her in a crowded room, as if they were the only two people in the world, the way he rubbed the back of her hand with his thumb as they'd go for long walks on Hampstead Heath. She was sure she'd seen love in Freddie's eyes. But the way Bertie told her, so earnestly, that she was being strung along, that she was being played with. His words had hurt, had felt so real. And the more Veronica thought about it, the more truth she thought she had seen. Freddie was flirtatious, charming and charismatic – not just to her but to all women. But Bertie had forced the point home, and Veronica had believed it. Bertie had been 'so ashamed' of his brother for the way he was toying with Veronica. And then, Veronica, under Bertie's helpful guidance, was encouraged to stop all contact, save what little of her dignity she had left.

Freddie nodded slowly and closed his eyes. 'My brother told you that? And you believed him?'

'Yes, he—'

'So that's why you just left me? That's why I never received an explanation? Just a cold, unfeeling note to tell me goodbye and good luck. That's why, less than a fortnight later you were seen stepping out with him?' He looked lost.

She nodded and put her hand to her mouth to try to hold

back the pained noise that escaped her throat. 'I didn't want to embarrass myself by confronting you. Far better to leave with dignity. He told me my heart would be safe with him. He told me you were talking about breaking it off with me. He told me he loved me. Then, later, he proposed. You didn't propose. You never told me you loved me. I didn't know how you felt and Bertie told me—'

'Lies,' Freddie cut in. 'Bertie told you a pack of lies and you believed them. All of them.'

'No,' Veronica cried. But she knew Freddie was right. 'Why would he do that to me, to you? Why would he want to ruin us?'

'He did it because he bloody well could. He did it to take you from me, because I wanted you, because he could see I'd fallen madly in love with you. I didn't propose, Veronica, because I wanted to make something of myself first, to prove myself worthy of you and earn a decent crust to support us. And then the bloody war started. Making permanent plans felt wrong. It felt unfair to you. What if I was called up? What if I was killed? And then, without a word of apology or explanation, you upped and left. Refused to return the messages I left with your parents, weren't at home when I visited. And only a short while later there you are, in the newspaper . . . *An Engagement is Announced* with my bloody brother.' He was shouting and paced the few feet in front of the daybed.

'I'm so sorry.' Veronica was shaking. She looked around her, feeling the weight of the living hell on her shoulders. 'I did this,' she whispered. 'I did this to us.'

Freddie flew to her and knelt down. 'I'm not angry with you, Veronica. How could I be? It's Bertie I'm angry with. Bertie I hate. My whole life he's tried to dominate me and I've always brushed it off. Thinking it didn't matter. Bertie, the older brother, the one to inherit everything. He was the one my parents pinned all their hopes on. The one who went off to parliament while I failed almost all my legal exams and was told to run Father's factory after he died. And only then because Bertie didn't want it. He had his eyes on bigger prizes. Bigger fish. But I didn't care. I didn't want this house. I didn't want the London house. I didn't want any of it. I only wanted you. And Bertie took you from me.' He looked into her eyes. 'No one has ever matched up to you, Veronica. I never gave anyone the chance. It was only ever you.'

For so long, deep regret had been building inside Veronica. She should never have allowed herself to listen to Bertie back then. But he'd been so convincing and then she thought she was falling for Bertie. But she wasn't. She had been lying to herself. It wasn't love. It was the comfort in moving seamlessly from one brother to the other. She thought she couldn't have Freddie's love, so she'd take his brother's. But Bertie didn't have any to give. It could all have been so different if she'd been stronger, had damned her dignity to hell and told Freddie she loved him. They could have been so happy.

She looked at the man she'd always loved. He looked defeated, older, a man who had been to war and had returned injured but alive. Just. Freddie was promising to help her, to go with her and protect her and, after all this time, after everything that had happened, he still loved her. She felt the same way.

'I feel as if I've been asleep and it's as though I've just woken up,' Veronica cried. She moved off the bed and onto his lap on the floor, where he pulled her closer to him, enveloping her in his arms. The feeling inside threatened to burst from within if she didn't tell him. 'I love you,' she whispered. 'I don't think I ever stopped.'

'I've always loved you,' he replied, a smile of happiness playing on his lips.

Then, before Veronica knew what was happening, she kissed him, a kiss that spoke volumes of love that had been lost for years and then found. But a stab of fear entered her heart as they gently pulled apart. Freddie rested his forehead on hers and closed his eyes.

Oh God, they would pay for this if Bertie ever found out. Veronica could feel it.

'We've been gone from the house long enough.' Freddie read her thoughts.

'You go first and I'll follow on in a few minutes. I don't think we should arrive together.' Veronica climbed up from Freddie's lap.

He kissed the tops of her hands. 'Not long now. We'll work out how to leave. Together.'

She nodded, but a feeling of dread had already taken hold.

Freddie tugged the door closed against the December weather and pulled his coat on and his collar up around his neck to protect against the coastal wind.

Veronica sat back on the daybed and took a few minutes to collect herself. She had tried to bury the love she'd felt for Freddie ever since she'd left him for Bertie. She told herself Freddie had been playing her for a fool. But it was she who had been the fool all along.

When she'd given him a few minutes' head start, she pulled her coat on and left the beach hut, standing on the hard, damp sand by the shoreline, listening to the waves crash onto the rocks at the edge of the small cove. She tried to push the feeling of anxiety far out to sea. The war was raging around them, but for the first time in a long while, Veronica felt a true moment of happiness. Freddie still loved her. She was leaving Bertie. Freddie had said he'd help her. And she and Freddie were leaving Tyneham together.

CHAPTER 14

Dorset, July 2018

'So now we know Veronica was still alive in the 1970s,' Melissa said, unclicking her seat belt. 'Your grandmother just told us. So that's kind of all I wanted to know. That she'd survived whatever was troubling her when that picture was taken, whatever it was that had given her that frightened look.'

But maybe that wasn't all she wanted to know. Melissa cast her mind back to the photograph. Veronica had a haunted look about her. It was one she'd seen plenty of times on her mum after a fight with her dad. While he'd never laid a hand on her, the abuse was present nonetheless. It had destroyed her mother's confidence. Melissa didn't just want to know if Lady Veronica was alive, she wanted to know if she was okay.

'You think it's him, don't you? Sir Albert. You think he was responsible for that frightened look?' Guy asked.

'Well, given the fact his knuckles are white holding her hand so tightly and what your gran said about him being a bit of a shit in general, I do now.'

'Okay,' Guy said, flicking the controls into drive. 'Come on.'

'Where are we going?'

'Tyneham.'

'Again? Why?'

'I wasn't that bothered before. But now I am. And there's someone there who might be able to shed a bit of light.'

They walked through Tyneham village. There hadn't been that many tourists the last time they visited, but now it was Monday and it was living up to its moniker of the ghost village. They walked into the church.

'He might be in here. He was last time,' Guy said.

'Who?' Melissa asked.

'One of the guides.'

'Hello again, young man,' the guide called Reg said as he saw them enter the church. 'Can't keep away?'

'Something like that yes. This is my friend Melissa. Melissa, this is Reg. He used to live here when he was a boy.'

Melissa shook the elderly man's hand.

'Reg Chatwell. Pleased to meet you,' he said.

Melissa introduced herself. 'You used to live here?' she asked.

'And now I'm back looking after tourists, for my sins.'

'It must be weird, seeing it like this?' Melissa asked, pushing her sunglasses up on top of her head.

Reg nodded. 'It is. It is. It's decayed and a bit of a mess, but it's a pleasure to see it at all. We thought it was gone forever, but the old girl is back, so to speak. So you've come again to have another look around?' he asked Guy.

'Yes and no,' Guy said. 'We wanted to have a look at a few of the boards again – the Standishes in particular.'

Reg made a face. 'Ah, everyone's always interested in the gentry, aren't they? No one cares about the poor old fisherman who lost his home as well, the dairy farmer who lost his livelihood and had to sell off his cattle by auction in under a month. What do you want to know about the Standishes?' He sighed.

Guy and Melissa exchanged a look. She felt reprimanded.

'Um, nothing much really,' Melissa said, aiming to placate Reg. 'We just wanted to have a look at the picture of Lady Veronica.

It's for a historical fashion thing that he's working on.' Melissa nudged Guy and Guy's eyes widened in confusion before he quickly nodded. 'Yeah, fashion and dresses through the ages. That kind of thing,' Melissa plundered on.

Reg eyed them keenly. 'Help yourself,' he said. 'I'll leave you to it.'

'Thanks,' Guy said as Reg walked off. Guy turned and stood in front of Melissa. 'Well, that went well,' he whispered. 'Fashion through the ages?'

She glanced over at Reg and stifled a laugh. 'I panicked,' she hissed. 'He sounded so annoyed that we were only interested in the Standishes. I had to say something. I couldn't just say, yeah, yeah, fishermen and dairy farmers, whatever, but was Albert Standish beating his wife?'

Reg glanced suspiciously back to them from his position by the church door as he welcomed two more visitors.

Guy took Melissa's hand, pulled her out of Reg's accusing eyeline and over to the boards. 'We may as well have a look while we're here, so we don't look like liars,' he said.

As they stood by the boards, both of them stared straight ahead at the picture of Veronica and Albert. Neither Guy nor Melissa spoke. Melissa could still feel Guy's hand around hers and she smiled to herself, stealing a glance up at his profile; he was incredibly good-looking. Melissa resisted the overwhelming urge to move her fingertips over the knuckles of the hand that held hers. He had nice hands – soft – and she felt a tingle run through her when she realised he wasn't letting go. They stood like that for some time, both staring straight ahead at the board. She was pretending to read the words so as not to disturb the moment. She wondered if he was doing the same. She looked down at his hand and he slowly looked down at her.

'Hold it tighter,' she said suddenly.

Guy laughed. 'What? Why?'

'Hold it so your knuckles are white, and so your fingernails are pushing into my hand, like that.' She pointed to the photograph.

'No, it'll hurt you,' he said.

She turned back to the creepy photograph and looked at Albert Standish again.

'Exactly.'

After having ruffled Reg's feathers they decided it might not be the best idea to approach him again right then. They left the church and wandered back to the car, walking close together. Melissa wondered if Guy was going to hold her hand again. It might have been her imagination, but she was sure her hand was still tingling where he'd held it earlier.

'I suppose I'd better get going,' Melissa said as they pulled into the inn's car park.

'Really? Big plans?' he asked innocently.

'No, not really. Applying for jobs. Doing the food shop. Not going on wild goose chases for wartime women who were probably fine.'

She smiled and their eyes met. How was he so handsome?

He was quiet and so she blathered on. 'Will you tell me if you find anything interesting? I don't know if you're going to ask your gran again. She seemed pretty tired from the first quick-fire round, so if you leave it then that's fine. But if you do ask, or if she mentions anything, will you let me know? I know Veronica's probably long-dead by now anyway, but still . . .' Melissa stopped speaking. Why did she always talk too much when she was nervous?

He nodded. 'I will. Gran was being too cagey for me to let it drop now. If I can't find anything out from a bit of gentle questioning, I'll see what else I can rustle up.'

Melissa looked taken aback. 'Are you going to keep looking?'

Guy nodded. 'I'll do some more research tonight and see if there's anything I can find in newspaper records. I've got some sites I subscribe to that might be worth looking at. I've exhausted official records, but there might be microfiche newspapers from the time or some that have been transferred digitally already.'

Melissa smiled. 'Will you let me know how your gran gets on as well? I hope she's on the mend soon. She's really lovely, you know.'

Guy nodded and ran his hand through his hair, seemingly unaware he'd pushed it completely out of place. Melissa fought down the urge to reach up and fix it for him.

'She is lovely. Listen, Melissa, would you mind if I called you when I get back to London? If you don't object, it would be really nice to see you again. If it's too soon after your break-up and you don't fancy it . . .'

Melissa smiled broadly and then bit her bottom lip, stopping the smile spreading. 'Like a date?' she asked.

'Like a date.' He laughed, suddenly interested in the cuffs of one of his shirtsleeves.

'I'd like that, yes.' Surprisingly, it *didn't* feel too soon. Which probably spoke volumes about her and Liam.

He looked up at her. 'Great.'

A painful silence descended, during which Melissa wondered if Guy was going to kiss her. *You've been single for one day, Melissa. One day. Pack it in.*

'Well, I suppose I should fetch my bag and then I'll head off,' she said.

He walked with her and carried her bag back to the car park for her. 'I'm sorry you're leaving,' he said quietly. 'I've enjoyed spending time with you.'

'Me too.' She was suddenly shy.

He loaded her bag into the boot of her car.

'Will you let me know when you've got back safely?' he asked.

She nodded and they swapped phone numbers. 'I guess I'll see you in London then?'

'Definitely,' he replied with a smile as she climbed into her car.

'Bye, Melissa,' he said as she started the engine.

She waved, pulled out of the car park and looked in the rear-view mirror. He was watching her go with his hands thrust in his pockets.

Melissa switched on the fan and processed the strangest few days she'd ever had. She wasn't expecting to be asked out by an incredibly handsome and lovely man quite so soon after having just been dumped. Fickle Liam clearly hadn't done quite as much damage to Melissa as she'd first thought. Liam who? Melissa laughed to herself and then her stomach twisted as she wondered how she was going to go about getting her things back from Liam's flat. Not that there was much. Maybe she could just sacrifice her few possessions, so she didn't have to risk seeing him again. Yes, that might be the best thing.

She recognised the road she was on as being fairly near the turn-off towards Tyneham. She pulled into traffic sitting behind a tractor and took the slow pace as an opportunity to think about Veronica. They'd asked Guy's gran and she'd been extremely cagey about the letters. She'd been fairly cagey about everything, really. If they did want to find out what *really* happened to the frightened-looking woman in the photograph, asking Anna was probably a dead end. The only route that remained was the guide at Tyneham, Reg. He'd grown up in the village and might remember the Standishes. But they'd made idiots of themselves when they'd seen him earlier on and he seemed like a grumpy sort.

Melissa edged the car forward. If she carried on, she'd soon reach the A road to take her very slowly back towards the motorways and London. If she hung a left, she'd find herself back at Tyneham again.

While she sat in the near standstill of traffic, she thought about her dad. About how it had been such a while since she'd spoken to him. After everything that had passed between her mum and dad, Melissa just struggled to be as close to him as she was to her mother. Both of her parents were so much happier now, apart, than they'd ever been together. Her dad's new wife was lovely, always sending Melissa a birthday present and inviting her to Christmas celebrations. She kept Melissa's dad in check where he needed it and his behaviour had mellowed with age. Perhaps he'd learned the error of his ways and was making amends in his second marriage? There was a small part of Melissa that wished her parents *had* been able to work it all out. But the decades of contempt, rather than love, had put paid to any chance of that happening. *No*, Melissa thought. *They were better off in their new relationships.*

The farm traffic carried on round the bend and the turning came upon her. It was now or never. Melissa looked at it longingly and then, after only the quickest of hesitations, wound the steering wheel and turned left onto the track.

She would quickly go to Tyneham. Just to see if she could extract any background information from Reg, who, in all likelihood, was probably a child at the time and knew nothing anyway. And *then* she was definitely going back home, back to normality and to forget all about her terrible holiday in Dorset, her crap ex-boyfriend and Veronica Standish.

CHAPTER 15

Tyneham, December 1943

Veronica followed Freddie at a distance after they left the beach hut and entered the house through the front door. Freddie was in the entrance hall. He had draped his coat over the back of one of the studded wingback leather armchairs; his hands held out in front of him towards the roaring log fire that was failing to warm the ice-cold entrance hall.

He turned and beamed as Veronica appeared. She returned his smile. Resisting the urge to run to his arms and embrace him, she started undoing her coat and moved towards his to collect it and hang it up. Neither of them spoke. The happiness shone from their eyes. As she approached him, she glanced around at the empty hall, worrying where Bertie might be.

From within his office, Bertie slammed the telephone down and Veronica jumped. Seconds later, he appeared in the front hall, glaring at her. He walked towards the fireplace and stood next to his brother. Bertie flicked open his silver lighter and matching cigarette case. He put a cigarette to his mouth and then lazily picked a piece of loose tobacco from his tongue and flicked it onto the hall floor. He looked at her through narrowed eyes.

'Where the hell have you been?' he asked, turning at the last second to look at Freddie.

'Me?' Freddie questioned. 'Walking, saying goodbye. I'm not sure when I'll be back here next.'

'You told me you'd be leaving, but yet here you still are,' Bertie said slowly, opening his arms wide to indicate his brother's ongoing presence.

'I'm feeling sentimental. I thought I'd stay until the end,' Freddie said, taking a cigarette from his silver case and flicking open his lighter. Veronica could see Freddie's jaw clench, but his pleasant smile remained fixed.

'All this leaving together business is turning out to be a nightmare,' Bertie said. 'We should have just gone. Damn the villagers. Damn solidarity. We've left it to the last minute. The removal company assures me they'll be here on the day, first thing, to pack up the beds and the last pieces of furniture. But if they're late and miss it . . .' Bertie trailed off.

Still holding Freddie's coat, Veronica listened from the far side of the entrance hall.

'God only knows why we have left it so late to finish here,' Bertie continued in clipped tones. 'The guns still need to be packed.' Bertie glanced around the hall, surveying items that should have been boxed up and sent on the moment the requisition order came through. 'Why are all the books still on the library shelves? The packing crates have been here for weeks.' His eyes bored into hers. 'You need to get on with it, Veronica.'

Bertie turned and left, slamming the door to his study behind him. Freddie's gaze followed his brother and then, when the door closed, he flicked his glance towards Veronica and his expression softened. She nodded. It was just a matter of time now.

Veronica climbed the stairs, unlocked her door and heard a rustling noise over her shoulder as she did so. Panic rose in her chest as she felt Bertie's presence loom. But she spun around and saw only Anna padding across the landing towards her. She exhaled a sigh of relief and both women entered Veronica's room.

Anna looked at Veronica questioningly.

'We're leaving together.' Veronica clasped Anna's hands and beamed with happiness. 'Freddie and I. He loves me. He never stopped.'

'The way he's been looking at you, it's no surprise.'

Veronica's face fell. 'Is it obvious? Do you think Bertie knows? Oh God, if he finds out before we have a chance to leave—'

'It isn't long now. Just be careful,' Anna said. 'Now, tell me what you have planned and how I can help.'

During dinner, Veronica was careful not to even so much as glance at Freddie. The overwhelming happiness threatened to explode from within her, but it was tinged with worry. She felt that somehow Bertie would know, would realise what was going on in his own house. His wife and his brother. And then all hell would break loose.

Whenever Freddie spoke to her, she answered him as joylessly as possible, hoping her one-word answers would throw Bertie off any scent he may be picking up. She must keep Freddie at arm's reach until they left. It was imperative, if they were to leave without a hitch.

Bertie poured glass after glass of wine, offering none to anyone and keeping the bottle within his reach. Veronica watched with shame as he leaned his head on his hand, his elbow slipping suddenly off the edge of the polished mahogany dining table. The table could easily seat thirty and the three of them were bunched together at one end.

Bertie lurched and eyed her angrily as if she was responsible for his embarrassment. He suddenly rose and walked towards the door. 'Goodnight,' he said over his shoulder.

Freddie looked towards the doorway as he and Veronica listened to the slow rhythmic thud of Bertie climbing the stairs. 'It's not what he says that scares me,' Freddie said in a low voice as he reached to pour himself a glass of wine. 'It's more what he doesn't say that I find the most sinister.'

Veronica glanced towards the door, making sure Bertie really had gone.

'Want to share this glass with me?' Freddie said, moving his chair closer to hers.

She shook her head. 'You have it.' After a few seconds, she continued, 'I'm sorry I'm being distant, but I must when Bertie's around. Anna said she could tell that you loved me, Freddie. What if Bertie can see it too? I'm worried. I couldn't bear it if anything happened to you because of me.'

'Nothing's going to happen to me,' he soothed, reaching out to touch her cheek. 'And nothing's going to happen to you either. We're leaving, together. I'd be gone from here right this moment if we weren't stuck out in the middle of the countryside without transport. We'll never make it through the valley in the dead of night in the blackout. We need to plan things. We need to find a way to leave. Unseen.' He leaned towards her and kissed her.

She wanted to savour his kiss, but instead she pulled away, glanced towards the door in fear, then gave him an apologetic look. 'Not in the house. We can't. William will help us leave. Anna will tell him. He was going to help me the last time.'

'The last time? You've tried to leave before?'

Veronica nodded, but offered no explanation.

'Come on,' he said, downing his wine. 'I'll walk you to your room.'

At her door, she resisted the overwhelming urge to kiss him, pull him towards her and take him in her arms, into her bed. What if Bertie saw? What if he was listening from his room?

Freddie smiled down at her. 'Goodnight, Veronica.' He backed away from her with a reluctant expression on his face and walked towards his own bedroom.

It was a strange kind of tapping, gentle at first and then slightly louder. Veronica wasn't sure if it was part of a dream in which she was far away from Tyneham or reality. After a while, she realised the tapping was on her door. A slow tap, then nothing and then it resumed again. She rubbed her eyes and sat up in bed while it continued.

Slowly, she tiptoed to the door, hugging herself against the bitter cold. It was dark and the fire had died out.

'Who is it?' It wasn't Bertie's usual hammering.

'Me,' a soft voice said.

Veronica smiled. *Freddie.* 'Go back to bed,' she whispered in return.

'Come on, quickly. It's absolutely freezing out here.'

'Have you any idea what time it is?' She laughed as she fumbled for the key and clunked it in the lock. As she opened it, in the darkness of the blackout, she smiled up at the shadowed face of the man she loved. Except, Veronica realised with horror, that it wasn't the man she loved at all as Bertie came in to focus.

'I thought if I tried a softer approach you might let me in.' Bertie had a triumphant smile on his face and he shoved her back into the room.

Veronica stumbled and then backed away when she found her feet. Fear shot through her. Bertie closed the door and stood against it, barring her exit.

She scanned the room for some kind of weapon, anything at all. Her eyes fell on the fireside tools. The poker. Bertie followed her gaze and gave a cruel laugh.

'Veronica,' he said, grabbing her and filling her face with alcoholic fumes. 'I'm your husband. I have a right.'

He started to undo his trousers and, as he looked down, fumbling with his belt, she broke into a run. But he was equally as fast, having realised the move she was making. He grabbed her from behind, hooked an arm around her waist and snatched at her raised hand. She wasn't quite pinned, but neither was she free. She fought with every muscle to throw him off, but he pulled her leg out from underneath her. Veronica fell to the floor,

131

landing on her elbow. She screamed as loudly as possible and clawed at him, feeling the flesh of his neck hook underneath her fingernails.

'You bitch,' he yelled as she fought against him, kicking and screaming, scratching and crying, and desperately hoping that by some kind of miracle she could wound him enough to stun him and free herself.

Suddenly the door burst open and Veronica felt Bertie wrenched from her. In the darkness, she heard knuckles connect with flesh as Bertie was punched hard in the face. Bertie flew towards her, his head lurched backwards and blood spattered across the room. Specks of blood landed on Veronica's face and silk nightdress as her husband landed against the end of the ornate four-poster. He crumpled to a silent heap on the rug.

Still on the floor, Veronica backed away across the room, breathless and shocked, frightened and angry with herself for having opened the door so easily to Bertie. Had he really been trying a new approach? Or had he bargained on her believing it was Freddie? Did that mean he knew?

Freddie walked out of the darkness and fell to his knees in front of her, hanging his head. He said her name quietly. Veronica pushed her hair away from her face, now wet with tears, and inched towards Freddie to hold him.

'I thought he was you,' she said.

'Dear God, he's a monster.' Freddie's face was anguished.

Veronica curled into him and stared at Bertie's misshapen form. She wanted to bury herself into Freddie's chest, but she was reluctant to close her eyes ever again.

Fighting her emotions, Veronica took charge. 'Let's move him. Take him back to bed. I want him out of my room.'

Freddie looked up at her as she rose. 'And then what?'

She fought down tears. 'I don't know.'

He nodded and exhaled loudly before rising to his feet and hauling his brother over his shoulder. 'Don't open the door again.

Not tonight. Not tomorrow night. I won't come to your room. For any reason. Understand?'

'Yes. Freddie, he said he hoped I'd open the door if he adopted a softer tone. He's never done that before. That's *why* I thought he was you,' she finished in a whisper, glancing at Bertie for any signs of movement.

'Do you think he knows?' Freddie asked, his eyes were wide and his tone strained under Bertie's weight.

'Possibly. But how could he?'

Freddie deposited Bertie on his bed for the second time in two nights. 'Do you think he's all right? I hit him rather hard.'

'Do you care?' Veronica asked. 'Because I don't. Not anymore. He's driven any love I thought I ever had for him away. All I have now is hate.'

'I hate him too.' Freddie closed Bertie's door. 'But he's still my brother. Oh Veronica, how have you coped with this for so long?'

'The worst is over,' she said.

She had no idea that the worst was yet to come.

CHAPTER 16

Freddie hardly slept. He listened all night long for signs of Bertie leaving his room to cause havoc. Checking his watch at six o'clock in the morning, he heard the maids Anna and Rebecca moving around, getting ready to light the fires.

Freddie walked down the corridor, tying his dressing gown tighter around his waist as he traversed the few feet to Bertie's room. He was ready to confront his brother, ready to accuse him of being the worst kind of man, ready to fight him if need be. Freddie may tire easily since he'd been shot, but he knew he could fight Bertie if forced. He deserved punishment. He deserved to live in fear of Freddie from this moment on. But for the sake of Veronica and her safety, Freddie would ride out the storm of Bertie's madness for a day or two longer. After all, Veronica had suffered it for years. As he opened the door and saw his brother's sleeping form on the bed, reason took hold. He and Veronica had twenty-four hours left and then they'd be gone. Freddie stood seething, boring holes into his brother with his eyes. But still Bertie slept on. Freddie swore under his breath, turned and left.

Washed, dressed, tired and hungry, Freddie glanced into Bertie's room an hour later and saw that his brother was gone. The bedding was thrown aside and the wardrobe doors left open, unwanted clothes for the day discarded on the floor for the maids to pick up. He heard movement from downstairs and braced himself to confront Bertie. He hadn't decided what he was going to say. Instead, he found Anna laying out the breakfast things in silver dishes.

'Where is everyone?' Freddie enquired.

'Sir Albert has already breakfasted,' she told him. 'Lady Veronica isn't yet down.'

'Where is my brother now?'

'I believe he's collecting the final rents from the tenant farmers and should be back soon,' Anna replied. 'And then, this afternoon, there are the last of the photographs being taken of all the villagers outside their homes before the departure. The Historical Society has organised it. Sir Albert will be here for that, if not before.'

'I see,' Freddie said, helping himself to breakfast. Real eggs. From real country chickens. What a treat. Not like the powdered nonsense he was forced to eat with alarming regularity. But even so, they tasted like lead in his mouth.

He sat waiting for Veronica, tapping his fingers nervously on the table. When she didn't appear for breakfast, he went looking for Anna. He found her in the kitchen, washing up at the large sink. She didn't notice him enter. Instead, an older lady looked back at him curiously as he stood in the doorway.

'Yes?' the new cook asked, staring at him. 'Sir,' she added as an obviously reluctant afterthought.

Freddie looked around at the kitchen, unchanged since his boyhood. The scrubbed wooden table where he'd helped the previous cook, Mrs B, make biscuits was still there. The simple copper pans were still hanging in their usual racks around the wall. He smiled. Some things never changed. Except Cook. His beloved Mrs B had long gone. Packed up at the start of the war and gone to her sister in Poole. Now there was this officious-looking dragon.

'I just need Anna for a few moments,' Freddie requested. 'If I may?'

Anna turned, wiped her hands on a cloth at the side of the old butler sink and left the kitchen. Cook eyed them both suspiciously as they stepped out into the hallway.

Some distance from the door, Freddie whispered, 'I promised Veronica I wouldn't go to her room. Will you tell her I've gone for a walk? She'll know where I'll be.'

Freddie left the house, pulling his coat on as he went.

Armed with a breakfast tray for Veronica, Anna knocked at the door and declared herself loudly.

'Freddie's gone out, but says you know where to look for him.' Anna laid the tray on the dressing table and sat on the edge of the bed. 'Here, eat this before you go. It's the photograph this afternoon. The Historical Society, remember?'

Veronica gritted her teeth. 'I only have one outfit left that's suitable,' she said, pointing at the jade two-piece skirt suit that she'd pulled out from the wardrobe. 'There's a dress for dinner tonight and then the black dress I'll wear tomorrow morning. Not too colourful. A good shade for disappearing into a crowd.'

'Not long now,' Anna said. 'Then you'll be free of Sir Albert.'

'Anna, I need to thank you. Now, while we are alone, while I have the chance. There may not be another time.'

'Hush,' Anna said. 'We'll see each other again. I'm sure of it.'

'I would like to believe that more than anything,' Veronica breathed. 'You've been everything to me, Anna, when I had nothing. You've kept me sane when I thought I was going to run entirely mad. You know,' Veronica said, 'even if I don't make it out of here, even if I fail . . . if something happens to me, I will never forget how you tried to help me. You and William. You're taking such a risk for me. If Bertie ever finds out—'

Anna waved her away with a smile. 'Ssh, don't be silly. You'll start me off.'

Veronica sensed Anna wanted to change the subject. 'Has your brother found other work yet, now he won't have the farm to look after?'

'William's joining up. He'll be called up anyway now our dad's farm's part of the requisition order. He won't be in a reserved occupation anymore, so he's getting a head start instead of waiting to be called up into a service he might not like. He's going to try for the Navy. He'll miss the sea if he goes too far inland.'

'It'll be a complete change of life for many,' Veronica said. 'The move inland, the move away from their homes, the tenant farmers with no farms to run. The shopkeepers losing their only way of earning money. They'll have to join up or . . . I can't imagine. It's going to be such a shock for so many, especially the elderly. What about you, Anna? Have you decided what to do?'

'I'm joining up too. I'll be eighteen in a few weeks. I want to do something for the war effort. The Wrens or the WAAF. I'm not sure yet. I think I'm finished with domestic service.'

'I should think so,' Veronica said.

Anna got up from the edge of the bed and went towards the door. 'I'd better get on.' As she reached the door, she turned and said, 'Freddie seems like one of the good ones.'

Veronica gazed at her breakfast tray. During the night, Veronica had awoken with a cold dread that Freddie's involvement in her departure would drag him down with her. They would forever have a life looking over their shoulders, never quite knowing if Bertie was looking for them. Never quite free. If Veronica left on her own, Freddie would still have a life to live. She knew what she had to do. She had to spare Freddie from a lifetime of running. 'He is one of the good ones.'

That's why she had to let him go.

He would be in the beach hut. She owed it to him to explain. She loved him. She loved him so hard, she knew her heart was going to break into a million pieces. Calling it off with him a second time, knowing this time that he really did love her, would be the hardest thing she'd ever have to do, but she had to do it. It would end before it had ever really started again, but it was for the best. She would take his offer to help her leave if he still wanted to give it. And then it would be *her* journey to make. She straightened herself up as she walked, resolving to leave by herself tomorrow. She would disappear forever. Or she would die at Bertie's hand.

Tramping across the grass and down towards the cliff steps, she heard a noise from the thicket in the distance. She stopped as the rustling got louder. She could see the shape of a young man in the foliage and then suddenly he lurched out, raised a gun and fired two shots. Veronica screamed, but she could barely hear herself over the sound of the gunshot.

The young man dropped his gun in shock as he saw her, while a small boy dashed past him and ran to Veronica's right to collect their kill. Clocking Veronica, the boy slowed down and then turned back to the young man with a look of horror on his face.

Her heart thudding in her ears, Veronica glared at the elder of the two. 'You could have killed me,' she shouted. 'What the hell do you think you're doing?'

The young man took his cap off and started running towards her. 'Lady Veronica, I'm so sorry. I'm so sorry. Are you hurt?'

'No, of course I'm not hurt, but you scared me,' she said, recognising him from the village now his hat wasn't shielding his face from her. 'John, if you're going to poach, you can't simply lurch out of the trees and just shoot. You didn't even check if Sir Albert was watching.'

John shook his head. 'I wasn't thinking. We're usually quick. No one usually comes here, this close to the cliff.'

'Usually?' Veronica repeated John's word. 'How often . . .? Never mind. It doesn't matter.'

Her breathing slowed and John looked at her intently. 'You won't tell him, will you?' John asked. 'Only, with the rationing, we never have quite enough and an extra bit really helps. Sir Albert never had his shooting parties this year and there's so many birds . . .' he trailed off. 'I've been feeding half the village,' he blurted out before biting his lip as if he'd said too much.

Veronica looked at the young man and then laughed. 'John, we're all leaving tomorrow. Take as much as you like. Take as much as you can carry.' She threw her hands up in the air to indicate how little she cared about the poaching.

John nodded at the younger boy, who resumed his run, scooped up the bird by its neck and looped back towards his older brother. 'This is my little brother Reg,' John said.

'Your brother has made you an accomplice, has he?' Veronica laughed, holding her hand out for Reg to shake.

Reg looked at her blankly, his arms by his side.

'He doesn't say much,' John said.

Veronica lowered her hand and smiled at Reg.

'But he's fast on his feet,' Veronica said pointedly.

'Which comes in handy,' John replied with a sideways smile.

Veronica shook her head in disbelief and stifled a laugh.

'You won't tell him, will you? Sir Albert. You won't tell him what you saw us doing?' John asked again.

'Of course I won't. Your secret is safe with me.'

'Where are you going?'

'What?' Veronica asked sharply.

'When you and Sir Albert leave with us all tomorrow. Where will you go?'

'Oh, we have a house in London. Sir Albert is busy at parliament and it suits him to be there permanently now we've lost Tyneham House for the duration of the war.' The lie rolled off her tongue too easily. In truth, she had no idea where she'd end up. But it definitely wouldn't be London. She would be nowhere Bertie would be able to hunt her down. It would need to be somewhere distant, somewhere he'd never think of looking for her, somewhere she could start again and get a job as a teacher or join one of the services and help the war effort. Maybe Scotland?

John coughed and the action snapped Veronica out of her thoughts.

'Where will you go, John?'

'I'm going to join the war,' he said proudly.

'Everyone's going to war. It's very brave of you,' Veronica said. 'Which service?'

'The Army. I'm eighteen. I'm ready to go and fight Jerry. Give him a taste of Britain,' John said, his chest puffed out.

Veronica reached out and touched his arm. 'You will look after yourself, won't you, John. You'll stay safe. For your mother.' He was so young. Just eighteen. A boy really. But ready to fight for his country.

'I'll do my best,' he grinned. 'I can't promise though. Are you worried about me?'

'Well, yes of course.'

'I think of you sometimes,' John said. 'How you helped me when I cut my leg falling off that horse. I was that embarrassed. But you were lovely, so lovely.'

'Oh,' Veronica said. 'Oh, John, I . . .' Veronica was lost for words. 'Thank you. But . . .'

'It's all right. I know. You're you and I'm me. You're married and I'm going off to fight. But I want you to know that I think you're wonderful. And, in another life, if you could have been mine, I'd never have treated you the way Sir Albert does.'

'John, stop.' Veronica's eyes were wide. Did the whole village know what Bertie had been doing to her? The shame.

'You know you're too good for the likes of him, don't you. He's a bastard, pardon my French. To you, to everyone. I'm not the only one who thinks it. My mum often wonders why you're still with him.'

'John, that's enough. Really. Please.'

'I'm sorry. I shouldn't have said anything. He doesn't know

what he's got. He's the luckiest man alive and he has no idea.'

'Thank you,' she said quietly.

'I won't see you again, will I?' John said.

'I don't suppose so, no, John.'

'Then I'll say goodbye now then. There'll be too much going on tomorrow to find you so . . . goodbye.' He reached down and took her hand within his, startling Veronica. He kissed her hand, a pained expression on his face, and Veronica smiled kindly.

'Goodbye, John,' she said. 'I mean it about staying safe.'

He smiled and put his cap on his head.

'Come on, Reg,' he said, turning to wave at Veronica one last time as he and the young boy headed into the thicket.

Veronica watched the young man and his brother until they were out of sight. She looked at her watch and hurried on towards the beach hut.

CHAPTER 17

'I didn't think you were coming.' Freddie stood as Veronica hurried into the hut. 'I was worried I hadn't made my message particularly clear to Anna.'

Veronica was flushed from almost galloping down the cliff steps. 'You did. I'm so sorry. I got held up.'

'Not by Bertie?' He looked at her with a worried expression on his face.

'No, no. He's still out. I didn't see him this morning,' Veronica said. 'Did *you*? Did he mention his actions last night? He denied it, I'm sure. Denied all knowledge. It's his usual way.'

'He'd gone by the time I was dressed, so I've no idea. I tell you, I was ready to have it out with him, Veronica. I was ready to kill him. He has to be stopped.'

'Not by us. Not by you. He's your brother.'

'It doesn't mean anything. Not anymore.' Freddie brushed her comment aside.

'You're wrong, Freddie. It means everything. He's not doing this to you. He's doing this to me and he won't be doing it for much longer.'

Freddie nodded and moved towards her, smiling a sad smile that made his eyes crinkle and a dimple crease in his cheek.

142

Veronica forced herself to move away from him when all she really wanted to do was kiss him and run her fingers through his hair, pulling him close to her. She shook her head and strengthened her resolve.

'Freddie, you must listen to me. I can't do this. Not with you. I want to. Please understand that I want to.'

Freddie's face fell. 'What?'

'I can't go with you tomorrow,' she said. 'I'm not mad enough to refuse your offer of help. I won't take your money, but I will borrow it, please. I need to set up somewhere new, somewhere far away from here – so far away that Bertie will never think to find me. Some highland village will probably do the trick. I'm going to take a different name. It's easy enough to pretend that I've been bombed out and get papers in a new name. If Bertie is to be believed, this war is wreaking havoc with paperwork.' Veronica realised she was going off on a tangent. 'But I can't go with *you*,' she said.

Freddie raised an eyebrow. 'Why ever not?' his voice was flat.

'Because I love you,' she said. 'Because I love you and I don't want to hurt you. I don't want to bring you with me on this . . . this fool's errand. I can run from Bertie. I can blend in and hide easily. But you . . . I don't think it's possible for both of us to do that.'

'You think I'm going to be in your way?' He stepped forward. 'Veronica, we can do this. We can do this together. I won't be in your way.'

She grabbed his hands and held them within hers, pleading with him to understand. 'No, that's not it. Not even close. You won't be in my way. I'll be in yours. Don't you see that?'

'What do you mean?'

'I can't ask you to come with me. I can't ask you to leave behind your life, your friends. I can't ask you to hide for the rest of your life, which you will have to do if we are ever going to stand a chance of outrunning Bertie. And if Bertie finds us together, it will be far worse than if he just finds me alone. He'll work hard to ruin your life as well as mine. He won't hesitate. I just know it. I can't ask you to sacrifice everything for me.'

Freddie closed his eyes, clearly exasperated. 'My God, you're impossible.'

Veronica raised her eyebrows.

'You don't get it, do you?' he continued. 'After all this time. After all these years? Was I not clear yesterday? Do you *still* not understand that I love you? You aren't asking me to sacrifice anything. What am I giving up exactly? Bertie? He's nothing to me. Not now. Not anymore. He's lost to me. He's lost to himself. He deserves to be alone. He doesn't deserve you and he doesn't deserve me. I can easily overlook the things he's done to me over the years. I don't care about any of that now. I really don't. But what he's done to you. My blood boils. I want to kill him. I'm coming with you, Veronica, because I love you. Because I've always loved you. I lost you once already. I won't lose you again. I won't. If running together is the only way we can be together, then I'll take it.'

She frowned.

'What's wrong now?' he asked.

'Don't do this because you think I need saving.' She spoke quietly. 'I don't need saving. I can save myself.'

She was still holding his hands tightly within hers and he slowly manoeuvred one hand away from her grip. He touched her gently on the cheek. 'I want you, Veronica. I want you forever. I'm not saving you.' He tucked a stray roll of her auburn hair back in to place. 'You're saving me.'

They stood looking at each other, drinking each other in until Freddie bent his head slowly and closed his eyes, kissing her softly and then deeper until she thought she was losing her mind. Freddie loved her and he still wanted to run away with her, even though she'd given him a way out of this madness. Her heart swelled. She couldn't be without him. She knew that now. She had no idea how she'd existed, these past few years. She would love him until her dying breath.

Veronica pulled back from his intense kiss and looked up into his eyes, conveying everything he meant to her with one desperate expression. She couldn't stop herself. She wanted him. She'd wanted him before, when they were first stepping out, all those years ago, but he'd been too much of a gentleman to attempt anything.

'Are you sure?' he asked, his eyes reading hers. 'Because if you're not, we don't have to—'

'Yes,' she breathed. She'd never been so sure of anything in her life. She moved her hands slowly to his shirt, undoing it and running her fingers across his chest until she uncovered his wound; red and white skin raised at the edges from the surgeon's efforts to remove the bullet. *How close had he come to death?* she wondered. And she'd had no idea about any of what he'd been through, no idea he'd been away fighting, no idea he had even been in danger. The wound was larger than she had expected it to be and she touched the skin around it softly with her fingertips. Freddie moaned and Veronica sprang back. 'Does it hurt?' she asked.

'No,' he said, clearly struggling to control himself. He took her hand in his and kissed it.

She started to move quickly, frenziedly, pulling at his clothes with him until he was down to his underwear. His taut body shocked her, or rather the effect it was having on her shocked her. She had thought that part of her had died long ago. She helped him with the small pearl buttons on her shirt as he fumbled over them and then discarded her green skirt. Hurriedly, she stepped out of her clothes and kicked them aside until she was wearing only her stockings and slip. He stood back and looked at her, failing to recover his breath.

'Bloody hell,' he murmured. 'You're so beautiful.'

She shivered in the cold wind that whipped through the beach hut and he pulled her close to him, kissing her. Slowly, he picked her up and lifted her onto the daybed, pulling the covers over them for warmth as he made love to her slowly. He watched her face intently. Through her gasps, she could see his worry.

'You aren't hurting me,' she whispered.

He nodded. 'I don't want to be like him. I don't want to hurt you,' he whispered as he stopped moving.

'You are nothing like him,' Veronica said, holding his face in her hands.

'I love you,' he said between gasps of breath as their bodies moved in time again.

'I love you,' she returned, her chest rising and falling in quick succession as she looked up into his eyes.

They lay together for a while afterwards. Veronica, in a haze of euphoria she had never felt before, wrapped her arms around Freddie and stared up at the ceiling through strands of his silky dark hair that had fallen over her eyes. She pushed it away and stroked it back into place, enjoying the feel of it between her fingers. His cologne was intoxicating and she closed her eyes, breathing it in, breathing him in, never wanting to let him go.

He held himself up on his elbows and gazed down at her. Veronica was so happy, she could cry. Instead, she smiled broadly and a small laugh escaped her lips.

'You have no idea how much I love you, Freddie Standish, how much I've missed you.'

CHAPTER 18

Dorset, July 2018

Reg was clipping up a photograph that had fallen down from the exhibit boards in the church when Melissa arrived. The day was drawing to a close and there was only an hour before the village was due to shut for the night.

'Hello again,' he said, raising an eyebrow. 'You really can't keep away, can you?'

Melissa gave him a little wave of acknowledgement as she walked over to him.

'Too many tourists making free and easy with their hands. That's our problem.' Reg indicated the photograph as he placed the final drawing pin in the picture. 'They can't just look. They've got to have a good old touch to boot.'

'They aren't the originals, are they?' Melissa pushed her sunglasses onto her head.

'Of course not. Copies. But I don't know why the powers-that-be can't see fit to put a laminate covering on the boards to stop the pictures dropping down. Now, let me guess.' Reg tilted his head to one side. 'Back for more fashion research?'

'I'm sorry,' Melissa said. 'That was a fib.'

'I know.' Reg laughed. 'I did rather guess you were telling me a porky. Your friend doesn't strike me as the kind of historian to go in for women's fashion documentaries. He's more tanks and battleships.'

'Is he?' Melissa asked.

'Yeah. You not seen his stuff?'

Melissa shook her head.

'He's good,' Reg continued. 'Makes it interesting, which you have to do if you're on telly, really. Now, what can I do for you? Mind if we sit? I've got some custard creams and a thermos of tea if you want to share a cup?'

Melissa followed Reg and sat in the heavy wooden pew in front. She declined the tea but took a custard cream and nibbled while he poured himself a cup of lukewarm tea. 'Been in here all day it has. Still, needs must.'

Melissa grabbed another biscuit when offered. 'Thanks. I don't really *do* biscuits. Bad for my waistline,' she said, eyeing up the packet and wondering if she could snaffle a third without looking like she was on a binge.

Reg was looking at her expectantly. 'Go on then. I can tell you're itching to ask me something.'

'I am. And I'm afraid it's not about dairy farmers or fishermen, if that's okay?'

Reg laughed into his thermos cup. 'I'll live,' he said. 'Fire away.'

Melissa took a deep breath. She felt like a lunatic again. 'I wanted to ask you what you knew about Albert and Veronica Standish.'

'Anything you want to know specifically?' he asked.

'Well, specifically, I suppose I want to know if she was all right, after the war. No, that's not strictly true.' Melissa's courage grew. 'Look at this picture,' she said, standing up. He stood and followed her. 'Look at their hands. His fingers are digging into her hand, he's holding her far too tightly, his knuckles are white. And then there's her face.'

Reg studied it hard. 'She looks scared,' he said slowly. 'I did wonder about this the other day.'

'Yes!' Melissa was excited now. 'Yes! This picture, it's not normal.'

Reg turned and walked back to the pew and sat down. Melissa followed and took another proffered biscuit.

'For someone who doesn't do biscuits you're making short work of this lot.'

Melissa smiled as she held the custard cream.

'So, what are you asking me then?' Reg said. 'Are you asking me if Sir Albert was nasty? Yes, he was, from what I can remember. Are you asking me if he hurt her? I've no idea, love. He wasn't a nice man. My mum used to hate him. She was quite scared of being anywhere near him. He used to come and collect the rents during the war after his estate manager went off to fight. My mum hated being alone in the house with him and whenever he was due she'd usually keep me back from school and pretend I was ill so she wouldn't be on her own. My dad would be too busy in the field. I was only six when the village got requisitioned, so I don't remember too much.'

Melissa was thoughtful. 'Do you remember anything about her? About them? Any background? I'm trying to work out where she went. If she was safe, I suppose. After seeing that picture, I had visions of him having killed her and then having got away with it. The whole scene just looked so eerie. But the only information that shows up after they left here is a clipping about Sir Albert standing down as an MP. Nothing about Veronica at all. It just all feels so wrong.' Melissa realised she was ranting.

'She was there on the day we all left. I remember that,' Reg said. 'One of my earliest memories is that day. There was two hundred of us, or thereabouts; all with bags packed. Carts and trucks provided by the army were loaded with our belongings to take us away. Hard to forget.'

He sipped his tea. 'I don't know much about what happened to them afterwards. Actually, I lie. I don't know *anything* about what happened to them afterwards. Before though . . .' He sat up straighter, a faraway expression on his face. 'I think it was the day before we were due to go, or maybe even a few days before, it's hard to remember, we saw her, Lady Veronica I mean, doing something she shouldn't have been doing.'

Melissa looked hard at Reg, waiting for more.

He continued. 'There were two of us kids. There was me, I was the baby at six, and then there was John. He was eighteen. He'd just got his call-up papers. I remember that well enough. I was off school. It was the Christmas holidays, but the school was being shut up for good anyway.

'We went off for a final explore, me and John. We would often poach from the Standishes. The odd bit of pheasant. My brother was a crack shot and I could run fast. He'd shoot, I'd grab, and we'd be gone.' Reg's eyes looked past Melissa, back to a time long ago. 'But on this particular day we knew we were leaving the village and so we went poaching for a slap-up final tea and thought we'd take our "borrowing" to a bit of a new level.'

He sipped his cold tea and made a face. Reg offered Melissa another biscuit. Her hand reached out, but then she changed her mind, realising she was inhaling them.

'What did you do?' she asked.

'They had a little hut down on the beach. It was their private beach, mind. More of a cove. It was about to be swallowed up by the army and their requisition order, so me and John went down to have a look. We'd been poaching and John said he wanted to see if the Standishes had left anything behind. My brother was head over heels in love with Veronica Standish. She'd once picked him up off the ground when he'd been thrown from our horse in the middle of the village; all his mates laughing at him. He thought she was the most beautiful thing alive. She was kind, I'll give her that. She was attractive too. That face,' he pointed over to the photo and whistled. 'I didn't have much to do with her though.'

Melissa could see why any man would be easily drawn to Veronica. She was stunning.

'Anyway. Ever since she looked after him, John had mooned around, talking about her and thinking about her and then talking about her some more until I thought I was going to have to rip my ears off just to stop having to listen to him. We shared a room and he was doing himself a repetitive injury thinking about her . . . If you get my meaning.'

Melissa laughed and screwed her eyes shut. Gross.

'Sorry to be crude. He was stepping out with a girl as well, but the moment Lady Veronica smiled down on him and helped him up, he'd forgotten this other girl and was a man in love. Doreen, I think she was called, this other girl. Might have been Jean? Anyway . . .'

Melissa wished Reg would get to the point. 'And you saw her . . . Lady Veronica?' Melissa nudged.

'Oh yeah. Well, we went to the beach hut one day, which was no small effort. Those bloody cliff steps were a nightmare. Don't think you can get to them now, mind. They're either fenced off still or it's all too overgrown. Anyway, down we went. Took us ages. I didn't know anyone was in there, but when we saw them we got the fright of our lives. I didn't know what I was looking at. I do now though. Ho, ho, I do now,' he said, smiling. 'But back then I just remember John pulling me away and shoving me all the way until we reached the village. And then I remember him running the last few lanes home, practically crying his heart out. I had a job to keep up.'

Melissa didn't understand. 'What was going on?'

Reg looked at Melissa as if she was stupid. 'What do you think was going on?' he asked, wiggling his eyebrows for effect. 'They were at it.' He sipped his tea with a triumphant flourish and then made a face, realising the tea was cold.

'Who were? Veronica and Sir Albert?'

'Well, at the time we thought it was Veronica and Sir Albert. I only caught her face before my brother threw me away from the window, but he watched a bit longer. He was devastated. John

151

thought she might actually secretly love him, based on their fleeting acquaintance. Oh, but he was deluded. Poor boy. This destroyed him for a while. He thought she was an angel. Seeing her *in flagrante* made him realise she was human like the rest of us.'

'Who?' Melissa repeated, verging on exasperation. 'Who was she having sex with?'

'Well,' Reg said, 'now we get to the good bit. John wouldn't speak on the journey home and I didn't know what I was looking at, at the time. But when we get through the door, he bursts into the kitchen, sees my mum and rushes over to her. I was standing in the doorway feeling a bit baffled and John pours his heart out to our mum, telling her he's just seen Lady Veronica having sex in the beach hut, how devastated he is, how he's madly in love with her, and can't believe she'd do this to him. Deluded see? Anyway, Mum can't get a word in edgeways and John says how he can't believe that Veronica's having sex in the beach hut with her devil of a husband when everyone knows what a monster he is, when I look round the corner and realise she can't possibly be having sex with her husband.'

'Why's that?' Melissa was utterly breathless.

'Because sat at our kitchen table, counting out the final rent money my mum had just given him, face as white as a sheet and eyes like saucers, was Sir Albert Standish.'

CHAPTER 19

Melissa couldn't believe it. Her mouth dropped open and she stared at Reg in disbelief. She didn't know which bit of the story to process first. Veronica Standish had been having an affair. Sir Albert had found out.

Reg looked fairly triumphant at having told a story that had shocked and amazed his audience of one.

'Bloody hell,' Melissa said. 'Did Veronica know that Sir Albert had found out?' she asked.

Reg shrugged.

'What did Sir Albert do next?'

Reg screwed up his face.

'Are you OK?' Melissa asked after a few seconds.

Reg opened one eye. 'This is my thinking face.' He closed his eye again and Melissa waited.

'I think he just got up and left. I don't remember anyone speaking at all actually. I do remember that he left the little pile of coins he was supposed to have taken. That was a big deal. My mum didn't touch them for hours. Kept saying he'd come back to collect them. But he didn't. They were still there when I went to bed. My last night in that little cottage.' He narrowed his eyes as he thought. 'There *was* something about a *note*. What was it?'

He shook his head. 'Can't remember now. Anyway, that's where my information ends, I'm afraid. We were all gone from the village the next day anyway and then we had much bigger things to think about. John got called up and he went off to war. He was an excellent shot, but the Germans were better and he died a few months later on D-Day.'

'Oh, I'm so so sorry,' Melissa said, reaching over the pew and taking his hand in hers.

'Thank you. He was a good big brother. He went off for training broken-hearted. My mum said he wasn't the same after the Lady Veronica incident. I was so young I can't really remember much about him other than a few things, including that day. That day I'll never forget.'

He stood up and stretched his back out. 'If there were consequences for Lady Veronica, I didn't know anything about them, I'm afraid. Like I said, the next day, we were all standing in the square listening to Sir Albert's speech, although I can't remember what he said now. She was there, I recall. Then we all slowly left the village family by family and we were never allowed to return. And that, as they say, is that.'

Melissa blew out a puff of air from her cheeks and exhaled the word 'Wow' very slowly.

'Wow, indeed.' Reg chuckled.

Melissa tried to process what Reg had told her. Veronica Standish had been having an affair right under Albert's nose and he knew. What the hell had he done about it? She remembered a time when her own mother had dropped a Waterford crystal fruit bowl at home and her father had flown off the handle, screaming and shouting for hours about how precious it had been, how expensive, how stupid she was. And that had just been a bloody fruit bowl. If her father, a man who wasn't notoriously violent but who had the shortest fuse Melissa had ever seen on anyone, could react like that over a bit of dropped glass – what in God's name had a man like Sir Albert done on the back of finding out that his wife was having an affair. Melissa dreaded to think.

'So, it was the next day you all left?' she asked.

'That's right. There or thereabouts. Maybe a day or two later. I can't remember, love. I've been to sleep since then.' He winked. Reg offered her another biscuit and she looked absently through it.

'No thanks. I wonder . . .' she said, getting up and walking to the final photo board. Reg, already on his feet, followed her. 'I wonder if this photo was taken before or after Sir Albert found out.' She looked at Albert's deadly expression in the Historical Society's photograph and at Veronica's face, full of fear. Of course he knew. Was Sir Albert planning his punishment or already exacting it? 'And you've no idea who she was sleeping with?' Melissa asked.

'Sorry, love, no idea at all. My brother thought it was Sir Albert. Was shocked to his core to find him sat at our kitchen table. But then we only saw the back of the man's head, so could have been anyone. And, remember, I was only six and had no idea what I was even looking at in the first place. As far as I was aware, John was mistaken and that was it.'

'Reg, you have been fab.' She hugged him tightly and he laughed with embarrassment. 'Thank you,' Melissa said.

'All I've really done is told you a sad story. If you find out who she was with in that beach hut, will you come and tell me? You've got me wondering now. Do you know,' he continued as Melissa walked towards the church door, 'I've still got my brother's letters he wrote home. He wrote them to my mum, but I've got all sorts of bits and bobs from when she passed away. I remember reading something in there about Lady Veronica. Probably just him moping about her. I've not read them since I was about thirty when my mum passed on. But I'll have a look when I've had my dinner. I'll give you a call if you like? See if I find anything interesting.'

'Yes please.' Melissa keyed her number into Reg's ancient mobile phone.

Reg looked at his watch. 'Time to lock up.'

Melissa helped Reg lock the church for the night and they munched the last of the biscuits as they walked back to their cars. A few of the other guides were milling around, preparing to leave.

'So,' Reg said as he eased himself into his car. 'Guy Cameron seems nice. You can't have been together long if you've not even seen any of his documentaries?'

Melissa felt her face redden. 'No,' she said. 'No, we're not . . . We aren't . . . We've only just met. We hardly know each other. I've only just come out of a relationship. It would be totally inappropriate.'

'Okay, okay.' Reg raised an eyebrow. 'You're protesting a lot there though, aren't you?' He chuckled.

Melissa cringed. Reg had a point.

'Goodnight, Reg. And if you find anything—'

'I'll call you, I promise.'

Reg was still chuckling to himself as he drove past her and out of the gate. She was grateful for the warmth of the sunshine outside after leaving the chilly church. She pulled out her mobile phone on the way back to her car but noticed she had no signal. Of course, she remembered Guy telling her that Tyneham didn't have a phone mast anywhere nearby. Time was knocking on and she was far too shaken by what she'd learned. Did she go back to Guy and tell him? Or did she drive home and call him from a motorway service station en route to London when she had a bit of signal? Choices choices.

Melissa stood by her car and turned to look back at the village in the orange glow of the early evening sun. Tyneham had taken a strange hold on her. She didn't want to leave Dorset. She didn't feel *done* with the village yet. What had started as a little stroll around a tourist attraction had turned into a quest. It was Veronica, Melissa pinpointed. Her story just got stranger and stranger the more Melissa found out. And it was Veronica's situation that made for uncomfortable comparisons, with that of Melissa's mother but also, in some very small part, with Melissa herself. If Melissa had been transported back to 1943, stepping in Veronica's shoes, would anything have been different? Yes, probably with the power of modern hindsight. Liam's surliness was unacceptable but Sir Albert's confirmed menacing behaviour was something else entirely. She strongly suspected he had been a violent individual and if it had been her, she would have clopped him over the head with a frying pan the first moment he'd raised his fists to her. And then she'd have done a runner. But in 1943, there wasn't the luxury of telephone helplines. And, unlike Veronica, Melissa had her own money, if not a huge amount, which made a new life a possibility in this day and age for someone like her. She sighed. It was feasible Veronica had been stuck with Sir Albert for a variety of reasons, not least social and economical. Leaving your husband wasn't the done thing, regardless of what they were like. Maintaining a stiff upper lip appeared to be the norm. And as a result of her dalliance, Veronica's punishment had been . . . what exactly? Melissa still had no idea what had happened to Veronica.

So she had been married to a man who had a nasty reputation. And now Melissa knew that Veronica had been having an affair and that Sir Albert knew this. That changed everything. So what happened next?

Melissa wanted to know who Veronica had been having an affair with. Whoever it was, they'd been present the day before the requisition because John and Reg had rumbled them in the beach hut. But it couldn't be one of the villagers because John would have recognised the man as one of his friends or at least someone he'd seen in church on Sunday or in a shop or something. There were only two hundred-odd people in the village. It was a small population. So who was it?

Melissa's logic ran out there and she wanted nothing more

than a sit-down and a large glass of cold wine. Actually, that wasn't true. She wanted nothing more than to sit down and tell Guy what she'd learned. She smiled, thinking about Guy, and then stopped herself as she recollected what Reg had said about protesting too much.

If she went back to the hotel and told Guy, she'd still be able to hit the road and make it home to London for a very late dinner and to crawl into bed. Maybe. And if not, then who cared? This was too important to her now.

Melissa got into her car and gave a little smile of anticipation and then winced as she crunched the gears, driving as quickly as the speed limit allowed towards the Pheasant and Gun.

CHAPTER 20

Guy was in the hotel's garden, sitting at one of the many wooden picnic tables that were scattered around the grounds. He had his mirrored Ray-Bans on and was nursing a pint as he read a newspaper.

As Melissa walked towards him, the evening sun cast her long shadow over his paper and Guy looked to one side, clearly waiting for whoever it was to change direction so he could continue reading. Melissa stopped in front of him. Although she'd only left him hours ago, she found she was overwhelmingly happy to see him again. Perhaps it was because he was the voice of calm in this whole crazy thing. Perhaps it was because he was, quite simply, a rather kind and incredibly attractive man. *Pack this in, Melissa*, she told herself.

When she stopped in front of him it obviously took him a few seconds to realise it was her. He smiled politely and as she moved to one side, the rays fell over him again.

Hi,' Melissa said with a smile. 'I didn't get very far.'

His slow smile turned into a broad one and he folded his newspaper up. 'No you didn't. I thought you were on your way back home?'

'I was.' She laughed and sat down on the opposite side of the picnic table. 'And then I wasn't. I went past Tyneham and I just couldn't resist seeing if Reg was still there. And, well,' Melissa teased, 'you'll *never* guess what I found out,' she said, leaning forward with enthusiasm.

Guy laughed and then leaned forward conspiratorially. 'You went back? I'm impressed. We'll make a historian of you yet. Go on then. I'm all ears.'

She told him everything she'd learned from Reg. Guy's smile quickly faded and then his mouth dropped open halfway through her story and stayed open until she finished. He coughed as his throat went dry. Melissa slowly pushed his pint towards him and he downed the rest of it in one go.

'Well, I'll be damned,' he said, when he'd finished. 'I mean . . . wow. Just wow.'

'That's what I said.' She looked around and signalled a waitress over. 'Large glass of Sauvignon please and a glass of ice to keep it cool.' The waitress looked at Guy as he ordered another pint, smiling at him unnecessarily. Melissa said 'thanks' pointedly to get rid of her. Guy gave Melissa a puzzled look and Melissa looked back at him as if he wasn't all there. Guy was totally oblivious to any female attention. It was almost as if he had no idea how attractive he was.

'Well, while you were on the road to London and then Tyneham and then back here again,' he said with a smile. 'I found something a little bit interesting too.'

'Really?' she said. 'Is it as interesting as my story about Lady Veronica shagging someone in the beach hut the day before the village got requisitioned?'

He pulled his laptop out from his bag on the floor. 'No. Close though.'

Guy opened his laptop up and searched for a folder. Finding it, he opened a screenshot, waited for the approaching waitress to deliver their drinks order and then spun the laptop round to her.

Melissa pounced on it and scanned down the screen. It was a newspaper clipping from January 1944. In it was a black and white picture of Sir Albert and Lady Veronica. They were standing a small distance from each other, only a few inches apart. She was in a pale evening dress and he in a black formal suit. *Sir Albert and Lady Veronica Standish enjoy a pleasant evening at Lady Newland's New Year's Eve Ball.*

Melissa stared at the page. Her smile disappeared and she looked up, past Guy and into the distance, thinking.

'I thought you'd be pleased,' he said, turning the computer round to check she was looking at the right thing. 'She's alive and well here. And at a party no less.' He tapped at the screen. 'Ta-da.'

Melissa was confused.

Guy continued, 'Whoever she was with in the beach hut, it obviously wasn't serious. Not serious enough to leave her husband for anyway.'

Melissa sipped her wine and looked down.

'What is it?' Guy asked.

'I'm not sure. It just doesn't seem to make much sense. I would have expected some kind of repercussion. A week or so after Sir Albert finds out his wife is sleeping with someone right under his nose, there the two of them are at a ball. They look like they've patched things up rather quickly. Why didn't she leave him?'

'It happens.' Guy shifted uncomfortably. 'People forgive. Things were different back then. Stiff upper lip and all that. Perhaps that was what brought them back together. Perhaps he realised what a complete sod he'd been and the two of them lived happily ever after?'

A wry smile formed on her lips. She thought of Liam and his long-term cheating. 'Not sure I could be that forgiving. What else did you find?'

'Oh. That was it, I'm afraid.' He indicated the picture on the laptop.

'This is hopeless.' Melissa glanced at her watch.

'Don't say you're leaving again?' He looked exasperated.

'No,' she smiled. 'I'll stay tonight. I've got enough time to find a cheap and cheerful hotel. Then tomorrow I'll head off.'

'I have a better plan,' Guy said. 'And don't fret, it doesn't involve staying in my room again. Just wait there a minute.'

Melissa watched him walk past her and looked at him curiously.

'All will be revealed,' he said over his shoulder. 'If my plan works that is.'

She sipped at her wine and put a few cubes of ice in as she turned to watch him walk through the garden and towards the hotel. He turned back and smiled at her as he went. He was cute. And, more importantly, he was nice. 'Oh, Melissa.' She slapped the palm of her hand against her forehead. She had broken up with Liam yesterday and twenty-four hours later was finding it far too easy to fancy another man. The last thing she wanted to do was jump out of the frying pan and into the fire.

Guy was taking an age and she swung round, stretching her legs out in front of her into the sunshine while leaning back against the picnic table. She drank her wine, closed her eyes, and enjoyed the rays.

Guy walked back across the grass, casting a shadow over Melissa. Her eyes sprang open.

'So what's this grand plan?' she asked.

'Left or right?' He indicated his hands, which he'd put behind his back.

She grinned and pointed towards his left arm. He produced a large key on an even larger wooden key ring.

'What's that for?'

'It's a present. If I told you I had to negotiate hard to get this, would you believe me?'

'No, I'd imagine you didn't have to negotiate at all because you waved your celebrity card at someone and they just gave it to you,' she teased.

He rolled his eyes and grinned.

'You didn't have to do that, Guy. I can pay for my own room.'

'I know. But I wanted to. It's just a small present. It's only for a few nights.'

'But I'm going home tomorrow!'

'Don't. Don't go home. Stay. Just for a bit longer.'

Melissa felt a little bit breathless all of a sudden as his eyes locked on hers.

'I'm enjoying myself far too much with you,' he said. Melissa felt the same but didn't dare say it.

He sat down opposite her and she swung her legs back underneath the table.

'I've not had this much fun in . . . well, I can't remember when. So you're doing me a favour, really,' he said. 'And even if we spend tomorrow discovering that Veronica and Albert Standish went on to have seventeen children and were blissfully happy living in the Caribbean then, marvellous, mission accomplished. We'll have got to know each other a bit better. I'll have taken a few much-needed days off work and you'll have had that holiday you were promised but never quite got because that ex-boyfriend of yours couldn't get off his surfboard.'

'Bravo,' Melissa said through laughter.

The waitress passed by and asked if they wanted refills. Now Melissa wasn't driving anywhere, she nodded.

'Yes please,' Guy said, without taking his eyes off Melissa. They were both smiling and his gaze was still on hers, making her feel a heady mix of excitement and nervousness at the same time. Melissa felt his little speech was a declaration of something but she couldn't quite place what. He just wanted to get to know her, spend time with her. He'd bought her a room for a few nights. He could have easily said there were no rooms and offer to have her stay in his suite again, but he'd been generous and gentlemanly and Melissa was trying hard not to like him quite so much.

'Thank you,' she said, reaching forward to take the key. 'But

I'm paying for the room.' She brushed aside the beginnings of Guy's protest. 'Only let's not tell the woman on the front desk, in case she takes the room back. What was in your other hand?'

He looked down to the side of the picnic bench where he'd placed the other item out of sight and then pushed it over the table towards her. It was a well-thumbed book titled *A Complete History of Tyneham*. Its spine was broken and plenty of pages were falling out.

Melissa fell on it. 'Where on earth did you find this?'

'It was on a bookshelf by the reception desk. There are a few local history books guests can borrow and that was sitting there.'

He got up and sat next to her to look at it, placing his sunglasses on the table. They read a few pages together in interested silence. Melissa could feel the heat from his body as he sat close to her. The faint scent of his aftershave smelled lovely. She tried to concentrate on the book. The pictures, where there were any, were grainy and dark and blown up larger than they should have been so they were pixelated and blurry. It was an amateur effort and they were both a bit disappointed. There was nothing particularly useful in there they hadn't seen on the boards or learned through other methods. There was a bit of backstory about the Standish family through the ages and how they came to have the house, which was gifted to them by Charles I for 'services rendered' along with a knighthood. Prior to that the house had been seized and redistributed numerous times throughout the religious chops and changes of the Tudor dynasty until the last family to own it before the Standishes lost all their money during the Stuart reign and the Crown seized it.

'Why don't we go out tomorrow and get some other local history books, see what we can find?' Guy suggested. 'There must be some more books on Tyneham with a bit more useful information.'

'And some with pictures we can see too.' Melissa closed the

book and handed it to Guy as her phone rang. She didn't recognise the number on the caller display.

'Hello?' she answered.

'Hello, love,' the male voice at the other end said.

'Reg! You rang! Did you find anything?'

'I've been having a little look through the box of John's things. I'm sorry to say . . .' he started and Melissa's heart sank, imagining he was going to say that he'd found nothing, 'that I've found something rather . . . er . . . downright nasty, I suppose is the best phrase for it.'

'Nasty?' Melissa sat up straight.

Guy looked up from the book and gave her a questioning look.

'John didn't have much time to write home, it would seem. He wasn't at war very long before he copped it at the hands of the bloody Germans. He must have known he might not make it back. So, in one of his few letters, he says something pretty inflammatory.'

'Really?' Melissa couldn't hide her curiosity.

'Brace yourself.' Reg took a deep breath as he read the letter out. 'There's a few bits of detail about how well he's eating and things like that. He knew what to say to keep Mum happy. Anyway, he gets to his confession in a roundabout kind of way.' Reg cleared his throat as he read John's words: 'Mum, I need to tell you something. About Lady Veronica. It's been eating me up. Mum, I didn't give Lady Veronica that warning note you wrote, telling her Sir Albert knew that she was up to no good with that man in the beach hut. I tried to. But I didn't. Now you, Dad, and Reg aren't living at Tyneham anymore, and now you're safe, I can tell you this. I couldn't before. I daren't. I hope you'll understand why.

'When you gave it to me, I ran as fast as I could. But Sir Albert had a head start. She wasn't in the beach hut anymore and when I got to the house, he saw me before I could go to the tradesman's entrance and ask one of the maids to fetch her.

'He said some terrible things to me. I was clutching the note for dear life and I'd screwed it into a little ball so he wouldn't see it. He wanted to know why I was there and I lied. I told him I was there to say sorry and that I was lying about what I saw, even though I wasn't. He laughed at me and said he knew I was trying to help, but it was too late for her now. He told me to leave and I tried to stand my ground, I really did. But, oh dear lord, he said things that scared me. About you.

'"There are things I've been wanting to do to your mother." That's what he said, if I ever went near Lady Veronica again.

'And then I could see her, inside the house. She was at the window and I couldn't get to her. I daren't. After what he said. I panicked. I ran. I didn't want him hurting you. Or worse. And when I got home and you held my shoulders and demanded to know that I'd given her the note, I lied to you. I said I had, when I hadn't. Because I didn't want him coming anywhere near you. I lied. I'm sorry.'

Melissa couldn't speak.

'He goes on to say other things about the war before he signs off,' Reg said. When Melissa didn't reply, he asked, 'You still there, love?'

'Yes.' Her mind was whirring and she couldn't think of anything else to say.

'Like I said . . . nasty,' Reg clarified.

'Very,' Melissa agreed. 'Very nasty indeed.'

'He was a monster. He was going to go for my mum, wasn't he?' Reg sounded far away.

From what Melissa had discovered about Sir Albert so far, she believed he probably would have tried to inflict some kind of punishment on Reg and John's mum, had John warned Veronica. Although in what way, she could only imagine.

'Yes, I think so,' Melissa agreed. 'Your mum wrote a note to Veronica to warn her,' Melissa spoke out loud, trying to piece it together. 'I don't blame John for not trying to get the note to

Veronica after running into her husband. I don't think I'd have done it either, to be honest.'

'Good,' Reg said. 'That makes me feel better. Mum tried to help her. But John didn't want to risk anything bad happening to our family.'

'Is there anything else in the box, Reg? Does John mention it again in another letter perhaps?'

'That was his last letter home before he died.'

'Oh no.' Melissa's hand flew to her mouth.

'You know, it's strange seeing his handwriting again after all these years. I can hear his voice in these letters. It's like he's still here . . .' Reg trailed off.

'I'm so sorry,' Melissa said. 'Thank you so much for finding that for me.'

'Melissa?' Reg asked. It was the first time he'd used her name.

'Yes?'

'What are you trying to achieve?'

Melissa felt horribly guilty for having had Reg look through letters that had resulted in his sadness. John's letter home had been poignant, revealing and his last. She listened to the slight crackle of the phone line. 'I don't know.' She sighed.

After she said goodbye to Reg, Melissa explained the phone call to Guy. They both inched together on the seat to discuss it without being overheard. By the end, as Melissa confessed how entirely awful and guilty she felt, she looked up to gauge Guy's reaction and found she was only a few inches from his face. He was wearing a serious expression and hadn't yet spoken. They were still in close proximity and while Melissa waited for him to say something, she wondered if it was her imagination that electricity fizzled in the silence between them. Melissa's eyes were drawn down to Guy's mouth. She wondered what it would be like to kiss him and in her current emotional state didn't care if it was appropriate or not given that she'd just been dumped.

The same waitress appeared, thumping menus they hadn't ask for onto the table. Guy and Melissa sprang apart. The moment was lost.

CHAPTER 21

They ate dinner outside. Every time they passed the salt or the water jug and their fingers touched, they glanced at each other awkwardly, apologetically. They talked into the night and Guy gave her his jacket when it became chilly.

'So what do you have waiting for you back in London?' he asked. 'You don't have to tell me if you don't want to, but what's the situation with your job?'

She sighed, reluctant to admit her life was boring and her working life even more so. 'I used to work in magazines. I hated it. I tried to get into journalism, but all I could get were jobs in advertising sales. Not even with the glitzy brands, just the classifieds at the back. And even then I was just doing the admin. I couldn't seem to get anywhere. I was in a cute little coffee shop near work one day and the girl who owned it seemed so happy, so chuffed not to be stuck in an office. Well, that's how I interpreted it. The music was playing, customers were chatty and queuing out the door. I wished I was her, or at least I wished I could be in there all day. I'm not saying I want to open a coffee shop, but I realised there was no point slogging it out on very little money for a job I hated. So when they offered voluntary redundancy, I leaped at it. I'm temping until I work out what I really want to do.' She glanced at him nervously. 'Do I seem like a mess?'

'No. You seem pretty normal to me.'

'Well, thanks.' She poured them both wine.

'Do you have any idea what it is you do want to do?' Guy asked.

Melissa thought. 'No,' she admitted. 'In an idealistic moment, the redundancy has brought me time. I don't think I want an office job anymore. I'm sure something else will turn up when I least expect it. It has to. Or I'll be broke very soon.'

She could feel herself getting tipsy and dared a question to change the subject.

'What's it really like to be a card-carrying celebrity? Do you get invited to loads of really swanky parties where the champagne flows all night?'

He laughed hard. 'Yeah, that bit's not so bad,' he admitted. 'But I much prefer to be at home, chilling in front of the TV, or with a good book. Or out on my boat.'

'Your boat? You're joking? I don't remember the last time I was on a boat.' She looked to one side and considered how different their lives were.

'I'll take you out on it if you like.'

'Oh, that's not what I . . . I wasn't fishing for an invite.'

Neither of them spoke for a few seconds. Maybe it was the ridiculous amount of wine she'd drunk, but she sensed the mood changing. They summoned the waitress for the bill. Melissa insisted she pay this time even though Guy fought it.

He glanced at his watch and then said, 'I think we should get some sleep. Tomorrow may or may not be a long day.'

She raised an eyebrow.

He just smiled.

'What are you—?' she asked as they left the table.

'No, don't ask. It's a surprise. A good one.'

She giggled a bit and realised the wine was messing with her. She was starting to feel silly.

Guy fetched her bag from the car and then walked her to her room, which was down the hall from his. She opened the door, looked inside and raised her eyebrows at the lovely space. How much was this going to eat into her redundancy package? With the tipsy euphoria of a lovely evening behind her and her disastrous holiday with Liam still fairly fresh in her mind, right now she simply didn't care how much it was going to cost.

'I'm really glad you convinced me to stay on a bit,' she said.

Guy lingered in the doorway and rubbed his shoe on the back of his leg. Melissa sensed something happening. But the gentleman in him had clearly taken over and he backed away from the door.

'Goodnight, Melissa. Sleep well.' He turned, and walked slowly to his room.

Melissa closed the door, sat on the edge of her bed and took her sandals off. She stared at the door, wondering if he might come back, wondering what might happen if he did. When a few minutes passed, she realised he was long gone and started undressing for bed, throwing various items of clothing out of her bag and slinging them on the floor while she searched for her pyjamas. She was a bit drunk and a bit annoyed. She realised she'd been hoping for some kind of kiss. She wondered if she was reading the situation entirely incorrectly. Perhaps he wasn't into her at all. Maybe he was just being nice.

The bed was soft and the Egyptian cotton duvet crinkled noisily when she snuggled under it; exactly the way hotel bedding should be. Before she had the chance to over analyse Guy's reluctance to kiss her or 'come in for coffee', something she hadn't even had the chance to suggest, Melissa had fallen fast asleep.

CHAPTER 22

Tyneham, December 1943

Later in the day, Veronica and Freddie worked together to pack the hundreds of books occupying the shelves of the library. They avoided looking at each other or touching each other or whispering words of affection in case anyone should be watching them from the doorway. Veronica basked in the glow of having been made love to by Freddie, of having found herself so utterly in love and loved in return. They didn't have long until they'd be gone together. She could not risk giving the game away now.

She looked out of the library's latticed windows and saw Bertie towering over a shivering young man in the gravel driveway. It was John, the boy she'd encountered poaching by the cliff steps earlier. There was something about his cowed demeanour that worried Veronica. Behind her, Freddie was helping to pack the last of the books. From the rolling wooden stepladder, he threw down the remaining volumes. Veronica spun around as the leather-bound tomes thudded haphazardly into the crate, then she turned back, held the curtain aside and peered through the gap.

'What's got your interest out there?' Freddie climbed down.

Veronica stood still. 'I think Bertie must know about John's poaching. Why John's come anywhere near the house, I don't know. I warned him explicitly . . . Oh the poor, silly boy.'

Bertie stood in the drive with his back to her. John's face was slack and he was looking intently at the ground. Veronica began to panic for him.

'What poaching?' Freddie enquired. 'Never mind. Do you want me to go outside and rescue the poor fellow?'

John's head slowly rose and he looked past Bertie and caught Veronica's eye. He looked desperately at her, widening his eyes as if to beckon her. She would be angering Bertie and she would pay for it, but she had to try to save John.

'No, I'll go.' Veronica summoned her courage. But by the time she stepped out of the front door and felt the crunch of gravel underfoot, John had gone. She stood watching his retreating figure with concern as he ran down the drive at breakneck speed and out of her sight. He had looked like he wanted to speak to her. She stood for a few seconds, wondering if he might turn back.

It was bitterly cold and, as her teeth chattered, Veronica wished she was wearing a coat or at least a thick jumper. She hugged herself as Bertie turned and bore down on her. His teeth were clamped together, giving him a determined look that Veronica knew all too well. *Oh God, he's started drinking already.* She began to back away and her heart sank even further as Bertie commanded her to stop.

'I heard something disgusting today,' he started. 'Something absolutely vile.' He waited for her to speak.

Veronica looked at his eyes, which seemed darker than usual and at his set expression, which unnerved her. She shivered both through cold and fear.

He taunted her. 'Veronica, Veronica, Veronica. What have you been doing?'

She stopped breathing. 'I don't know what you mean.'

Bertie nodded slowly and his lips curled into a malicious smile. 'Yes, you do.'

Veronica chewed her nails. Behind them, the dull thud of a horse and cart sounded and a few seconds later animal and driver came in to view. As they turned into the drive, Veronica could see that, alongside the driver, the cart also held a passenger in the form of a middle-aged man. She silently thanked them. Whoever it was had saved her from whatever train of thought Bertie had been taking.

She moved back from Bertie and he grabbed her hand, yanking it from her mouth and clutching it tightly as he pulled her next to him.

'You don't get to leave that easily, I'm afraid,' he said as the cart came to a stop in front of them.

The horse whinnied as the passenger climbed down. The man was wearing a dark brown suit that looked as if it had seen better days during tight clothing rationing. The elbows of his suit were threading. He fumbled with a large press camera; its oversized light proving cumbersome. He started to drop the camera and Veronica rushed forward to help but was pulled back by Bertie.

Veronica went rigid as Bertie's grasp tightened so hard she could feel the circulation leaving her fingers. She was unable to fake the part of the bright hostess now. A lump formed in her throat as she realised why he was behaving like this: Bertie knew.

The man introduced himself, but Veronica barely heard a word. He was speaking about suitable locations for photographs for the Historical Society archive and was busy gesturing at the various angles of the house. Veronica's head thudded and as Bertie led the man to his preferred location around the far side of the house, he pulled Veronica along behind him. She stumbled and felt her feet drag. She righted herself and tried to keep pace with Bertie, who was still clutching her hand tightly. Thoughts flew wildly around her head.

Bertie's hand yanked at her arm. 'All right, old girl?' he said with a bright smile that was all for show for their visitor.

'No,' she whispered. 'I need to lie down. I don't feel well.'

'Oh, I'm sorry to hear that,' the photographer said, coming to a sudden stop. 'Of course you must—'

'She stays,' Bertie interrupted and turned to face Veronica. He cocked his head to one side. 'She stays,' he repeated with an acid smile.

The photographer was hesitant, but nodded, eyeing Veronica curiously.

'Here is good enough,' Bertie said as he led them round to where the rose garden met the gravel walk.

'I think the light might not be the best—' the photographer attempted.

'Here will be fine,' Bertie commanded. 'Let's get on with it, shall we?'

'Of course, Sir Albert,' the photographer said as he moved towards them. 'Now, if I may position you both like so.'

Bertie's hand clutched Veronica's. She tried to wiggle her fingers free, but it only served to spur Bertie into holding her tighter. He dug his nails into her hand.

'You're hurting me,' she whispered as the photographer resumed his position behind the camera. 'Please, Bertie.'

But Bertie's jaw was clenched. She knew she couldn't reason with him. Not now. She put up with the pain. It would all be over soon.

'Just bear with me while I make it ready.' The photographer tapped his camera and began fiddling.

Bertie chose his moment and started speaking quietly, so quietly that the winter wind coasting in from the cove threatened to drown him out.

'Imagine how I felt when I found out that the very thing you can no longer bear to do with me . . .' he started.

Veronica drew in a sharp breath.

Bertie slowly bent his head; his mouth near her ear. Veronica recoiled as his lips brushed her earlobe. Her eyes widened and fear gripped her. She knew what he was going to say. He closed his fist around her hand until she thought her fingers were going to break.

'. . . You were caught doing only a few hours ago, with my brother,' he finished and lifted his head in the direction of the camera.

The light bulb flashed. 'We're working perfectly, sir,' the photographer said. 'Let's call that the test picture, shall we?' He made the camera ready for the next photograph, but Veronica moved away and turned, her hand still held within Bertie's unfailing grasp. 'Oh, you appear to have moved Lady . . .'

'I think you're finished,' Bertie said. It wasn't clear if he was talking to Veronica or to the photographer.

'Right. I see,' the photographer said and began profusely thanking Bertie. 'The Historical Society will be so pleased—'

'You're dismissed,' Bertie told the photographer, his eyes never leaving Veronica's frightened face.

The photographer blustered, mumbling his deferential thanks as he packed up his films and equipment. He turned towards the waiting cart and disappeared out of sight around the side of the house.

Bertie let go of Veronica's hand and she rubbed it to soothe the pain.

'Bertie, I . . .' She clamoured desperately for words that would soothe, but she knew it was too late for lies.

He held his hand up to stop her and silence fell between them. Veronica stood her ground and tried not to show her fear. She tried to make herself taller as Bertie tilted his head to one side.

'I always suspected you still had feelings for Freddie,' he said. His voice sounded darker, more menacing than Veronica had ever heard it before.

He began pacing around her slowly as he spoke. She stiffened as his feet crunched on the gravel around her.

'Even on our wedding day, I could see you looking around for him. How do you think that made me feel?'

The years of hatred mixed in her mind with Freddie's confession that he had never stopped loving her. She had allowed herself to be fooled by Bertie. There was no room for lies anymore.

'You forced us apart,' Veronica cried. 'You played with us, like we were toys in your sick game.' Veronica's eyes met Bertie's as he rounded on her. 'Why?' she cried. 'Why?'

'Because I could,' he replied.

Veronica blinked. It was the most honest thing Bertie had said to her in years. If Veronica could trust Bertie, she'd have placed her head in her hands to cry, but she couldn't allow herself that luxury. Not now. She needed to stay alert to any sudden move he might make. She might be able to outrun Bertie; she'd been fast at games at school. But could she reach Freddie inside the house? Could she get to him in time? She had to try.

'I always could play with Freddie,' Bertie confessed. 'It's a gift. I'll admit it got boring, for a while. And then he fell in love with you. And it became interesting again.' Bertie's lips formed a curl of a smile. 'He didn't seem to need me anymore. Didn't seem to need my seal of approval. Didn't seem to have any time for me. My little brother, the reprobate, didn't want the sanctuary of his big brother. I never cared much for Freddie until then. And I wondered what I could do to change it all back. It was you. You were the problem. But then it dawned on me. Wouldn't it be fun to play with both of you?' Bertie paused as if expecting an answer and then continued.

'I could see he loved you, but could you see that? I didn't think so. He'd always been too reserved. I saw the way you looked at him though. The light in your eyes. If I killed that light, who knew what might happen. Maybe he'd need me again. And then the most miraculous thing happened.' Bertie laughed loudly. 'I honestly didn't mean for it to.' A sick kind of mirth flowed through his words and tears of laughter wet the corners of his eyes. 'You started to fall for me. I don't know how I did it. It was spectacular. It certainly wasn't my intention. I didn't want you. It was far too easy to convince you that Freddie was playing you off with other women. Far too easy. And then I managed to get you alone one too many times, whispering silken words in your ear. And before I knew what was happening, I'd proposed and you'd accepted.

'Do you know how hard it's been, keeping something this monumentally satisfying to myself all these years? It's been very hard, Veronica.' He stamped his foot with each word that followed to emphasise his point. 'Very hard indeed.'

Veronica fought the urge to throw up. Her stomach heaved and she put her hand to her mouth. Had she really been that easy to persuade? Bertie had been convincing – so convincing. She realised, sickeningly, that Freddie hadn't given up on her too easily. She had given up on him.

'The moment we were married, you hated me,' Veronica cried. Her eyes met his.

'No, darling,' Bertie replied. 'I hated you long before that. But what I didn't realise was that I hated Freddie too. I'd like to say he had always been in the way, but he hadn't. As my younger brother he was simply . . . there. No more, no less. He was always the quiet one; the boring one. Went off to the beach hut whenever he could to sit alone and read. What a crashing bore. And yet, he was clearly my parents' favourite. Nothing I could do would ever change that. But maybe, just maybe, if I married first, produced the long-awaited grandchild — the heir . . . perhaps then I could change their minds about me.

'As the older child, so much was expected of me. I fulfilled all of their bloody ambitions and did they ever tell me how proud they were? I did far better than him at exams, and then at life. Freddie failed at everything he touched. Except bloody cricket, his one and only love. Until he met you. I thought removing you might liven things up a bit – liven *him* up a bit. But instead I took you from right under his nose. You slipped straight through his fingers. And he didn't do a damned thing about it. I thought that was my comeuppance. He didn't seem to want to play the

178

game. But I was wrong. I got saddled with you, Veronica. *That* was my punishment.'

Veronica fought tears down.

'But after a while you rather suited my needs. For all your other foibles, I had a pretty wife to show off in London. And then Freddie buggered off to the war. Oh,' he said, a look of mock concern on his face, 'you did know about that, didn't you?'

Veronica clenched her jaw, balled her fists by her side, and gave Bertie a look that removed any doubt that she hated him.

Bertie's tone softened, but Veronica didn't trust it. 'Your insistence that you thwart my sexual advances was getting boring. And I do so hate to be bored. So I wrote to Freddie, inviting him here to say farewell to the old place.' Bertie waved in the direction of the house. 'I didn't think the requisition was going to go ahead or else I'd never have bothered. Imagine my surprise when he actually turned up. I thought it would be fun, watching your nerves finally shatter under his predictable, lovesick gaze. But then you reciprocated, as I have just found out. I had no idea you had the ability to feel anymore. What I was more surprised about though, Veronica, was finding out the two of you had done *that!*'

Veronica's head was foggy and she felt her courage die, replaced with worry and fear as words dripped from his mouth like poison. She glanced around at her escape route back to the house. She needed to warn Freddie, to tell him that Bertie knew. Veronica slowly backed away, inch by inch.

But as she started to turn, Bertie's hands flew to her hair, clasping at a great chunk of it. He pulled it tightly as if he intended to rip it out. Her head flew back and she had no choice but to look up into the darkening, cloudy sky. Her eyes watered at the pain in her scalp.

'I have put up with this behaviour for far too long,' he said.

'My behaviour?' she shouted. '*My* behaviour?'

He pulled her hair tighter. There was nothing for it. She readied herself to scream, to fight, but he suddenly let go of her and stepped back. She stumbled, just managing to right herself and turn to him as she rubbed her head. A sickening smile had formed on his face.

Veronica's eyes darted wildly. If she ran, he would grab her, but if she could scream loud enough and long enough, she might just be able to raise Freddie's attention, even from the other side of the house. She opened her mouth to scream, but he grabbed her around the waist and pulled her against him. She cried out in pain and thrashed at him.

'I wouldn't do that if I were you,' Bertie began.

She didn't grace him with an answer.

'I know what you're doing,' he shouted over her thrashing.

They were only twenty or so feet from the corner of the house. If she could just loosen his grip.

'And what you've been planning, all this time. Tomorrow is it?' he asked.

Veronica took in a sharp breath of air and slumped helplessly into him.

He knew she was leaving. She was no match for him and Bertie held her arms down tightly with one arm and casually lit a cigarette with his free hand, flicking his silver lighter closed with a snap. 'The day you think you're leaving me.'

'Oh God,' Veronica breathed the words and then instantly regretted it.

'Oh, you thought I didn't know? Did you think I hadn't over-heard you and silly little Anna?' Bertie carried on without waiting for an answer. 'Why do you think all of your belongings suddenly disappeared? I didn't think you had it in you, to be honest. Finding out you were getting ready to disappear into the mist was by far the most exciting thing I've ever learned about you, Veronica. It opened my eyes. I could almost respect you for it.' He inhaled on his cigarette and blew the smoke out of his nostrils. 'Almost. But not quite. If only you hadn't done *that*, you whore. All of this might have ended quite differently.'

He spun Veronica around to face him. She tried to stare him down, but she felt her courage die.

'So now we come to the question of what happens next.' Bertie breathed smoke into her face, only inches from his.

Veronica waited. It didn't matter what came next. 'I'm leaving.' She struggled against him. She was leaving. There was nothing he could say or do that would change that. She would never stay. Never.

'I wouldn't be too sure of that,' Bertie said, flicking the end of his cigarette on to the gravel. 'Listen carefully, Veronica, because what follows is what is *actually* going to happen. To you and me and to my darling little brother.'

At his mention of Freddie, defiance flooded Veronica's senses. She gritted her teeth.

'We are going to walk back to the house together. You are going to be the picture of the calm and dutiful little wife that I always thought you were until you started spurning me. And you are going to end it with Freddie. You're going to send him away and tell him you're never going to see him again. I don't care how you do it. But you will do it, Veronica. You *will* send him away. Today. Now.'

An involuntary laugh escaped her lips. 'You're mad, Bertie. You're stark raving mad.'

But her laughter was cut off as he pushed her back and then placed his fingers around her neck. She only just managed to stay upright as she gasped for breath. He let go. Veronica coughed and rubbed at where he'd choked her.

Bertie waited silently for her to collect herself and lit another cigarette in the interim.

Blinking the tears of pain away, she cried, 'And why would I do something like that?'

'Because if you don't send Freddie away,' Bertie said, 'I will walk inside the house and I will kill him.'

CHAPTER 23

Dorset, July 2018

The curtains were partially open and the bright sunshine woke Melissa the next morning. Blinking into the light, she sat up and reached for the complimentary bottle of mineral water on the bedside table. She drank every drop of it and then wished she hadn't as she realised she should have saved some for the paracetamol she was going to have to knock back. Her head was thumping after the amount of wine she'd drunk with Guy at dinner last night.

Throwing her face under the cold tap at the sink, she guzzled water with the headache pills and looked at herself in the mirror. What a state. How much had she had? It wasn't *that* much. She'd been trying to counteract the damage from the custard creams, so perhaps salad for dinner had been the problem. Actually, perhaps the wine had been the problem.

She went down to breakfast and Melissa's heart lurched when she saw Guy sitting at the table. He was wearing tortoiseshell glasses and he looked completely different, like some kind of sexy academic. His hair flopped over his face where he hadn't bothered to fix it in place. If anything he looked even better this morning, unlike her.

'I didn't think it was you for a second,' she said, sitting down.

'I normally wear contacts, but I'm too bleary-eyed this morning.' He pushed his hair up out of his face.

'I think I might have drunk a bit much last night,' she confessed.

'Me too,' he said. 'But with some strong coffee and a few paracetamols, we should survive.'

He poured Melissa a steaming cup of coffee, which started working almost the instant she sipped it.

The waitress brought toast and they both descended on the white bread, ignoring the healthier granary option. They perused the menu and both went for a full English.

When the waitress left, Guy leaned forward. 'This idea I had last night might not be the best thing now. In hindsight, it's actually probably a terrible idea.'

'What is it?'

'I mentioned my boat yesterday. I keep it here. I wondered if you wanted to go out on it?'

Melissa's alcohol-ridden stomach churned at the thought of bobbing up and down on the high seas. 'Eurgh, really? Now?'

'Perhaps not.' Guy lifted his glasses up, rubbed his eyes, and laughed. 'How about this afternoon? I need to go and see Gran this morning. You don't have to come with me. You chill here in the sun or sleep off your hangover.' He gave her a sideways smile as he put his glasses back on. 'And I can catch you later if you like? Bring a swimming costume.'

'Okay,' she said slowly. 'But I'd like to come with you to see your gran. If you'd like the company?'

'I would like that.' He smiled broadly.

'I don't want to be in the way. I don't want to upset her. She seemed a bit . . . off before.'

'She was just a bit tired and I think she's in pain, although she's so stoic she won't actually say. I think she'd appreciate some female company. My mum's been coming and going since she arrived in Dorset, fussing as usual, but Gran and Mum don't really get on. Mum's staying with a friend while she's down here.

Mum's the dreaded daughter-in-law. Come with me, I'm sure she'd like it.'

After drinking about a litre of coffee each and polishing off everything on their breakfast plates, Guy and Melissa felt ready to face the day. They arrived at the hospital and went into the geriatric ward, where Anna had been moved.

'Oh, it's you two! Lovely! Have you seen where they've put me?' Anna was incensed as Guy walked in, accompanied by Melissa.

'It's quieter in this ward,' Melissa said.

'Of course it is, dear, it's the geriatric unit. God's waiting room.' Anna kissed Guy on the cheek and gave Melissa a smile. 'I am pleased to see you, darling Guy,' she said. 'Your mother is a fusspot. I've sent her off to get a magazine for me. That should keep her busy for a few minutes. But I see you're back.' She indicated Melissa. 'So . . . you two. You must tell me what's going on between you. Quick, before your mother returns and starts fussing again. Are you . . .?'

Melissa felt her face flame and Guy fidgeted beside her in one of the plastic visitors' chairs.

'No, Gran. She's just, um, we're just friends.'

'Oh well. She's a very pretty friend. Do you have a boyfriend, dear?' Anna turned back to Melissa.

'Er . . . No.' Melissa sat up straight under the rapid questioning. 'I did. A few days ago. But now I don't.' Melissa cringed and then wondered why she'd said it quite like that.

Anna looked enquiringly for more information, but Melissa kept her mouth shut.

'Interesting,' Anna said.

Guy's mother returned. 'Oh, darling, you're here. How wonderful. And you've brought a friend. How lovely to meet you.'

Melissa extended her hand to Guy's mother. 'Hi, I'm Melissa.'

'I've heard all about you from Anna,' Guy's mother said, holding her hand tightly after having shaken it. 'I'm Catherine.'

As Catherine smiled warmly, Melissa could identify elements of Guy in his mother's face. They both shared the same warm expression when they spoke and the same shade of brown hair.

Turning to Anna, Catherine said, 'I bought you a *People's Friend* and *Good Housekeeping*. I couldn't decide between them, so I bought both. Can I get you anything else? Can I sort your pillows a bit better for you? What about a cup of tea from the coffee shop? I can go back downstairs. It's no problem.'

'No, thank you, dear,' Anna said to her daughter-in-law in a strained voice, clearly annoyed by the fussing.

Melissa jumped up. 'I could do with coffee, so I'll go and grab some. What does everyone want?' She was desperate to leave after the embarrassment of the boyfriend question. She took orders and made herself scarce.

'She's very pretty,' Anna said to Guy. 'Do you like her?' There was no mistaking the hopefulness in his grandmother's tone.

Guy nodded. 'Yes, I do. She's lovely.' He moved quickly on. 'We've kind of got a bit involved in investigating . . .' he was going to say *Veronica Standish* but changed his mind and said, 'the history of Tyneham.'

'Go on,' Anna said. 'I can see you're itching to ask me something.'

Guy's mother looked curiously between them.

'On the last day,' Guy said, 'who else was there? Who else was there that usually might not have been?'

'No one was there, darling. Just us.'

'Oh . . . I heard that Veronica might not have been a hundred per cent faithful to her husband and we suspect it wasn't one of the villagers, so I wondered if . . .'

'Who told you that?' Anna snapped.

Guy's eyes widened in surprise at his grandmother's tone. 'It's a long story, but . . .'

'There's no story at all, I'm afraid. You've been led up the garden path,' she said in an annoyed tone.

185

'I know it was a long time ago, Gran, but could you think back to that last day,' he ploughed on bravely. 'Was there anyone there who shouldn't have been there? Who wasn't normally there? Did you hear a rumour that Veronica was with someone, in the family's beach hut, down in the cove, or anything like that?'

'What you are suggesting is utterly unsavoury, Guy,' Anna baulked. 'I'm surprised at you, a logical man who prides himself on facts and figures. What kind of gossip have you been listening to?'

'I'm sorry, Gran,' Guy said, disappointed at having been thoroughly chastised. He felt like a child again, having been told off for eating too many sweets before his Sunday lunch. 'I'm like a dog with a bone,' he said. 'I'll drop it now. There is one more thing though. I found this.'

He pulled his laptop out of his bag and waited for the screen to come to life. He spun it around and showed her. She leaned forward and looked at it. Slowly she smiled as she saw the photograph and read the caption. *Sir Albert and Lady Veronica Standish enjoy a pleasant evening at Lady Newland's New Year's Eve Ball.*

'It's from a newspaper from January 1944,' Guy said. 'I thought you might like to see it.'

Anna's eyes widened. 'Well I never,' she said and then offered no further comment.

'Have you seen it before?' Guy asked.

Anna shook her head. 'No. No I hadn't.'

Guy was confused at his grandmother's reaction. 'She looks fine, doesn't she?' Guy asked.

'Yes, dear, she looks just fine to me.'

'That's what I thought,' Guy said and snapped the laptop shut.

He described his grandmother's reaction when he and Melissa were back in the car.

'Do you think we might be barking up the wrong tree?' he questioned.

'Yes, all the time,' she replied. 'I'll admit I thought he'd done something horrific to her. But obviously not now. He's just dragged her to some New Year's Eve ball, quit parliament, and then . . . well, I don't know what happened next, but your grandmother said Veronica wrote to her and was fine. So . . . I feel like we're being led on the trail of something, but I don't know what.'

'I feel the same. Something's amiss. But I think whatever it is that we find out, we're not going to like it.' He glanced at her from the driver's seat. She was looking down, chewing her lip. 'You all right?' he asked.

'Yeah, no, maybe.'

'Do you want to stop?' he asked.

'No!' Melissa looked up quickly. 'No, not at all. It's just . . .' It was on the tip of her tongue to tell Guy about her mother's unhappiness in her marriage, the non-stop fighting between her parents, the perpetual unhappiness. She wanted to tell him why she felt so invested in Veronica, in this woman she'd never met, in finding out she was okay. In another life, it could have been her mother, it could have been Melissa herself.

But she couldn't. Not now. Not yet. She didn't know him well enough. She couldn't put that on him.

'Don't worry. I'm just being silly. Cóme on. Let's go and do something fun. Let's go book shopping.'

Oswell's Bookshop was a secret haven. Situated in a side street in Lyme Regis, Melissa felt as if she had stepped back in time. Rows upon rows of books jostled for space, all stacked haphazardly on shelves that had been put up too close to one another.

She looked at Guy. He looked as if all his Christmases had come at once.

'How did you find this place?' she asked.

'I used to come here years ago. The owner's a friend of Gran's. She used to bring me here every now and again for a new book, and then we'd go and get ice cream and sit on the beach.'

Melissa looked at Guy's wistful face. He'd clearly disappeared back to his youth. 'How old were you?'

'I think I was about ten the last time Gran and I did that. It was before we moved away when Dad got a job overseas in banking. I was packed off to boarding school and we hardly ever came back here again. Not until I was an adult really and I came back of my own volition. I love it here. I always have. There's something about Dorset. It's got the best of everything: beautiful coast, stunning countryside. Anyway,' he said, 'the local history section's over here,' he finished quickly as Melissa eyed him smilingly.

An elderly gentleman appeared from behind a beaded curtain at the back of the shop. 'Well hello,' he said when he spotted Guy. 'What a treat to see you again.'

Guy greeted the owner and they shook hands, exchanging pleasantries about Guy's return after years away and Anna's health.

'And who is this lovely young lady?' the owner asked.

'Melissa, this is Mr Oswell. Mr Oswell, this is my friend Melissa.' They shook hands. 'You have a wonderful shop,' she said.

'Thank you. I love it. Although I'll confess it's getting a bit much for me now in my old age.' He turned to Guy conspiratorially, 'I'm considering closing up and retiring.'

Melissa listened as Guy remonstrated about what would be the loss of an excellent bookshop.

'I feel like I've been running this place since the dawn of time,' Mr Oswell finished. He switched on an electric desk fan and then turned back round. 'Now, what can I do for you both?'

'We're after books on Tyneham village, if you have any?' Melissa said.

'I think I have one or two, over there.' Mr Oswell indicated a low shelf, and as Melissa bent to look, Guy took himself off around the shop.

Melissa turned and he gave her an embarrassed but happy look as he spotted a few of his own books on the shelves. Mr Oswell gave Guy a pen and encouraged him to sign them.

A delivery arrived and Guy offered to help lug the books in, rolling up his sleeves and going outside to lift the large boxes into the shop and up onto the counter.

While Guy worked, Melissa produced the only three books on the shelf about Tyneham and placed them on the counter next to the delivery.

'Which one do you want?' Mr Oswell asked.

'I'm taking the lot please.' If there was information to be found, she wasn't taking any chances by leaving behind a book that might contain what she needed.

'Lovely. Thanks very much,' he said.

'All of them?' Guy queried as he hauled another box in.

Melissa shrugged. 'Yep.'

She paid, but they stayed to help Mr Oswell open the delivery boxes, unpack all the books and then crush up the packaging. Guy kicked it into a small shape for easy storage and carried it out the back.

They said their goodbyes to Mr Oswell and Guy promised not to leave it so long next time.

Melissa looked up at him as they walked through the streets.

'What?' He unrolled his sleeves and looked down at her.

'You're one of the good ones, do you know that?'

'Yes I do,' he said sheepishly. 'My mother tells me daily.'

Melissa laughed. A woman approached him and Melissa was shocked how close the lady stopped, right in Guy's personal space.

'Hi! Oh my God, it's you. Do you mind if I take a photo with you?' the woman asked and automatically stood next to him.

'Of course.'

'Would you mind?' the woman asked, holding her phone out for Melissa to take a photo. When the woman had gushed a bit more, Guy said goodbye and he and Melissa fell in to step again.

'You're just so nice. Too nice. There's got to be something wrong with you. What is it?' Melissa probed.

Guy looked away and into some shop windows.

'Nice guys finish last, remember?' he said quietly

Melissa wondered what on earth he meant and looked at him curiously.

They walked towards the waterfront, past the row of beach huts in various pastel shades and along past the long stone Cobb, which Melissa recognised from a TV adaptation of Jane Austen's *Persuasion*. On one of the small docking areas was a large white powerboat with a blue flash along the side and a canopied area for the captain. A man with a hamper greeted them on the jetty. Guy discreetly handed him a banknote and the man wished them a good afternoon's boating.

Melissa's eyes almost popped out of her head. She'd been picturing a dinghy. This was a shiny speedboat. She tried to play it cool and not let her facial expression give her surprise away, as if people took her out on flashy boats all the time.

When Melissa didn't speak, Guy asked, 'What do you think? Fancy a cruise along the coast?'

She aimed for nonchalant. 'Sure, why not.'

He jumped in and then reached back to help Melissa, holding her waist as she stepped from the jetty. As she landed, they came face to face and their eyes met. They stood for a second and Melissa felt her stomach flip. When he finally let go of her and turned away, Melissa moved quickly into the boat and sat down on the white leather seats at the back. She looked up at the clear blue sky and wondered how her holiday from hell had suddenly picked up so nicely. She looked over at Guy, working around the boat, removing buoys and ropes, and she smiled.

'Can I do anything?' she asked.

'No thanks,' he murmured as he produced a set of keys on a floatation key ring. 'I've got it covered.'

Guy unlocked small cupboards, retrieved maps and charts and then sat himself down at the controls.

'Ready?' He turned to her, as he put the key in the ignition.

She nodded and smiled widely in anticipation, excitement getting the better of her.

He cruised slowly out of the harbour and when they were safely in open water, he slid over on the seat and then turned back. 'Come up here with me.'

She sat next to him, the small leather bench giving them no space. Melissa tried to ignore the electric sensation she received when their legs touched.

He put his hand on the throttle. 'Would you like to have a go? I'll do speed, you do steering.'

'Only if you're prepared for me to crash your very expensive boat.'

'You'll be fine,' he said, laughing.

He pushed the throttle forward slowly and Melissa settled in behind the wheel. The sun blared down and her hair whipped behind her as he built up speed. She giggled. He looked at her and gave her an expression of mock-fear, eyes wide as he threw the throttle forward and the boat accelerated.

Melissa squealed with excitement and gripped the wheel tighter as the speedboat moved over the water. After a few minutes, when the sea became slightly bumpy and the boat began bouncing on the waves, Guy reduced the speed and put one hand on the wheel, offering to take over. His fingers brushed against hers and she felt a flicker of excitement. She was having far too much fun.

As Guy steered and consulted a map of the Dorset coastline, Melissa stayed in her seat next to him instead of moving to the rear of the boat again.

They cruised past the sheer white cliff face at West Bay and Guy pointed out landmarks that Melissa was unfamiliar with. They sped past the long stretch of Chesil Beach and the famous Portland Bill lighthouse. They left Weymouth behind them and eventually Lulworth Cove came into view. They both turned in their seats to look back from the edge of the cove.

'It's a real beauty spot,' Guy said, idling the engine. There were at least twenty boats in and around the cove with people swimming in the crystal-clear water around their vessels.

'Wow,' Melissa said. 'It's beautiful. Like the Caribbean.'

'You should see the village.' He pointed up the hill behind the cove. 'I'll take you there one day if you like.'

Melissa wondered if one day would come, if they'd see each other again after these frantic few days ended.

'Did you bring your swimming costume?' Guy asked, shaking her out of her thoughts.

'I did. I'm wearing it underneath my clothes.'

'Good. I think we can find somewhere quieter than here.' They cruised past Lulworth and after a few minutes Guy consulted his map and furrowed his brow. 'It should be this one.'

Melissa got up and peered across the clear sea towards a small, unremarkable inlet with a little shack situated near the rocks.

'But I can't make out if . . .' He trailed off, looking through his technical binoculars. 'Yes, look, the beach hut's a wreck and the cliff steps are a bit dangerous, but I think it's the one.'

Melissa looked blank and then she stood up to get a better view. 'Is this Tyneham Cove?'

Guy nodded, folding his map up and shoving it back inside the cupboard. 'I thought it might be nice to see it. This is the only access to the beach now. There's no way through from the village these days, probably due to those awfully frightening steps.' He nodded in the direction of the cliff.

'I'd imagine they'd kill a few tourists quite nicely,' Melissa said.

He handed her the binoculars, but she held them down at her side as Guy manoeuvred the boat as close to the cove as he could without scraping it on the rocks underneath. He killed the engine and threw the lunch hook over the side to keep the boat in place.

'The cove is much smaller than I imagined it would be.' Melissa peered into the distance and then into the water, looking down at the depth. 'Can we swim over and look?'

'I don't think there's much more to see, but if you can brave the water, we can go over.' He leaned over the boat and dipped his hand in and shuddered. 'It doesn't matter what time of year it is, British seawater is always stone cold.'

'I thought you were a hardy boaty type?' Melissa raised an eyebrow and smiled.

'I am.' Guy played at mock-defensive. 'But I'm usually on a boat rather than actually in the drink.'

'Oh, where's your sense of adventure?' Melissa took her top and shorts off and kicked her sandals to the side of the boat. She was wearing a white bikini and she noticed Guy's eyes flick over her before looking purposefully out to the cove again.

She threw her top at him and it hit him in the face. He laughed, but by the time he'd brought the T-shirt out of his eyes Melissa had jumped overboard and had started swimming.

'Oh my God, it's freezing.' She turned round to face him while treading water. 'Are you coming?'

He was already wearing a pair of dark-blue Ralph Lauren swim shorts. He unbuttoned his white shirt and took it off, exposing strong upper arms and a hard-looking chest.

Melissa was surprised and tried to stop staring. *Wow. Mr Historian works out.*

The water was calm and became even more still the further into the cove they swam. Melissa soon felt soft sand under her feet and made her way out of the water. She noticed Guy trying his best not to stare at her while she stood on the beach, ringing out her hair. She regretted the white bikini now. It was supposed to have been something sexy in which Liam could admire her in the cottage garden, something that might have sparked her former boyfriend's interest in her again. But Liam had never been at the cottage. It wasn't for public display. She'd had no intention of going *out* in it. But when Guy had told her to bring her swimming costume, it was the only one Melissa had packed for her holiday. She prayed that it wasn't see-through when wet and she peered down to try to check. She thought it looked fine.

Droplets of water ran down her as she looked over the old stone dragon's teeth that had become smooth through years of being lapped by the unforgiving sea.

'What on earth are these?'

'Coastal defence.'

Melissa frowned, none the wiser.

'To stop German tanks from coming ashore, should we have ever been invaded.'

Melissa's eyes widened. 'It could never have got to that stage, surely?'

Guy gave her a look that said otherwise. 'They got pretty close. I wrote a book last year about Hitler's planned invasion.'

Melissa gave him a knowing smile before moving towards the beach hut. 'Of course you did.' Behind her, she heard him laugh.

On close inspection the hut was even more of a mess than it had looked from the boat. It had been over seventy years since it had last been tended to. The roof was half off, the clapboard walls disintegrated and battered. Shelves that may once have held books and ornaments were on the floor, rotten with water damage, and the front door was missing its glass panes and hanging off its hinges. The small curtains were all but gone; the only sign they had ever been there at all was a scrap of frayed, dirty fabric hanging from one solitary curtain ring, blowing in the summer breeze where the windows had long since blown in. The floor was intact but the damaged walls were rich with graffiti.

'Some of the graffiti looks as if it's been there since the latter years of the war,' Guy said. 'Perhaps soldiers came here to relax, swim, drink, smoke . . .'

'And destroy,' Melissa said unhappily.

Broken beer bottles littered the floor among paint cans. Out of the corner of her eye, Melissa saw Guy wince as she tentatively walked through the debris to take a closer look at the graffiti.

'Be careful.' He reached a hand out instinctively towards her. 'You never know if there might be needles.'

'Some of this graffiti's modern. Who comes all this way just to tag their name on a wall of an old beach hut? Or shoot up? What's wrong with kids these days?' Melissa asked.

Behind her, Guy's shoulders shook with laughter. 'You sound like my gran.'

'She's got a point,' Melissa returned. 'Honestly. Why ruin a perfectly good beach hut?'

'It probably wasn't perfectly good for much longer after the Standishes left,' he said gently. 'If it was lucky enough to survive the army's antics, it would have been a miracle. Then all the natural weather in the past seventy-five years, the 1987 storm for example.'

'It's just such a shame. This might be the only place Veronica Standish found something resembling happiness, and there's just nothing left of that now. It's a wreck.'

She turned and picked her route back through the smashed bottles, moving past Guy as he stood in the doorway. He held out his hand to help her, wincing again as her bare feet brushed broken glass. Melissa barely noticed.

They swam back and climbed on to the boat. As Melissa stood, drying off, she looked back sadly at the cove and the ramshackle beach hut. She wasn't sure what she had been expecting, but when she'd pictured it all in her mind, it hadn't looked anything like that. Guy respectfully moved away, giving her a few moments to herself. Behind her, he clicked open the hamper.

Forcing herself to cheer up a bit, Melissa turned. 'What's in there?'

'A bit of a late lunch.' He pulled out crusty bread, pork pies, Scotch eggs, sausage rolls, various dips, fruit, cheeses and chutneys. 'Gosh,' he mumbled distractedly, looking into the hamper and pulling out a half-bottle of chilled champagne and a punnet of strawberries. 'I only asked for a picnic suitable for a first date and we've got a banquet.' Guy looked up to see Melissa's mouth had dropped open. 'What's wrong?' he asked.

Her mouth closed and she smiled slowly, seawater dripping from her as she wrapped the towel round her body.

'First date?' she asked.

Guy's eyes shot to the side. 'I was using it as an example for the deli,' he bluffed.

Melissa was smiling curiously at him. Before she could quite work out whether Guy actually might like her, he stepped forwards, dipped his head and kissed her slowly and deeply, his hands touching her lightly on her waist. Melissa's eyes closed and she thought she might pass out. Every part of her body was tingling. She clasped her arms around his neck.

Another boat approached the cove and some of the teenage passengers on board wolf-whistled and jeered in Guy and Melissa's direction. They sprang apart.

'I couldn't resist,' Guy said, threading his fingers through hers.

Melissa stood on tiptoes and kissed him quickly on the mouth. 'At least no one's taking pictures,' she said, waving at the leering teens.

'The youth of today aren't interested in someone like me.' Guy gave her a shy smile. 'Come on, let's get out of here and eat back at the dock.'

Regardless of whether it was a first date or not, Melissa couldn't think of a more perfect way to spend it.

CHAPTER 24

He took her hand, led her up to the controls and they sat close together while he steered them back to the harbour. She nestled in against him and he placed an arm around her shoulders. Whenever Melissa looked up at Guy, he was smiling out to sea. Melissa was equally as happy. How had this happened? How had she found herself being kissed by Guy on a speedboat after only having known him for a few days? *Because he's a nice man, Melissa. And you've not had much luck with those.*

As they pulled up alongside the jetty and he tied the ropes to secure the boat, they unpacked the picnic and sat eating on the dock, legs dangling over the edge as they watched the sun go down. He popped the cork on the champagne and it flew out into the water.

Guy looked around. 'I hope the harbour master didn't see that.'

'This is all very smooth,' Melissa said as he poured the half-bottle of champagne into plastic flutes and then placed a strawberry in each.

'I try.'

After the picnic, they walked back to his car, hand in hand. Melissa looked up at Guy and he smiled whenever he caught her eye.

'You know, I've wanted to kiss you since I first met you,' he whispered. His lips brushed her ear and she felt her legs weaken.

'Really?' She squeezed his hand tighter. 'I had no idea.'

'You must be blind then,' he laughed. 'I thought I was making it a bit too obvious for a while.'

Back at the hotel, he kissed her at the door to her room. Melissa's insides melted as she backed against her door and he moved with her. Maybe it was the champagne or maybe it was the exhilaration of the day, but she was adamant she'd never been kissed quite like that before.

'Meet downstairs later?' he asked huskily, backing down the hallway. She nodded, then reluctantly watched him disappear inside his room.

Melissa closed the door and squealed with happiness before heading into the shower.

Guy was down in the bar before she was; a stack of paperwork alongside his laptop on the low table in front of him. He was on one of the oversized squashy brown leather sofas, relaxing in jeans and a T-shirt and looking thoroughly gorgeous. He'd kicked off his deck shoes and Melissa noticed how nice his feet were.

He held out his hand to her and when she took it, he pulled her next to him on the sofa. She snuggled in and inhaled his scent. He smelled fresh and clean, like expensive soap. He glanced around to see if anyone was looking in their direction and, on finding the coast clear, he kissed her.

'Do you mind if I get on with a little bit of work?' he asked when they came up for air. 'My next book isn't going to write itself, sadly.'

Melissa nodded. She could barely speak. She touched her mouth where his lips had just been.

Neither of them were hungry for dinner after the late picnic, so they just ordered coffee. When she'd recovered, Melissa pulled out the three books about Tyneham that she'd bought and clunked two of the heavy tomes on the table.

'Light reading,' she quipped.

He picked one up and read the blurb on the back.

'What are you working on?' she asked. He handed the book back to her.

'It's a book charting those who made the voyage out to Dunkirk in the Little Ships when they went to help the BEF evacuate in 1940. There'll be a TV show to coincide later in the year.'

She raised her eyebrows. 'You know, I might start taking more of an interest in history now.' She settled into the sofa and started reading. Guy grinned, then immersed himself in his work; his brow furrowed as he typed furiously on his laptop, hunching over the coffee table to do so. Occasionally, he pushed sheets of paper around to find a note he needed.

Melissa couldn't help wondering where all this was going. After the ridiculous fiasco of her non-relationship with Liam, was she ready to jump into something new? If this dalliance with Guy was going anywhere, then it was going to have to go there slowly. Very slowly. She glanced at him over her book and wondered if he had other ideas. What if, to Guy, Melissa was just a holiday romance? He'd asked to meet her in London, but that was when he thought she'd been leaving and perhaps that had never actually been his intention anyway. What if he had just been being polite?

She tried to focus on her book, flicking through pages upon pages of some rather lengthy facts about Tyneham's farming successes and lists of those in census records before finding a semi-interesting chapter about the graves of those buried in the churchyard. The villagers had been reluctant to leave for many reasons, but for some, one of their main worries had been leaving their lost spouses and family members behind in the churchyard, not knowing if they'd ever be able to pay their respects again. Melissa realised with sadness that until the village had reopened this week that they hadn't been able to visit their graves since 1943.

She looked up thoughtfully and spotted someone taking a picture of her and Guy. *Jesus, really?*

Melissa sipped her coffee and moved on to a chapter about the village cricket team and how it had disbanded at the start of the war when most of the young men had been called up or had voluntarily joined the army. A few photographs showed a couple of winning matches and there was a picture of the cricket team grouped together. The date showed the team holding a winner's shield in 1937, two years before the outbreak of war. The photo had been taken too soon; one of the men was out of focus, as if he'd just run into the frame at the last second. His face was slightly blurry, but there was something about the foppish dark hair that struck her. She scanned the picture caption and was surprised to read the name at the end.

She sat up straight and said, 'Who the hell is Freddie Standish?'

CHAPTER 25

Tyneham, December 1943

In the grounds of the house, Veronica's skin prickled with cold and fear. Bertie's triumphant smile cut through any last hope she had of leaving him.

She swallowed and her eyes widened in disbelief as she looked at Bertie. 'What?' she cried. 'You're going to kill him? You're going to kill Freddie? Your own brother? You couldn't. You wouldn't.'

'Wouldn't I?' He gave her a sideways look as he inhaled on his second cigarette. 'You really think I wouldn't do that? What are you comparing it to? All the other things I've ever done in this house?'

Veronica's eyes darted about wildly. This couldn't be happening. This wasn't how this was supposed to end. She was supposed to be leaving. With Freddie. They were running away. They were finally going to be together.

'I don't believe you.' She shook her head. 'Even you wouldn't do that.'

'You do believe me, Veronica. It's just that you don't want to believe me.'

'How?' she asked.

Bertie looked confused. 'What do you mean?' He tilted his chin up towards her.

'How are you going to kill him?' she asked incredulously.

Bertie laughed. 'If it's details you want . . . the hunting guns are still here. Packed up and ready to go if any of the remaining staff have done what they've been bloody instructed to do, but still here. If you go inside the house and do as you've been told, you'll save both your life and Freddie's. If you don't . . .'

Veronica gulped as Bertie shrugged and tailed off. She put her hand to her neck again, the sting of his grip still present. She was silent, stalling for time. Her mind was blank. What could she do? How could she fight him? How could she stop him? She looked at Bertie's face. She'd never seen him look so calm. For the first time in a long time, he appeared to be a man entirely in control and he knew it. He would kill Freddie. Veronica could see that now. He'd almost killed her countless times. He was capable of killing his brother. She had to save Freddie. It was too late to save herself.

'What will happen to me?' she asked.

'You?'

Veronica nodded. 'What are you going to do with me? *To* me? After.'

'Nothing.'

'Nothing?' she repeated. 'I don't under—'

'You're coming with me to London and wherever else I want to take you, where you will play the part of the dutiful, loving wife. You will cause me no further trouble. You will look elegant at parties. You do not get to leave – to make a fool of me. You will do whatever I want and, more importantly . . .' He stepped forward and ran a finger down her neck and towards her chest, eyeing her hungrily even as she closed her eyes and recoiled, 'you will carry out your wifely duties as and when I command.'

Tears sprang anew in her eyes. Bertie waited for her to respond. There was no way out. She could see that.

'How do you know I won't leave you?' she asked, a tinge of defiance creeping back into her voice.

'Oh, that's easy enough to sort.' He waved his hand casually as if he was batting away a fly. 'You won't leave the house without my say-so. I won't go as far as locking you in your room, unless I find I have to, but you will go where I go when I want you to, and when that's not possible, you will stay indoors unless otherwise instructed. I have a mind that we might need some additional staff. A few people I can rely on to keep an eye on you.'

She closed her eyes for a few seconds as she realised the format her life would take. From this moment on, there was only pain, imprisonment, and despair. She knew she wasn't going to be able to survive Bertie's brutality. He'd almost killed her one too many times in the bedroom when his mood had been dark and his body had been too overwrought with alcohol.

'No,' she cried. 'You can't do this.' But she knew he could. There was no point carrying on. She could end it all, if she was brave enough. She had no idea at this moment in time if she was. The one thing she did know was that she had to save Freddie.

Bertie led Veronica back to the house, clutching her hand tightly and dragging her behind him. She didn't know how her legs carried her. Her entire body felt weighted. As they came into the front hall, the fire flickered in the grate. Veronica stood by it, staring into the logs in a daze. She had no idea how cold she'd been outside until now.

As the fire danced in Bertie's eyes, he stood opposite her. 'You know what you have to do,' he snarled. 'Even one hint of a warning and I remove Freddie from our lives permanently. Do you understand? You have to see it from my point of view,' Bertie reasoned in a lighter tone and stepped forward to stroke Veronica's face. She gritted her teeth as he touched her. 'He's defiled my wife. It's no more than he deserves.'

Veronica's shoulders shook as she burst into tears. She wiped them away quickly in case Freddie appeared. Bertie looked on with a sympathetic expression that was almost five years too late.

Then suddenly he moved to the boxes in the hall that held the newly packed guns and pulled out what he was looking for, assembling it expertly.

Veronica looked on, horrified, at the gun. How was this happening?

'Go on then.' Bertie loaded bullets and snapped the rifle closed, nodding his head to usher Veronica onwards. 'Get rid of him.'

Bertie pushed Veronica along the hallway and into his office, where they could both hear Freddie packing the heavy ledgers. He thrust her through the door and stood back out of sight.

Freddie looked up from packing as Veronica entered. He cast her a loving expression and then appeared to check himself, glancing around in case Bertie was nearby to witness it. If only he knew how close Bertie really was. Veronica could feel his malevolent presence emanating from close behind her. She looked at the floor, hoping beyond hope that this was all a horrific nightmare, one from which she'd wake any moment now.

'What's wrong?' Freddie asked, his smile fading as she continued looking at the floor. He reached inside his breast pocket and took out his silver engraved lighter. He put it on Bertie's desk while he fumbled in his pocket for his cigarette case.

Veronica tried to speak but her mouth had gone dry. She licked her lips and knew that she needed to be convincing and fast if she was going to save Freddie's life before Bertie changed his mind and shot his brother regardless.

'Freddie.' Her voice shook and she hoped he couldn't hear it. 'I've come to a decision about my future. And I'm sorry to say it doesn't involve you.'

Freddie narrowed his eyes and smiled uncertainly and then the smile faded to be replaced with curiosity. He stopped fumbling with his cigarette case.

'What?' he asked. 'Not this again.'

'It's for the best. Regardless of whether you love me or not, it would be wrong of me to encourage you any further. If I left with you tomorrow, it would only be because I needed you. Needed your help.'

'Which I'm willing to give,' Freddie confirmed, missing the point.

'But that's not enough. It's not enough for either of us.' Veronica heard Bertie's feet shuffle gently and she started to panic further. She knew if Freddie doubted her for even a second, she would cave. She would blurt out the truth and beg him to run, which he wouldn't. Not in time. And then he would die.

'Veronica, why are you doing this?' Freddie sounded exasperated. 'Why now? Why at all? You know how I feel about you. I want to be with you.'

Veronica took a deep breath. 'But I don't want to be with you.' She looked him straight in the eye and mustered her strength. 'I don't love you. I'm sorry to say it, but there it is. What happened in the beach hut . . . it shouldn't have happened. I was . . . I don't know. Your news about going to war. About being shot. It struck me. I felt sorry for you. And you helped me, when I needed you. With Bertie, I mean. You were just in the right place at the right time. That's all it was—'

'No,' Freddie interjected. 'No. I don't believe you. You love me. I know you do.'

She looked away momentarily. 'I thought I did. But I'm afraid I don't. I realise that I would be treating you terribly cruelly if I allowed you to continue thinking that. I shouldn't have said it. I didn't mean it.' A lump formed in the back of her throat.

He stepped towards her and Veronica stepped backwards in response. Her face was impassive. 'Don't think this isn't the hardest thing I've ever done. But it's also the most honest,' she lied.

Veronica could sense Freddie wavering. All she needed was a seed of doubt. He exhaled. 'Why?' he asked. 'Why now?'

'I want to do this on my own.' She sped up. 'If I leap from one brother to the next, yet again, I wouldn't forgive myself.' Veronica almost believed herself.

Freddie was silent and he looked at the floor. His brow furrowed. 'But Bertie?' he questioned. 'You can't . . .'

Veronica shook her head. 'I'm not going to stay with him. Tomorrow. After the speech. I'll leave then as I had always planned.' She grimaced, knowing Bertie could hear her. The next sentence she uttered louder and more forcefully: 'But you need to go. You need to be far away from here. Now.'

Freddie's gaze rose from the floor and his voice rose with it. 'Now?' he queried. 'You want me to leave now? You break it off with me, for a second time, and you expect me to just do as you ask and leave?' His voice rose. 'Why are you doing this?'

'I've told you why, Freddie. Stop clinging on to something that never really was.' She hated the necessary cruelty of her words and the pain she was causing him.

His eyes widened and he rubbed the palm of his hand across his mouth. 'I don't know why I even came here,' he said quietly.

She could hear the agony in his voice and she dug her finger-nails into the palm of her hands repeatedly, nervously.

'This isn't the same as before,' he said. 'This is different. Before, you were lured away by the promise of greater things that turned out to be lies. But now, what? I don't understand. Help me understand.' He looked at her imploringly.

'I don't have to help you understand, Freddie.' Veronica didn't know how her nerves were holding up. Her heart was thudding. 'I just need you to go. You're holding me up. I can't leave if you're still here. Don't you see that. I need to make plans. You need to leave. Now. I'm sorry I led you on. I really am.'

'You think you're doing this to spare me, Veronica. But you aren't. I can take it. I can take the hell of running from Bertie forever. We can do this together.' He finished uncertainly, as if he knew the game was up.

'It's not enough, Freddie. You're not enough,' Veronica finished with more courage than she felt. It was brutal. But she had no other option. She had to save him. She thought of the ease with which Bertie had assembled the gun and knew she was doing the right thing.

Freddie nodded and looked away. He laughed bitterly as he walked towards the door. Veronica panicked. Was Bertie still there? How would he explain the gun to Freddie? Or would he just eschew all explanation and simply fire at Freddie? *Please God, don't let Bertie hurt him.*

'I'll never stop loving you, you know. You're ripping me to pieces again,' Freddie said as he passed her.

She tried to rise taller, to make herself feel a strength that wasn't real while avoiding his gaze.

'Good luck, Veronica.' His voice broke as he spoke and she closed her eyes against the tears that threatened to fall.

Moments later, she heard the front door open and close, signalling Freddie's departure. Behind her, from the other side of the hall where he'd moved out of sight, Bertie laughed. Veronica put her hand to her mouth to muffle the wail of despair and relief that threatened to escape her lips. Freddie had left her life forever. Whatever happened to her next, at least she'd saved the man she loved.

CHAPTER 26

Dorset, July 2018

In the hotel lounge, Guy looked up, his eyes conveying confusion at his surroundings. He'd obviously been miles away, out to sea with the Little Ships.

'Er, sorry?' He blinked, refocusing on Melissa.

'Who the hell is Freddie Standish?' she repeated.

She held the book out to show him. He looked from the image of the assembled cricket team to the caption, clearly puzzled. 'A typo maybe? A shame we can't see his face. Although it sort of looks like Sir Albert. But it's hard to tell. Maybe a cousin or younger brother, perhaps?'

'Younger brother?'

'Mm.' Guy was distracted by his work. 'Albert inherited it all, the farmland, Tyneham House and the houses in and around the village. If there was a brother, he was bound to be younger. If that's who this man is.'

Melissa looked at the dark hair with curiosity. Guy bristled next to her, shaking his head when she dog-eared the page.

There was nothing else in the rest of that particular book and flicking through the other two she got the feeling they were going to prove fairly useless too. The mysterious man had only been mentioned once and even then it was simply a picture caption.

If it was a typo, it was a pretty big one. Albert to Freddie wasn't an easy leap. If it wasn't a typo, the fact that so little space was given to him across three local history books suggested Freddie Standish, whoever he was, really wasn't that important at all.

While Guy continued typing on his laptop Melissa flicked back to the first book and looked at the blurry image again. She had a feeling about him that she just couldn't shake from her head.

The minutes ticked by and Melissa gave up on squinting at the picture. She gathered the books into a small pile and sat back while Guy closed his laptop and put his paperwork into his bag. He leaned back on the sofa and then shifted his body so he was facing her.

As she turned towards him, strands of hair fell over one of her eyes and Guy reached forward to brush them away, tucking them back behind her ear. Melissa felt hot all of a sudden. She made a little gasp, only slightly audible, as his hand slowly touched her ear and brushed delicately down her neck. He pulled back suddenly and clenched his jaw, glancing around to see if anyone was watching them.

Confusion coursed through Melissa.

'I'm sorry.' Guy leaned forward to take a final sip of his coffee and changed the mood between them entirely.

Melissa laughed nervously while a strange veil of panic replaced confusion. 'Why are you sorry?'

'I don't . . . I mean, we've only just met. I'm not a fan of rushing things.'

'I agree.' Melissa wondered where this conversation was going. Surely she wasn't being dumped before anything had actually got off the ground? That would be a new low.

'I really like you, Melissa.' He exhaled loudly and ran his hand through his hair. 'I don't want to move too quickly and ruin whatever is happening between us.'

Melissa suddenly felt fuzzy. This was a feeling she wasn't used to. A man liked her enough not to rush into anything. 'I agree,' she said again. 'That sounds like a good plan.' She wasn't used to dating gentlemen.

After he'd kissed Melissa goodnight at her door and returned to his own room, Guy leaned against the back of his door and exhaled loudly. He'd resisted the overwhelming urge to try to take her to bed. He was a man, after all. And she was gorgeous. He was pleased that she'd agreed they should take things slowly and respected that she hadn't invited him inside for a drink. He wasn't sure he'd have been able to resist an actual invite if one had been issued. He'd meant what he said. He did want to take it slowly. He liked Melissa and he wasn't going to mess it up the way he'd messed his last relationship up by rushing in too quickly and allowing himself to be swept along too fast. That way led to madness. Not this time.

He paced the room, moving towards the window, and stopped to look up at the clear night sky. His mood shifted as he stared outside and he reached for a small bottle of whisky from the mini bar. His favourite brand was there and he smiled, realising his assistant Philippa had probably organised that particular placement for him. What would he do without her to arrange his high-impact work schedule? But while he rejoiced in Philippa organising his work life, he didn't even want to think about who had managed his personal life for the past decade and how badly that had ended. He ran his hand through his hair and shook his head as he realised what a complete fool he'd been when it came to relationships.

Inside his laptop bag a stack of papers had been silently beckoning him. He'd been putting them off for the best part of a month. Why? He had a vague idea. Perhaps because it wasn't a decision that relied on facts, figures, statistics, and easily explained historical events.

He rifled through the bag until he found a large brown envelope. He pulled out the documents inside and flicked through where the little neon tags marked where he needed to sign. Without hesitation, Guy unscrewed the lid of his Montblanc pen and signed his name with a flourish. He'd allowed this to fester for far too long.

He sat down in the chair and looked at the last page as the black ink dried. For all the emotions he thought he was going to feel, he didn't think it would be relief or freedom. But both flowed through him rapidly. A large smile formed on his face as he sealed the envelope and threw it towards the door of the suite as a reminder to post it in the morning. As it landed on the thick carpet, it made a satisfying thud.

Guy tipped the whisky straight into his mouth from the bottle, bypassing the cut-glass tumbler. He kicked off his shoes and put his feet up on the desk, leaning back and savouring the taste of the alcohol. Tomorrow was a new day.

CHAPTER 27

The knocking was getting louder. If it was in the depths of Melissa's dream, then it needed to stay there, far out of reach of reality.

Knock knock knock. It sounded again. Her eyes opened this time and she tried blinking sleep out of them. When that didn't work, she rubbed her eyes and rolled onto her side, slowly acclimatising and blinking herself awake. She groped for her phone and pulled at it to check the time. It was still attached to its charger and it pinged back out of her grasp as if it was on a bungee cord and fell to the floor.

The knocking sounded again and Melissa sat up as she realised someone was hammering at the door to her hotel room. She sprang out of bed and went to the door, yanking down the pyjama T-shirt she was wearing. She'd kicked her way out of her pyjama bottoms during the night, it had been so hot. But a thigh-skimming top and a pair of knickers was not suitable attire to wear to answer the door, so she decided it was best not to open it. 'Yes?' she called.

'It's me,' Guy called back. 'I've been knocking for ages. I thought you might have died in there.'

'Sorry,' she called back.

'Are you going to open the door?' He laughed.

Melissa looked down at her thighs. *No.*

'Sure, just give me a sec.' She ran to the bathroom and grabbed the fluffy robe from the hook behind the door. She glanced in the mirror and tried to smooth her bed hair down. Covering up with the robe, she pulled the hotel door open. 'Hi.' She smiled.

'Hi,' he returned and leaned against the door frame. One hand was thrust casually in his pocket. 'So,' he started, 'I called room service for some breakfast. They're bringing it to my suite. I wondered if you wanted to join me?'

Behind him came the clang of a room service trolley being rolled down the corridor.

'Definitely,' Melissa replied and gestured for the waiter to bring the trolley to her room; she didn't fancy prowling the corridor in her dressing gown.

'Thanks,' Guy said to the waiter and handed him a tip as he left.

Melissa looked at the trolley that was piled high with fruit, croissants, and Danish pastries, two toast racks with white and brown bread, pots of jams and preserves, and two silver domes covering hot plates. A pot of tea, a cafetière of coffee and one extra silver pot sat on the tray.

'What's that one?' she asked as Guy pushed the trolley inside the room and closed the door behind him.

'Hot chocolate.' Guy grinned. 'Just in case. I went ahead and ordered a little bit of everything off the menu. I wasn't sure what you might fancy. I'll eat whatever you don't.'

Melissa looked on hungrily. 'That's a lot of breakfast.' She took a piece of toast and jam and paused briefly as she watched Guy tuck into an entire full English, followed by two slices of toast. For a toned man, he had a healthy appetite.

'What do you want to do today?' Guy said as he threw his napkin down onto his empty plate. 'Does the hunt continue?'

Melissa nodded, eyeing up the croissants.

'I guess so. I want to know who the mysterious Freddie Standish is.'

'Ah, he of the grainy, pixelated little picture. All right.' Guy stood. 'You finish breakfast, get dressed and I'll meet you downstairs. We'll search some local records as well as the online ones and see what we can find.' He lifted a grape from the fruit bowl, threw it high in the air, positioned his head back and caught it deftly in his mouth.

'Smooth,' Melissa said as Guy headed towards the door.

'Thanks. That could have gone horribly wrong. There's nothing like a grape to the eye to really impress a girl.'

Melissa laughed.

'Melissa?'

Her head shot back up to see that Guy's face was serious.

'I'm really glad you stayed,' he finished.

She smiled. 'Me too.'

Melissa walked downstairs in cut-off shorts, T-shirt and flip-flops. Guy was nowhere to be seen and the receptionist eyed her critically while she waited for him. Melissa smiled, but the woman behind the front desk ignored her.

'I don't suppose you've seen—?' Melissa asked.

'He's in the garden,' the icy receptionist cut in.

'Thanks. Have a good day.' Melissa rolled her eyes.

Guy was pacing up and down, speaking into his phone with a concerned look on his face. Melissa sat in the sun a little distance away from him to give him privacy and waited for him to finish. A few minutes later, he stabbed at his phone to end his call. He ran his hand through his hair and frowned.

'You okay?' Melissa enquired.

'Not really,' he said. 'That was my mum. I need to go to the hospital. Gran's not doing so well.'

'What's happened?'

'I'm not sure. Overnight she seems to have taken a turn for

the worse. The nurses weren't happy and the doctor was just doing his rounds when my mum called. Can we postpone our research?'

Melissa felt so guilty that their quest had taken him away from Anna. She was poorly and he should be with her. What were they doing? There were other things in this life more important than tracking down a frightened-looking wartime wife.

'Yes, definitely. Your gran's health beats that hands down. You go.'

Guy ran his hand through his hair again. 'Okay, thanks. I'll see you later.'

Melissa nodded. Guy bent down, kissing her. It felt electric, exciting. He lingered, his eyes closed, and then he grinned as he stood back up.

'Bye.' He waved as he turned.

Melissa smiled at his kiss as he walked away. She exhaled deeply, attempting to get her breath back. While her track record with men had, so far, not been great, no man had ever made her stomach flip the way Guy did.

She felt bad for him. She had no grandparents now and could well remember her nanny's sad demise all those years ago. She'd been at university and had missed the very last days of her nan's life. There were so many things she wished she'd asked her about. Hindsight was a wonderful thing. Melissa was glad Guy was spending these days seeing his family.

She glanced at her watch. Time was knocking on. She needed to be proactive now. Just because Guy was an expert historian didn't mean she couldn't do some research herself. She'd rinsed the internet for all it was worth when it came to Veronica and Albert, but maybe the mysterious Freddie Standish might lead somewhere.

Melissa fetched her laptop from her room and sat in the sunshine on the terrace. Connecting to the hotel's hazy Wi-Fi service, she opened up a genealogy website and reluctantly put her credit card details in to pay for access. As the different options opened up in front of her, Melissa's eyes glazed over. First and last names were a breeze. Melissa input *Freddie Standish* into the relevant fields. Location, dates, categories, and subcategories started to flex her brain. She typed in *1943* and *Dorset* and clicked go. Nothing. Nothing of any use anyway.

Tapping her foot, she hunched over the screen and tried again but unticked the box for 'name variation'. She only wanted Freddie Standish. Not Stanton or Stanbridge or anything else. Birth records, death records, and census records all drew a blank. There was nothing that matched a Freddie Standish. She sat and stared out across the hotel's garden wondering what to search for next.

She moved the mouse to kick-start the screen and then, on a hunch, replaced *Freddie* with *Frederick* in the search field, typing as fast as she could. She hit enter.

CHAPTER 28

As the page loaded, it displayed zero relevant results. Melissa could have screamed. They made this all look so easy on *Who Do You Think You Are?* How were there no results? What was she doing wrong? Maybe it was a typo in the book after all. Maybe Freddie Standish wasn't a real person.

Melissa slammed the laptop lid down just as a waitress approached her. She glanced at her watch. 'Bloody Mary, please,' Melissa said without hesitation. Dead-end research was thirsty work. It was a wonder Guy wasn't an alcoholic.

She sat for a moment and wondered what other route was available to her. Would there be anything in a library that wasn't online? Maybe other local history books might show something interesting about Veronica and Albert.

She made a snap decision. 'Actually, sorry, can I cancel that drink?' Melissa asked.

She looked up the nearest library on her laptop and then gathered her belongings and strode purposefully towards her car.

It took about half an hour of winding through lanes to reach the library. Melissa wondered the last time she'd been inside one. Probably at university? That was shameful.

The single-level Victorian red-brick building had once been a

217

school and the words carved into the stone above the front door showed it had been the Girls' Entrance. The laminated sign Blu-tacked on the inside of the door explained that it was now a community library – run by volunteers just three days a week.

Melissa nodded hello to the lady who was single-handedly running the premises and then perused the shelves. The local history books were plentiful, but Melissa wasn't really sure what she was looking for. A book about Tyneham would be excellent – especially if it wasn't one of the three that she had already bought. But there was nothing.

Melissa sighed; it sounded as loud as a scream in the close confines of the quiet library.

'Can I help you, dearie?' the female volunteer asked kindly. She was middle-aged with bobbed hair and glasses.

'I'm not really sure actually,' Melissa replied. She was despondent and she knew she sounded it. 'I'm looking for . . .' What was she looking for? *I'm looking for a woman in a photograph from the war that was in an unhappy marriage. Her husband found out she was having an affair and then she disappeared without trace a month later.* No. That wouldn't sound particularly normal. Start small. Then work up to it. She thought of the pixelated Freddie Standish.

'I wonder if you have any books about local sport. Cricket in particular.'

The volunteer looked up as she thought. 'I don't think so. We have a few almanacs, but they're quite old. Pre-war, I think. Only little home-made pamphlets by enthusiasts of the time. Mementos really. They rarely get a look-in, but I'm sure they are here somewhere. What is it you are looking for?'

Melissa tried not to get too excited at the thought of pre-war local cricket books, which would have ordinarily bored her to tears. 'A name. Someone called Freddie Standish.'

'Is he a famous batsman? I'm sure I've heard that surname before.'

218

'No, he's not famous. He was a resident of Tyneham before the requisition. He played for the local cricket team in the thirties, but I can only find one reference to him, so I just wanted to check that he was real. That the name wasn't a typo,' Melissa clarified.

'We learned about Tyneham in school,' the volunteer said. 'I remember the big house was taken as well as the village. They reopened it last weekend – the village, I mean. Don't think they've opened the house yet though. Have you been to have a look? I'm going next week. You might find something interesting about him there.'

Melissa grimaced. 'It was visiting Tyneham that got me into all this mess in the first place.'

The lady looked strangely at Melissa as they walked round to an archive shelf. The volunteer pulled a box of pamphlets out of a small Perspex storage box. 'These aren't official library property. My granddad was a local cricketer and used to keep the odd bit of local sporting memorabilia and a few of these crept into the library when he died. I can't remember the last time we looked at these. But let's see.' The little yellowing leaflets were made of thick paper but were crumbling at the edges. They were basic in their presentation and the librarian hadn't been lying when she'd said they were a home-made job. Melissa's hopes of them proving useful died.

'What are these exactly?'

'Some are almanacs of the big cricket teams in Dorset and there's references to a few matches for each of the seasons – players and the like.' The telephone rang in the office and the librarian gave the box to Melissa. 'I hope it proves useful,' she said as she went to grab the phone.

Melissa shunned the desk. It was too small for her needs. She sat on the scratchy carpeted floor tiles and leafed through the contents of the box, laying each pamphlet out methodically in chronological order. She ran her finger over the old typewriter ink and then started reading. The big county cricket match sheets were a dead end; Freddie's name wasn't listed in any of them. But after a few minutes flicking open the smaller pamphlets, she found a list of team members for various local cricket teams. Tyneham was listed through the 1920s and 30s with the players' names, positions and ages. Melissa was disappointed to see that a few years were missing. The pamphlets showed the various teams Tyneham had played against along with the final scores throughout the seasons. There was nothing relating to Freddie in the nineteen twenties, but then as Melissa started on the nineteen thirties lists, there he was. Her eyes almost popped out of her head. Freddie Standish was on the Tyneham cricket team from 1932 to 1937. Like the other players, his age was displayed. In 1937, Freddie Standish had been twenty-six. He wasn't a typo. He was real. Melissa made a whoop of joy.

She pulled out her mobile phone. Her first thought was to message Guy. Whoever this Freddie Standish was, he was young. Given there was nothing else to go on at the moment, a lead was a lead, however apparently useless it looked. Her phone had been on silent all day and as Melissa looked at it there was already a message from Guy.

I'm going to stay at the hospital for the rest of the day. Gran's stable but sleeping a lot. I'd appreciate the company if you're bored, but if not, no problem. Guy xx

Melissa read it twice and her heart went out to him.

The volunteer approached Melissa. 'Anything I can help you with?'

Melissa started placing the pamphlets and faded sheets back in the box.

'Thanks, I found what I was looking for. He's listed. Aged twenty-six in 1937, so it says.' Melissa felt proud of her find.

'Not long before the war,' the librarian mused. 'He'd have been twenty-eight when he went to war, if he went in 1939. That's a good age. But not one to say a life had been fully lived.'

'No, I suppose not.' Melissa looked down at the floor.

'So, who was he then?'

'Something to do with the family that owned Tyneham House. He just intrigued me. He cropped up when I was . . . looking for something else. I think he may have been a brother or a cousin. But he's a regular on the cricket team so I'm not all that sure he would be a visiting cousin now.' Melissa didn't want to tell this woman that she was on the hunt for Lady Veronica Standish. The idea of Veronica having had an affair with a man who two of the village boys swore was her husband seemed like gossiping about a friend. Talking about Veronica like that to this stranger made Melissa feel disloyal.

Melissa took a picture of her find on her phone, thanked the librarian, popped a five-pound note in the collection tin that went towards repairs and funds and said goodbye.

She had found Freddie but now she had no idea what she was looking for next. As she walked back to her car she realised this was all just a massive distraction from real life. The prospect of looking for a job and having to return to her crappy little flat did not fill Melissa with joy. Standing in the sunshine in the library car park, she thought about this holiday that had turned into an adventure. Was it only an adventure because she was forcing it to be? She'd hit a dead end, surely? Was finding Freddie Standish getting her closer to discovering what had happened to Veronica? Maybe nothing had happened to Veronica. Maybe nothing had happened to any of them. Melissa was annoyed she wasn't getting anywhere.

She would go and see Guy and keep him company.

En route to the hospital, Melissa wondered if it was time to make a decision. If she couldn't get any further finding out what happened to Veronica, she would have to stop obsessing about it and start thinking about her own life. She'd been putting off serious job-hunting for long enough. Her heart just hadn't been in it. But Guy had made the last few days fun, exciting, and enjoyable, and she loved being with him. If this was going to go somewhere, then wasn't it best that it started in the realms of reality? Her real life had beckoned her a few days before and she'd ignored it. Perhaps if Guy didn't have any other immediate ideas about what they should look for next, it was time to go home?

CHAPTER 29

'Hi,' Melissa whispered to Guy as she approached Anna's bedside.

He rose and took her hand. Melissa looked down and was concerned to see that Anna looked paler and thinner around the face than she had before.

'What's happening?' Melissa asked. 'How is she?'

'Fine, I think. Tired though. You came.' He smiled. 'I didn't expect you to. But I'm really glad you did. Thank you.'

'No problem. I wanted to talk to you. Guy, I think I should . . .' She was about to tell him she thought it was time for her to go back to London, but Anna stirred.

Guy moved away from Melissa and stood over his gran, watching her with a concerned expression on his face. When Anna settled, he turned his attention back to Melissa but the worried look prevailed. 'Sorry, you were saying?'

Melissa shook her head. 'Nothing.' She squeezed his arm gently. 'It'll keep.'

After a while, Guy whispered, 'I've been thinking. I wonder if we should look Freddie Standish up.'

Melissa gave him a knowing look as she sat down. 'I had a go today actually. Online I couldn't find anything. I have a new-found respect for your job. Even when information is listed as being

223

available on those websites, it's not simple to work out what you're supposed to be doing.'

Guy smiled knowingly and sat beside her.

'So I went to the local library . . .' Melissa told Guy what she'd discovered and showed him the photo of Freddie's almanac listing that she'd taken on her phone. 'It may be something or it may be utterly irrelevant, but I think he's definitely a brother. I find it hard to believe a visiting relative would be a regular on the cricket team, unless they were really hard up for players and drafted relatives in from across the county.'

Guy looked impressed. 'Okay,' he said. 'This is a working theory. What if the man that was seen with Veronica was mistaken for Sir Albert for one very simple and obvious reason?'

Melissa interjected. 'They were only seen by a distraught teenager who may have been mistaken and a small child who didn't know what he was looking at anyway.'

Guy gave her a withering look. 'Play along would you?'

Melissa laughed.

'And what if,' Guy continued, 'the only reference we can find to anyone who may look remotely like Sir Albert is this Freddie chap. Same last name. Same sort of age. A bit of a regular in the village at one point. Shame that image you found in the book was so blurry.'

'But we don't even know if he was there or not – when the house was requisitioned,' Melissa reasoned.

'Hmm,' Guy nodded. 'There is that.' Guy looked thoughtfully into the distance towards the end of the hospital ward. 'You know,' he said suddenly. 'There is an easy way to find out who he actually is.'

'Don't say birth records, I've tried that,' Melissa offered. 'I've even tried name variations, which threw up fifteen billion results. None of them useful.'

'But now we have an age for him, it should make it easier. We

224

know the year of birth. If he was twenty-six in 1937, then he was probably born in 1911. Why not try it.'

'If Veronica did have an affair with Sir Albert's brother, that's juicy stuff. But what good will that do us? Finding out if Freddie was a brother?'

Guy slumped in his chair. 'Oh, I don't know. I'm out of ideas now. Worth a shot though.' He pulled his phone out. 'We can't do an awful lot from here, but if I give my assistant Philippa the information she can pull birth records for us. She'll have the answer in minutes.' He looked at his watch. 'She'll have left the office by now, but she'll pick it up first thing.' He tapped away on his phone.

'You can't use that in here,' a nurse said as she walked over. She gave him a look that said she knew who he was and Guy gave her a devastating smile in return.

'Sorry, I'll go outside. I need to make a few calls.' He turned to Melissa. 'You okay here for a bit? I'll come back with coffee.'

Melissa nodded. 'Take your time. I'm not going anywhere.' Although she really should be going home now, albeit reluctantly.

The hospital ward was quiet. Most of the patients were asleep or reading magazines. There were no other visitors; a fact Melissa found odd.

'Where is everyone?' she whispered to the nurse. The nurse narrowed her eyes as if she didn't understand. 'Other visitors?' Melissa explained.

'It's not visiting hours for another half an hour yet. We let him in today a bit early. Actually, he's been here most of the day.' She nodded her head towards the door through which Guy had left the ward.

Melissa smiled. If ever there was a time for special treatment, this was it. When the nurse left, Melissa glanced at Anna whose eyes were on hers.

'Oh, you're awake,' Melissa said.

Anna smiled. 'Just this second.' Her voice sounded thin and

raspy and Melissa stood up to pour her some water. Anna sipped delicately.

'Can I do anything else?' Melissa enquired. 'Guy's just stepped out to make some calls, but I can go and fetch him.'

Anna shook her head. 'Leave him be. He's been here all day.'

Melissa took the glass from the elderly lady and then sat back down and smiled. She felt awkward being there now. 'How do you feel?'

'Like a train has hit me. The oxygen helps.'

'Oh, would you like . . .?'

'No dear. Stop fussing.'

Melissa laughed. 'Sorry.'

'What have you been doing today?' Anna said slowly. Her voice rasped and her chest rose and fell in quick succession while she spoke. Melissa winced just looking at her. 'Tell me something not hospital-related, please.'

Melissa wasn't sure how much she should say. 'I've been reading some local history books. About Tyneham.'

Anna smiled. 'Anything interesting?'

'Yes and no,' Melissa volunteered.

'What was the interesting part?' Anna asked.

'Nothing much really.' Melissa wondered if she was feeling brave, if she should chance it. 'I found Albert's brother. Playing in a series of local cricket matches.' Melissa wasn't sure how this was going to go down.

'Oh yes?' Anna said.

Melissa's bravery grew. 'Freddie Standish? Quite a batsman apparently.'

'I wouldn't know. I don't know anything about cricket. I never knew the Standish brothers until I started working at the house. And even then, I didn't know Freddie.'

Melissa's excitement grew at Anna's confirmation that Freddie *was* Albert's brother.

'He wasn't there that often?'

226

'Only once, in my time. At the very end.' Anna sounded far away.

Melissa's eyes widened. 'Was he there the day of the requisition?' Melissa tried not to let excitement tinge her voice.

Anna's eyes drifted towards the end of her bed. 'No, he . . . visited towards the end and went . . . the night before the requisition,' she finished quickly. Her gaze drifted back to Melissa. 'He likes you, you know,' Anna said.

Melissa had slowly been inching forward in the plastic hospital chair. Without realising it she'd been holding her breath. 'Er, sorry?' she exhaled, feeling deflated. Her mind had been forced away from Tyneham suddenly.

'My grandson.' Anna looked at Melissa curiously. 'Guy. He likes you.'

'Oh. Right.' Melissa was excitedly processing. Her heart was racing. Freddie *was* Albert's brother. And he *was* there at the end – well, the night before, which was as good as in Melissa's opinion. Was it Freddie that Veronica had been with in the beach hut? Who else could it be? Albert knew that Veronica had been with someone. If it was his own brother, did Albert know that too?

'Guy reminds me very much of my husband.' Anna interrupted Melissa's thoughts. 'Sometimes qualities skip generations, you know. Guy's father is lovely, but in a different way. Thinks nothing of sending his wife in his place to check on me. Considers that a job well done. But in Guy, I see his grandfather almost entirely.'

'In what way?' Melissa asked absent-mindedly as she tried to process the information about the Standishes.

'Guy thinks with his head *and* his heart. He may overanalyse a situation until it drives you mad, but in the end it's his heart that will rule any decision.'

Melissa smiled, starting to pay attention. She liked the sound of that. 'How did you meet Guy's grandfather?'

It was Anna's turn to smile. 'In an air raid. Not long after Tyneham was requisitioned. I'd turned eighteen and had just

227

joined up. I was off to join the WAAF. I was that excited about being able to play my part in the war that when the siren went for the raid I don't think I even moved. I was too busy grinning from ear to ear looking at my papers. He was home on leave and as he ran past me on his way to take cover from the bombs, he simply grabbed my hand and pulled me along with him to safety. We talked for hours in that shelter, unaware of anyone around us. He was a bit older than me. His parents were very well-to-do, but in the middle of a war none of that seemed to matter very much at all. Nor did it after. He was incredibly kind. Very handsome. Guy's just like him. Guy's not a closed book, but neither is he renowned for wearing his heart on his sleeve, so I can see . . .' Anna sounded tired and she trailed off.

'See?' Melissa prompted.

'That he likes you very much indeed.' Anna yawned sleepily.

Melissa could feel her cheeks reddening. She didn't know how to reply to that. She looked at Anna, but the elderly lady was closing her eyes as she drifted back to sleep.

Guy gave Melissa a curious look as he returned. 'What was that about?'

'Nothing much,' she fibbed and looked at him thoughtfully, trying to stop a smile spreading on her face.

Guy stretched and yawned. 'Coffee shop's closed, would you believe it? I'm taking a few things to Gran's to wash for her in a bit. Mum's on her way to take over. Keep me company?'

At Anna's house Melissa put the wash on while Guy filled the kettle. He sniffed the milk dubiously and then washed it down the sink. 'It'll have to be black coffee, I'm afraid.'

They sipped their drinks at the old Formica table in the kitchen while the whir of the washing machine provided a monotonous soundtrack.

'So Sir Albert did have a brother,' Guy said once Melissa had relayed what Anna had told her. 'Interesting. You know, the more

I wonder about Veronica sleeping with someone in the beach hut and the more you keep on about Sir Albert's brother . . .'

'Yes?' Melissa smiled. She knew where this was going.

'When Reg's brother saw Veronica with someone, he would have known if he was looking at someone he knew, someone from the village. The village wasn't that big; everyone knew everyone. John only saw the back of the man's head, but he thought it was Sir Albert. It could have easily been the brother.' Guy sipped his coffee. 'He was there, after all. Gran confirmed that.'

Melissa nodded. 'It's all guesswork though, isn't it? I mean, we'll never know what really happened and we can't find any of them after the requisition. Every time we move a bit further forward, it feels as if we get to another standstill.'

Guy looked thoughtful. 'Can I ask you something?'

Melissa looked at him warily. 'Yes,' she replied, one eyebrow raised.

'What is it about Veronica that's got you so hooked? I mean,' he clarified, 'I'm forever on the hunt for an interesting story, but . . .' He left the question hanging in mid-air.

Melissa stiffened and thought about what she should say. That this was some kind of therapy? That she needed to know Veronica had got away from what sounded like a hellish existence? She wondered if she should risk it? No, she'd only frighten him off.

'You've converted me,' she said. Avoiding frightening him was probably the sensible option. 'I'm becoming an amateur sleuth and it's all thanks to you.'

He laughed and it turned into a yawn. 'God, I'm tired.'

'Do we need to collect anything for your gran?' Melissa asked, grateful to change the subject.

'We'll hang this washing out, grab Gran a couple of extra nightdresses and then make a move?'

Melissa remembered where she'd seen the nightdresses before in Anna's room. She also thought of the memory box she'd found and wondered if she should say anything about the oddly blank postcards. They sat in silence sipping their instant coffee.

'I'll get the nightdresses,' she said, washing up her coffee cup and placing it on the draining board.

Melissa had found the clothes Guy had asked her to locate in the bedroom and was absent-mindedly playing with the pink ribbon on one of the nightshirts while staring up at the memory box on the shelf.

Guy swung his head round the door. 'All set?' He looked in the direction of her gaze. 'What's that?'

Melissa was torn between fibbing outrageously by claiming not to know and confessing that she'd already looked inside on her prior visit. 'It's a memory box.'

'Really?' He moved towards the wardrobe. 'How do you know?'

'I looked inside. Last time we were here. I was on the hunt for writing paper.'

'Anything interesting in there?' Guy asked. He slowly reached up and took the box down, positioning it on the bed.

'A few postcards. Just bits and bobs really.'

He prised the lid off and looked inside.

'Guy, you're snooping!' Melissa cried.

'Oh right,' he scoffed. 'Pot calling the kettle black.' He gave her a grin and then poked the contents around the box, sitting down on the bed while he took out the stack of postcards. 'They're all blank.' He sounded disappointed. 'Stamped and addressed, but blank. That's weird. Don't you think?'

Melissa agreed. She sat on the bed and folded the nightdresses up, laying them on her lap while Guy flicked through the stack of cards.

'Hello.' He pointed to the bottom of one of the postcards. 'Look at this.'

Melissa took the postcard. Her eyes widened as she read the tiny script at the very bottom. The slanted handwriting wasn't in the main text box; it had been written at the bottom next to the printed words identifying the cover image. Melissa had only flicked through the batch of cards the first time she'd looked and the writing was so small it wasn't surprising she hadn't spotted the faded ink. At the very bottom of the artist postcard, dated March 1944, the words simply said:

Thank you. For everything. Even though it ended the way it did. Veronica. x

CHAPTER 30

Melissa looked at Guy, whose eyebrow was raised as he flipped the card back and forth slowly. 'Well, well, well,' he said. 'Gran said she received some letters and such from Veronica throughout the years.'

He started leafing through the postcards, scanning for more writing and handing them to Melissa to double-check, but all the remaining postcards were blank.

'Where's the postmark from?' Guy asked.

Melissa looked at the stamp. 'Inverness. Two months after Veronica and Albert were spotted at that swanky-looking ball.'

'Gran wasn't lying then, Melissa,' Guy said softly. 'Veronica was okay . . . in the end.'

'I guess.' But Melissa was uncertain. '"Even though it ended the way it did?"' she read the postcard out loud again. What did that even mean? That didn't imply happiness. Melissa remembered what Reg had confirmed, that Albert was nasty. The implication seemed to be that Veronica suffered both emotionally and physically at his hands and that certainly looked the case in the photo of Albert holding Veronica's hand far too tightly. Melissa held on to the image of Veronica's frightened face in the photo. 'I just don't understand what would possess her to be with him.'

Guy gave her hand a squeeze then tilted his head. 'What's that?' he asked, looking in the box. He let go of her hand and reached over, pulling out an old ornate brass key. He turned it round in his hand.

'I doubt that opens anything in a post-war bungalow,' Melissa said. 'It looks old. Victorian?'

Guy didn't reply. He was thinking – turning the key over and over. He slowly put it back in the box, then changed his mind, and took it out again. Pocketing it, he replaced the postcards, put the lid on the box and put the box back in the wardrobe.

Melissa raised her eyebrow. 'What are you thinking?'

'I'm not sure. Not at the moment anyway.'

She knew she needed to go home, but even thinking about it made her stomach feel tight. She just didn't want to go. She felt happier throwing caution to the wind and staying in Dorset, with Guy, just for a few days longer, even if the cost of the hotel room was draining her bank balance. She felt she had more to do, more to discover. She couldn't leave now.

'I'll tell you what *I'm* thinking,' Melissa said. 'It's been a long day. My brain hurts and I'm starving. Let's deliver this care package to the hospital and go and find somewhere to eat.'

Melissa and Guy were reading their menus at a hotel at the top of the hill that overlooked Lulworth Cove. Melissa couldn't help staring in wonder at the view. It was magnificent; the cove a near-perfect circle of azure blue sea with only a small inlet fenced in by thin green cliffs. She could barely concentrate on the choices of fresh fish and local produce.

'Wow,' she said. 'How did I not know about this place?'

Guy laughed. 'You're very welcome. I told you I'd bring you here.'

The last of the sun was shining down, offering them a beautiful view of the almost Caribbean-looking sea. 'Lulworth Cove was beautiful when we sailed into it before, but seeing it from inland is just breathtaking,' Melissa said.

Guy nodded. 'If you like this, you'll love Durdle Door.'

Melissa looked at him blankly.

'It's a rocky arch in the sea, essentially. You can swim through it. It's huge. Fabulous beach. And yes, it *is* better looking out to sea rather than in to land, I suppose. But please don't tell any of my yachty chums I said that.'

The doors of the hotel were wide open, letting the last of the evening sunlight cast a glow upon the diners. Melissa put her elbow on the table, resting her chin on the upturned palm of her hand and taking in the view.

'It's just magical. You know,' she said, dragging her eyes away and on to Guy, who was looking at her and smiling. 'I was having a terrible holiday this time last week. Meeting you, well, you've made it fun. Different. Special,' she dared.

He reached over and touched her hand. Melissa watched as his thumb started stroking the skin in between her thumb and forefinger. Despite the summer breeze through the open doors, Melissa suddenly felt hot.

Guy's eyes were fixed on hers. There was a small smile playing about his lips and Melissa looked up just in time to catch it.

A waiter suddenly appeared, thrusting his hand in between them, lighting the candle. Melissa sat up straight and Guy moved back, letting go of her hand. Since he'd kissed her on the boat and then again at the hotel, he'd made no further move on her. She knew they were starting whatever this was slowly, but the candlelit dinner was only serving to get her hopes up. Realisation crashed down on her that a relationship with someone as lovely and as well-known as Guy was probably not likely. This would end up a fling.

Melissa breathed in deeply and exhaled slowly. Whatever this was, she was determined to enjoy it while it lasted. If it was all over at the end of this rather hopeless quest to establish what happened to Veronica all those years ago, then so be it. She'd found out the hard way that if a man didn't want to be with you, there was very little you could do to fight it.

'These scallops are delicious.' Melissa scooped up a little bit of crumbled black pudding from the side and offered Guy her fork. He leaned forward to sample some. Melissa smiled once he'd swallowed and he was finding it hard not to be even more drawn to her. He'd told himself that taking it slow was for the best all round. His last relationship had gone too fast. It had engulfed him, carrying him along on a rip tide he was unable to swim out of. It had ended badly, as most people had told him it inevitably would. And, as a result, Guy was now finding it hard to trust his own judgement. If he hadn't allegedly been an adult, he'd probably have driven Melissa round to a few of his friends' houses to gauge their opinion. But he *was* an adult and he was just going to have to man up and see if he couldn't at least work this one out for himself.

The sun dipped low in the sky as they walked down to the shoreline of Lulworth Cove after dinner. They weren't alone: the last of the sunseekers were enjoying the final rays some way off round the bay. Laughter and the sound of glasses clinking drifted across the cove towards them. The water lapped at the edge of the sand and Melissa took her sandals off and crept over the pebbles. She placed her feet in the water and stood as the sea gently tickled her ankles.

Guy took off his deck shoes and joined her, reaching down to hold her hand. They both stared out at the sea in the fading distance. He slowly turned towards her and she lifted her head. He closed his eyes, but it wasn't to kiss her. It was because a sinking feeling was now gnawing at him. He had to tell her. He had to be honest. It had gone too far already.

'Melissa,' he started, opening his eyes. He wished he'd met her ten years ago, instead of—

But he was cut off from his musings as he felt Melissa's mouth on his. Softly and slowly she kissed him. He couldn't remember the last time he'd felt this strong attraction to someone whilst feeling quite so uneasy.

When they eventually pulled away, it was to the sound of the revellers on the other side of the cove, who had packed up and were trudging over the pebbles in order to leave the beach.

He looked down at Melissa. 'Come on.' He bottled it and he detested himself for it. 'Let's get out of here.'

Melissa nodded and took the hand he offered as they overtook the other tourists.

The drive back to the hotel was laced with unspoken words and sexual tension. Melissa's hand was on Guy's on the gearstick; her fingers threaded over his as he drove. Classic FM was playing quietly in the background. She looked over at Guy. He had seemed so tense on the beach after they had kissed, but he looked more at ease now. She smiled. This was all starting to feel far too perfect. She was sure any second now it was all going to go horribly, horribly wrong. She doubted her confidence was strong enough to take another romantic beating quite so soon.

'Nightcap?' Guy suggested as he held the door of the hotel open for Melissa. She spotted a vacant leather sofa and sent Guy off to secure it as she bought a whisky for him and an amaretto for herself. She sat next to Guy and sipped her liqueur, turning her body towards his and wondering what he was thinking. He'd seemed so open, but now it felt like he'd retreated a little bit. Was it her imagination that he'd been a bit quiet towards the end of the evening?

He raised his hand and touched her cheek. Melissa closed her eyes as his thumb gently caressed her face.

There was a new tension between them. She was pretty dense when it came to men, but even Melissa could feel this.

When she opened her eyes, he was looking at her strangely. She felt her heart thud in her chest as he moved closer towards her and kissed her.

Guy eventually lifted his head to check his surroundings and to presumably ensure they weren't being observed. Melissa's breathing quickened. He looked down at her, his gaze roving from her eyes to her mouth.

If she misjudged this, she'd look a complete idiot. But he was giving her a look that was unmistakable and reciprocated. Melissa had no idea how long they sat gazing at each other.

'Do you want to go upstairs?' she eventually asked. The moment she said it, she felt instantly shy.

A man waiting to be served at the bar was eyeing them with amusement. Guy nodded at Melissa, holding her hand as they both stood up and moved towards the door that separated the hotel residents' area from the bar. Safely through the door, Melissa pulled Guy towards her and kissed him again. Guy seemed suddenly unsure what to do with his hands.

'Do I . . .' He swallowed. 'I mean, should I go and get something?'

'Something?' Melissa was confused.

He ran his hand through his hair and gave her a sideways smile. 'I think the gents' loos have a dispenser. I'm afraid I don't have anything. I wasn't expecting . . .' he trailed off.

She nodded, glad he was as nervous as she was.

Guy turned on his heel and headed towards the dividing door, taking change out from his pocket on the way. 'Stay there,' he instructed with a smile from the door. 'Just . . . don't go anywhere.'

Melissa giggled and put her hand up to her mouth. She stood against the wall by the staircase leading towards their rooms. She could feel her heart racing and she bent over, placing her hands on her knees to calm herself.

After a minute or so, the door opened and she stood up and tried her best to look totally calm, trying to hide her nervousness.

But it wasn't Guy. An elderly couple appeared, laughing and talking loudly.

'I'm sure that was Guy Cameron,' the woman said to her husband. 'He rushed past us at about a hundred miles an hour. You never pay attention when it matters,' the woman chastised her husband. They briefly glanced at Melissa as they passed her.

'Goodnight,' they said.

'Goodnight,' Melissa replied, aiming for calmness but stifling a smile. Guy had been rumbled.

Guy burst through the door just as the couple reached the turn on the stairs. Melissa's finger flew to her lips to silence him. He looked at her curiously, slightly out of breath. He smiled at her and patted his pocket, Melissa assumed to indicate a successful mission. He laughed, dipped his head, and looked up at her through his eyelashes.

When the couple had gone, Melissa held out her hand. 'Come on,' she breathed.

Guy took her hand and clutched it as they went upstairs. He unlocked the door to his room and they walked in.

Tension buzzed between them. Melissa stood in the room not knowing quite what to do. Guy closed the door and turned to face her. The atmosphere changed immediately. They looked at each other. Neither said a word. Guy suddenly took charge and walked towards her, leaning in and kissing her, his hands in her hair and then lightly stroking her neck until she thought she would melt.

They kicked their shoes off as they headed towards the bedroom of his suite.

Shedding their clothes quickly, they pressed themselves against each other and fell down on the bed, kissing. Melissa couldn't remember the last time she'd felt this kind of burning desire. She wanted him, desperately wanted him.

She tried hard not to let the moment end too soon, grasping the bed sheets as he made love to her. His hair fell into her eyes and brushed her face. She threaded her fingers through his hair and pulled his face towards her, kissing him and wrapping her legs around him as they moved in time together. Guy lifted his head, his eyes searching for a sign and as she let go of everything only a few seconds before him, she'd never felt so free.

CHAPTER 31

When Melissa woke, it was to find herself naked and alone in Guy's king-size bed. The sun was blazing through the chink in the curtains and directly into her eyes, blinding her. Ordinarily on holiday she'd dive back underneath the duvet, but this wasn't an ordinary kind of holiday. She was in Guy's bed, after having had the kind of sex that had never happened to her in real life.

The only downside was that she was alone. She was also phenomenally hot. She got up, thrusting her hand through the gap in the curtain in order to open the window. The shocking chill that rushed through from outside helped and she peeked out, hiding her naked body behind the curtain, to see bright sunshine on one side of the opposite field and dark rain clouds gathering on the other. It had been so hot for so long that the weather was long overdue a push on the reset button.

She turned back towards the room. Her clothes were nowhere to be seen, having been shed in a frenzy the night before. Melissa deduced they must all be in the sitting room on the other side of the door. Guy's discarded shirt was crumpled next to the bed and Melissa put it on, hoping he wouldn't mind, and opened the door.

Guy was freshly washed and shaved and Melissa thought he

looked far too sexy in his dark shorts and pressed short-sleeve shirt. He looked up and gave her a broad smile. He was on the sofa, hunched over the coffee table, which had a breakfast tray piled high with goodies. But when Melissa appeared, he leaned back and stretched his legs out under the table.

'You're a sight for sore eyes.' He raised his eyebrows at her. 'That shirt looks better on you than it does on me.'

'That's because it barely covers anything.' She looked down at the thigh-skimming shirt.

He smiled. 'True. I left you to sleep in. You looked so peaceful. Do you want coffee?'

Melissa made appreciative noises as she took the proffered cup. Her clothes from the night before were folded and on the arm of the sofa.

'So this is where my clothes were hiding.' Melissa put her coffee down and made a move to reach for them, but Guy intervened and gently took her hand, pulling her down onto him. He held her face in his hands and scanned her eyes.

'Do you have any idea what you're doing to me?' He looked serious. 'Thank you,' he said.

He looked like he wanted to say something else, but when he didn't, Melissa said, 'You'd better not be thanking me for sex.'

His mood changed and he smiled broadly in return, planting a kiss on her mouth. 'No.' He pulled back and smiled. 'Despite it being bloody fantastic.'

'You know, I don't usually do this kind of thing,' she said, threading her fingers through his. 'Sleep with people so soon after meeting them.'

'Me neither,' he agreed. 'But I've been thinking about this. Really, the amount of time we've spent together this past week must be the equivalent of about six dates by now. Just, very close together.'

She kissed him. 'I like that,' she said. 'But I think the idea of taking things slowly and what happened last night are two very different concepts.'

An expression that Melissa couldn't quite work out – worry maybe – passed over Guy's face. 'Yes, I realise that,' he said. 'But given what happened last night, I'm not complaining.'

Melissa giggled, hopped off him and scooped her clothes up, pulling her shorts on and bundling the rest under her arm. 'I'm just going to pop back to my room, shower and put fresh clothes on. I'll be right back.' Melissa noticed the key from Anna's memory box on the table by the tray. 'Any bright ideas about what that might be for?' she asked.

'A few, yes,' he answered mysteriously.

'Go on then.' Melissa leaned against the door frame. 'Enlighten me.'

His eyes met hers, but he didn't speak.

'You're not thinking . . .?' Melissa said.

'Fancy an adventure?' Guy replied.

By the time they dragged themselves away from the comfort of the suite, it was almost midday. Melissa climbed into the passenger seat of Guy's Range Rover as he started the engine. Above them, the skies darkened as the rain clouds passed overhead and Guy glanced down at his shorts with a look of concern.

'I don't think I'm suitably attired for today's weather,' he said, throwing the controls into drive.

As he drove out of the Pheasant and Gun's car park, Guy groaned as the orange light flashed on the dash, indicating low fuel. Ten minutes down the road, he pulled the Range Rover into a petrol station and Melissa stood by him as he refilled. He held her in one arm and nuzzled her freshly washed hair while he held the petrol pump in the other hand. 'You smell great,' he murmured.

'I'll get this.' She indicated the petrol pump. 'You're doing all the driving around, so let me pay for the fuel at least.' He started to protest about the price of filling up a Range Rover, but she waved him away.

The numbers were whizzing around on the machine, but Guy let go of the trigger. 'All done,' he said. 'Thanks.'

She suspected he was fibbing, that the tank could have held much more but that he wanted to spare her the expense.

As Melissa walked across the forecourt to pay, Guy stood by the front of the car and waited for her.

Inside the petrol station, Melissa hummed distractedly as she stood in a five-strong queue. The man in front of her was holding a tabloid newspaper and had it open at a page full of photos. He showed it to his wife.

'Look. It's that bloke you like,' he said. 'Been a bit of a naughty boy.'

Melissa looked inside her wallet and half wondered which celebrity had been up to no good now. She pulled out her credit card and tried to remember how much was already on it that month. Her paper statement would be at home and she had no idea what kind of damage she'd done to the card recently. Along with all the bills that would be draining her bank account, paying for the fuel was a stark reminder that she really did need to reassess her work choices. The redundancy money wasn't finite, sadly. After what had happened last night with Guy, maybe she wasn't about to do a runner back to London just yet, but she could use this time wisely and work out what it was she did want to do. After all the hard work trying to hunt down Lady Veronica, Melissa categorically knew she could strike 'historian' off her list of possible new employment ideas. But this all felt like a fresh start and she was perhaps now, finally, mentally ready to find something she actually did want to do.

'They never can keep it in their pants.' The woman in front of Melissa looked at her husband pointedly, waving the newspaper at him. The husband bristled and Melissa stifled a laugh, glanced up with a vague interest and peered over the couple's shoulders at the paper to see who they were referring to.

'Oh my God,' Melissa cried as she looked at the images. The

couple spun to look at her. Melissa felt the blood drain from her face.

Cold with fear, Melissa backed out of the shop and went into the forecourt, lifting the clear plastic lid that held the newspapers. Hands shaking, she flicked through until she found the page.

'No, no, no,' she repeated as she tried to take in the words that accompanied the images. She stopped breathing as her eyes darted over the pictures. They were of her and Guy. They'd been taken last night in the bar when they'd been kissing. There were five pictures laid out on the page in a six-square grid showing Guy and Melissa in various stages of kissing on the sofa. The fifth image was of them leaving hand in hand through the door that led to the hotel bedrooms. The photo caption was something mucky, leaving no doubt about what was occurring between them.

She struggled not to throw up as she looked at the final image of the six. A cold feeling descended on her. It was a picture of Guy and a blonde woman, smiling, done up to the nines on the red carpet of a TV awards ceremony. His arms were round her waist and she was pouting at the camera. The headline above the article read *No More Mr Nice Guy.*

Melissa staggered back a few paces as she read the words. No, this couldn't be happening. This wasn't real. She looked across at Guy, who was leaning casually against the bonnet of his car. He gave her a wide grin and then, on seeing her expression, his smile faded and he stood up straight.

'What?' he mouthed at her, frowning. 'What's wrong?'

She walked towards him, clutching the newspaper tightly in her shaking hands. She stopped, about five feet from him, and stared at him.

'What's wrong?' he repeated, closing the distance between them.

Unable to speak, Melissa thrust the paper at him. He took it, glanced at the images and then closed his eyes, letting his arm with the newspaper drop.

'I can explain,' he said.

Melissa found her voice. 'Don't bother.'

'Wait. Please wait. It's not like that. Let me explain.'

She backed away slowly as Guy lifted his head and looked at her, panic on his face.

'You're married,' she shouted.

CHAPTER 32

Melissa turned and ran. Guy stalled for a few shocked seconds. He loathed himself. He looked down at the sheet of newspaper and swore loudly at the images that faced him. Why hadn't he just told Melissa from the very start? He moved in her direction, but stopped when he was hailed from behind.

'Oi, mate,' the garage attendant came out of the shop and yelled. 'Where do you think you're going? You've not paid for your fuel or that paper.'

Guy grabbed his wallet and swore when he found no cash inside. He wanted to just thrust the man a fistful of notes and be done with it. But instead he had to suffer the shame of going inside the shop to pay with his credit card. The couple with the newspaper had recognised Melissa from the images and wasted no time in telling the rest of the shop what was going on. The customers and staff had watched Melissa and Guy with much interest and their expressions were now a mix of wide-eyed and mocking as Guy walked past them to pay. One had his phone out and was filming him.

'Piss off,' Guy said. 'Just, piss off.'

'Oh dear, looks like you're in serious trouble now, son,' the man clutching the tabloid said. His wife looked lividly at Guy, who didn't venture a response. He clenched his jaw while he paid, feeling the eyes of the other customers boring into the back of him. He stared directly ahead as he walked past the rows of colourful chocolate bars and bright magazines and wrenched open the door. The petrol station forecourt smell was stale and fume-ridden, but he'd never gulped down so much air so thankfully in his life.

Agonised, he put his hands into his hair as he looked around. The long road stretching past the petrol station was devoid of pedestrians; Melissa had vanished and pursuing her on foot would be futile. Guy leaped into his car, which now felt empty without Melissa, and he drove along the country lane painfully slowly until he eventually spotted her. She was sitting on a bench inside a churchyard, her head in her hands. Guy parked and got out, praying she wouldn't make a run for it.

Melissa heard Guy calling her name. Her head shot up and she stood, wiping tears from her face and dragging smudged mascara onto her fingers. She tried to walk past him on the shingle path, but he reached for her arm.

'Don't,' he said. 'Don't go.'

'Go away.' She pushed his arm aside, angry at how quickly she'd moved from one cheating man to another. Two adulterous men in the space of one week was definitely a new record, a whole new level of humiliation. She didn't know how this kept happening to her.

Guy looked pained and his face was empty of any colour. She thought back to that first kiss on his boat when he'd told her he'd planned a picnic for a first date. Melissa felt sick remembering last night. What the hell had been happening this whole time? He'd been having nothing more than a casual fling with her in Dorset while his wife was elsewhere.

'No.' He stepped forward and barred her way on the narrow path that ran alongside the twelfth-century church.

Melissa stepped onto the grass to get round him, tripping over a tilting gravestone in her desperation to get away. He grabbed her to steady her and she flung his arm away.

'Let me explain and then, if you still hate me, you can leave and you never have to see me again,' he said.

She swung round and looked at his face, wracked with pain, his eyes pleading with her. She stayed silent and clenched her hands to her sides, controlling the urgent need to punch him. Instead she waited for a veiled excuse as to why Guy Cameron thought it was fine to cheat.

'Go on then. Make it fast.' She spat the words out.

He sighed and his shoulders dropped. 'I am married, yes.'

Melissa began walking again.

'But we're getting divorced,' he called after her retreating figure.

She faced him, uncertain if he was telling the truth.

'I signed the divorce papers this week. I don't know how long it will take.' He ploughed on. 'But it will all be over soon. We've not made an official announcement, so this newspaper can't possibly know that my marriage has been over for ages. It's all spiralled horrifically out of control now.' He pushed his hand through his hair and then let his arm drop to his side.

Melissa felt numb and her head was throbbing in the heat of the day.

'I was strongly advised by my publicist not to tell anyone until it was all signed and over and done with. We just wanted a clean break. The last thing we needed was for anyone to say anything to the gossip columns. And look how that turned out. But I should have told you, especially after last night,' Guy continued. 'You and I were getting on so well. Then suddenly we were getting on very well indeed and I knew I could trust you, but I didn't want to ruin things by telling you. And then last night happened, which was . . . Christ, it was amazing. But I like you, Melissa. I do really like you. And there didn't seem a good moment to just blurt out *by the way, I'm in the middle of a really nasty divorce*. Somewhere along the line, between meeting you and last night, if there was an opportunity to tell you, then I missed it. I'm so sorry.' He stopped talking and looked at her. His eyes searched hers. 'Melissa, please say something.'

'I don't know what to say. Are you really getting divorced?'

Guy nodded.

Melissa looked at him, trying to work out whether she could trust him. Could she? She had no idea.She spoke quietly, uncertainly.'Am I just a rebound for you? An easy shag while you figure out what your life looks like as a single man?'

He stepped forward, his face serious. 'No. Absolutely not.'

There was silence between them.

'Am I a rebound for you?' he asked eventually. He looked shocked at the prospect.

'No, of course not. I liked you the first time we met.'

He smiled. 'The first time?'

'Maybe the second time.' Melissa smiled back. 'You should have told me,' she said helplessly.

'I know. I wanted to forget it was all happening. It's been going on so long now that I just want it all over and done with.' He pushed his hand through his hair and then let his arm fall down by his side.

Melissa walked back to the bench. She sat down with a thump. Guy followed and stood awkwardly in front of her. He gestured to the space on the bench and when she didn't object he sat down beside her. Melissa looked at him as her anger faded to disappointment.

'How long have you been married?' Melissa's voice was flat.

'Ten years,' he said.

'What the . . .?' Melissa hadn't been expecting that.

'Maria and I met at university and married when we were twenty-two. We were young. Too young,' he explained.

Melissa exhaled loudly. 'What happened?'

She didn't want to hear any of this, but at the same time she needed to know absolutely everything.

Guy shrugged and his shoulders sagged heavily. 'I'm afraid it's the usual story: we grew apart. After a while, we just completely ran out of conversation. I could see I bored her whenever I talked to her. She didn't enjoy anything about history. Neither did she care about what I did with my days. She didn't do an awful lot with her free time sadly and didn't seem to have too much to talk about when she did find something to do. We were young and so it didn't become apparent until much later that we had almost nothing in common. My career took off straight after university and I suppose she rode my coat-tails a bit. I didn't mind. It took me a long time to see that she loved the little bit of fame I'd garnered and everything that came with that: the lifestyle, the travel.' He laughed bitterly. 'The money.' He kicked at a stone with his shoe. 'Mainly the money, actually.'

'Oh.' Melissa was lost for words.

'I was working so hard, travelling a lot and she'd given up her job so she could travel with me. A couple of years ago, I suggested we try for a baby. She said she wasn't ready. I respected that.' Melissa looked bleakly at the clumps of grass that were growing through the gaps between the paving stones by the bench.

'When we talked about it again, she said she didn't want children at all now. That hit me hard. It wasn't because she didn't like children, or didn't want me to father children with her, apparently; it was that she didn't want to be saddled at home with a child while I got to *live the high life* as she put it. I offered to tone down the travel and she said she didn't want to be stuck at home at all. She asked who the hell would pay for the houses and cars if I turned work assignments down.' He sighed before continuing. 'We went to marriage counselling, but in the end we just fell apart and she walked out on me. Or rather, I thought she had. She was seeing someone else. I've still no idea who. Then she came back to me, a few months later, and begged me to take her back. She said she'd give counselling a better try this time. So we got back together. I was too much of an idiot to see she still didn't want me though. She just wanted the lifestyle she'd been used to.'

Melissa looked up at him. He had a pained expression on his face and she felt sorry for him. Like her, he had been cheated on. She put her hand on his and held it while he stared straight ahead towards the low wall dividing the churchyard from the lane. He summoned a small smile at her touch.

'She made an effort for a while and so did I. I booked the counselling, but she was angry and didn't want to go. We argued about it and she told me she was seeing the man she'd left me for the first time and that they had more in common. So that was that. And now here we are, getting divorced. I've been holding on to the divorce papers for a while. It's not that I can't let go – I swear, I'm ready to never see her again – but every time I looked at them I just felt like a failure. I thought if I signed them, I'd be admitting that most of my adult life had been a disaster. Yes, my books, TV work, lectures were all going well. But that's career. That's not real life, not what you go home to every day. But what I went home to every day had never been good. It wasn't love. For either of us. I was too scared to admit it or too busy to realise it. One of those.'

He paused and then, 'I'm sorry.' He turned to her. 'I *should* have told you. I found myself falling for you and I didn't know where it was going to go, or if you even felt the same, and then yesterday . . . well, yesterday confirmed it. I felt like you'd just blown into my life from out of nowhere. You're incredible, Melissa.' He put his hands on her tear-stained face and looked into her eyes. 'I know we've not known each other very long but I think . . . I think I'm falling in love with you.'

Melissa's mouth dropped open, but no words came out. She was amazed. She had no idea how she felt about him. Not now. Her brain hurt. She was too confused.

'It's a lot to process,' she said, unsure herself if she was referring to the declaration of love or the news about the divorce.

His hands dropped from her face.

'I understand if you can't trust me,' he said. 'But I promise, if you forgive me and give me a chance, I will never lie to you or keep anything from you again.'

Melissa exhaled. She didn't know where to start. 'I think I just need a bit of time,' she said, rising from the bench. She needed space. She couldn't think with him sitting next to her.

He looked up at her as she stood in front of him; the pained expression back on his face. 'Of course. Shall I drive you back to the hotel?' He stood with her and thrust his hands in his pockets. He looked lost.

Melissa shook her head. She couldn't deal with his well-bred manners right now. 'No. I'll walk, thanks. I need some fresh air.'

He nodded and Melissa could feel his gaze on her back as she walked away. Her emotions were all over the place; she felt as if she was Alice falling down the rabbit hole.

She stopped at the end of the lane and looked blankly at a signpost, trying to remember which way they'd driven moments before, but she couldn't click her brain into gear. She stared ahead as she walked the way she thought she'd come, through a canopy of trees that had formed themselves over the years into what she had always called a tree tunnel when she was a child. Melissa concentrated on putting one foot in front of the other, barely aware of other cars whizzing past every few minutes. She had been falling for Guy. She could see that now. But a week ago, there'd been Liam. And although Liam had turned out to be a complete bastard, it had taken her a while to work that out for herself and, even then, it had only been cemented when she'd spotted his name on the suspicious restaurant booking. Like almost everything remotely unsavoury in her life, she'd avoided addressing it until the last possible moment.

Eventually, the turning for the hotel came into view and Melissa stopped at the entrance and sat down on the warm brick steps, thinking, mulling over all the obvious points that had got her to this situation. She was still here, in Dorset, when she should really have been back in London, job hunting. Up until the events of last night, it hadn't been the fledgling romance with Guy keeping her here. Well, maybe in part. But the mystery of what happened all those years ago in Tyneham between Veronica and Albert Standish was troubling her. She and Guy were on the trail of something. But it wasn't only that. It was Veronica herself. The similarities between the unhappy relationship Veronica had been subject to echoed those between Melissa's own mum and dad. Almost, but not completely. Thank God her mum had finally seen sense and left. But it had taken years of unhappiness. And then, in the end, when she hadn't been expecting it, she'd found a kindred spirit in the man who had become Melissa's stepdad.

But the scars of her childhood had meant that Melissa had forever been scared of going into any relationship, feeling that if she ever spoke out of turn, she'd be shouted at the way her dad had instantly shouted at her mum. It had never seemed worth it, the knowledge that an argument must be just around the corner, leading to eventual heartache and pain. She was sure, in part, that's why all her relationships had been destined to fail from the outset. Easy to please Melissa, never speaking out even when Liam had ditched her almost every day on their so-called holiday. She needed to change this kind of pathetic behaviour.

The black clouds moved overhead and raindrops started falling, splattering onto her face and dampening her T-shirt, but it wasn't enough to make Melissa move inside.

Her thoughts turned to Guy. He'd looked distraught at having kept his divorce from her. He'd been lost under the weight of it all. They'd started out whatever this was, not with lies and deceit, but with something else, a quiet inability to share what was really troubling them both deep inside. But did people share that kind of thing when they'd only just met? Melissa had no idea. The short time they'd spent together told Melissa almost everything she needed to know about Guy. Until the frightening revelations in the newspaper, he'd seemed perfect. Almost too perfect. It was probably a bit of a relief that he wasn't. At least she knew now and at least she wasn't *actually* being cheated on. Again.

Guy had poured his heart out to her, telling her about the breakdown of his marriage and then he'd told her he was falling for her. And Melissa's only action had been to walk away, leaving him looking lost. The more she thought about it, the more she wanted to kick herself for having been less than understanding. Avoidance and running away were nasty habits. She couldn't seem to stop herself. She'd avoided sorting her terrible job for an embarrassing amount of time and in the end had just run away from it, without having found another one. And now she was avoiding Guy.

What an idiot she'd been. Guy had confessed his deepest troubles to her and if Melissa didn't want to send this relationship the way all her others had quickly gone, she needed to do the same. She needed to tell him why she felt she was so messed up. She liked him, she really did, and she just knew in her heart he was different to any of the other men she'd been with before. A slow feeling crept in that he was worth taking a risk on.

Melissa's phone vibrated in her pocket. Her best friend Imogen was calling.

'Just checking in. You okay?' Imogen said when Melissa answered.

Melissa smiled. 'I will be. Any second now.' It was the truth.

'Atta girl. Want me to hunt Liam down? Do the world a favour and remove him from the gene pool?'

Melissa couldn't help it, she laughed so hard she snorted. 'No thanks. I like my friends *not* on remand.'

'You never know. I might get parole?' Imogen suggested.

Melissa stood up and started walking towards the road. She was going back to the church. She was going back to find Guy and to apologise for just leaving like that. Right now, she couldn't have given two hoots about Liam.

'I've got these fabulous new ceramic kitchen knives,' Imogen continued. 'They're really sharp. I could cut something of his off really quickly – if you get my drift. He'd never see it coming.'

Melissa scoffed. 'I have to go, Immy. Can we discuss your homicide plans later?'

'Fine, fine, I'm going. But only because you're laughing. Call me if you need me? Okay?'

Melissa agreed before ending the call and pocketing her phone to protect it from the rain. She felt so lucky that she had such a good friend in Immy. And now, maybe, if she didn't mess it up, there was Guy.

As the rain grew heavier, Melissa quickened her pace, but just as she ran towards the road, Guy's Range Rover pulled round the corner and into the hotel car park. Melissa sprang out of the way as Guy slammed on his brakes inches from her.

He got out with a look of concern that he'd almost run her down and opened his mouth to speak. But Melissa got to him first.

'I'm sorry,' she said as she approached him.

He shielded his eyes against the rain. '*You're* sorry? Why are *you* sorry?'

'I shouldn't have just left like that. I'm always running away, avoiding the issue,' she said, wiping raindrops from her eyelashes. 'It's easier than having to face the real problem, easier than having to talk about it.'

He smiled. 'You've used that thinking time well.'

'It was high time I did do some thinking. I'm so sorry for what you're going through,' she replied.

'So am I,' he said. 'But you shouldn't have found out like that, Melissa. Not from a bloody newspaper. Those pictures. Christ. What a mess.'

'Oh God, those photos. It's a good job I don't have a faint heart.' She stepped closer.

'I want to be with you, Melissa. I've let this get so out of hand. You aren't the only one who runs away. I've held off on this divorce for as long as possible. I've put it off long enough. I think I'm only ready now to finally start thinking about it all. I'll fix it. The newspaper. I'll sort it all out. I'm so sorry.'

'It doesn't matter.' She blinked the rain out of her eyes. 'Really it doesn't.'

They stood in the rain and she told him about her parents, about how it had made her feel over the years, about how worried she always felt going into any new relationship that it was all probably going to end in tears regardless.

'And now there's the hunt for Veronica and her situation. What did she go through in that house with her husband? Did she ever find happiness? I need to know that she did.'

Guy opened his mouth to speak, but Melissa hadn't finished pouring her heart out.

'I've never managed to open up to anyone I've ever liked,' she continued, 'and now, because I'm obviously so distant when it comes to anything resembling a human emotion, I just seem to push people away, instead of addressing the issue, scared of it ending in a blazing row. So it festers and then ends anyway. I don't want to do that to you,' she confessed. 'I really don't. I don't want to push you away if there's an issue, simply because it's easier than having a discussion.'

She looked up at him, expecting him to look shocked and worried as to what he'd got himself into. But he looked at her in a way no man had ever looked at her before. She had no idea what the look was or what it meant, but he nodded.

He pulled her towards him. 'Thank you,' he whispered.

'What for?'

'For telling me that.' He pushed her rain-soaked hair back from her face. They looked at each other through the rain and as a taxi pulled up, a couple ran out and made a mad dash towards the hotel. Guy and Melissa ignored them, remaining rooted to the spot.

There was nowhere else she wanted to be right now but the

car park, soaked to the skin in the relentless rain, with him. He kissed her and as his arms wrapped around her waist she felt all the weight and the agony of the past few hours lift from her shoulders and disappear into the atmosphere. Without realising how, the pair of them had inched gently towards his car. Their bodies were pressed together as they kissed and she felt a deep stirring within her.

It was as if he'd realised it was happening to him too and he looked at her, his eyes heavy, his look longing. Without speaking, they held hands and made their way into the hotel and up to his room. They peeled their wet clothes from each other and left them scattered on the floor of his suite. With the rain lashing at the windows, he made love to her so differently to the night before. She couldn't explain how, but it felt more honest, as if the two of them really knew each other now. They held on to each other for a long time afterwards and as she trailed her fingers along his smooth back, they gently drifted off to sleep.

A short while later, Guy's stirrings next to her woke Melissa. The duvet was in a tangle around them.

'Your hair's gone wavy,' he said as he gently pulled a lock of her hair and watched it spring back.

'It's the rain,' she groaned.

'There is something about kissing in the rain that will tend to lead to this kind of thing.' He gestured towards the crumpled bed sheets before leaning over and kissing her. He pulled back and looked into her eyes. 'Thank you for allowing me to explain.'

Melissa had no time to reply. Guy's phone vibrated on the bedside table and he grabbed it. He made a face and stabbed at it, rejecting the call.

'My publicist,' he said. 'Probably giving me her damage-limitation report.'

'It's okay,' Melissa said. 'You should probably speak to her.'

'I know,' Guy nodded. 'Just not at this moment.'

*

Melissa returned from her room where she'd put on dry clothes just as Guy finished dressing. He picked up his wet trousers to shake them out and hang them on the back of the chair, but something fell out of the pocket and onto the carpet. It was the brass key from Anna's memory box. He picked it up and held it in his hand. In the other hand, his phone vibrated again. This time it was a text message. He read for a few seconds and then paraphrased.

'It's my assistant, Philippa. She's asking me if I've seen the papers today.' Guy coughed nervously. 'Anyway, she also says she's got copies of both Freddie and Albert's birth certificates. She's sending copies by email when she's back in the office. She said it was quite easy to find Freddie when she realised that wasn't his real name and that it was Albert's certificate that helped her.'

'What does *that* mean?' Melissa asked.

'I have absolutely no idea whatsoever. She gets into the spirit of a mystery though, doesn't she? We'll have to wait for the email, but you were right about Freddie not being his real name.'

'I knew it.'

Guy walked over to the window and looked out at the incessant rain. 'I think it's clearing.'

Melissa wasn't so sure.

He looked down thoughtfully at the key. 'I think we should head back to Tyneham.'

Melissa looked from Guy's face to the key and then back again as she realised what he had in mind.

'Oh no.' Melissa covered her eyes. 'You can't be serious.'

He nodded, raising an eyebrow. 'How do you feel about a spot of breaking and entering?'

CHAPTER 33

Tyneham was almost deserted as the rain fell heavily. Only a few vehicles were left in the car park and as Guy and Melissa arrived, the last few tourists were making a dash back towards their cars. The inclement weather had put paid to any more visitors today.

Guy rummaged in the boot for his large golfing umbrella and pulled it out with him, dashing round to cover both he and Melissa as she climbed out of the car. The rain lashed down around them at an almost horizontal angle and they were quickly getting soaked through.

'This is biblical,' Guy muttered.

'We're just going to have to run for it,' Melissa replied. 'Have you got the key?'

Guy tapped his pocket. 'Come on then.' He held the umbrella over them with one hand and Melissa's hand in his other as they broke into a run.

By the time they arrived at the front door of Tyneham House, they were drenched. The umbrella had flipped inside out in the strong wind that was whipping up from the coast and Guy had been forced to fight it closed while they ran the remainder of the avenue.

In the sanctuary of the large, brick and wood porch, they stood and caught their breath. Melissa wrung her hair out, thick strands of which had clung to her face and neck. She grabbed her band from her wrist and put her hair up into a high ponytail, wringing it out for a second time. She looked at Guy and laughed while she continued to catch her breath. He was shaking the water out of his own hair like a dog.

Melissa leaned against the gothic-arched porch and the stones moved, forcing her to leap away from it and turn to look at the failing structure.

'How is this place still standing?' she asked. In a way, she was glad it was chucking it down so she'd been forced under cover. It meant there had been no time to stand in the driveway and admire the building. If there had been any thinking time, she wasn't so sure she'd be doing this now. There was something still so desperately sad about Tyneham House. Melissa felt a strange mix of something pushing her far away from it, while at the same time she was also curiously drawn towards it. 'Remind me why we're doing this?' she asked.

Guy put his head to one side. 'We don't have to, you know. You asked me where my sense of adventure was. Well, here it is.' He brandished the key. 'Do you want to do the honours?'

'No,' she said, still making the same face. But she reached over and took the key gingerly. 'Here goes.'

There were two keyholes in the large, dark wood front door. One looked as if it might be original and the kind of key that would fit it was not like the one Melissa was holding. She imagined the kind of key that might fit that keyhole would be a ten-inch long wrought iron that would be so oversized that even she wouldn't be able to lose it. The second keyhole, slightly further down the door, was a more modern addition, perhaps Victorian or Edwardian.

As Melissa slipped the key into the hole, she was amazed that it fitted. It felt a little loose, but it slipped in easily. She tried to turn it, but it wouldn't budge more than a millimetre or two. She tried the other direction, but still no joy.

'Oh,' she said. She'd been expecting to feel relieved, but was actually disappointed.

Guy watched. 'Can I try?' he asked.

Melissa moved aside as Guy tried to turn the key. He swore when he realised it wasn't going to move.

'It's not the right key,' Melissa said.

Guy stepped back, taking the key out of the lock with one hand and running his other hand through his wet hair. He sighed and looked out of the porch as the rain continued to fall around them. 'Well, that's that then,' he murmured.

'I guess so,' Melissa agreed.

Neither of them moved for a few minutes. Melissa was waiting for the rain to slow before they headed off and she assumed Guy was doing the same.

But he stood up straight. 'It may not be the end of the adventure.'

'No?' Melissa was wary.

'There's a loose window panel further round the house.' Guy raised an eyebrow suggesting mischief.

'You really want to break in?' Melissa asked. This was a side to Guy that she hadn't seen. She liked it.

'I do now, yes. We're here, aren't we? We aren't going to do any damage. Just have a little look.' He dangled the key in front of her. 'And see if this opens anything . . . interesting.'

Melissa scoffed. 'It probably opens an old silver cabinet or a larder where they kept the tea hidden from the servants back when it cost a million pounds a spoonful.'

Guy laughed, then pulled out his phone. 'Damn,' he said. 'I forgot there was no signal down here. I was going to check to see if Philippa had emailed. See what Freddie's birthdate is so we can track him down. We'll just have to look later. That will be something fun to do while we dry out at the hotel.'

Melissa wasn't sure Guy's idea of fun and hers were completely the same.

He put his phone away, looked at her and smiled. 'So, are we doing this then?'

Melissa thought for a moment and then groaned. 'Oh God, all right then.'

Guy propped his umbrella into the recess of the porch and looked around in case they were spotted. But there were very few tourists remaining in the village and the guides were presumably all busy in the church and the school, staying dry.

They reached the side of the house, where Guy remembered the loose panel had been.

'What are you looking out for?' Melissa asked. 'Afraid of getting caught?'

'Of course.' Guy laughed. 'However,' he said, locating the panel board in question, 'as of this morning, my public reputation is now that of a total bad boy so why not add breaking in to Ministry of Defence property to my charge sheet?'

Melissa laughed nervously. What kind of sentence did breaking in to MOD property carry? She wasn't keen on the idea of going to prison.

Guy pulled up the 'Danger, Keep Out' board. The nails were missing from the bottom left-hand corner and those that remained were loose, so the board had some give in it when Guy lifted it up.

'I'll hold it while you climb through first,' he said.

Melissa peered inside. It was pitch-black. All the other boards were doing their job of keeping the window areas tightly shut. The glass was missing, however, and the interior stank of damp. She took her phone out of her pocket and put the torch function on, shining it inside, but she had no time to assess before climbing in.

'I don't mean to hurry you, but this is not easy to hold up.' Guy's voice was strained.

Melissa shoved one end of her phone between her teeth, leaving the torch-end shining into the house as she climbed in. Small shards of glass stuck up on the window pane and she avoided them as best as she could, kicking one dangerously sharp-looking piece out of the pane altogether to avoid either of them slicing their hands.

She leapt down on to the floor and felt the crunch of broken glass underneath her feet where the window had given in some time ago. The board was heavy, but Melissa pushed it out from the inside as hard as she could so that Guy could climb in.

When both were inside Tyneham House, they held their phones out, shining the torchlights around the room. It was a pathetic attempt to brighten a large, pitch-black space. Melissa looked down at the broken glass and wished she wasn't wearing sandals now. Her toes were dangerously close to the shards, where almost all the windows had given in over time.

'Be careful.' Guy shone his phone torch down.

'The wood must have warped in the panes, smashing the glass out,' Melissa said.

She was expecting a repeat of the devastation of the beach hut but reminded herself that kids with spray cans were unlikely to have been able to get into the village over the years, let alone the house. The village had only just been reopened and before that it was under heavy guard to protect citizens from being shelled on the gunnery ranges. She still kept an eye on the floor for needles as she walked. Just in case.

Melissa tried to remember the photographic boards in the church – one of which had shown the layout of the house. But it was hard to make sense of her surroundings in the dark. The room they were in was empty of furniture, giving no hint of what its purpose had once been. 'Where are we?' she asked.

'It looks like a sitting room or a dining room perhaps? The wood panelling is exquisite,' Guy replied. He started to move off to take a closer look, then turned back to take Melissa's hand. 'We don't want to lose each other in this place,' he said.

Every move they made echoed around the empty room. The wooden floor looked relatively intact and as she shone her torch upward Melissa was surprised to see the ornate plasterwork ceiling still held the ceiling roses and intricate details. Bits had crumbled to the floor over the years, but the majority was intact. She looked up at it until her neck started to hurt.

Guy whistled. 'That's beautiful.' He squeezed her hand.

'Let's see what else there is,' she said.

The door that led off to the entrance hall was wide open and they cast their lights around the hallway. Like the first room they'd been in, the floor was thick with dust. Melissa smoothed some away with her shoe to expose large black and white tiles. She looked up to see that Guy had moved a short distance away, shining light onto the large fireplace. Melissa could imagine a huge mirror hanging above the stone surround, but now there was nothing but flaking paint on the walls. The fire and grate had survived decades of abandonment. Above her, in the centre of the hallway, an ornate chandelier was heavy with cobwebs. Melissa shuddered. There was something about this house that Melissa couldn't quite put her finger on.

The stairs at the end looked more inviting, holding promises of treasures upstairs. Melissa touched the bannisters. Underneath the dust was smooth mahogany. The feeling of desolation struck her again. She thought of the elusive Veronica. *Where did you go?* Veronica would have touched this as she moved on the stairs. So would her husband – Melissa wasn't so keen on that thought.

Behind them, the door to the first room creaked as it slowly started to close, stopping just shy of the door catch. A chill went through Melissa and her eyes widened. Guy spun round from his position by the fireplace to look.

'It's just the wind,' Guy broke the silence. 'It's blowing a gale out there.'

'Yeah, I know,' Melissa said, unconvinced.

They climbed the stairs, which were sturdier than Melissa had thought they were going to be, and went to look in some of the upstairs rooms. Most of the rooms housed the same panelling as those downstairs. Where once there had probably been rugs and carpets, there were now only the exposed floorboards. Doors that were sticking, Guy shouldered open, taking care not to break them off the hinges. But there was nothing exciting in any of the bedrooms.

Melissa fell in love with an en suite bathroom that housed a claw-footed cast-iron bath. The thin marble tiles that lined the floor and walls made the room feel even colder than the rest of the house and were in stark contrast to the dark mahogany that lined almost every other room.

The middle floor held no other riches and at the end of the long corridor a small door led to the servants' staircase.

'I *still* haven't asked Gran if she lived in or if she travelled in daily,' Guy said.

'Shall we go up?' Melissa looked up the stairs.

Guy might have nodded, but in the darkness Melissa could barely see.

'I take it that's a yes?' Melissa laughed as he started up the stairs.

When they reached the top of the stairs and entered the servants' landing, fragments of light were cast onto the corridor from some of the open doors where the MOD hadn't bothered to place window boards this high up. The corridor was narrow as they reached the top and ran through the middle of the house, with rooms shooting off either side.

Even with the marginal daylight, they kept their torches on. Where there should have been summer sun filtering through the windows at this time of day, there was only black cloud and the relentless clattering of rain on the gabled roof outside. The initial excitement had worn off and now all Melissa felt was cold. She and Guy wandered in and out of rooms, finding nothing of interest until they came to the room on the far end of the corridor. With a bit of effort, Guy shouldered it open and said 'Wow' as the door banged into the wall behind it.

'This must be the luggage room,' he said. Stacks of leather suitcases, old dressmakers' dummies, a gramophone, school travelling trunks and various other detritus of days gone by met their eyes. In the corner, various cricketing paraphernalia including kneepads and moth-eaten jumpers were discarded on the floor. Guy picked up one of the cricketing jumpers and as he did so they both jumped as a door slammed downstairs.

CHAPTER 34

Melissa said a very unladylike word.

'It's still the wind,' Guy said, replacing the dusty kneepads. But Melissa could see the unflappable Guy Cameron was now slightly on edge.

'Okay.' Melissa wasn't at all sure it was the wind. 'I wonder if we should leave?'

Guy reached for her hand. 'Getting spooked?'

'A little bit.'

'Me too.'

'Don't say that. I'm relying on you to be the strong one.'

Guy laughed. 'Why did I suggest we do this? Let's just peer around the kitchen and then make ourselves scarce. I doubt there's much more to see, but the old Victorian range cooker will probably be there still.'

Melissa was beyond caring about range cookers. She was starting to get a bit worried. A strange and uncomfortable feeling had been creeping on her since the door had first creaked and now with the slamming downstairs she just wanted to go.

They went back downstairs, entering the darkness again and navigating their way across the hallway and past the fireplace by their torchlight. They peered inside another large but long room.

'If the first room was the sitting room, then this was the dining room, judging by the length of it,' Guy suggested.

Melissa didn't care. As Guy peered into the remaining downstairs rooms, shining his torch slowly along the spaces from side to side, Melissa turned and kept an eye behind her.

'Let's just check out this range cooker and then go, shall we?' she asked.

'Sure,' he said, turning his phone torch on to her. She blinked in the face of the light. 'Sorry.' He instantly lowered the torchlight. 'This way, I think.' He gestured towards the far end of the house and Melissa reluctantly followed behind him, shining her torch and glancing round frantically.

The kitchen left a lot to the imagination. Where once there had probably stood a Victorian cooker range, there was now a 1930s Aga. Guy looked disappointed.

'They were obviously a modern bunch. The Standishes, I mean, to have that,' Guy said.

A few copper pans were hanging on a rack but, far from gleaming and shiny, they were tarnished and streaked with dark brown damp as if they'd been dipped in wet clay. Melissa shone her phone light around some of the kitchen dresser units and free-standing cupboards, which had obviously been of no use to anyone since the requisition, having been left behind. She paused to look at an old Victorian wooden laundry rack on a rope system, wound round a double-ended hook on the wall. She wondered at something so old that had survived the generations, survived requisition and was still here over a hundred years later, left intact amongst the devastation.

Guy wrestled with the Aga doors, trying to look inside. Melissa couldn't work out why and so she left him to it. She moved across the large kitchen space, crossing the floor around the old scrubbed pine table. She imagined some poor kitchen maid, peeling and chopping and then clearing away, ready for the servants to have their meal.

Melissa shone her phone onto a thick wooden door and gave the round metal handle a turn. Nothing. She moved away and then looked back at it. So far it was the only door that had either not been left wide open or that wouldn't open with a bit of brute force. Melissa tugged at the round knob again, twisting it in both directions.

Guy joined her. 'Shall I give it a go?' Shouldering it was no use. The door, if it moved, would open towards them, not the other way. He handed Melissa his phone, put one foot on the door frame and then yanked hard. Still nothing. 'Curious,' he said. 'I wonder what's in there.'

'Probably nothing after all this time. Or maybe,' she said, feeling mischievous, 'it's where they kept the family jewels. And they've been hiding in this cupboard for decades waiting for TV historian Guy Cameron and his now, rather unwilling, sidekick Melissa Turner to discover them and reveal their whereabouts.'

Guy rubbed his hand across his chin, thinking. Melissa was holding one phone in each hand, shining light on the door to show the doorknob and keyhole underneath it. She watched him thoughtfully. Suddenly, Guy put his hand into his pocket and pulled out Anna's key. He slipped it into the door. It fit. He looked at her; his eyes wide. 'Let's see if it turns.'

Slowly, he started to turn the key in the lock. It stuck at first. But with a bit of gentle jiggling into place and a strong hand, it started to turn. Melissa realised she was holding her breath, shining both torches on to the lock as she watched Guy twist it firmly and slowly. The snap of the lock clicking out of place and recessing into the door shocked her. Melissa's mouth dropped open as she exhaled loudly and Guy turned and looked at her again.

'Bloody hell,' he said. 'I wasn't expecting that to work.'

Melissa didn't reply. Her eyes were on the door, which for some unknown reason she was expecting to fly open all by itself.

'Right,' she said with a false tone of bravery. 'Let's open this

269

then.' Melissa handed Guy's phone back to him, stepped forward and turned the handle and when it didn't instantly move she tugged at it with all her might. It creaked as it opened and she was instantly reminded of all the horror movies Liam had forced her to watch, even though he knew she hated them. When a door creaks like that, you don't look inside. You close it and run away.

But it was only darkness that met her on the other side. They shone both their torches inside and were surprised to see a brick wall about six feet away. But directly in front of them, stretching down into darkness, was a wooden staircase.

'Why does my grandmother have a key to Tyneham House's cellar?' Guy murmured.

The last thing Melissa wanted to do was go down there, even with two torches and Guy for company. It just felt like a terrible idea. Guy moved past her and peered down as far as he could see. He pushed at the first wooden step with his foot. It creaked horribly.

'Seems safe enough.' He shrugged. 'Shall we give it a go?'

'Are you kidding? Did you hear that creak? Don't you think we should tell someone where we are before we do that?' Melissa's voice was high. 'It seems a bit clichéd that we both go down there.'

Guy looked past her and into the abyss. 'There's no phone signal, remember. Perhaps I'll just go down, have a quick look and then we'll leave. My grandmother has been keeping the key to this room in her memory box for over seventy years. I just want to see what's so important down there. I need to satisfy curiosity now – while we're here. I'm certainly not coming back again.'

He put his foot on the step and winced as it creaked again. He withdrew his foot and sighed. 'Perhaps not.' He kicked at the door frame and a splinter of rotten wood came off. 'Why the hell does she have this key?'

Melissa groaned. Guy was right. This probably *was* the only chance they'd get to find out what was so important about this cellar. She suggested something she wasn't at all comfortable with. 'I'll go. I'm lighter.'

'Wait a minute, I don't think . . .' Guy interjected.

'Don't panic. I'll be careful.' Melissa gingerly placed one foot on the top step. It creaked, but not as much as it had when Guy's foot had been on it. 'See? Nothing to worry about,' she said with a brightness she didn't feel. She trod as lightly and as slowly as she could down two more steps.

'Stop,' Guy said as Melissa continued. 'This is a terrible idea.'

'Stay there,' Melissa called back. 'I'll be fine.'

The creaking continued with each step, but Melissa gave herself a stern talking-to. There was no reason to panic. Old buildings always creaked. She just needed to keep hold tightly of the bannisters with her free hand.

She stopped and lifted her torchlight up from the wooden stairs and down into the room below. She could just about make out the cellar's nearest brick walls but couldn't yet see the furthest one. She could see the flagstone floor beneath her though and knowing she was within reach of the floor gave her some small comfort. Not long now. But as Melissa stepped onto the next step an almighty crunch sounded underneath her. Wood splintered and her foot went through the stairs, her body juddered into the spindly bannister and the rotten staircase gave way underneath her, detaching entirely and hurtling towards the ground. As she hit the floor and crumpled into a heap, she could hear Guy shouting her name. But then the sound became quieter, further away, and her eyes slowly closed.

There was something cold against her face. Melissa blinked slowly and pushed the palm of her hand onto the cold flagstone floor, trying to lift herself up. Why was she lying on the floor? Her legs were higher than the rest of her body. But she had no idea why. Where the hell was she?

She put her hand to her head and felt blood in her hair. She was in darkness and her eyes weren't adjusting. The ringing in her ears started to clear and she could hear someone shouting at her. Had she been in some kind of explosion?

Melissa dragged herself forward, released her legs from underneath something heavy and sat up. She tried to focus on the darkness around her. Her eyelids felt heavy and she coughed, her dry mouth producing a dust-filled splutter. Melissa lifted her head and looked up. A small light shone some way above her from the direction of the shouting and when the ringing in her head had started to dissipate, the shouting from above became clear.

'Guy?'

'Oh thank God. Thank God. I thought you were dead. Are you hurt? Are you bleeding? Have you broken anything? Talk to me.' He was laying on his front on the kitchen floor above, his head, shoulders, and arms visible as he shone his phone torch down on to Melissa. 'Jesus Christ,' he said as the faint light scanned across her.

Melissa slowly glanced around and suddenly realised what had happened. Large shards of wood had scattered around the room where the upper stairs had splintered. To one side, the entire bottom half of the staircase was intact, but on its side. Melissa was sitting in the middle of the debris.

'I'm okay,' Melissa said and then groaned as she tried to move. A searing pain spread across her chest. 'I think I've broken some ribs.'

'Can you move? How the hell am I going to get you out?' Guy looked at the distance between them and then shone his torch around the kitchen. 'I'm going to get one of the volunteers,' he said.

'No!' Melissa called back. 'I'm fine. If you go, you'll have to tell them what we've been doing.' She coughed and dust scratched the inside of her throat. 'Is there anything you can use or throw down to me?'

Guy disappeared from view. Above her, there was the sound of something heavy being dragged.

'Are you able to move out of the way?' he shouted. 'I'm going to have to lower one of these kitchen sideboards down. That will give us some height for me to drop down, lift you up and out hopefully.'

'You can't do that,' Melissa cried.

'Why not?'

'You'll damage it.'

Guy's head appeared at the cellar entrance above. He indicated the collapsed staircase. 'I think we're well beyond that at this point, don't you? I need you completely clear.' His voice was strained and Melissa thought he sounded angry.

She moved slowly out of the way through a mix of shuffling and crawling, one hand clamped to her ribs. She backed into the cold stone wall and called up that she was out of the way.

The dragging continued above as Guy hauled the sideboard across the floor. Melissa put her head back on the wall and then winced in pain. She hunched forward instead and waited. She thanked God silently that both she and Guy hadn't gone down the stairs. How long would they have been down here before anyone had found them? Would anyone have ever found them?

The sideboard became wedged at the entrance to the cellar and Guy barged it through. Shards of wood splintered off the edges of the sideboard and the door frame as he rammed the unit through the door. He angled the cabinet on to its side and tilted it so it was upside down. Above her, Melissa could hear him swearing. He took the sideboard legs in his hands and gripped them tightly.

'This is phenomenally heavy.' His voice shook as he spoke. He slowly levered it off the edge, leaning back and straining to hold it. He only managed to lower it a few feet before his grip failed and the unit slipped entirely from his fingers and crashed onto the cellar floor. Guy laid down on his front and looked into the cellar, shining his phone torch onto the sideboard. He gave an exultant, 'Yes.' The unit, while at an awkward angle and now missing a great chunk, had mostly still held together. 'Are you all right?' Guy called to Melissa as he lowered himself down through the hole. With his body dangling, he let go of the edge and landed on his feet on the upturned furniture.

Melissa was sat in the corner. He took his phone out of his back pocket and shone it on her face.

'As fine as can be expected,' she replied as she blinked in the light.

'Oh shit,' he said, kneeling down and looking at her. 'You're incredibly pale.'

'I'm okay,' she said. 'I think it's just the shock of it all. And I think I've lost my phone.'

Guy put his forehead on Melissa's and his hand in her hair. 'The phone is the least of all our worries. Thank God, you're okay,' he said. 'I thought you might be dead. You didn't answer me at first.' He pulled his hand out of her hair and looked at his wet fingertips with horror. 'Melissa, you're bleeding!'

'It's not much,' she said, touching the place where Guy's hands had just been. It was damp with blood. 'I didn't land on my head. I think I just knocked it on the floor or the stairs at some point.'

'We need to get you to hospital. Come on. Gently does it.' Guy stood up and lifted Melissa, placing his arm around her waist. 'Can you stand while I turn that sideboard round? It'll make it higher for me to climb up and then pull you through.'

Melissa nodded. She wondered how her ribs were going to withstand all that. She held the torch for him while he kicked bits of staircase out the way and turned the furniture upright.

The torch was casting a faint light into the far corner of the room. Melissa squinted to see what was over there, but Guy's body was casting a shadow as he moved.

'It might be best if I lift you up and then I'll boost you gently through.'

But Melissa wasn't listening. 'What's all that?' She pointed to the far corner and held the torch out where she could see lumps of large furniture had been stacked.

Guy turned his head and shrugged dismissively. 'I don't know and I honestly don't care. Up we go.'

'Wait a second,' Melissa said, touching her sore ribs as she walked towards the corner. 'Maybe it's treasure,' Melissa laughed and then winced at the resulting pain.

The torch threw a spotlight into the corner of the room. Stacked up against the wall were piles of old leather travelling trunks and half-height wine racks. The racks weren't lined up as they would be in an ordinary fashion if they had held wine but were instead stacked haphazardly at odd angles, as if someone had thrown them there in a hurry.

Melissa crouched down, wincing at the pain in her ribs, and peered through the bottle-shaped holes in the racks. There was something at the back, but she couldn't tell what it was in the dim light and her arm wasn't long enough to reach through to investigate. It was a pile of frayed fabric, from what she could see, but it gave no other clue as to what its purpose might be and what it was doing there.

'Is it covering something?' Guy crouched down to join her and squinted through the racks.

'I'm not sure.' Melissa coughed as dust flew up from the racks as she withdrew her hand. The cough reverberated through her pained ribs and she cried out.

'Right. Enough of this,' Guy sounded exasperated. 'We're going.'

'Not yet,' Melissa said. 'Help me move these racks. I think there *is* something else back there.'

CHAPTER 35

Tyneham, December 1943

The village was eerily quiet and the dull, winter light was fading. In the distance Freddie could see outlines of boxes and crates piled up outside individual homes, ready for the movers that had been hired by the army to ensure a smooth and seamless evacuation.

Freddie stood at the end of the tree-lined drive that divided the grounds of the estate from the threshold of the village. His legs had brought him this far, but suddenly he felt unable to move. He put his head in his hands and sat on a tree stump as the winter evening darkness descended. He wanted this feeling to end. He was in a nightmare. He must be. This couldn't be real. Veronica had broken his heart once before and it was happening again now. But reluctance to leave engulfed him.

Would he ever see Veronica again? He doubted it and the thought crushed him. He would never stop loving her. But tomorrow she was running from Bertie and if she was clever enough neither he nor his brother would be able to find her. She would be gone from him forever. It was clear she neither wanted nor needed him. And he couldn't fight such a vehement dismissal. Darkness encircled his heart. He'd lost her. He knew it.

But something stopped him from moving. The moment he

got up and continued his journey into the village, it would all be over. He didn't know what to do. He couldn't sit here all night and he couldn't walk all the way to the train station in the blackout. It was miles. He was freezing. His mind was a whir and he couldn't think straight.

He pulled his coat around him and looked down at his suitcase. He'd left the few items he'd come all this way to collect. Sod the cricket bat. He'd thought it was his possessions he'd wanted, but it was always the thought of seeing Veronica that had been the driving force of his visit.

In the distance, he watched the moon glinting off the duck pond and failed to force his mind on to other things. He was delaying having to move, having to make a decision, and he knew it. The moment he got up, it would be the end. He would never again see the woman he loved and his family home was being requisitioned tomorrow. Freddie had never felt so alone.

He closed his eyes and tried to pretend this wasn't happening. The longer he sat, the colder he got. He looked at his watch. He had no idea how long he'd been there. Half an hour? An hour?

He felt his body creak as he stood up. He gave one final glance back at the house. It was in blackout and he could just make out its pale walls in the faint moonlight. He patted his pocket, then pulled his cigarette case out and fumbled with it, his cold fingers not quite working properly. He could see steam from his breath in the chill air as he pushed a cigarette in between his lips. He reached for his silver lighter, but it wasn't in its usual place. He tried his inside pocket on the other side, but it wasn't there either. His trouser pockets held only his wallet. What the hell had he done with his lighter? Had he left it behind in the house? It was another thing to mourn.

He sighed, angry with himself for having been so careless. It was the last remaining vestige of his parents. He had nothing else of them, and he'd mislaid it. He kicked at the tree stump and then regretted it. The pain seared like a blade through his frozen foot. He closed his eyes and resigned himself. As much as he despised the idea of returning to the manor, he was going to have to go back for it.

But as he turned towards Tyneham House, he knew without doubt that the lighter was not the real reason he was returning. Nothing Veronica had said had made any sense. She'd told him she didn't want him if he only wanted to rescue her. She'd told him she'd always loved him and that if only she hadn't listened to Bertie back then she'd never have left him. They'd made love. They'd promised to love each other forever. And now she'd rejected him. Cruelly and quickly. She'd been eager for him to leave.

Freddie's head spun as he relived their final conversation. He'd been so stupid. Just like last time, he'd let her go far too easily. He hadn't fought for her at all. He wouldn't lose her again. Not this time. He quickened his pace until he was running up the driveway. He clutched his chest as he ran; his wound aching in the cold.

Damn the consequences. Damn Bertie to hell. He would fight for her this time. If need be, he would fight Bertie for her. He would confront his brother about his behaviour and he would save the woman he loved from the monster she had married.

There was one thing Freddie was certain of as he approached the front door and grabbed at the handle: he would leave with Veronica. Even if it killed him.

CHAPTER 36

Dorset, July 2018

Despite the freezing-cold temperature in the cellar, Guy was breaking a sweat. He'd just lugged five seriously heavy and over-sized wine racks out of the corner of the room and piled them up against the adjacent wall.

Melissa held the torch while he worked. She'd offered to help and he'd tried hard not to laugh. It was going to be difficult enough to get her out of the cellar without her doing more damage to herself.

He was only moving this lot to placate her. He didn't know why his grandmother had been holding on to the cellar key for the past seventy-odd years and right now, with a collapsed stair-case behind him and an injured woman in front of him, he simply couldn't care less. The reality of having broken into an MOD-protected house that was strictly off limits was unnerving him.

'My career will be shot to bits if people find out about all of this.' He gestured at the staircase.

'Don't be silly,' Melissa laughed and then clutched her ribs. 'Renegade bad-boy TV historian Guy Cameron breaks into a manor house, destroys half of it and then rescues the girl from the wreckage. Your career will go *stellar*.'

Guy rested as he looked towards the sixth and final wine rack. 'I'm glad you can see the ray of sunshine amongst it all.' He smiled. 'But I think we should take a second to remember exactly who it was who crashed through the staircase, shall we?'

'Have some sympathy.' Melissa's shoulders shook with laughter. 'I think I've actually broken some ribs.'

'Well, we'd be halfway to the hospital by now if you weren't making me do this.' He grimaced. 'Tell me,' he said, gripping the edges of the final rack but looking directly at her, 'does the dangerously attractive TV historian get the girl?'

'Perhaps.' He heard the smile in her voice.

'That's good enough for me.' Guy heaved the last rack out the way. 'Say what you like about the Industrial Revolution, but they built things to last back then. They're ridiculously heavy.' He dusted his hands off on his shorts.

He looked at Melissa, who was peering towards the travelling trunks as she inched forwards slowly. His heart lurched. He didn't know what he'd have done if she'd been seriously injured, or dead. It didn't bear thinking about.

'I'm glad you're okay,' he said. He thought anything else would sound trite.

'So am I,' Melissa teased.

He reached towards the trunks and started to move them one by one. There were only four, so it wasn't as arduous as the wine rack task. They weren't pushed up against the wall, but just a couple of feet shy of it. Behind the final trunk something had been wedged in and was covered in a frayed fabric.

Guy hauled the last trunk further out so they could both see what was behind it. He pulled at a bit of the fabric, but it was wrapped around whatever it was covering. He pulled again, a bit harder, loosening it, and it came away in his hands.

He heard Melissa's loud gasp before he fully registered what he was looking at.

Then it became apparent what the shape in front of him was.

Guy swore loudly and sprang back, knocking into one of the wine racks.

Melissa was standing still, her hand had flown to her mouth and her eyes were wide.

'Oh my God. That isn't what I think it is?' she cried from behind her hand.

Guy didn't instantly reply. He swallowed and then said, 'I think so, yes.'

'It's not real . . . is it?'

There was silence and then, 'I think it might be, actually.'

Positioned on the floor at an awkward angle was a skeleton.

CHAPTER 37

Tyneham, December 1943

It was Veronica's only consolation that Freddie had left. He would be safe and Bertie could never hurt him now.

Bertie entered his study, propped the gun by the door and laid his hand hard on Veronica's shoulder. 'It's for the best,' he said.

At his touch, Veronica sprang back. She wiped the tears from her eyes and watched him carefully. Bertie reached out and touched her face, wiping fresh tears away with his fingers. She recoiled again. She wanted to throw up. Her head was dizzy and she leaned against his desk to steady herself.

Bertie threw her an angry look and walked towards his decanter, poured a large whisky and drank it in one go. He refilled his glass.

'Not going to ask me how many of these I've already had?' he asked. 'Not interested anymore?'

When it was clear his question wasn't rhetorical, Veronica gritted her teeth and enquired how many.

'A lot. But not nearly enough, darling. Not nearly enough.'

He looked her up and down as he drank, his eyes rested on her chest and his gaze drifted down her body slowly as he leaned against the empty bookshelves. He looked nonchalant, as if he hadn't a care in the world. *But then, he didn't, did he, not really,*

Veronica thought. *Not now anyway.* Bertie always got his own way in the end.

'May I have one of those?' Veronica asked. She needed something to steady her nerves. She wanted to curl up on the floor and cry. Maybe Bertie had been right all along. Maybe drinking to oblivion did hold all the answers.

Bertie smiled a slow, curious smile and poured Veronica a whisky. He held it out to her, then pulled it back towards his chest as she stepped forward for it, before he finally gave it to her. Veronica realised she'd never be free of Bertie's games.

She raised her eyes slowly from the glass and looked at her husband. His own eyes were locked with hers. She knew for certain in that moment that he'd won. He would never let her run. There would only ever be one way to escape him.

The appalling realisation arrived and a state of calm veiled itself over her. She looked at the tumbler, which suddenly held the answer. She would drink as much as she could and then she would walk down to the beach. She would walk into the waves and she would let the tide take her.

'May I have another?' she asked as she drained her glass. The liquid burnt at the back of her throat and all the way down into her stomach.

He filled her glass almost to the top and eyed her curiously when she didn't protest.

She drank as much as she could before she started to feel sick. Whisky was vile. A third glass would be unbearable. But if she was going to do this, she'd need to be as out of her senses as possible. She'd always thought suicide was for cowards, but she realised now it would be the bravest thing she'd ever done if she was to go through with this. What was the alternative? A life of rape and brutality, sick games and hatred at Bertie's whim? No, she couldn't possibly continue like this. Death was preferable. She tipped back the remainder of the drink.

Bertie poured them both another glass.

Veronica started to feel dizzy. She wondered if she'd already drunk too much. Would she even be able to get down to the beach? What if she slipped and fell down the steep cliff steps? She'd break her neck. Veronica laughed and put her hand to her mouth as she realised that would be the most preferable solution to all her problems.

'What's so funny?' Bertie narrowed his eyes.

Veronica shook her head. 'Nothing.' She smothered a smile and then felt tears prick her eyes again. So this is what hysteria felt like.

'Tell me,' Bertie demanded.

'No,' she dared, sipping the last awful drops of brown liquid.

Veronica turned and put her crystal tumbler on Bertie's desk. But she'd been overconfident, thinking Bertie had already done the worst he could do. In one quick step, he was upon her. He grabbed her hair and pulled her backwards so her back arched the wrong way. He hooked his foot around her legs as he spun her round and pushed her onto the desk. The glass tumbler fell to the floor and smashed. It all happened so fast. Veronica was feeling flush from the whisky, her senses dulled. By the time she realised what was happening, it was too late to fight back.

CHAPTER 38

Dorset, July 2018

Whoever it had once been was in a seated position, their head hunched over towards their knees. Their clothes were virtually intact but frayed through age. Seeing a skeleton fully dressed was almost comedic, like something you see in an advert or biology lab. Guy was having trouble processing what was in front of his eyes.

'We need to go and tell someone,' Melissa said.

'Yeah,' he replied, his voice flat.

Slowly, he let go of Melissa's hand and bent down over the skeleton.

'How long do you think they've been down here?' Melissa asked. She was wide eyed, unbelieving.

'A long time.' Guy clenched his jaw, reached out and touched the fabric of the wool jacket that was on the skeleton.

'What are you doing?' Melissa cried. 'We shouldn't touch anything. This is so awful.'

'Yeah,' Guy repeated, but opened the jacket up to look at an inside pocket. Fragments of a blouse or a shirt, thinned by time but covered in something thick, dark, and crusted, brushed his fingers. 'Jesus Christ.' Guy shuddered as he accidentally touched the skeletal ribs. He felt inside the jacket pocket, but there was nothing in there.

'What are you looking for?' Melissa asked.

'Some kind of ID.'

'You don't think . . .?' Melissa trailed off. 'It's not . . .?'

Guy glanced up at her and then looked back at the body, before moving on to the other pocket. Inside, his hand brushed something hard and metal. He dug deeper for a second object. Slowly he withdrew an old, tarnished cigarette case and its accompanying lighter and held it out to show Melissa.

*

Tyneham, December 1943

Bertie was pinning Veronica awkwardly on the desk, his hands now on her shoulders, holding her down. She raised her knee, but Bertie slammed his body onto her.

'Tell me what is so funny,' he demanded again.

She'd seen him in a great many states over the years, the majority of which were alcohol-induced. And while he'd clearly been drinking this afternoon he was in nowhere near the same sort of inebriated state he usually got himself into. No, this time he was naturally violent.

'Bertie, please,' she begged, knowing it would do no use. 'What are you doing? You're hurting me.' The starkness of her situation sobered her slightly

'What am I doing?' he laughed. 'Surely even someone as glacial and as frigid as you knows what I'm doing?'

'No!' She tried to sound stronger than she felt. 'Not like this. Upstairs,' she said, playing for time, looking for a way out. 'The servants, Cook, Rebecca, Anna, they'll hear us in here.'

'Cook and Rebecca have gone. I dismissed them. And I don't care if Anna hears us.' He dug his fingers into her. 'I'll take it in any way I can. You've been dishing it out so freely to my brother . . .' He whispered into her ear, 'It's my turn now.'

She turned her head around, her eyes darting wildly for anything she could use to hurt him. The desk was almost clear of items, Freddie having considerately packed most of them away. A few letters remained at the end of the table, stacked neatly and ready to be packed. Next to them was an ivory-handled letter opener. But she couldn't move her arms to grab it.

'We can start this marriage again,' she lied, trying to buy herself time. 'But we have to do it properly. You want something from me and I'm prepared to give it. But not like this. If you want to hold me down . . .' She blinked back tears. 'If you want me to do as you ask, then I will. But not here, not like this. Please, let's go upstairs.'

Bertie looked curiously at her, almost as if he believed her; he released his hold on her, just enough. As she felt his fingers unclasp from her shoulders, Veronica's survival instinct took over. She turned her head to the side, moved her arm over her head and grabbed the letter opener by its handle.

But Bertie had realised just in time that she was paying him lip service and as she threw her arm forward and lashed out at him, he sprang back from her. Her legs suddenly freed, she slid off the desk and landed on her wobbly feet. She wasn't used to whisky. She'd drunk too much. She was almost upright and she slashed towards Bertie again as she finally managed to stand to her full height.

She caught him on his cheek and Veronica's eyes widened in fear as Bertie roared like an animal. Blood trickled from the cut and ran down his face. She'd surprised herself as to how deeply she'd wounded him. But having paused, she'd lost her advantage. She was no match for Bertie. He pushed her backwards onto the desk, slamming her head into it. But she kept hold of the letter opener and as Bertie lunged down on her she aimed it for his chest.

She closed her eyes in horror as she prepared to feel the blade tear through his skin. But, instead, Bertie landed his knee into

287

her stomach, winding her. Veronica cried out and her hand flew down to protect herself. He grabbed it and slammed it into the desk two, three times, until her knuckles bled and she let go of the letter opener.

'No,' she cried as it fell to the floor. Despair set in. Bertie would kill her now. She knew it. He would punish her, but he wouldn't stop there. She looked into his eyes, which were almost black with rage. She pushed her free hand into his chest to attempt to push him off, but it was no use. He landed his knee into her stomach again and Veronica cried out in pain. Tears fell down her cheeks and rolled past her ears onto the desk, but she wasn't aware of anything other than death shadowing her.

Cowed, pinned, and in agony, she closed her eyes and tried to think of Freddie, the man she loved. But Bertie's hands moved down. It was clear he still had other intentions and he yanked her skirt up around her waist, fumbling with his trousers.

'No,' she cried again as she tried to push him off. Her face suddenly stung as Bertie slapped her hard.

She knew if she carried on fighting, it would take longer to die. She tried to disappear inside herself. Her thoughts of Freddie comforted her as she silently begged Bertie to kill her quickly. Let it be over. Just let it end.

Veronica turned her head to the side facing the study door so she didn't have to look at Bertie's face. A movement in the doorway caught Veronica's attention and she saw Freddie's face.

'Oh God, no,' she cried. 'No.' She realised with horror that she wasn't imagining Freddie. He was there, in the doorway. His face was set purposefully, but even in that split second Veronica knew it was too late to stop what happened next. Bertie's hackles were up the moment Veronica uttered the fateful cry and he was more than ready for what followed.

Before Veronica could shout, warning him to run for his life, Freddie had flown across the room, knocking the gun over as he ran towards them. He launched himself at his brother, but Bertie was faster. Veronica, faint and already in so much pain, struggled to get up, struggled to help Freddie. But she could only watch, screaming in horror, as Bertie landed blow after blow on Freddie's chest. As the man she loved crumbled to the floor under Bertie's relentless attack, she knew she was watching Freddie pay the price for having fallen in love with her.

CHAPTER 39

Dorset, July 2018

Melissa shone the torch on the cigarette lighter. Where once the sterling silver of the cigarette case and its accompanying lighter would have been bright, both were now entirely tarnished through age. Guy was holding them out in the palm of his hand and Melissa reached down and picked up the cigarette case first. She handed Guy the torch and then prised the case open. If any cigarettes had been inside, they were now a mix of dust and tobacco. Melissa snapped it shut and then turned the cigarette lighter over. One side was smooth, but the side that had been face down on Guy's palm had something engraved on it. Guy shone the torch onto it and Melissa ran her fingers over the words.

Through the tarnish, the wording was clear and she read it out to Guy. '*To Alfred, on the occasion of his 21st birthday.*'

It took a few seconds for her to realise the significance of the name. She read it again to double-check. Alfred. Not Albert.

'Alfred,' Guy reasoned in a sad voice. 'We've been looking for a Freddie or a Frederick. But his name was Alfred.'

'No!' Melissa cried. 'Why did it have to be Freddie?'

Melissa couldn't contain the disappointment that welled inside her and she half fell, half sat on the floor, wincing in pain and still clutching the lighter and the cigarette case. She looked over at the body and tears started falling down her face.

'Why him?' she asked. She was angry suddenly. 'Albert killed him.'

Guy sat down next to her. 'You don't know that,' he sighed. She leaned in towards him and he put his arm around her.

'He must have done. He knew about Freddie and Veronica. He knew they'd been together in the beach hut. He was a violent monster. If he didn't kill him then who did? And why?' Melissa started crying again, angry with herself for reacting like this. She was emotionally overwrought. She was in pain and she had just stumbled across a dead body. 'I wanted to find Veronica. I wanted to find Freddie. But not like this,' she said between sobs.

'I know,' Guy placated. He stroked her hair while she cried and Melissa was grateful he was letting her cry it out without trying to encourage her to stop.

When she managed to pull herself together, she looked up at Guy, who stroked the remaining tears from her face with his thumb. She wasn't sure if she was in a position to think clearly or not.

'I don't want to be here anymore,' she said, handing Freddie's cigarette case and lighter back to Guy. He put them in his pocket.

'Neither do I.' Guy helped Melissa up from the floor. She looked back at Freddie's body and closed her eyes. She felt helpless. She was over seventy years too late to do anything and now they were just going to leave him there. She couldn't work out what else to do.

With a great deal of effort on both their parts, Guy managed to get Melissa up to the floor above. Guy was breathless with the exertion as he followed her up into the kitchen.

Melissa leaned against the Aga and tried to ignore the pain in her ribs.

'I don't want to leave him there.' Tears threatened to fall again. 'Not like that.'

'I know,' Guy soothed.

'But I think we have to. For now,' Melissa reasoned after a few minutes' silence. 'We can't even go to the police.'

Guy's head snapped up as he looked directly at her. 'Why on earth not?'

'Guy,' she tried to be gentle. 'We need to find out why your grandmother has kept the key this whole time.'

Guy looked as if he was in a daze. He didn't speak for a minute or two.

'Guy?' Melissa prompted.

'Yeah?'

'I don't want to be a drama queen. But I think I should probably see a doctor. And we need to think about all of this quietly, together, before we do anything rash.'

'Of course,' Guy said, snapping to his senses. 'You need to go to the hospital. Come on,' he agreed.

The increasing pain in Melissa's ribs was starting to overshadow the daze of having found poor Freddie.

'It's all just so desperately sad,' Melissa said. 'And none of it makes any sense.'

Guy stood by the entrance from the kitchen to the hallway and looked back over his shoulder at the doorway to the cellar. They had closed it but not relocked it. Unspoken between them, they knew they both felt that locking Freddie back inside the cellar was the wrong thing to do. Neither of them wanted to leave him down there now that he'd finally been found after all these years.

Melissa reached out and took Guy's hand as they walked through the dusty corridors and back through the main entrance hall. Guy held the window board out for her and helped her back through the way they'd come. The pain in her chest seared, but it was nothing compared to the way she felt about Guy. He was in the middle of a divorce to a woman who'd played him for a complete fool, his name had been ruined in the newspapers and now there was this – his grandmother had been keeping secrets from him and a man had died.

Even though Guy had apologised profusely about the confusion in the newspaper, and for not telling her about his divorce, she hadn't been entirely sure if she could trust him not to hurt her. He'd told her he was falling for her and she thought it was true. But she hadn't been sure if she felt the same way. Or rather she was trying to talk herself out of feeling the same way. Up until now. She'd almost fallen to her death and Guy had come after her. He'd have moved heaven and earth to have saved her. She looked at him as they walked towards the car. Now wasn't the right time to say it back.

CHAPTER 40

After the euphoria of realising she was falling in love with Guy eventually gave way to the pain ricocheting through her chest, Melissa felt drained. She couldn't stop thinking about that dreadful cellar. Had Freddie died down there, having been locked in? Or was he already dead and had been moved there with the intention of hiding his remains? The arrangement of the trunks and the wine racks suggested the latter.

In the car journey to the hospital, Melissa stared out of the window but took in nothing of the beautiful Dorset coastline as it merged into rolling green fields. Her mind was on Freddie. The brother that died. And Veronica. Veronica who had fled the house, or had been forced to flee – leaving Freddie to his fate. How could Veronica do that to Freddie? How could she leave him to die? But what if she knew nothing about it and had left, oblivious to Freddie's fate and his final resting place in the cellar? But then where had she gone afterwards? Melissa wanted to scream. She wanted to know that Veronica had achieved the happy ending she deserved. She wanted to know that she'd had the confidence to leave and to start a new life for herself, just like Melissa's mother had tried to do. She felt like she had all the answers to a crossword puzzle, but no idea where to put them. She must be having a nightmare; from which she'd wake any second now.

As they turned on to the road that approached the hospital, Melissa asked, 'How has he been down there, undiscovered, all this time? How are we the first to find him? I know the room was locked but . . . still.'

Guy didn't reply immediately. He shook his head by way of an answer and it was only a while later when he finally found a parking space in the busy hospital car park and switched the engine off that he spoke. 'The army never moved into the house. Or the village for that matter. They just wanted to clear the way for the gunnery range to fire shells safely. Even now there are no plans to open the house to the public. It's been deemed too expensive and difficult to make it usable.'

Melissa thought of the crumbling porch and the collapsed staircase and agreed. 'So it's perfectly feasible that if we hadn't found him . . .' She trailed off.

'He might never have been found,' Guy finished. 'Well, not anytime soon.'

Melissa shivered. It was cold now and she was in shorts and a T-shirt. They were filthy and dust-covered. And Guy looked how she felt.

'Let's get you in,' he said as he noted her pained face.

Melissa was triaged, during which an uncomfortable question was asked enquiring how she had sustained her head and rib injuries. Neither Guy nor Melissa had considered getting their story straight and they looked so entirely shifty when asked that the nurse was under the distinct impression that Guy had contributed heavily to Melissa's injuries.

Melissa's small head wound was attended to and after being assessed for concussion or something more serious she was given some pain relief and a time to attend the X-ray clinic to have her ribs looked at. As the nurse handed her the card for the X-ray department, she also gave Melissa a leaflet about recognising domestic abuse. Shocked, she took it and wondered if Veronica's life might have turned out differently if someone had ever done the same for her; or if Melissa's own mother's marriage might have come to an end far earlier than it had done if a leaflet had been thrust at her.

Weary beyond belief, Melissa rested her head on Guy's shoulder in the X-ray department, waiting for her time slot to roll around.

'I can't tell you how happy I am that they don't think it's too serious,' Guy said, shifting on his plastic chair.

Melissa just nodded. She was in no mood for conversation. She thought of Anna in one of the wards upstairs. It was only early evening. Visiting hours were soon, although Guy's celebrity status seemed to have gained him the equivalent of an access-all-areas pass to the geriatric ward regardless of the time of day.

As if reading her thoughts, Guy's eyes flicked to his watch. He sighed, then hunched forwards, putting his head in his hands. 'What do I say to her?'

'Tell her the truth,' Melissa said. 'Tell her what we found.'

Guy nodded, his expression set.

'Or you don't have to say anything at all,' she said softly as she thought of Anna, looking frailer at their last visit than she had the one before. This sort of information would be too much, surely?

'Pardon?' Guy asked, looking confused.

'Whatever happened to Freddie, it was a long time ago. A lifetime ago. You don't have to do anything. You can just leave it. It doesn't matter,' Melissa said, but she wasn't sure she meant it. It mattered a lot to her. And they'd come this far. Freddie was dead. Veronica had disappeared. Why? Why had all of this happened?

Guy stood up suddenly, dropping his phone and attracting the attention of the other patients in the sterile-looking waiting room.

Aware of this, he knelt down to pick it up and came face to face with Melissa.

'It does matter,' he whispered. His face was agonised as he placed his hands on her knees. 'It matters because my gran has kept this key for over seventy years. And I want to know why.' Guy turned and left the waiting room, leaving Melissa behind with other patients who were now taking a keen interest in the both of them.

Melissa fidgeted, looked at her watch, and at the appointment time on the X-ray card. She had an hour. She couldn't let Guy do this alone.

He was strides ahead of her, walking purposefully through the hospital corridors. With the painkillers kicking in she was coping better with the cracked ribs, but breaking in to a run was well beyond her. 'Guy,' she called. 'Wait.'

He stopped in front of the lift and pushed the button to hail it. He clenched his jaw and his eyes had taken on a steely expression that frightened her.

'Go easy on her,' Melissa said.

'Why are you here?' He sounded worn out as he turned towards her.

'What do you mean?' Melissa stepped back, startled.

'I mean now. Here, with me. Melissa –' he looked exasperated '– every fibre of your being should be telling you to run. Every bone in your body should be shouting to get the hell away from me.'

Melissa's mouth fell open. Guy got in the lift and Melissa darted in after him.

'Did I blow it by telling you I'm falling in love with you? Actually don't answer that.' He put his head in his hands. 'I'm sorry, Melissa. We shouldn't be together. I'm going to do you a favour and let you get on with your life. You shouldn't be with a fuck-up like me. I didn't tell you I was getting divorced and then your picture ends up in the papers, where you are wrongly accused of being the other woman in what the papers thought was a happy marriage. And then, I almost got you killed by letting you convince me *you* should go down the stairs instead of me. You could have died. Because of me.'

Melissa started to speak, but Guy continued, so she closed her mouth.

'I'm sorry, Melissa.'

As the lift came to a stop and they exited, Guy fumbled in his wallet. Melissa raised an eyebrow as he held a handful of banknotes out for her.

'Get a taxi back after you've been given the once-over here. I've really enjoyed getting to know you this past week. These past few days with you – I don't know when I was last this happy. Until the cellar. I'm sorry I couldn't make things work between us.'

Melissa's confusion grew and when she didn't speak or reach out to take the money, he lowered his arm.

'Bye Melissa.' He touched her face and their eyes locked. Her stomach plummeted. 'Look after yourself.' He turned and walked down the corridor towards the geriatric unit.

Was he serious?

'Don't I get a say in any of this?' Melissa asked.

He turned around. A row of plastic chairs was fixed to the wall and Melissa sat. She was drained both mentally and physically. Guy stood a few feet away.

'I know we haven't known each other very long,' she said. 'But I like you. Rather a lot, actually. You're kind and funny. You're lovely. You make me laugh and you make me smile. And I've not done anything with you that I wouldn't do again. In a heartbeat.'

'I'm sorry.' He shrugged again. He made those two words sound so final.

'You told me you were falling for me,' she said. 'I take it you were lying.'

He sat down next to her and closed his eyes.

298

'I meant it,' he said.

'But you don't mean it now?'

'Of course I do.' He sounded pained.

'Then don't push me away. Not now. Not like this.'

They sat in silence for a few moments. Guy's head was in his hands and Melissa watched him. She realised she was holding her breath.

She took a deep breath and touched his hand. He pulled his hands from his face and looked at her.

'I love you,' she said and then smiled. It was a lovely feeling. She bit her lip to halt her wide smile and then said it again.

Guy looked up. 'You don't have to say it just because—'

Melissa cut him off. 'I'm not. Trust me.' She laughed. She couldn't believe how this day had turned out.

He touched her face and a wide smile spread across his face. Her stomach flipped. He was far too handsome for his own good.

'I love you,' she repeated, loving the way it sounded, the way it felt. 'It's probably the wrong time to tell you that.' She glanced up and down the hospital corridor.

'It's not.' He shook his head. There was laughter in his eyes. 'It's the perfect time.' He leaned towards her and kissed her. Something inside her melted and she knew she didn't want to be without him.

When they reached her room, Anna was sitting up in bed. She had an oxygen mask over her face, but Melissa could see her warm smile behind it. Still, Anna was looking more and more frail. She had a stack of unopened magazines in front of her and a cup of tea was going cold.

'Hello, my darling,' Anna mumbled, holding her hand out for Guy. Guy took it and held it tightly, a thin smile on his lips. It looked like an effort of will for Anna to raise her hand from the bed and Melissa noticed how thin her skin looked, almost translucent.

Anna gestured that she'd like help removing the oxygen mask and Melissa delicately unhooked the strings and placed the mask on Anna's lap.

'It's lovely to see you.' Anna clutched Guy's hand and squeezed it lightly.

Guy just nodded and Melissa looked at him to see tears slowly filling his eyes.

'My darling grandson, I'm not dead yet,' Anna smiled.

Guy laughed and wiped his eyes as a nurse appeared.

'Just a few quick checks,' the nurse said as she held Anna's wrist and took her pulse before preparing the blood pressure monitor.'

Melissa stood. 'We'll get you a fresh cup of tea.' She looked at Guy pointedly who rose and followed her.

Something had struck Guy as they stood in the queue at the hospital coffee shop. 'Why do you think Sir Albert stood down as an MP a few weeks after the requisition?'

Melissa shrugged as she ordered two lattes and a tea. 'Because he was an erratic, murdering piece of shit? No idea. I can't make head nor tail of any of this.'

'Guilt, probably,' Guy mused. 'Took himself out the limelight so he could bury himself away and pretend it had never happened.'

'None of this feels real,' Melissa said as she handed Guy his coffee. 'Or it feels too real. I can't work out which. We said we were on the trail of something, but neither of us knew what, and we knew that when we found out, we might not like it.'

'We certainly got that right.' Guy made a disgusted face as he sipped his coffee and then went off to find sugar on the condiments stand.

Melissa looked at Guy as she wondered how it was they had got to this point. If she hadn't seen Veronica's stricken face in the image, if she hadn't noticed Sir Albert's menacing glint and tight hand around his wife's, Melissa wouldn't have cared less about

Veronica Standish. She'd never have gone into the cellar. And they'd never have found Freddie Standish's body.

'What a mess,' she said. 'I just wish none of this had ever happened, that we could leave poor Freddie down there – as much as I hate that idea – never tell anyone and pretend we were never there.'

Guy looked into his coffee. 'So do I. But you know we can't.' He reached over and touched her hand. 'We found a dead body, Melissa. We've bought ourselves a bit of time, but we are going to have to tell someone eventually. The state that place is in, someone's going to go in there at some point to survey the building to either refurbish it or knock it down. They'll know people have been down there recently. And also' – he looked even more worried – 'your phone's in there somewhere. They'll know that you, specifically, were there.'

His phone vibrated in his pocket and he pulled it out and read the text message.

'It's Philippa. She's emailed over the birth certificates.' He closed the text message window. 'It's all academic now anyway, isn't it? Going back in time to try to move forward. We've found Freddie now.' Guy sighed. 'Poor bastard. And birth certificates will hardly help us discover what happened to the other two.'

All the same, he clicked open his email as they walked towards the door of the ward. He started swearing about the poor signal in the hospital building and Melissa could see he'd had enough today. He just wanted to talk to Anna.

'Here, let me,' Melissa suggested.

Guy willingly gave Melissa the phone. The first attachment opened painfully slowly. A copy of a birth certificate loaded up bit by bit. It was Albert's. Among other details in columns, including father's name and occupation, Albert Standish was listed as having been born at the family's London house on 20 August in the year 1911. The time of birth was listed as 2.15 a.m.

'That's strange,' Melissa said as they arrived at the ward doors.

Guy stood and started pacing. 'You don't usually see the time listed on a birth certificate, if I remember mine correctly,' Melissa finished.

Guy glanced down at the phone and read the old-fashioned writing but looked none the wiser. He felt in his pocket and pulled out the cigarette lighter and looked at the name on it again. 'Alfred. Poor old Freddie. What on earth did he have the misfortune of doing in order to end up dead in the cellar of Tyneham House?'

Melissa closed the attachment with Albert's birth certificate and opened the second one. She glanced up at Guy as he paced. He was still holding Freddie's cigarette lighter, flicking it open and shut repeatedly, while looking towards the ward entrance.

'Do you think we could look at that later?' Guy gestured towards his phone. He stopped pacing and looked back at her anxiously.

'Just a sec. It's almost loaded.' Melissa stared at the phone as the certificate came up line by painful line. She started tapping her foot, impatient for the information to appear.

A near-perfect copy of Albert's birth certificate loaded on the screen. She zoomed in to look.

'Oh, it's the same one twice,' she said. 'I think your assistant might have made a mistake . . .' Melissa's voice trailed off as she read the information in one of the columns again and then checked the name of the baby that had been registered. But it wasn't the wrong one.

Alfred Standish was also listed as having been born at the family's London house on 20 August in the year 1911. Freddie's time of birth was 2.45 a.m.

Melissa frowned, uncomprehending. But then her head snapped up and she stared at Guy.

Guy had resumed pacing but stopped when he saw her face. 'What?' he asked.

Melissa couldn't believe it. She couldn't speak. She turned the phone around and showed Guy.

'What the . . .?' Guy frowned, then he looked at Melissa. Their eyes locked and Guy's expression turned to astonishment as he too realised what he was looking at.

Freddie and Albert were twins.

CHAPTER 41

'Twins?' Guy mouthed. He was having trouble comprehending. 'Twins.' He held his hand out for his phone and Melissa passed it back. Guy flicked between both birth certificates and then looked up at Melissa, his eyes wide. 'Jesus Christ.'

He clicked off the screen and looked at the text of Philippa's email, scanning it for further information.

'It makes sense when she said that by finding Albert's certificate first it made it easier to find Freddie's. The time is only listed on a birth certificate for multiple births. When she saw that there was a time on Albert's certificate, she must have known straight off that Freddie was a twin.'

'Your gran never said they were twins.'

Guy's voice took on a harder edge. 'Gran has said hardly anything. Has she had the key this whole time? Has she always known about Freddie being in the cellar? I need to talk to her.'

'Gently,' Melissa called after him. 'Please, Guy.'

He pushed through the ward doors and walked past the nurses' station without even registering the women behind the counter, who looked delighted to see him as usual. Melissa gave a polite smile out of habit as she hurried past.

Anna looked slightly brighter when Melissa and Guy arrived with her tea.

'Thank you, my darlings,' she said, taking a sip. 'Ooh that's lovely. Not like the dishwater I'm being served here.'

'Sorry it's in a paper cup,' Melissa said. 'When do you think they'll let you out?' She didn't want to storm in and shock Anna with their discovery, but she could see Guy fidgeting. For once, he was the impatient one.

'Not for some time. They don't think I'm strong enough for anything at the moment, but fingers crossed,' Anna said with a small smile.

Guy started to speak, but Melissa cut him off and he closed his mouth. 'What did the nurse say? Was she happy with how you were doing?'

'She's not very happy with my breathing. She's not very happy with much, actually.' Anna attempted a laugh and coughed repeatedly. Melissa helped her with the oxygen mask and Anna held it over her face for a minute, letting the strings hang loose. Guy and Melissa sat in silence while Anna breathed deeply.

Eventually, once Anna had placed the mask in her lap, Guy spoke. Melissa felt a flicker of fear and suddenly wanted to be anywhere other than here. Whatever had happened in that cellar, whatever Albert had done to his brother, there must be a reason why Anna had the key.

'Gran,' Guy started. 'I need to talk to you.'

Anna nodded. 'This sounds serious.'

'It is.' Guy ran his hand through his hair.

'Gran?' He sat up straight and looked directly at her. 'What happened just before the requisition?'

Anna didn't reply immediately, but when she did she said, 'Why are you asking me about this again?'

Melissa could see it was no use. They weren't going to get there gently.

'We found the key,' Melissa started. 'I'm sorry.'

Guy reached into his pocket and pulled the key out, holding it towards his gran.

Anna looked at it. She reached out to touch it and then withdrew her hand. Melissa couldn't read her expression. The elderly lady had looked at the key so blankly that Melissa couldn't tell if she recognised it or its significance.

Anna held her tea out for Melissa to take. Melissa's glance flicked to Guy as she placed the paper cup on the roll-out table. His brow was furrowed and he looked about ten years older.

'It's the key to the cellar of Tyneham House,' Melissa prompted.

Anna exhaled loudly and then closed her eyes. 'I know,' she whispered.

Guy shuffled forward on to the edge of the plastic visitor's chair and said quietly, 'We went down there. We found him.'

Anna drew a sharp intake of breath and put her hand to her mouth. Her eyes were still closed.

'What happened, Gran? I don't want to upset you. But we need to know.'

'You found him?' Anna whispered.

Melissa nodded and then crouched down to the side of Anna's bed and touched her hand gently. Cannula tubes were sticking out of her hand and Melissa dodged them and slipped her hand underneath Anna's to hold the elderly lady's. 'We just knew something wasn't right. We wanted to know if you knew what happened.'

'Why?'

'Gran,' Guy said, his tone tender. 'We found a dead body. Isn't that reason enough?'

Anna closed her eyes and was silent for so long that Melissa wondered if she'd drifted off to sleep. Just as Melissa started to rise from her crouching position Anna asked, 'What did he look like, after all these years?'

Guy flicked a glance at Melissa. 'A skeleton,' he said. 'But fully dressed. In a suit.'

'Sort of real,' Melissa said quietly. 'But not real at the same time.'

Anna nodded, raised her watery eyes and eventually said, 'God forgive me. It was an accident.'

Guy started to speak, but when Anna continued he stopped.

'You have no idea what it was like, living in that house. That last week was the very worst.'

Guy and Melissa exchanged looks.

'I wished I wasn't living there. But I'd promised to stay for her.' Anna looked blankly at the far wall of the hospital ward.

'For Veronica?' Melissa asked.

Anna nodded. 'Sir Albert was a drinker, you see. Couldn't stop. But couldn't hold it either. It became a . . . problem.' Anna coughed and reached for the oxygen mask.

After a few moments, she continued. 'He was a menace. If he didn't get his way, you know, then he'd take it out on her verbally, or he'd give her little shoves if she got in his way, or reach out and take her hand sharply. And that was just in public or in front of the house staff. What he did to her behind closed doors . . . well . . . it's different now isn't it? There's more help.'

Melissa thought again of the domestic abuse leaflet that the nurse had passed her. She thanked God that times had changed. Just about.

'Women are stronger now, perhaps, and there's more help available, for some at least. Most people seem better equipped to see what's happening to them these days,' Melissa offered.

'You'd be surprised, dear. Has Guy mentioned his soon-to-be ex-wife?'

Melissa nodded and Guy's head shot up.

'Abuse comes in all shapes and sizes. It's not always physical. But Sir Albert's abuse of Veronica was mental and physical. It had been going on for years. Veronica was leaving him.'

'Really?' Melissa's eyebrows lifted.

'It took her a long time to realise that's what she needed to do. And she tried, several times. But timing was never her strong point and she always lost her chance – especially the last time she tried. In the last few days before the requisition. Someone arrived and she missed her opportunity to leave.'

'Freddie?' Melissa offered.

Anna nodded. 'Freddie.'

'What happened?' Guy asked.

'Freddie arrived and it changed everything,' Anna said. 'They used to be lovers, before the war. Veronica told me that Sir Albert talked her out of a relationship with Freddie.'

'And into one with him?' Melissa asked. 'Was she so easily swayed?'

'She could be, I suppose. She was strong in many ways. Kind to others, too. But she had no confidence and when Sir Albert told her Freddie had no intention of marrying her and that she meant next to nothing to him, she was embarrassed and ashamed. Sir Albert coaxed her away and then soon after he proposed.'

'But it wasn't true – about Freddie, I mean?' Melissa asked.

'No, dear. Freddie loved her. Might I have my tea back?' Anna asked.

Melissa handed the tea to her and she gulped it down thirstily.

'She drove Freddie away on purpose this time.' Anna was quiet. 'Sir Albert threatened Freddie's life and so Veronica sacrificed her happiness with Freddie for a lifetime of hell with her husband.'

'This is terrible,' Melissa cried and then looked around to check no one was listening. 'But he didn't go? Freddie didn't go?'

'No,' Anna said, remembering. Tears sprang into her eyes. 'He came back. Oh, may God forgive me.'

Melissa thought of Freddie in the cellar and tried to hold back tears. 'What happened?' she asked.

'Why do you have the key?' Guy cut in. His head was in his hands.

'I was supposed to go back,' Anna answered. 'When the requisition order was lifted. When the war ended, I was supposed to bury his body properly. I could confide in my brother, William. I was going to ask him to help. The cellar door was sturdy and the lock was secure. The army weren't moving into the village, they mainly wanted to use the house for training and to shoot around it, so hopefully they weren't going to pay too much attention to a locked cellar door. And if they did, then the body was hidden quite well. But he wasn't supposed to be there this long. We all thought we'd be moving back within a matter of years.'

'Who killed him?' Guy was blunt.

Anna narrowed her eyes. 'Oh, Guy,' she said. 'My darling grandson. Albert was killing them both. It was all happening so fast. By the time I arrived . . . her head, the desk . . . there was so much blood I couldn't see how she was still alive.' Anna looked haunted as she relived the event. 'She was moving so slowly, I thought she was going to die. But they, the two of them, the brothers, they were fighting, each of them trying to get a stronger grip on the other, each of them hitting one another over and over and over. I picked up Sir Albert's gun.' Anna paused, closing her eyes briefly. 'I wasn't sure what I was going to do. I might have tried firing a shot to startle him, to shock him. But I was frightened, so frightened. I wasn't capable of handling a rifle, and I don't know how, but somehow I fired it. I only wanted to save Veronica. And I wanted to save Freddie. I wanted to make them stop fighting. I never meant for it to end like that.'

Melissa was breathless hearing the tale that had led to a man's death all those years ago.

'And poor Freddie died,' Melissa declared, feeling flat and exhausted.

'No.' Anna shook her head, vehement, and a tear ran down her face. 'No. I didn't kill *him*.'

Guy sat up straight, realising the significance of Anna's confession.

Melissa's mouth dropped open before she whispered, 'You killed Albert.'

CHAPTER 42

Tyneham, December 1943

Veronica felt a weight on top of her. She was being crushed. She was aware of a bang, but it sounded so far away. It was only when the sound was accompanied by something heavy landing on her that she vaguely understood what had happened.

Then there was silence. Pain seared through her head where Bertie had slammed it into the desk. Her dizziness was still present as her eyes struggled to focus. Veronica moved her head and a mop of someone else's hair brushed against her face. Bertie was on top of her, lying on his back and at an awkward angle. Veronica opened her mouth to scream, but no sound came out. Or if it came out she was unable to hear it. There was ringing in her ears – such loud ringing.

She started to push Bertie off, but his body was limp. She called his name and shook him, but there was no response and so Veronica pushed him as hard as her remaining strength would allow. His legs were draped over the side of his desk and his lifeless form finally slumped onto the floor with a thud. Veronica summoned all her energy and turned slightly on to her side in order to get into a less painful position to sit up. As she did so, she looked down and saw that she was covered in blood. Her clothes were smeared in it from her chest down to her knees. She sat up and turned towards the door. Anna's eyes were staring straight through Veronica and her hands, still holding the gun, were shaking.

Freddie was on all fours, facing her, his breath rasping. He lifted an arm to his chest. Between thick, exhausted rasps, his eyes were on Bertie's lifeless form.

'Freddie,' Veronica cried. He stared as if he was in a trance and at her call he looked up at her and blinked but, winded, seemed unable to speak. Then, coming to his senses, he climbed slowly to his feet and walked uncertainly towards a shaking Anna. He gently pushed the barrel of the gun towards the floor. Anna's grip was tight and Freddie had to prise her hand from the gun, finger by finger, while she stared wide-eyed and shocked at Bertie's body.

Veronica moved round on the desk and slid off. Her stomach hurt where Bertie's knee had made repeated contact. She put her hand to her head, which was in agony, and found her hair sticky with blood, smears of which were on the desk where her head had been slammed repeatedly.

As Freddie took the gun from Anna, he held it low and then turned to face Veronica as he put it on the floor. His eyes were pained and he still hadn't spoken. He looked at her bloodstained dress and then down to the floor where Bertie's lifeless form lay. He and Veronica stared at each other and then at Anna, who burst into tears, breaking the silence of the room. Veronica staggered forward to take Anna in her arms.

Veronica had often found it hard to believe Anna was only seventeen. But now the girl looked so young and so small.

'Thank you,' Veronica cried into Anna's hair. 'Thank you.'

Anna, shocked, was still unable to reply and sobbed into Veronica's shoulder. Eventually, as Anna pulled back to wipe her eyes, Veronica saw blood had transferred from her dress onto Anna's clothes.

Freddie put both his hands onto his head and stared down at

Bertie's body. Slowly he moved towards his dead brother, bending over him to check for signs of life.

Bertie's shirt was soaked with blood. Freddie slumped down onto his knees next to his brother.

'I'm sorry,' Anna cried. 'I'm so sorry.'

'Anna, you saved me.' Veronica stood, glancing between the twins. One dead. One alive.

'I've killed him.' Anna burst into tears again. 'I didn't mean to. I only wanted him to stop. He was going to kill you.'

'I can't believe he's dead,' Freddie said quietly.

Veronica looked down at her bloody dress. 'You saved me, Anna,' she repeated.

'But I didn't mean to kill him,' Anna cried. 'I didn't.'

Veronica touched Anna's shoulder and held her gently. 'It's all right. It will be all right.' Veronica had no idea if anything would be all right ever again. She had wanted to be free of Bertie, but not like this.

'I don't know what to do,' Anna said. 'Who do we tell?'

'No one,' Freddie said as he looked up at the women. He looked at Veronica with meaning and shook his head slightly. Veronica could see panic in his face.

Catching Freddie's glance, Anna's mouth dropped open. 'But we have to tell,' she said. 'I've killed someone.'

'You saved us.' Freddie climbed slowly to his feet.

'But . . .' Anna trailed off.

Veronica held Anna's hand while she tried to piece together what they should do. The pain in her head was addling her mind, but one thing she did realise. 'Anna, if we tell anyone what's happened, you'll hang.'

'No,' Anna said. 'Not if I confess. Not if I tell them it was an accident.'

Veronica was definite. 'No,' she said. She looked down at Bertie's body and wondered what in heaven's name they were going to do now.

'But . . .' Anna started again. 'We have to. We *have* to do something.'

'We do have to do something.' Veronica touched her head again and felt thick blood still oozing in amongst her matted hair. She reached out to the empty bookshelves to steady herself, her hands leaving a trail of blood on the wood. Anna grabbed Veronica round the waist as Veronica slumped against the shelves, weakened by her ordeal.

'We can't let Anna hang for this. Not for him,' Freddie said in a quiet voice as he looked down at his brother.

'Then I'll do it,' Veronica straightened. 'You get Anna away, Freddie. Go. Now.'

'No.' His voice was hard. 'I won't allow that. I should have stopped my brother years ago. I should have stopped him tonight. This is all my fault. I'll go to the police.'

Veronica rushed to him, but dizziness prevented her from walking straight. 'No,' she said. 'What if they don't believe you? What if they don't believe it was an accident?'

As she ran into his arms, her foot made contact with something small but solid. Freddie's lost cigarette lighter flew across the floor and landed against the wood panelling. Veronica picked it up. It was spattered with blood and she turned it over in her hands and instinctively wiped it clean. Was it Bertie's or was it Freddie's? Identical cigarette lighters for identical twin brothers. Only the engraved names highlighted the difference.

She looked down at the lighter in her hand and at the wedding ring on Bertie's finger. She realised what she had to do. Bertie had put them all through hell for years. His final act would not be to condemn one or all of them to death. The requisition order would take effect in a matter of hours. There was very little time. She felt sick at what she was about to suggest, but Veronica was sure this was the only way they would finally be free of Albert. And the only way they would all be saved.

CHAPTER 43

Dorset, July 2018

Freddie's cigarette lighter looked dull in Guy's hands, the shine long since gone.

'But . . .?' Melissa trailed off, wondering how Freddie's lighter had come to be on the body, wondering how it was that Sir Albert was in the newspaper cutting from a New Year's Eve Party a few weeks later, wondering how he'd come to resign from parliament if he was already dead.

Guy shook his head. 'This makes no sense.'

'I know. Punishment was different back then. I would have hung, of that I'm sure. Neither Freddie nor Veronica would let me confess to the police.'

'But,' Melissa spluttered, 'it was self-defence, or defence of Veronica and Freddie. Something like that.'

'Nowadays we'd call it something like that,' Anna said. 'But back then, I'm not sure it really existed. If I'd confessed, Freddie said he was going to come forward to confess too and so did Veronica. But if we had, well, one of us would have hung, if not all of us.'

Melissa gulped and put her hand to her throat.

'We stood, discussing who would confess for so long that we were in danger of being found out. The requisition deadline

315

loomed. The army was preparing to fence off the house and village. As the landowner, Sir Albert was expected to say a few words to the villagers. We had to move fast. We were all in shock. It wasn't what any of us wanted, a man's death and a body to hide. I'm not at all proud of what happened. I wanted to tell the truth.'

'So Freddie—?' Melissa asked as realisation dawned.

'Freddie pretended to be Bertie.' Anna looked down in her lap. 'He swapped his lighter and cigarette case for Bertie's and he removed Bertie's wedding ring and wore it. It's not what he wanted for the rest of his life, but he did it. He said that no one would miss *good-for-nothing Freddie Standish*. But if Bertie suddenly went missing, an MP no less, then questions would be asked and a hunt would begin. It was easier this way.

'None of the villagers had seen Freddie there on that last night. No one even noticed when Freddie wasn't there, ostensibly, that last morning. It wasn't even mentioned. People were too wrapped up in being evicted. But "Bertie" was there. "Bertie" gave the final address to the villagers. "Bertie" and Veronica left. No one ever mentioned Freddie again,' Anna finished.

'I can't believe it's so neat and tidy,' Guy said. 'For something so mind-bogglingly awful.' He looked at Anna and his elderly, frail grandmother looked back at him.

'I killed a man when I was seventeen, Guy,' Anna said between rasping breaths. 'He was the devil. But it was an accident. I've had to live with it ever since. And I've kept Veronica and Freddie's escape a secret too. I never told anyone. Not even your grandfather.' Anna nodded to Guy.

'But why were you expected to go back? Why was it you who took the key? Why not them?' Melissa asked. 'Why not Veronica and Freddie?'

'I volunteered. It was all my fault. My mother and father were only moving a few miles away and even though I was signing up to do my bit in the war I'd be closest to Tyneham when the war

316

was over, when we were told we'd be able to move back. My brother William had plans to return home and continue farming after the war had ended. He knew what Sir Albert was like. And I knew I could trust him to help me when the time came to move the body. Veronica and Freddie left the area. They had to. They tried to live a normal life, but they couldn't do it around people they knew. The picture you showed me of them at the New Year's Eve ball in 1944 amazed me. Such a risk. I think they must have realised that soon after,' Anna said. 'Tough for Freddie to play the role of Albert in public. It must have been hard for them both.'

'So a few weeks later Albert stood down as an MP. I mean, Freddie stood down.' Guy blinked, clearly still getting his head around it all.

'And then they were never seen again,' Melissa said.

Anna nodded. 'I assume they were scared. I assume they changed their names if you couldn't find any records of them. Easy to do in the war. Paperwork was atrocious. They moved around a bit, judging by the locations of the postcards, which I received periodically from various locations. They were presumably just to let me know she was fine. I knew they were from her, even though there were never any words. Other than just one.'

'*Thank you — For everything,*' Guy recalled Veronica's words on the postcard.

'Yes, that one. That was the only one she risked with any writing. I think they must have suffered, long after. People accused Freddie of being the reprobate brother for most of his life, but he was the best of men. He moved his brother's body. They'd never had a good relationship. Bertie had bullied him since childhood from what I could gather. But I would imagine hiding his own twin brother's body would have had some sort of lasting effect on poor Freddie. And then they were permanently running, keeping away from anyone, wondering if anyone might ever notice the swap.'

'Well I never.' Guy shook his head.

317

'So if anyone ever did find the body, they'd think it was Freddie?' Melissa clarified. She thought she just about understood all of this.

'As we did,' Guy confirmed.

Anna coughed hard and reached for her mask. Eventually she said, 'Bertie, as an MP and gentry, could have bought himself out of any situation that arose. The body of *Freddie* Standish would have been discreetly forgotten about.'

'Their being identical twins explains why the guide Reg and his brother swore blind that Veronica was in the beach hut with her husband,' Guy said.

'And why they were so confused as to how Sir Albert was in their house at the same time. Frightening their mother. It was his twin brother, Freddie, down at the hut the whole time.'

'Very few of us knew Freddie before, remember. He'd left years ago. It was easy for the villagers to forget a man who was of no real significance anymore. He just faded from memory. My brother William knew him. But they were a different class and didn't communicate often after Freddie left the village originally, as men often don't. They grow up and move on. And confidences between William and his friends weren't shared between he and I. Although he did try his hardest to help get Veronica out when I asked him to.'

'Sir Albert never mentioned his brother?' Guy asked. 'Never talked about his twin?'

Anna nodded. 'Not to me. I was just a servant. And Sir Albert categorically did not socialise with the villagers. Always thought he was better. The older ones would have remembered Freddie, I'm sure. But he was never mentioned in everyday conversation in Tyneham House. The hate ran that deep with Sir Albert. There were never family photographs out. Just old family portraits of generations of long-forgotten Standishes. Freddie had been removed. I never knew about him until he arrived before the requisition.'

'Come on now. Let Mrs Cameron rest.' A nurse wandered over

and put her hand gently on Melissa's shoulder. 'You know it's not visiting time yet and you can see she's tired.'

Guy stood and looked down at Anna. 'I'm sorry, Gran,' he said when the nurse had left.

'Why are you sorry?' she asked. 'I should have told you when you started asking questions, but I wanted to protect Veronica and Freddie, as much as myself. I don't know if they are alive now or not. They were much older than me, so I think probably not. The postcards stopped in the seventies, so maybe one or both of them passed away as old age encroached. And if they changed their names, well, I like to think they were all right until the end. Happy together and finally free from Bertie.'

'Me too,' Melissa said. 'She managed to be with the man she really loved. And who loved her. That was all I wanted for her – the woman in the photograph who looked so frightened.'

Anna smiled at Melissa. A moment of understanding passed between them before Melissa excused herself to attend her X-ray appointment.

'I'm sorry that I've upset you,' Guy said to his gran once Melissa had left. 'Because I kept on. Because you did something to save someone.'

'And it resulted in rather a mess,' Anna said. 'Guy, what are you going to do?' Anna spoke quietly.

'Do?'

'About what you've found. About what I've told you.' Her voice was calm.

Guy rubbed his mouth with his hand. He thought of all the things he should do. All the right things to do. And he knew what path he would take.

'Nothing. I'm not going to do anything. What good would it do?' He shrugged. Guy reached down to take Anna's hand. 'Gran, I love you. I'm so sorry all this has come out now. I'm so sorry I forced all this out. I'm sorry I wouldn't let it rest.'

'Darling, I'm glad, really,' she said. 'It was time. I've never felt so light.'

'We'll work out a plan, Melissa and I. Maybe we'll go back, sneak in, and bury him properly. Hide Bertie's body forever.'

Anna winced. 'Don't do anything. It's not your burden. It was always mine.' She squeezed Guy's hand. He was aware how fragile her hand felt against his. 'Guy, I'm very proud of you. Everything you've achieved. The man you've become. You do know that don't you?'

A tear struck the very corner of his eye and he brushed it away and swallowed. 'Of course.' Guy gave his grandmother a gentle hug and kissed her on her forehead. 'I'll see you tomorrow,' he said. 'And Gran? Don't worry, will you? We'll sort this.'

Anna nodded. 'Now run after that lovely girl.'

When Guy had left, the nurse returned and gave Anna a smile. 'He's a lovely chap, your grandson.'

'He is.' Anna gave the nurse a determined look. 'Do you still have those payphones on wheels?'

The nurse gave her a curious glance and nodded.

'Would you fetch me one please, I should like to make a telephone call.'

CHAPTER 44

'Melissa Turner?' the radiographer called and Melissa withdrew her head from where it had been resting on Guy's shoulder. She gave him a look that she hoped conveyed love and sympathy for the dilemma he was now in and stood up to follow the clinician. Guy gave her a thin smile and then closed his eyes, resting his head back on the wall.

Melissa's head was spinning. What on earth were they going to do about Bertie's body? Guy was right. Leaving it there wasn't really an option. Guy had explained the conversation he'd just had with Anna. Melissa had agreed with him. They needed to work out how best to move forward while still protecting Anna.

'You're a very lucky woman.' The radiographer's voice snapped Melissa from her thoughts. 'The nurse who triaged you was under the impression you'd broken almost all of your ribs on one side, but actually you've only broken two of them and nothing appears out of place or moving dangerously towards your organs.'

The radiographer was matter-of-fact and it was just what Melissa needed. Along with some more painkillers.

'How did you hurt yourself?' the radiographer asked as Melissa moved to leave.

'I fell down some stairs.' It wasn't strictly a lie.

Guy looked like death as he drove them back to the hotel. His face was ashen and his hair a mess. They were both still covered in dust and there was a cobweb in Guy's hair. What must the hospital staff have thought?

Neither of them spoke on the return journey and the desolate silence continued as they walked through the hotel, attracting raised eyebrows from the girl behind the reception desk as they passed her. She had a copy of this morning's newspaper open at the story about Guy and she gave Melissa a dirty look.

When they were both clean and freshly dressed, Melissa opened a window and breathed in the fresh smell of grass. There was something about a rainstorm that she loved. It made everything clean and new again.

Guy poured them both a stiff drink from the minibar and when they'd finished they stared into the distance, holding each other on the sofa in his suite until they eventually drifted off to sleep in each other's arms.

Guy's phone rang on the coffee table in front of the sofa and they woke with a start. The sun was already up, but in the height of summer that could mean it was anytime from 5 a.m. onwards. Melissa moved as fast as her sore ribs made possible to allow Guy to lean forward. As she blinked into the sunlight, she glanced around for the painkillers.

Guy coughed, his voice gravelly as he answered, 'Hi, Mum. What time is it?' He glanced at his watch and, obviously seeing the earliness of the hour, sat up straight. 'What's wrong?'

Melissa rubbed her eyes and looked on. The phone call didn't sound good.

'Shit. No.' Guy ran his hand through his hair and was silent while he waited for his mum to speak. 'Oh God.' His voice was strained. 'Okay. Don't worry. I'll be there as soon as I can.' He said goodbye and hung up. His face was worry-stricken.

'What's wrong?' Melissa asked.

'It's Gran.' Guy stood up. 'She's taken a turn for the worse. Mum's been called in to the hospital. My dad's on his way down from London.'

Melissa stood and reached out to touch his arm. 'Oh no. Oh, Guy. You should go. Quickly.'

Guy looked around the room as if he'd lost something, then put his hand to his forehead. His eyes were wide and he looked as if he was descending into shock.

Melissa grabbed Guy's car keys from the side table by the hotel room door. 'Come on,' she said.

Guy and Melissa walked at speed through the hospital corridors. He was holding Melissa's hand tightly and her other one was clutching her ribs.

Guy caught sight of her out of the corner of his eye and slowed down. 'I'm dragging you. I'm sorry. Are you okay?'

'I'm fine.' She gave his hand a squeeze.

When they stepped out of the lift and turned towards the entrance doors to the ward, there were two uniformed police officers chatting outside, waiting to be admitted.

'The nurse said this Mrs Cameron's some relative of that posh historian off the telly. That Guy Cameron,' the first officer said. Melissa stopped dead when she heard the words.

'Oh, my wife loves him. Remind me to get a picture with him if he's here and if this all turns out to be a wind-up.'

They looked up and spotted Guy and Melissa standing still about ten feet away. Melissa wasn't sure why, but her first instinct was to run and to pull Guy back safely with her.

'Keep going,' Guy hissed to Melissa and she started up again towards the doors. 'Excuse me,' Guy said as he reached past the officers and pushed the buzzer to the ward. It was only 7 a.m. and the doors were usually open by now.

Guy gave the officers a thin smile and turned back towards Melissa. He clenched his jaw as he looked at her with a worried expression.

'It'll be okay,' Melissa mouthed, although even she wasn't sure at this point if any of this would be okay. What were the police doing here?

'Er, Guy Cameron, isn't it?' the first police officer asked. 'Recognise you off the telly.'

Guy turned around, jaw still clenched, and nodded.

The officers introduced themselves. Guy didn't introduce Melissa and she felt as if he was almost trying to push her protectively behind him, but she stood her ground.

'Well, this is a strange one, I'll admit,' the second officer ventured. 'Not had anything quite like this before, I don't mind saying.'

'Like what?' Melissa asked.

'And you are?'

Melissa introduced herself and Guy moved forward to push the buzzer again, pointedly ignoring the officers.

'They just asked us over the intercom to wait outside for a while. Some kind of emergency inside,' the first officer said. 'Shouldn't be too long.'

'Right.' Guy gave his thin smile again and stood near the door, beckoning Melissa over by holding out his hand for her.

'I think we're actually here to see someone related to you.'

Shit. Melissa looked up at Guy and he exhaled loudly.

'Okay,' Guy said. 'What about?'

'Well, I think we'll speak to her privately first and then I'm sure she'll tell you,' the first officer said.

'If it's not a massive wind-up,' the second officer said under his breath.

A harassed-looking nurse opened the door. 'Gentlemen, I'm sorry to say there's no point . . .' She trailed off when her eyes flicked from the uniformed officers towards Guy and Melissa. 'Mr Cameron. Please, step inside. I'm afraid I need to talk to you.'

The officers looked uncomfortable and drifted into the ward's entrance to await further information. They raised their eyes to the nurse, who gave them a very small shake of her head that Guy missed, but Melissa caught.

Oh no, Melissa thought. *Oh no*. Melissa squeezed Guy's hand as they were led into a small office. A nurse signalled for him to sit down, but he remained standing.

'Please wait here for just a moment.' The nurse left.

Guy turned to Melissa. 'Where's Mum? What the hell is going on?'

But Melissa had a terrible feeling she knew what was going on and she really wanted to be wrong.

Guy's mother entered the room clutching tissues to her face, her eyes red and puffy.

'Mum?' Guy's voice wavered.

'She's gone,' his mum said.

'No!' he cried as he gathered his mum in his arms. She sobbed into his chest.

The nurse stood by the door, giving mother and son time. Melissa slumped into a chair. As Guy looked over his mother's shoulder at Melissa, his face wore an expression of absolute disbelief.

'I'll give you a few minutes and I'll come back with some tea,' the nurse said.

'What happened?' Guy asked his mum.

'The nurse said they were unhappy with her breathing last night and she was deteriorating rapidly. They mentioned pneumonia and that her heart wasn't able to cope. She was gone by the time I arrived this morning.' Guy's mum sniffed. 'I've been sitting with her a few minutes. She looks very peaceful. Like she's not really gone.' Guy's mum broke down and tears stained Guy's shirt as he held her again.

'I'll let you two be alone.' Melissa started to rise.

'No, please stay.' Guy's mother collected herself. 'Stay for Guy, please.'

The nurse returned with a tray with three cups of tea and Guy asked her to confirm what his mum said. He brushed tears away from his eyes as the nurse explained, using far more complex terminology, what had happened to Anna overnight and how heart disease in the elderly wasn't curable.

When Guy and his mother had comforted each other, Melissa looked at the nurse and asked the dreaded question. 'Why are the police here?'

The nurse looked uncomfortable. 'After you left, last night,' the nurse said, nodding at Guy, 'your grandmother asked me if she could make a phone call. She asked me to phone the police.'

Guy sat down in a chair and rubbed his hand over his eyes. 'Go on,' he said from behind his hand. Melissa looked at him. His eyes were closed. He knew the reason why she'd made the phone call.

'She said she needed to tell them something that couldn't wait any longer, that it was something she should have done a very long time ago.'

Melissa exhaled. Anna had been planning to confess. After all this time, she still wanted to confess. She'd intended to spare Guy the anxiety of dealing with Albert's body. She had been planning to remove the burden entirely from her grandson.

Guy looked at Melissa and the nurse's eyes followed their interaction. Melissa looked away at a nondescript point on the wall.

'I don't suppose you know what it was about?' the nurse asked.

'I'll talk to them in a minute,' Guy said. 'For now, I'd like to see my gran please.'

While Guy and his mother sat with Anna's body, Melissa prowled the corridor, giving them time. If she had smoked, now would be a great time for a cigarette. She stopped pacing and smiled politely as the two officers brushed past her. One cast her a confused look, the other patently ignored her.

'Wait,' Guy called from the ward doors.

The officers spun round and Guy approached more sedately than Melissa was sure he felt.

'While you're here,' Guy said, 'I need to tell you something. This might not be for you at all. It might be a job for the military police given its location.'

The officers looked confused.

Guy continued, 'Yesterday, I was somewhere I shouldn't have been. I was taking a bit of a risk with my life and, well, with my career too no doubt. However,' Guy said, pointedly avoiding Melissa's gaze, 'I broke into Tyneham House and went into the cellar.'

Melissa watched the officers' faces. It was clear that neither of them knew what Guy was talking about.

'The old village that was requisitioned during the war? Anyway, I found a . . . skeleton down there.' Guy was choosing his words carefully. He made it sound less exciting than if he'd found a five-pound note.

One of the officers raised his eyebrows. The other started scribbling quickly in his notebook.

'It's old. Very old. No idea how long it's been down there. At least since the war,' Guy mused. 'I think it's the body of Freddie Standish, one of the brothers who lived there for a while.'

'What makes you say that?'

'Because I found these.' Guy handed the lighter and cigarette case to one of the officers.

Melissa's heart thudded in her chest. She could see that Guy was thinking on his feet.

'I know, I know. I shouldn't have removed them,' Guy said when the officer looked flustered. Guy placed the items inside an evidence bag that the officer produced from his pocket. 'One for your cold-case team, I suppose?' Guy asked.

'Unlikely, given the age of the body, if it does turn out to be wartime. We'll hand this over to those who need to know and we'll be in touch. We'll need a statement about how you came to find it, mind.'

'I understand,' Guy said. 'Happy to help in any way I can and I should mention I dropped something down there: my friend's phone, which I'd borrowed. Oh, you might want to inform your forensic team, before they go in, there's a slight issue with the cellar staircase.'

The first officer nodded and made a note, while the second one narrowed his eyes. 'Any idea what it was your grandmother wanted to speak to us about?'

Guy shook his head. 'None whatsoever. I'm glad your journey wasn't wasted though.' Guy indicated the evidence bag.

The officers said goodbye and then the second officer turned back and walked towards him. 'Oh, one more thing, Mr Cameron.'

A slight look of panic crossed Guy's features. 'Yes?' he asked tentatively.

'Could I get a picture with you? For the wife. She's a huge fan.'

CHAPTER 45

Requisition Day, December 1943

Veronica stood shivering in front of the gathering of over two hundred faces in the village square and desperately hoped none of them had heard the events of last night. Each one of the villagers was a familiar face and each looked expectantly at her and at Freddie, who was gripping her hand in fear. He looked as frightened as she. Veronica glanced into the crowd at Anna, who gave her an encouraging nod.

Anna was back in the arms of her family, where she should have been all along, if only she'd gone when first told. Veronica thanked her silently for staying. If Anna hadn't been there last night, Veronica would be dead. But she was alive, and despite what had happened she knew she finally had a chance for a better life. Anna's brother William stood by his sister, his head angled to one side, eyeing his old friend Freddie curiously. Veronica looked into William's eyes as his gaze drifted to hers. The young man who knew she'd been trying to run away acknowledged her and then turned his gaze back to Freddie, who was studiously ignoring him. Did William know it wasn't Bertie standing next to her? If he did, there was nothing to be done now. It was a risk worth taking. They would face this for the rest of their lives. But

William was the only one in the crowd who gave more than a cursory look to the brother who shouldn't have been there.

No one had liked Sir Albert. The villagers' attendance at this event had been deemed obligatory by the vicar. In just a few moments, the crowd would be gone and this would all be over. She would be free.

To Veronica, Freddie's fear was palpable. He was worried that he couldn't do it; that he'd never be able to pass as his brother. It wouldn't be easy. But she would always be alongside him, for the rest of their lives, until they grew old and grey. She would love him until she could no longer breathe. They were doing this together. It was their only choice if they were all going to get out of here alive, Anna included.

Just a few words of encouragement were all that the villagers needed to assure them they were doing the right thing. It was something they could be proud of – giving the village to the troops to help them win the war. They were doing something that would go down in the history books as an act of sacrifice for their country.

'Sir Albert?' the vicar prompted, indicating it was time for the speech.

The man at her side nodded, stepped forward a few paces and Veronica moved with him. He squeezed her hand tighter. Her fingers brushed over the thick gold wedding ring he was now wearing and she shuddered, remembering what had happened inside Bertie's study.

Veronica felt dizzy again and put her free hand to the back of her head to feel the large lump that had formed. She had managed to wash away most of the blood, of which there had been plenty, but a few traces of thick, oozing red liquid still appeared on her fingers when she pulled them out of her hair. She wiped it off on the black fabric of her dress. Black for mourning. She felt it appropriate given that today marked the death of the village.

Freddie looked down at her, adjusting his grip, his expression blank, as if to check she was still there, as if he still couldn't quite believe what was happening. And then he looked back towards the crowd to speak.

CHAPTER 46

Dorset, Autumn 2019

The view from the terrace down to the beach was Melissa's favourite from the house, with its panoramic sweep of the coastline. They had bought it last month, just over a year after Anna had passed away, when both Guy and Melissa realised that Dorset had a pull on them neither could ignore. The sun was just rising and had streamed into the room so brightly that at 7 a.m. she'd crept out onto the terrace to watch as the bay lit up below. She and Guy hadn't got round to buying garden furniture yet, so Melissa stood against the metal and glass balustrades and stared down to the sea. The terrace balustrade was the only modern addition the previous owners had installed to the Victorian beachside cottage. Early morning surfers scrambled down to the beach and a gathering of wild swimmers greeted each other. Melissa shivered for them. Autumn was almost over and the air had a slight chill to it at this time of day. She pulled her robe around her tighter, fancying that the sea was always cold in Britain, regardless of time of year. But then, what did she know? She sipped her coffee and smiled as a strong pair of arms encircled her.

There had been a frightening moment last year when the MOD had called Guy in to ask awkward questions. Why he'd taken it upon himself to venture inside Tyneham House had been the question at the top of their list. Afterwards, Melissa had joked that it was his celebrity status that had earned him some wrapped knuckles instead of a fine or even a prison sentence. In truth, neither of them knew what the punishment should really have been for breaking into the manor house. She shuddered to think.

A year after the discovery she and Guy had made in Tyneham, Melissa thanked her lucky stars for her new life in Dorset. She knew now what real love was. She had found it with Guy. And all those years ago Veronica had found it with Freddie. True love, with its everlasting appeal of give and take; and trust, was surely one of the most important human needs. It was to Melissa. It had been for her parents, when they too, had eventually parted from each other and found the right person. Funny how it wasn't always with the person you thought it would be.

Guy, bleary-eyed, smelled the coffee cup pointedly and she laughed, turning in his arms and handing it to him.

'We really need to get curtains for the bedroom windows soon,' Guy said. 'The sun has woken us up every day since we moved in.'

Melissa looked over Guy's shoulder at the cottage. The inside was a wreck, but they were planning to work on it slowly, when Guy wasn't travelling and when Melissa wasn't busy with Mr Oswell in his bookshop, getting the finer details of ordering, profit and loss sheets and understanding the needs of his nearest and dearest customers. The rooms in the cottage would come together, slowly. It was the sea views from almost every window that had won them both over. Melissa had been only too happy to wake up early every day, sip coffee and stand quietly, admiring the view. It was something she'd never been able to do in the London rat race. It would never get boring.

'So,' Guy said. 'Today's the day.'

Melissa nodded.

'I might pop in and say hi to Oswell Books' new owner. I hear she's incredibly sexy. I might take her out for lunch.'

Melissa smiled. 'I'll be far too busy to entertain you. I might take Mr Oswell out for lunch instead though, actually. I'll tell you all about my first day as owner later. I think it's not going to be all that different to the past few months when I've been learning the ropes. I'm glad he's staying on part-time though. I'm absolutely dreading doing this on my own.'

'You're not on your own, Melissa.' Guy nuzzled her neck. 'Well, I'll let the two of you enjoy the first day of your new working arrangement together then. I'll keep out the way. However . . .' Guy spun Melissa around slowly so she could see the view again, and handed her the coffee cup. Melissa sipped the remaining coffee. 'Obviously the first thing you'll do is put my books somewhere really prominent in the shop,' he said as he kissed her neck. 'Eye-level. So they fly off the shelves, creating a stampede, if you will.'

'Of course,' Melissa said. 'We've got a mortgage to pay after all.'

EPILOGUE

Scotland, December 1948

'Count to ten and close your eyes. I'll hide.' Veronica giggled and ran as fast as her legs could carry her to the oak tree that stood proudly at the end of the grounds. When settled behind its shielding trunk, she stamped the snow from her boots and then regretted the action and the resulting noise that had reverberated dull and echoing around the thick white garden. She winced, expecting to be found within seconds.

'Found you!' the little girl cried out and clapped her mittens with glee.

Veronica groaned but in truth there was nothing she loved more than seeing joy on the little girl's face. 'Well done, Anna.' She bent to adjust her daughter's woolly bobble hat, which was falling over her eyes. 'One more go and then we'll have to return to the house. It's growing dark.'

The little girl nodded. 'My turn to hide.'

'All right then.' Veronica watched her daughter scamper off, her boots making little marks in what few patches of virgin snow remained.

Little Anna turned. 'Mummy, you aren't supposed to watch me hide. That's cheating. You have to close your eyes.'

Veronica laughed. 'Sorry.' She turned back towards the pale,

335

buff-coloured stone house and looked up at its chimneys as they pumped smoke and the comforting smell of a log fire into the air. Her attention was caught by the back door opening and she smiled as Freddie stepped out, buttoning up his coat as he walked towards her.

'I brought your scarf out for you.' He draped it round her neck and kissed her. She smiled into the face of the man she loved and he slipped his gloved hand in hers. 'We still need to put out a drink and a mince pie for Father Christmas.'

Veronica nodded.

'Father Christmas prefers a gin and tonic, by the way.' Freddie grinned.

'Does he now?' Veronica gave Freddie a knowing smile as he looked over her shoulder. 'Where is she?'

'Behind the potting shed this time.' Freddie smiled.

'Mummy,' Anna shouted from behind the wooden structure. 'It must be longer than ten seconds by now. Aren't you coming?'

Veronica and Freddie turned as their daughter tried to re-hide herself behind the shed. Together they ran to find her.

Author's Note

My reimagining of the requisition of Tyneham merges many of the facts with fiction. The two hundred and twenty-five villagers were given about a month to pack up and move in December 1943. Under the cover of official secrecy, there were few clues available to the outside world as to what was happening in the sleepy coastal village. The main indications were the urgent auction notices in the newspapers for farming machinery and livestock owned by those who worked the land around the village.

Tyneham sits at the bottom of a long and winding valley and leads down to a beach, Worbarrow Bay, which I renamed Tyneham Cove and where I imagined Veronica's beach hut. Both the village and the bay were taken in order to train troops for D-Day due to their proximity to the already existing Lulworth gunnery ranges in the hills above.

While most of Tyneham is a ruin, St Mary's Church and the small single-room schoolhouse are the only remaining buildings intact. Both are preserved entirely as fascinating museums and relics of a former time. The school officially closed long before the requisition. When the coastguard station at Worbarrow Bay closed in 1912 and the coastguards and their families left the village, there were few children of school age left to attend and in the early 1930s the school closed.

The once beautiful Tyneham House, home of Veronica and Albert in my story, was home to the Bonds, the owners of the house and the village. The house was requisitioned earlier in the war and one of its uses was to house members of the WAAF (Women's Auxiliary Air Force). Sadly, the house no longer stands. In the 1960s it was demolished, deemed to be structurally unsafe. Although, there are those that believed, like the church and school, that the house could easily have been preserved.

While the Tyneham of my story reopens to much fanfare in recent times, in reality and under much pressure from former residents, the village reopened for sporadic visits many years ago, but only on specific days of the year. However, sadly, Tyneham remains relatively unheard of. As do the other English villages requisitioned during the war for training purposes, including six villages in Norfolk now comprising an Army training village and Imber in Wiltshire.

For the purposes of my story, I imagine the small population of Tyneham leaving together, in solidarity. But in reality the villagers removed themselves family by family shortly after the requisition order arrived. They took only what they thought they would need for the remainder of the war, having been told they would be able to return when the war was won.

By the final day, hardly anyone was left, but the last occupant to leave pinned a note to the church door.

Please treat the church and houses with care. We have given up our homes where many of us have lived for generations, to help win the war to keep men free.

We will return one day and thank you for treating the village kindly.

However, shortly after the war, Tyneham became subject to a compulsory purchase order and today the population remains at zero.

Acknowledgements

I couldn't have written this book without the unending support of my wonderful husband, Stephen, who put himself in charge of the children's bedtimes almost every evening for a very long time so I could write.

Likewise to my wonderfully supportive mum, dad and in-laws, who volunteered for child-care duties when I was knee-deep in edits and proofs. I thank you.

My fantastic daughters, Emily and Alice, are a constant source of fun and amaze me daily. I'm very grateful I get to be both a mum and a writer, two of the best jobs in the world.

To my brilliant agent Becky Ritchie. Gosh, what can I say? You are endlessly positive and cheerful, work at lightning fast speed and found the most wonderful home for *The Forgotten Village* with Avon. For your ideas and support, thank you. Thanks also goes to the wonderful Alexandra McNicoll and her team, for finding great foreign publishers for *The Forgotten Village*.

It is my outstanding editor Rachel Faulkner-Willcocks who deserves so much praise for making this book what it is. Her thoughtful suggestions and fantastic ideas shaped the book entirely. Rachel, you felt like a real partner in crime and I am so grateful to you and to all at Avon for the fantastic behind-the-scenes work that goes into turning a manuscript into a book.

In 2016 I was lucky enough to get a coveted place on the Romantic Novelists' Association (RNA) New Writers' Scheme. I owe a huge thanks to the RNA and to Alison May in particular, who provided excellent feedback on an early draft of this book as part of the New Writers' Scheme.

Also through the RNA I've found some wonderful writing buddies. To my friends in the Chelmsford Chapter and especially my Write Club friends: Tracy, Peter, Sue, Karen, Nic and Snoopy, big thanks for writing chat, advice and lovely friendship.

And to you, the reader, the biggest thanks of all for buying a copy of *The Forgotten Village*. I hope you enjoyed reading it as much as I loved writing it.

To keep in touch with me on social media follow me at:
www.lornacookauthor.com
Facebook: /LornaCookWriter
Instagram: /LornaCookAuthor
Twitter: @LornaCookAuthor